NEVER DARE A WICKED EARL

NEVER DARE A WICKED EARL

RENEE ANN MILLER

ZEBRA BOOKS
KENSINGTON PUBLISHING CORP.
http://www.kensingtonbooks.com

ZEBRA BOOKS are published by

Kensington Publishing Corp.
119 West 40th Street
New York, NY 10018

First Printing: February 2018
ISBN-13: 978-1-4201-4457-4
ISBN-10: 1-4201-4457-X

eISBN-13: 978-1-4201-4458-1
eISBN-10: 1-4201-4458-8

10 9 8 7 6 5 4 3 2 1

Printed in the United States of America

To my husband, John.
Thank you for your love,
unwavering support, and for
washing the dishes all those times
I dashed back to my laptop after dinner.

ACKNOWLEDGMENTS

This book wouldn't be possible without the support and help I've received throughout this journey. Thanks to the From the Heart critique group for taking me under their wing and sharing their knowledge. A shout-out to Ana, Ashlyn, Averil, Barbara, Christine, Christina, Deborah, Diane, Dylann, Kathleen, Linda, Miguella, Tess, Wendi, and Wendy for not only helping me with my writing, but for your friendship and invaluable advice. Thanks to the Romance Chicks for our daily chats. Hugs to John, Johnny, Becky, Bubby, and Adriana for your smiles. Mom and Dad for your love. Heartfelt appreciation to my agent, Jill Marsal, for believing in my writing. Last but not least, a huge thank-you to my talented editor, Esi Sogah, and the Kensington team. You all rock!

Chapter One

London, November 1875

A bottle of Highland whisky was supposed to make a man forget his regrets. Hayden Milton, the Earl of Westfield, blew out a heavy breath. As usual, he'd managed little more than to undermine his equilibrium. Carefully he set one foot before the other as he lumbered through the fog and darkness shrouding Brook Street.

He peered at the heavens above. "Can you forgive me, Laura?"

Too late to ask his wife for forgiveness. Five years too late. The dead could not offer absolution.

Shaking away his maudlin thoughts, he made his way to the front door of his town house. His hand hovered over the handle as he eyed a drooping potted holly on the top step.

Where the blazes did that come from? He stepped back and looked up at the hazy structure. One, two, three, four . . .

This was not his residence—unless someone had removed the fifth floor during his absence. Was that possible? The inane question brought about the realization he must be more inebriated than he thought. He stared at the nearly identical town house next door. One, two, three, four, five. He glanced at the step. There was no holly, sickly looking or otherwise.

He took another step back.

Blast it! Lady Bedford's residence. The old battle-ax would expire from a seizure if he crawled into her bed naked. A vision of himself snuggling between the sheets with the wart-faced matron flashed before his eyes. He shuddered.

In front of his own town house, he set a steadying hand on the wrought iron fence. Thank God Celia would be asleep. He didn't wish the child to witness him listing like a ship on the high seas.

Footfalls shattered the silence of the small hours.

He turned as a diminutive woman burst through the gloom. She stopped directly in front of him, her face tipped downward. One pale hand clutched the hood of her black cape, anchoring it to her head. The woman lifted her face and a pair of slanted green eyes peered at him.

Adele.

At one time, her catlike eyes had intrigued him, but their affair had been brief. She teetered somewhere between senseless folly and complete madness. Too volatile—even for him.

She raised her arm and moonlight glinted off the dueling pistol clasped in her hand.

Ah, so my day of reckoning is upon me? "Adele, my dear, has it come to this? Murder?"

A feral smile curled her lips. "Oh, Hayden, I don't intend to kill you."

Though she spoke slowly, her words were slurred. Apparently, he was not the only one who'd numbed his mental capacities with liquor, or in Adele's case, a tincture containing opiates, a habit she favored.

Grinning, she lowered the gun. Its barrel, previously

pointed at his chest, now aimed at his manhood. She let out a low, bitter cackle. "No, dearest, I merely wish to maim you."

Only a woman would think of gelding him; a man would aim right for his black heart.

Adele arched a brow.

Did she expect a reaction? Had she thought he'd fall to his knees and plead for his life? Not likely. At least not on the anniversary of his wife's death. His own demise seemed a fitting turn of events.

"You bastard, say something," she hissed.

Go ahead, do it, the words echoed in his mind, teasing the tip of his tongue. Was he as mad as Adele or had the liquor pickled his brain?

He glanced at Celia's bedchamber window. For the child's sake, he needed to keep his wits about him. He'd stood over his wife's grave and promised to do his best for the child. He wouldn't fail Laura. Not again.

His gaze returned to the antiquated pistol. The ornate gun probably weighed close to five pounds. Adele's hand already trembled from the effort to hold it still. He'd a better chance of surviving if she kept the barrel pointed low—away from his chest and abdomen.

"Sweeting, why don't you give me the gun and accompany me inside? We'll sit and chat about what I've done that has you so distressed." He inched closer.

She stepped back. Her wide-eyed expression looked deranged. She waved the gun. "Stay back, Hayden. I swear I'll shoot."

He raised his hands, palms out, as a movement beyond her shoulder caught his attention. A short figure walked toward them. The person appeared distorted, a body too narrow in comparison to its upper girth. The figure stepped under the illuminating light of a lamppost.

Damnation. Young Jimmy McGivney.

The newsboy carried a bundle of the morning paper hefted on his narrow shoulders. At any moment, Adele would hear Jimmy's footsteps scraping the pavement behind her. He couldn't risk the unstable woman turning on the lad and shooting.

He leapt forward to grapple the gun away from her.

Flint struck steel. The flash of powder igniting dispersed the darkness. A deafening sound reverberated through his entire being and the scent of sulfur filled his nose. As if someone kicked his legs out from beneath him, he fell forward and slammed against the pavement. His breath exploded from his lungs.

The cold, damp ground permeated his upper body, contrasting with the heat burning through his lower half, burrowing into the core of his marrow. The warmth waned. Seeped out of him until it pooled on the pavement below him, leaving an astringent, knifelike pain in its wake.

His eyes drifted closed, and Laura's lovely face flashed before his mind's eye. *Forgive me, my love.*

Adele's retreating footsteps clicking against the pavement drew his mind back to the present. He forced his heavy lids open. A bright, almost blinding light besieged him just before a strange warmth and darkness settled over him, sucking him into a state of peaceful, mindless oblivion.

Chapter Two

Sophia Camden swung open the door and dashed into the Earl of Westfield's opulent bedchamber. The dark room didn't smell like a typical sickroom. It was absent the stale odors of sweat, liniment, and excrement. No, the air smelled of soap, fresh linen, and beeswax—of wealth and servants and immunity to the ravages besieging the poor.

As she made her way across the room, she held up a small paraffin lamp, illuminating his lordship thrashing about in a massive four-poster bed. He tossed and turned as if he wrestled with the devil himself, and the profanity he spewed would have scorched even Lucifer's ears.

Fever? A knot settled in her stomach. She should have checked on the gentleman when she arrived late last night—ignored the housekeeper's warning not to disturb him until morning. With a sense of dread racing up her spine, she placed the lamp and her black medical bag upon a low chest of drawers and rushed to the bed. In the near darkness, shadows marred Westfield's features, but she discerned his eyes were closed.

"Shhh . . . relax, Lord Westfield." As if she'd uttered some magical incantation, his rambling ceased, and his flailing body stilled. She pressed her palm against the moist skin of his brow. Warm, but not feverish. A tense breath eased out from between her lips.

Thank goodness. Just a nightmare. Understandable after being shot. The newspapers had reported a cloaked woman fled the scene. Westfield claimed to have not known his assailant.

She leaned forward and straightened his tangled blankets. A masculine scent drifted upward. It reminded her of pomanders, the clove-studded oranges she'd placed about her grandfather's studio to mask the pungent odor of turpentine and paint. The spicy, familiar scent was soothing.

Soothing? What little she'd learned about his lordship since arriving here remained far from that. The housekeeper had offered little information. However, after Mrs. Beecham led her upstairs to a bedchamber across the corridor from Westfield's suite of rooms, she'd sent in a young maid with fresh sheets. Alice had been much more disposed to gossiping, softly chirping away like a young skylark who'd suddenly realized God had blessed it with the melodious gift of song.

Alice informed her she was Westfield's third attendant in less than three days—a fact Westfield's sister had omitted when she'd hired Sophia.

She pinched her lips into a straight line and smoothed the richly textured navy damask counterpane.

Westfield's large hand shot out and caught her wrist.

Her breath snagged in her throat.

His eyes blinked open. Westfield's viselike grip eased as his fingers skimmed the sensitive skin of her wrist. The gentle, almost lover-like touch scattered gooseflesh over her body and a spark of current fluttered in her belly.

"Who are you?" he asked.

The deep, raspy tone of his voice added to the odd sensations barraging her. She willed the unsettling feelings aside. "It's only five in the morning, Lord Westfield. Try to sleep."

He released her and shifted up on his elbows, allowing more light to shine on his face. Not enough to clearly see much more than the dark stubble that shadowed his square jaw, giving him a dangerous, almost piratical look.

"I asked you a question, madam."

"Miss Sophia Camden, my lord. I'm to tend to you during your convalescence . . . to act as your nurse."

"Nurse? What happened to that fool-headed attendant who was here yesterday?"

"Attendant?" she prevaricated, not wishing to repeat the story Alice disclosed.

"Come, Miss Camden, surely you've heard something."

Oh, yes, I've heard plenty. Enough to know you're beyond wicked.

"Miss Camden?" His voice was softer now, more compelling. She had a feeling his tone could change like the wind or the seasons, depending on his mood. And that he could wheedle the truth from even the most obstinate person, if he so chose.

She sighed. Best to get this revelation over with. "It's rumored he resigned late yesterday evening after you placed him in a headlock while threatening to shove his face into your bedpan."

"He deserved it." There was no hesitation in his voice. No remorse.

"I'm sure he did, my lord." Unless Westfield was a ninny, he couldn't miss the disbelief and condemnation dripping from her tone.

He expelled a heavy breath. "I don't need to explain my actions to you, Miss Camden."

"Indeed, you do not."

"You are not needed here, madam." He waved a dismissive hand toward the door.

"Sir, you've had two attendants. One stayed barely a day before resigning, and the man we just discussed supposedly left with nary a word except some nonsensical rambling he uttered as he fled down the stairs. It was believed you might show less distress to a female nurse."

"And what dunce thought that?"

"That would be your sister, Lady Prescott."

"Edith. Confounded woman. I should have known."

"It would be best if you returned to sleep. I have a medicine that will help calm you."

"I don't need calming," he snapped.

"You were tossing and turning in your bed, and if you continue to do so, you might tear the stitches in your thigh." She strode to her medical bag and removed an amber bottle of tincture, along with an inventive little utensil called a Gibson spoon. It was designed with a clever lid so one could avoid spillage when one's patient was not in an agreeable mood. Apparently, it was needed here. After filling it, she returned to the bedside and inched the spoon to his mouth.

His head jerked back. "What in God's name is that?"

"The medicine I spoke of. I assure you Dr. Trimble prescribed it. Please open your mouth."

Settling against the headboard, he folded his arms over his chest.

Stubborn man. Without further thought, she pinched his nose closed.

He opened his mouth—most likely intent on giving her a piece of his mind—but before he uttered a word, she slipped the spoon between his lips, tipped it back, and withdrew it in one fluid movement.

Coughing, he drew the back of his large hand across his mouth and gaped at her.

His sister had said to use a firm hand. Perhaps that had been a bit extreme. But it was done and there was nothing she could do to take it back. She spun around, retrieved her lamp, and strode to the door. As if the devil prodded her further, she lifted the medicinal spoon in the air in a bold gesture of fond farewell. "Good night, my lord, I bid you pleasant dreams."

"Why you insolent little . . . imp," he bellowed, his obvious shock flaring to rage.

She pulled the door closed.

"You're dismissed, Miss Camden!" His raised voice carried easily through the wooden door. "Do you hear me, madam? You are fired. Discharged. Bloody well sacked!"

Hayden lowered the sheet off his face and narrowed his eyes against the bright deluge of light streaming through the bedchamber's windows. Who dared to draw the curtains open so early?

Celia? No, his sister had taken the child to her town house, insisting he needed to rest. *Mathews?* Tugging down his nightshirt, he opened his mouth to call to his valet. He snapped it shut. Standing before the hearth, with her back to him, stood a slender woman dressed in a dark navy gown topped with a white pinafore. She wore what appeared to be a starched doily with wings atop her head.

He frowned. What was Mrs. Beecham doing dressing the maids in such odd-looking hats? What had happened to those old thingamabobs they'd been wearing before . . . mobhats or mobcaps? Whatever one chose to call them, they were as ugly as sin, but this starched atrocity lacked improvement.

A foggy memory of an insolent nurse tugged at him. The fine hairs on the back of his neck stood on end. Surely, that had been a nightmare. His gaze swung to the chest of drawers and the amber bottle and medical bag set atop it.

Hell, not a dream! He cleared his throat.

The woman spun around.

The first thing that caught his attention was the porcelain bedpan clasped in her hands. The second thing was her eyes. They were dusted with long lashes that swept outward, elongating their almond shape, and so dark, that at this distance, he couldn't discern her pupils from her irises.

He examined the rest of her face with its straight nose and full, wide mouth. Her skin was far from fair, and her hair, pulled into a chignon, was as black as a moonless night. She looked Mediterranean. Lovely in a foreign, exotic way.

A sharp pain shot up his leg, reminding him of the last time he'd allowed himself to become involved with a woman with unusual eyes set in an attractive face. He ran his hand over his bandaged thigh and silently cursed that lunatic Adele.

He bestowed the woman with a scowl meant to terrify.

She smiled.

He narrowed his eyes.

She stepped closer.

Baffled, he scratched his head. Perhaps it wasn't the same woman. She didn't appear the least bit repentant, and he was doing everything to intimidate her—short of baring his teeth and snarling like a rabid dog.

"Good morning, Lord Westfield. I hope you slept well."

By God, the she-devil! He recognized her soft, cultured voice and the faint, enticing scent of lavender and lemon drifting off her skin.

"Didn't I sack you?"

Laying the bedpan upon the counterpane, she tipped her head sideways. Her dark, expressive eyes widened. "Did you?"

"You bloody well know I did."

"Are you ready for your breakfast, my lord?"

Didn't this woman realize he was the Earl of Westfield? A man one dealt with quite prudently, if one had to deal with him at all. A man revered by some, despised by others, and feared by many. He cocked a brow. The affectation usually sent his servants scattering like marbles across the prow of a heaving ship.

Her serene smile didn't waver. "Before you breakfast, I'd like to redress your wound."

"Are you hard of hearing?" he asked in an elevated voice.

"No, my lord."

This had to be someone's idea of a wicked joke. "Ah," he said, feeling enlightened. He peered beyond her to the open doorway. "Lord Simon Adler is hiding in the corridor and having a jolly good laugh over this, isn't he, the bounder?"

She followed his gaze to the door. "If he is, I'm not aware of it."

He raked his hands through his hair and slumped deeper into his pillows. He'd not prayed in years, but he contemplated asking for divine intervention or, better yet, a lightning bolt.

"Listen carefully to what I'm going to say, madam. You—are—sacked."

"You cannot dismiss me."

He inspected her attire. Though her hat was an oddity, her other garments didn't contradict her sanity. Her dress was not on backward, her buttons were correctly fastened, and she didn't wear her drawers atop her head. Nevertheless, she suffered some disorder of the mind if she thought he lacked the authority to discharge her.

"This is my house, madam. I assure you *I can* dismiss you. Now remove yourself from my premises."

"My lord, your sister retained me, and Lady Prescott

informed me that only she may dismiss me." She started to fold back his counterpane.

"What the devil do you think you're about, Miss . . . ?" Damn, the woman had him so rattled her name eluded him.

A wan smile settled over her visage. "Miss Sophia Camden."

"Miss Camden, my sister is apparently trying to cast me into an early grave by sending you here. Furthermore, she has no authority in my house. She cannot force your services upon me. Moreover, if you touch my bedding again I'm going to pull you down, brace you over my legs, and set my open palm to your derrière."

Red suffused her honey-colored cheeks. "Y-you wouldn't dare."

"It would be a grave error on your part to dare me. I have a terrible weakness for them."

She stepped back and placed her hands on her hips. "Your wound is in need of re-dressing, and since I'm the only one here qualified, I implore you to let me attend to it. Dr. Trimble will not call on you today."

He pointed at the door. "Out!"

With an exasperated expression, she turned and picked up her medical bag.

"Miss Camden."

She spun around.

He jerked his chin toward the medicinal bottle. "Take that bitter concoction with you."

She slowly shook her head. "No, I wish you to keep it. For if your wound festers and septicemia sets in Dr. Trimble will need to amputate your leg, and once the anesthesia wears off you'll be pleased to have it. Indeed, you'll take a fancy to that concoction." She strode to the door.

The devil take her. The conniver attempted to manipulate him. As if taunting him, another knifelike pain stabbed at his thigh. He gritted his teeth. "Miss Camden," he called as she stepped over the threshold.

She pivoted around.

"I wish you to attend to my leg before you leave."

Her expression remained impassive as she set the medical bag down, returned to the bed, and folded back his blankets, exposing his legs. Her adept hands began removing the bandages.

"Have you experienced any numbness in your leg or foot?" she asked.

"No."

Her fingers removed the last strip of cloth. She examined the thin cotton that covered the ghastliest area of his puckered and sutured skin. She didn't appear repulsed.

"Do you work on a surgical ward, madam?"

"I do not."

"Then tell me what medical training you've received."

"I have spent the last couple of years working with Dr. Trimble. It is from that employment, along with reading in his extensive library, that I have gained my knowledge. I am Dr. Trimble's medical assistant."

"I've met Trimble's assistant. Pudgy man with a crag-laden face and leathery skin." He swept his gaze over her. "You've had a miraculous transformation."

"That is Mr. Bailey. He's Dr. Trimble's *surgical assistant*. I assist Thomas . . . I mean Dr. Trimble with his female patients."

A woman assistant? He'd never heard of such a thing. The warmth of her fingers skimming his thigh and the heat they evoked drew Hayden's gaze back to the wound. He reached out to scratch the marred skin.

"No, no, do not touch." She elbowed his hand away. "I've read Dr. Joseph Lister's study on antiseptic principles. Keeping the wound clean is imperative. I only uncovered the dressing to discern if the injury was seeping. Fortunately, it is not."

Crossing his arms over his chest, Hayden nodded. Not only had God endowed Miss Camden with stunning eyes, she was intelligent. His gaze slid over her. She wore a gown devoid of embellishments, and if her starched collar went any higher it would be lethal. Worse, not a single tendril escaped the stranglehold of her chignon. It looked too austere, more suited to a matron of advanced years, and though not in the first blush of youth, she wasn't much older than twenty-three, possibly twenty-four.

She bent a little farther over his leg, and he cocked his head to the side to get a better view of her shapely bum. A favorable asset, indeed. That single sight, alone, tempted him to let her stay. His gaze shifted to the bedpan. No, he'd not have her shoving that deuced thing under his arse every day, let alone removing it. He still had some pride left.

"I shall dispatch a note to Dr. Trimble informing him I'd prefer a male attendant."

"My lord, why not give me the opportunity to prove my competency? A so-called trial period. Shall we say ten days?"

"No, Miss Camden, no trial period."

She finished bandaging his leg and looked him squarely in the eye. "Consider it a *dare*."

Wasn't she a sly little imp with a great deal of cheek, using his own words against him? The mischievous glint in her dark eyes sent an odd, nearly forgotten jolt of excitement through him.

"A dare, you say?"

Her tongue darted out to wet her lips, and she smiled—a pretty, full-mouthed smile that dimpled her cheeks. "Yes, my lord."

Hayden scrubbed a hand over his chin while contemplating her. He always fancied a battle of wits against a worthy adversary, and this was possibly just what he needed, since lying in this godforsaken bed bored the hell out of him. And he could always have his valet assist him with his more personal needs.

"I accept your dare, madam."

As if she'd outsmarted him, her smile grew wider.

"Miss Camden, you understand a dare is only entertaining when the loser offers a forfeit. We must make this interesting and place a *bet* on the outcome."

"A bet?"

"Indeed. If you complete the ten days, I will add a substantial bonus to the pay my sister has promised you. Furthermore, I will not dismiss you until your services are no longer required. However, if you resign before the allotted time . . ." He tapped his finger to his chin. "I'm not sure what my prize should be, but I shall think of *something* worthy of my victory."

"I have no desire to place a wager on the outcome, but if you insist, we could make a gentleman's bet."

Had she not heard that contrary to his birth, he was not a gentleman? "Ah, apparently, you are not so sure of yourself," he goaded.

She nibbled her lower lip.

"Forget it, Miss Camden. You would lose anyway."

A spark of anger flashed in her eyes. She thrust out her hand for him to shake. "I'm quite sure of my abilities. I agree to your terms."

He grasped her delicate hand. A pleasant warmth settled against his palm. He was going to enjoy giving the efficient Miss Camden a go-around she would never forget and ultimately claim the victory and his forfeit.

"May God be with you, Miss Camden."

Chapter Three

Sophia tried not to swallow the lump forming in her throat as she stared at the devilish gleam in Lord Westfield's blue eyes.

When she had entered his bedchamber this morning, she'd expected to see a craggy face harmonious with the vulgar-tongued devil who had snapped at her during the early morning gloom. But the light of day revealed the unexpected. Westfield was perhaps thirty, a good five years younger than his sister, Lady Prescott. And if one could label a man beautiful, the word seemed apropos. His brown hair was wavy, his jaw square and stubborn, and his high cheekbones pronounced, but not too angular. And his eyes were a fascinating color. Not a diluted blue but an intense shade, like an artist's rendition of the Mediterranean Sea.

Still holding her gaze, Westfield ran a hand over his darkly bristled jaw.

What the deuce had she got herself into daring this rascal? She could practically see the cogwheels turning in the man's head as he calculated his next move. A move he hoped would leave her owing him a forfeit. Her stomach knotted.

"Miss Camden, you said you assist Dr. Trimble with his female patients?"

She nodded.

"So, you don't usually attend male patients?"

Perhaps she shouldn't have admitted that. Did he think it made her less qualified? "I work predominately with women, but I attend children as well, including boys."

"A boy's body is not the same as a man's."

So this was his game. The bounder thought he'd scare her off with immodest talk. "Anatomically, my lord, boys are not much different than men. Of course, there are the obvious differences. Their muscles are not as defined, they have less body hair, and they are still experiencing growth."

"Exactly what is still growing?" The scoundrel flashed a boyish grin. An illusion. Such a bold question attested to the fact.

"Their stature of course."

"Obviously, madam, but can you not offer me something more specific?"

Wicked, wicked man! "Indeed, my lord. Their feet."

He let out a hearty laugh. "That's not the answer I was seeking, Miss Camden, but possibly Dr. Trimble's anatomy books aren't as comprehensive as you believe."

"Dr. Trimble's journals and illustrated books are rather detailed," she responded tartly.

"Really? Perhaps next time Trimble is here, I shall ask him about his infamous books. I will inform him how you told me all about their *detailed* illustrations, inciting my interest in them."

Heat burned her cheeks. The scoundrel was beyond the pale, twisting her words around. Well, Thomas would not believe him. She moved to the foot of the bed, intent on pulling Westfield's bedding back over his body. He trapped the navy blue counterpane under his good leg, then flashing a smile, he folded his hands behind his head.

"Miss Camden, I'm in need of a hot sponge bath. And you, my dear woman, are about to get a true lesson in anatomy." He motioned with his chin to a door at the side of the room. "You'll find a clean nightshirt in my dressing room."

The smile on his face clearly revealed he thought he'd won. That, at any moment, she'd scurry out of his bed-chamber, down the stairs, and out the front door as her predecessor had. The unscrupulous man was in for a shock. "Yes, right away."

He blinked. "You're going to bathe me?"

"Did I not mention, my lord, Lady Prescott wishes me only to deal with your medical care? The honor of bathing you shall fall soundly on your valet, Mr. Mathews."

"Damn Edith and her prudish morality," he mumbled.

Sophia tapped her fingernail against the side of the bedpan, drawing his attention to the porcelain bowl. "He will assist you with the bedpan as well. I trust the urge to shove someone's head in it has passed?"

He scowled.

"If you'll excuse me, I shall inform him you're ready for his assistance." Sophia curtseyed and exited the room.

She pulled the bedchamber door shut and leaned against the hard surface. Closing her eyes, she expelled a heavy breath as the memory of Lord Westfield's body flashed before her. Never in her life had she seen a man with such an impressive physique. In truth, Thomas's medical books with their abundance of illustrations *had not* prepared her for dealing with a man who possessed legs like Michelangelo's *Creation of Adam*. It had been rather difficult to feign indifference.

And now she'd foolishly allowed the man to up the ante and add a wager to her dare. Why had she acted so impetuously? It would have made sense if she needed the funds, but she did not. However, his lordship's reticence to let her tend to him had made her feel inadequate, reminded her of Great-Uncle Charles's cruel words about her limited worth. She'd wanted to prove her competence. To show his lordship she could care for him as well as any man.

But to dare him was rash. To add a forfeit lunacy! The scoundrel would use every wile in his arsenal to thwart her. This would not be a means to prove her intelligence, but a game to ease Westfield's ennui. She straightened. Well, she'd not turn back now and owe him some unknown prize. She had contended for years with Great-Uncle Charles's sharp tongue; surely, she could survive whatever Westfield heaved upon her.

But she needed to raise the stakes.

She spun around and rapped on Westfield's bedchamber door.

"Enter," his deep voice called.

With shoulders squared, she marched to the foot of his massive bed. "If I win the dare, my lord, there is something else I want."

He arched a dark brow.

She gathered her courage and barreled forward. "Do you know Russell Gurney?"

"From the House of Commons? Of course."

"Mr. Gurney hopes to change the law that excludes women from taking the examination to be physicians. If I last the ten days, I wish you to support his efforts."

His blue eyes widened. "Do you wish to be a physician, Miss Camden?"

She stiffened her back and held her chin high. Whenever she revealed this fact, she opened herself to derision, especially from Great-Uncle Charles. But everyone she'd loved had died, and perhaps if she became a doctor, she could stop others from losing those most important to them and experiencing the loneliness that sometimes crept over her.

"I do, my lord. One who treats women."

The room grew quiet and even though his lordship's face didn't show scorn, a bead of sweat trickled down her back.

"Very well, Miss Camden. If you win, I'll throw my political weight behind this issue."

The air held in her lungs eased out. "You will?"

"Whatever else I am, madam, I am a man of my word." He grinned. "But first you must complete the dare to avoid owing me a forfeit."

She intended on winning. Yes, she'd prove her competence and tenacity, no matter how much his lordship tried to unsettle her. She had to. The stakes had become too dear. With his lordship's political muscle, she might just attain her dream of becoming a physician.

The following morning, at nine thirty sharp, Sophia strode to Westfield's bedchamber door. Yesterday, his lordship and she had engaged in a battle of wits throughout the day. He had complained incessantly, cursed like a sailor three sheets to the wind, and asked her a multitude of tedious and wicked questions about human anatomy. She'd refused to answer him, and he'd flashed that boyish grin of his, knowing he unsettled her.

Fortunately, his lordship had spent the better part of the evening preoccupied with ledgers, folios, and documents all scattered about his bed like the leaves of a maple on a winter's day. Peculiar behavior for a man linked to a coterie of nobility known for their indolence and frivolity.

She rapped a quick staccato against the thick oak door and entered his bedchamber with a fair amount of resolve. Westfield's large frame was sprawled, belly down, over the massive bed, and he stirred upon her entering. She moved to the windows and flung the heavy blue curtains wide. The room flooded with the grayness of the stark morning.

Grumbling, Westfield dragged the counterpane over his head.

She cleared her throat. "My lord, I have an appointment at eleven o'clock, and I wish to examine your leg before I leave."

From under the bedding came a low disembodied voice. "Miss Camden, you walk a fine line between insolence and outright madness waking me this bloody early." He lowered the counterpane off his head, clutched his injured thigh, and rolled onto his back.

Even with his hair in disarray, the man looked appealing. What would it be like to wake up next to such a virile man? She tamped down her wicked thought.

He narrowed his already heavy-lidded eyes. "I'm not going anywhere, madam. You may examine me upon your return."

Evidently, she was destined to struggle through another day of combative behavior. So be it. Without responding, she entered the bathing room, washed her hands, and collected fresh bandages.

She returned to find Westfield had rolled back onto his stomach and appeared fast asleep. Did he believe she'd concurred with his mandate? Well, he was in for a shock. With a swift tug, she sent the heavy counterpane and sheet flying to the foot of the bed.

She sucked in a breath. Westfield's nightshirt had ridden up and over his hips to reveal his taut bum. Gracious, his gluteus muscles were so developed one could bounce a coin off them.

"Shall I roll over, Miss Camden, so you can ogle my bits as well?" Westfield asked, his deep voice muffled by his thick pillow.

She swallowed. How long had she been staring? She darted to the foot of the bed and flung the sheet upward.

Westfield rolled over and peered at her with a lopsided grin. "Tsk-tsk, Miss Camden. Who would have guessed you're a naughty girl?"

She set her hands on her hips and scowled at him. "And you are no gentleman. Now please pull your nightshirt down, so I may examine you."

His grin widened as he adjusted his nightshirt. "Ah, I think you've examined me well enough."

Her cheeks warmed. "Do not flatter yourself. I have a job to do, and you look no different to me than the children I tend to. In fact, from what I could see, you . . . you reminded me of *little* Edward Shore."

Westfield's smug face faltered. "Who the deuce is little Edward Shore?"

"One of Dr. Trimble's patients. The poor mite took ill last week, and I helped his mother bathe him with cool water to reduce his fever."

His lordship's color dimmed a shade causing him to resemble a man suffering with a case of the collywobbles. He'd probably never had such an unflattering comment heaved upon him. No, she bet his lovers practically swooned over that fine bum of his.

"Oh, my lord, you appear disconcerted. I do not wish you to fret over little Edward, for he has fully recovered."

"How old?"

"What?"

A nerve twitched in his jaw. "How old is *little* Edward?"

She tapped a finger to her chin. "I believe he is nine. But he's a wee little thing who looks no more than seven." Sophia bent down, averted her smiling face, and began to unwrap his bandages.

She expected a pithy retort, but Westfield remained silent, which didn't bode well.

Dash it all, what's he thinking? "After I change your bandages, I'll bring your breakfast tray before I leave."

"Where are you going?"

"I volunteer at the Whitechapel Mission and Dispensary in the East End. Dr. Trimble and I go there one day a week."

Westfield's face twisted. "Whitechapel? It's the bowels of hell. Will Trimble remain with you while you are there?"

"Sir, are you concerned for my welfare?"

"Will he remain with you?" he repeated, his jaw tense.

"Yes, I expect his carriage at eleven o'clock." She finished examining his thigh, moved into the bathing room, and set the soiled clothes in an enamel pail before washing her hands. She stepped back into the bedchamber. "I shall return shortly with your breakfast."

"Miss Camden, what lunatic, besides Dr. Thomas Trimble, considers that paste I'm fed breakfast?"

"My lord, many people start their day with a bowl of hot porridge."

"And what did you eat for breakfast?" His tone betrayed he thought it something magnificent.

"For the past two mornings, I've been served porridge, along with the rest of the staff."

He frowned. "Do they eat it every day?"

It sounded as if the thought sickened him. "I'm not certain, but it's possible."

"Well, I want something substantial."

Sophia looked at his tightly set jaw. She wasn't in the mood to argue with him, and a return to his normal diet might improve his disposition. Though unlikely. "All right, I will inform your chef you may start eating your regular fare."

"And tell Mrs. Beecham I wish to speak with her. Feeding the staff porridge every day is unconscionable."

His disgust over his staff's breakfast surprised her. She nodded and exited the room.

As she passed a hall mirror, she surveyed her frazzled face. Good grief, what had she been thinking, gawking at Westfield's bum as if it were some fine antiquity on display at the British Museum? No wonder the scoundrel had looked so pleased with himself. She pressed her fingers against her flushed cheeks. Blast it all, the man looked nothing like little Edward Shore. He was magnificent, and he knew it!

A half hour later, Sophia made her way up the stairs carrying Westfield's breakfast tray. As she stepped off the landing, she saw his valet closing the master's bedchamber door.

Mathews, a balding man well into his forties, started upon seeing her, and then turned several shades of red before settling on the color of a ripe tomato. The man looked ready to swoon. She rushed forward. The covered platters on the tray rattled and the Sevres creamer tipped precariously. "Mr. Mathews, are you ill?"

The valet shook his head, pulled a white handkerchief from his pocket, and dabbed it across his shimmering brow. His hands trembled like a man suffering the ravages of palsy.

"Miss," he said, stuffing his dampened linen back into his pocket. "I must insist you give me the tray and let me bring it into his lordship."

Sophia eyed him keenly. "Mr. Mathews, I assure you I can handle whatever nonsense his lordship throws at me." She gave him a smile, hoping to reassure him. "Would you be so kind as to open the door?"

He took a deep breath. "I shall accompany you, Miss Camden."

Sophia gave a brisk nod, and Mathews slowly swung the door open.

She crossed the threshold. The bed was empty.

What the deuce! Silly, silly man. Reckless to be up and

gallivanting about. Her gaze shifted to an open doorway. A private sitting room? Yes, from where she stood, she could see a settee and several chairs done in the same opulent navy damask as the bedroom's curtains and counterpane. Like the bedchamber, the walls were white with thick moldings and wainscoting.

"Mathews, if that is Miss Camden send her in."

Something in the lighthearted tone of Westfield's voice, along with Mr. Mathews's unease, sent a foreboding sensation skittering up her spine.

What in heaven's name is Westfield up to? She strode to the doorway, stepped into the room, and nearly tripped over her own two feet.

Westfield lounged on a chaise, wearing nothing but a thin sheet wrapped around his lean waist and a self-satisfied smirk on his lips.

Chapter Four

Sophia's throat grew dry. Up until this point in her life, she had thought no man's chest could be as magnificently formed as Michelangelo's *David*. She'd seen a cast of it at South Kensington Museum, but looking at Westfield, she realized the young David's body somehow paled in comparison. Westfield's shoulders were broader, his pectoral and abdominal muscles more developed, and unlike the statue, his skin was warmly hued, while below his navel a thin band of hair trailed beneath the sheet.

His smile broadened. "Ah, Miss Camden, I'm as hungry as a horse."

She tried not to leer. "Where is your nightshirt, my lord?"

"I was warm, so I removed it. And since I resemble *little* Edward Shore, whom you recently attended and bathed, I figured you wouldn't mind."

She turned to the valet. "Mr. Mathews, would you please be good enough to get his lordship a nightshirt?"

"I'm not putting it on. If you wish to work here, you'll have to contend with me in the nude. Of course, you could *resign*."

As Mathews scurried into the dressing room, Sophia distracted herself by setting the breakfast tray down on a large mahogany desk. She glanced at the numerous landscapes that dotted the walls of the private sitting room. An impressive collection. Her eyes moved past a Canaletto of the Thames to another landscape of the river. It was one of her grandfather's paintings. Her chest tightened. One of the few she'd regrettably sold. She fought the urge to step up to it. If she had known Westfield owned it, she would have included it as part of her prize for completing the dare.

Mathews rushed back into the room, holding a nightshirt.

Westfield scowled at the valet. "Mathews, are you as hard of hearing as Miss Camden? I said I do not wish to wear a nightshirt." With an impatient wave of his arm, he motioned the man away.

The movement caused the cording in his upper arms to twist and his pectorals to harden. Sophia couldn't look away. She'd overheard someone on Westfield's staff say his lordship was a member of the London Rowing Club. Could the repetitive movements of such an activity have developed him to this extent or had God felt generous?

A foreign heat warmed her belly while a contradictory shiver prickled her skin. *This will not do!* She strode to Mathews, took the garment out of his unsteady hand, and turned back to Westfield. She tried not to act overwhelmed by his nakedness; however, she couldn't stop her gaze from perusing the thin ribbon of hair that trailed downward until it—

Westfield cleared his throat.

Her gaze snapped back to his face.

The scoundrel smiled at her like some merry Andrew at a carnival. As she tossed the nightshirt onto the chaise, she noticed a set of crutches leaning on the wall. Ah, so that was how he'd maneuvered about. Where had they come from? She looked at Mathews.

The valet's cheeks turned red and he averted his face.

She gathered up the crutches.

Westfield narrowed his eyes. "What are you doing with them?"

Ignoring his inquiry, she returned to the desk and leaned the crutches against the wall. "You should not be out of bed, my lord."

There were two silver-domed platters on the breakfast tray. She lifted one of the lids, revealing several thick slices of bacon and three eggs. A savory aroma permeated the air. "I believe your chef has outdone himself. Mr. Mathews, doesn't this look tasty?"

"Yes, miss," he responded, once again, mopping his limp handkerchief over his brow.

Sophia began to cut the bacon into bite-sized pieces. She stabbed a piece with the tines of the fork and lifted it into the air. "I'm not giving you this tray of food until you put your nightshirt on. In fact, it looks so tempting, I'm going to start eating it myself, so the longer you take to dress, the less there will be."

His lordship glared at her, then swung his legs down, and tried to stand. He cringed.

"I wouldn't do that. You'll tear your stitches and slow down your recovery."

He slumped back down. "Miss Camden, if you dare eat even one piece of my—"

She placed the piece of bacon in her mouth and slowly drew it off the tines. "Mmm. I don't know what you pay Monsieur Laurent, but your chef is worth every pound. This bacon is cooked to perfection." She turned to the valet. "Mr. Mathews, would you care to join me?"

The red that flooded Mathews's face drained away. The valet swallowed, and his Adam's apple visibly bobbed convulsively as the man's gaze shifted to Westfield's gaping mouth.

"Mathews, if you eat one jot of my breakfast or even

take a whiff, you shall find your scrawny arse on the street. Now, you ruddy well better get my food from that confounded woman and bring it to me!"

The poor valet appeared ready to swoon again. Sophia knew the man couldn't comprehend why Westfield didn't sack her as he most likely did anyone who did not cower before him.

Not wishing to place the valet in the middle of the battle, she said, "My lord, this is between you and me, and I shan't relinquish this tray until you put your nightshirt on."

"Mathews, get my crutches," Westfield barked.

She flashed Mathews an apologetic expression. "My lord, what is it you expect Mr. Mathews to do? Wrestle them from me?"

"Yes, by God, if that's what it takes."

Mathews's mouth fell open, and his gaze swung back and forth between them as though he observed two tennis players at Hampton Court. "I-I believe I'm being hailed. I'm coming!" the valet said, and bolted from the room.

"Damn you, Mathews. You spineless rotter. You probably wouldn't have won a tussle with this termagant, but at least you might have given it a go!" He turned his angry glare back on her.

She smiled and lifted another dome with great fanfare. "Oh, sausages. How divine."

"You she-devil. Don't you dare."

"Did you know Monsieur Laurent has left for market?" She shook her head at him. "No, you poor soul, confined as you are, you would not. But surely you must realize what it means?" Without waiting for a response she continued, "It means there is no one in the kitchen to cook up more of this hearty fare."

If possible, Westfield's visage took on an even more lethal edge.

"Oh, don't fret. I'm sure there is some porridge left in

the kitchen." She scrunched up her nose. "Though it does have a terrible propensity to crust and thicken when it sits about."

Westfield reached out and grabbed his nightshirt. He looked like a man barely contained. He drew the garment over his head and onto his body. "You, my dear girl, are lucky I cannot walk, because if I could, I would throttle your slender little neck."

A frisson ran down her spine. Westfield's hands were massive. They looked capable of snapping not only her neck, but grinding stone to dust or bending steel. She battled down such unsettling thoughts and dabbed at the corners of her mouth with the pressed linen napkin from the tray. "I'll ring for a clean fork and napkin."

"Never mind, just give me my food," he said, buttoning his nightshirt.

Sophia felt a pang of regret when he fastened the last button.

"Be warned, madam, I shall remove my nightshirt as soon as I'm done eating."

"Hayden!" a female voice gasped from the doorway. "Surely, you cannot be serious."

Westfield slumped against the pillows cushioning the chaise and rubbed the back of his neck. The sharp look in his eyes was gone, replaced by an unmistakable affection for the woman who entered his private sitting room.

"Tell me, Edith, have I been such a terrible brother you felt it befitting to shackle me with this accursed woman?"

Lady Prescott sighed. "Hayden, should not the question be what lunacy persuaded me to retain such a sweet and gently bred woman to tend to you? I should have hired a charwoman from one of the East End infirmaries with ham-sized hands and a vocabulary befitting a sailor."

Westfield's sister plucked the kid gloves off her fingers. They were a deep green, like her fashionable walking dress with its bustled back and layered swags. The woman patted her brown hair, swept up into a chignon. "I'm appalled by your behavior. It is beyond the pale, even for you." She turned to Sophia. "Do forgive my brother's immodesty, Miss Camden. I pray it shan't happen again, but I did forewarn you that your charge would not be easy. Yet, I never imagined . . ." Her ladyship steepled her hands and tilted her face heavenward before looking back at Sophia. "My dear, I hope you are not about to resign."

"No, Lady Prescott, I would not dream of abandoning his lordship. I fear his confinement has piqued his temper and brought about some oddity of behavior, but we can only hope and pray it will be relieved with my fastidious care."

With a hand on her bosom, Lady Prescott heaved a sigh. "Good, my dear. I knew I could count on you." She waggled a finger at her brother. "We must thank the good Lord that Miss Camden has a great deal of Christian charity in her, Hayden. You should feel ashamed."

"Presently, dear, all I feel is hungry." He motioned to the tray. "My breakfast, Miss Camden."

Sophia placed the bed tray upon his lap and turned back to Lady Prescott. "May I inquire how you are faring, my lady?"

"Quite well. My cold is all but gone."

Sophia smiled. "I'm pleased to hear it."

Westfield raised a fork laden with bacon. His hand stilled. "Edith, I'd offer you some breakfast, but Chef is at market. Would you care for some hot chocolate, tea, or some toast?" He slipped the fork into his mouth.

Sophia gently cleared her throat. "I'm sorry, my lord, I don't mean to be impertinent by correcting you, but Monsieur Laurent hasn't left yet."

Westfield nearly choked on his bacon. "What?" he

asked, coughing down the meat as though it had grown a cloven hoof. "I thought you said Laurent was at market."

She pressed her fingers to her cheek. "I do beg your forgiveness if I was somehow unclear. Mr. Laurent is not due to leave for another hour."

Sophia thought Westfield would throw one of his dishes at her, but instead he grinned.

"You are a worthy opponent, Miss Camden. Very worthy."

Lady Prescott stared at her brother. "Opponent? What in heaven's name are you prattling about, Hayden? Is he feverish, Miss Camden? Should Dr. Trimble be summoned?"

"Edith, I'm fine. I have no fever, and I do not wish to see Trimble. Now, dear, do you wish for some breakfast?"

Lady Prescott took an exaggerated breath. "No, I'm fine." She settled into the upholstered chair by the chaise.

"If that will be all," Sophia said. "I must take my leave so I may accompany Dr. Trimble to Whitechapel."

"Miss Camden," his lordship said, "I am not in the habit of employing people who make their own schedules."

"Oh goodness, Hayden." His sister swatted at his arm with her gloves. "*I am the one* who retained Miss Camden, and she made me aware of her previous commitment to the mission." Lady Prescott turned to her and smiled. "I think it rather commendable you and Dr. Trimble give so much of your time to those less fortunate. You do recall, Hayden, I am a patroness for the Whitechapel Mission, and it is supported by some of those closest to my heart?"

Looking disinterested, Westfield pierced several pieces of sausage with his fork. "Indeed, my dear. You, Trimble, and Miss Camden are angels doing God's work."

Was the nobleman so insensitive to the hardship of the indigent? One only had to visit the East End to see their plight. She'd seen factory-girls whose hands were cut and scarred from machinery, and men whose bodies were twisted and crippled from the laborious work they partook in, but worst of all, she'd seen dirty, badly nourished children with no hope in their eyes.

Doubtful Westfield had ever set foot in Whitechapel or anywhere thereabouts. She thought of her sister and niece—of the filth they'd called home. She clamped her mouth shut and resisted the urge to tell his lordship what she thought of him. Instead, she nodded and turned to Lady Prescott. "It was good seeing you again, my lady."

"You too, my dear."

As soon as Miss Camden left the room, Edith glared at him.

"Do you get pleasure in letting others believe you are indifferent? Why do you court condemnation? You are a generous man. The mission's greatest benefactor, yet you shroud the fact."

"You think the high sticklers would forgive my transgressions if they knew of the alms I bestow upon the poor? Has my money bought me absolution? Erased the fact I abandoned my wife not even a month after Celia was born? How fanciful you are, dear."

Edith's face flushed. "There were extenuating circumstances. If Laura had told you the truth, you wouldn't have left her or Celia."

He narrowed his eyes. Edith was about to cross an unspoken boundary if she wished to place blame at Laura's feet.

"Hayden, you are kind and caring, yet everyone who knows it must remain mute. Others would see you in a different light if you could forgive yourself instead of seeking out their derision. I know why you are acting this way toward Miss Camden. You wish her to tell people how wicked you are. When will you feel worthy of forgiveness?"

The memory of Laura's tear-streaked face appeared before his mind's eye. He didn't deserve forgiveness. "I should have figured out what Father had done to Laura, yet I was blinded by my own sense of betrayal."

"It is difficult to accept that Father would force himself on someone. That he would do it to his son's betrothed is incomprehensible." Tears glistened in Edith's warm brown eyes.

"Do you doubt Laura's last letter to me? That it was Father who got her with child?" Hayden couldn't force his mouth to say the word *rape* aloud. His stomach curdled. He shoved his dish of food away.

"Father was nothing if not cruel at times, especially to those he considered beneath his station. Your decision to marry a simple country girl infuriated him. Yes, I believe it. One only has to look at Celia to see the resemblance to our family. But you wouldn't have left Laura if she had told you—"

"She knew I would have taken pleasure in sending him to the devil." His hands flexed. Too late. The bastard was dead. As was his wife.

Edith gasped. "You wouldn't have."

"It appears my wife knew me better than you. So she suffered in silence, and I walked away."

"Because you thought her unfaithful. How were you to know the truth, Hayden? What were you to conclude? She gave birth to a child you knew wasn't yours. Most men would have reacted the same way. You need to forgive yourself. Otherwise, I fear you won't be content until you are dead. It is the only thing that explains why you started a relationship with that madwoman Adele Fontaine."

He glanced away.

"Oh, Hayden, it was only a wild guess, but your expression confirms it. I saw you and her standing before Claridge's Hotel a few months ago. Quite insane to engage in a dalliance with such an unstable woman. You live your life as if it has no future. You are reckless. If you do not care a fig for yourself, at least think of those who love you. Think of your commitment to Celia. I know after Laura's death you vowed to care for the child."

"I have always presumed Celia would be well taken care of if something were to happen to me. Am I wrong to believe that you would welcome her permanently into your home?"

"You know I would. I love her. But *you* are the only parent left in her life."

"Parent?" he echoed.

"Hayden," she said softly, placing her hand atop his. "You are her father in every way that counts. Celia has lived with you since Laura's death. She loves you dearly, and you love her. When you told me what Laura's letter revealed, I promised I'd take the secret to my grave. I'll never disclose it to her, nor anyone else."

He averted his face, knowing it reflected his torment. Edith was correct; he loved Celia as if she were his own. But was it enough?

After Laura's death five years ago, he'd toyed with the idea of asking Edith to raise Celia. Edith would have made a fine mother, yet sadly, she was childless. However, the moment he'd seen Celia in the nursery at Wincombe Manor after Laura's funeral, he'd felt a connection to the child.

He remembered her nurse, a good-natured, elderly woman saying, "Say hello to your papa, Celia." The woman had set her frail hands against the child's slender back, propelling her forward. Celia, only three, had turned and latched on to the nursemaid's legs as if the devil himself stood before her.

"That's fine, Miss Penworthy," he'd said, taking a seat in the corner of the large room. "Celia hasn't seen me in a long time. We need to become reacquainted."

For three days, he sat in the nursery every moment the child was awake. On the first day, she occasionally glanced at him from where she sat playing on the floor, as if he were an oddity or something out of place, such as a bug floating in one's soup.

On the second day, while he sat in the same chair, looking over the estate books, Celia had surreptitiously tiptoed toward him. She'd ducked under the table and brushed her little hand over the cuff of his wool trousers as if the coarse fabric intrigued her.

He'd peeked under the table and given her a gentle smile, and she'd scurried away.

However, on the third day, seeming to feel braver, she'd approached him. As if wishing to confirm he was not a figment of her imagination, she'd poked him in the ribs with her tiny index finger. He'd wanted to reach out and hold her, to place her on his knee, but he'd resisted, believing he would only succeed in frightening her off. Instead, he pretended her touch tickled, and they smiled at each other.

And that evening, after she'd eaten her dinner, she climbed onto his lap, a book in her hand, and peered at him. And it was then he'd known: he would take her back to London with him and care for her as best as he could, for surely there was a modicum of love left in his heart for this innocent child.

"Hayden." Edith's voice drew him back to the present. "Please be more prudent in the future, if not for your own sake, then for those who love you." His sister stood and smoothed out the skirt of her dark green gown. "Now, I must be off. Celia is here with me. I promised she could visit with you before we leave to go shopping."

He nodded.

Smiling, as if they had not broached any subject more benign than the weather, Edith bent down and kissed his cheek. "I pray you will take what I have said to heart."

He patted the top of Edith's hand. She was right: if he didn't change his ways, he'd not fulfill his graveside promise to Laura to care for Celia, and he'd fail his wife *again*.

Chapter Five

Sophia stepped out into the cold November air and ascended the servants' stairs to the pavement in front of Westfield's house.

A fashionably dressed gentleman stood before Lord Westfield's front door under the portico. His eyes were nearly as dark as hers, and his angular face was not quite handsome, but arresting.

He tipped his hat to her. Daylight slashed across his face, revealing a scar on his left cheek.

The front door opened. "Lord Adler," the butler said. "Come in, sir."

Adler? Oh, she'd heard his name before. Scandal nipped at the nobleman's heels like an overanxious dog.

The sound of a man clearing his throat drew her attention. She turned to see Thomas standing next to his carriage. He held out his hands, and she moved forward to place hers within his, pleased as always to see her closest friend and employer. "Thomas, how are you?"

"I'm well. How are you, Sophia?"

"Fine." She climbed into the carriage and settled against the blue plush interior.

He followed her inside and arched a brow—a clear indication of his disbelief.

The carriage jerked as the coachman urged the two horses to start up the street. Ignoring Thomas's inquisitive gaze, she stared out the window at the grand façades and the spattering of fashionably dressed pedestrians. Unbidden, a vision of Westfield lounging on the chaise, light glinting off his sculpted chest, flashed before her eyes.

"Sophia?"

She gave a slight start and turned to find Thomas peering at her.

He grinned. "You haven't heard a word I've said, my dear."

"Thomas, please forgive me," she replied, feeling foolish for having lascivious daydreams over a man she didn't even care for.

"A penny for your thoughts."

She studied her hands folded in her lap. "I was wondering if those supplies I ordered for the dispensary have arrived." Guilt swept over her. She had always been completely truthful with Thomas, but sharing one's baser daydreams . . . that she would not do. Not even with her trusted friend, who knew more about her than anyone else in London.

She'd told him about growing up in Chelsea with her parents, grandfather, and sister, Maria. That diphtheria spread through their house, sparing only her and Maria. How they were sent to live with their only other relation—their father's uncle Charles.

She'd been twelve when she arrived in Northumberland. She still recalled Great-Uncle Charles's words upon seeing them. "Have them scrubbed," he'd said to the housekeeper. "They look like gypsies." At the time, she'd not understood why their olive skin bothered him. Mama had been even darker, and Papa had called her his Italian goddess.

Only years later, did she learn Great-Uncle had expected Papa to marry a proper English miss—a member of the nobility. It hadn't mattered that Aletta Gianni was the daughter of the revered painter Vincente Gianni; Mama was still an immigrant with no ties to the English peerage. And Great-Uncle's thwarted hope of having ties to the aristocracy had made him cruel to both her and her sister. Nothing they'd done was good enough.

"Has Westfield been unbearable?" Thomas asked, once again, interrupting her thoughts.

"Unbearable?" she echoed.

"Sophia, you know what I mean." Exasperation deepened his tone. "He's an arrogant man. I wish to know how you're faring."

A commotion outside the carriage briefly caught Thomas's attention. He gave an impatient-sounding sigh. "You have not answered my question. Is he treating you with respect?"

"Thomas, I assure you I can handle Westfield."

"Does he know that?"

She laughed. "I daresay he's learning."

A smile resurfaced on Thomas's handsome face. "I'm pleased to hear it." His posture relaxed, and he settled against the squabs. Holding her gaze, he continued, "However, I would be greatly relieved if you did not return to his residence."

Sophia arched a brow. "You don't care for him, do you?"

"I don't know him well enough to like or dislike him, Sophia. But the rumors of debauchery and immorality . . . I wish you had not allowed Lady Prescott to talk you into attending the man."

"I thought you abhorred gossip."

The carriage swayed as they turned onto Whitechapel High. "I do, but . . ." He tugged his hat off his head and crushed the rim in his hand. "It is not all gossip, Sophia.

He has a child. She was born only seven months after the nuptials. A few weeks later, he was here in London acting like an unfettered young buck."

"Oh," she mumbled.

"I'll give him credit for taking responsibility. He obviously got the woman with child. She was not of his social standing. But I cannot excuse his shabby behavior afterward or the way he flaunted his infidelities. He abandoned the poor woman in the country. She died near five years ago."

Sophia stared at the nerve twitching in Thomas's jaw. He may treat the highborn, but it was clear he possessed little tolerance for their ilk.

Sophia bit her lip. "Where is the child?"

"Celia lives with him, but Lady Prescott has taken her to her residence so Westfield might rest. The child's lovely. Precocious and smart." He smoothed the rim of his hat. "I wish you to be careful. I hear he can be charming when he wishes to be."

Sophia's mouth fell open. "Thomas, is that what you fear? That he will try to seduce me?" She laughed softly. She was tempted to tell him that Westfield had already sacked her, and she remained in his employ only because she'd dared the scoundrel. But Thomas would call it folly, just like Great-Uncle Charles called her ambition to become a physician a foolish venture, and she didn't wish to be criticized. She'd experienced enough disapproval from that cantankerous relation to last her a lifetime.

"Do not worry about the man seducing me. Westfield has no desire in that regard. He hasn't even tried to be charming. In truth, he does not care for me, nor I for him, but we shall muddle through our differences as best we can."

Sophia returned her gaze to the window—to the grave faces of the people looking at the fine equipage as it made its way through Whitechapel. She should spend her time thinking about these people. Not waste her thoughts pondering a highborn nobleman who was a rogue.

"Christ, if you don't look like a man who's had his bollocks twisted into a knot," Lord Simon Adler announced, stepping into Hayden's sitting room.

"If you've come here to insult me, you unsympathetic sod, you'd best turn your hairy arse around and leave," Hayden bit back.

Laughing, Simon unbuttoned his black town coat and settled himself into one of the fireside chairs. "I just saw a vision of beauty exiting your house. Have you hired Celia a new governess?"

"No. Did the woman have a taut chignon, cold eyes, and disapproving scowl?"

His longtime friend plopped his legs atop the ottoman and grinned. "No. Glossy hair, enchanting eyes, and extremely kissable lips."

Hayden harrumphed. "My new nurse is anything but kissable. Stick your tongue in her mouth and you'll find yourself mute."

The corner of Simon's lips twitched. "A termagant, eh? Why, old chum, she sounds like your type."

Hayden ran his hand over his thigh. "I've learned my lesson."

Simon gave him a sympathetic look. "I warned you about Adele. Do you intend to eventually tell the authorities, or do you wish to handle this matter more discreetly?"

"Her brother has sent her to the Continent. Hopefully, to some asylum. I've told Kent that as long as she remains there, I will not disclose her identity. I do not wish to add fuel to the spectacle presently being played out in the newspapers." He had to start thinking about Celia and Edith.

"Will your pretty nurse be returning shortly? I should like to make her acquaintance." His friend grinned.

Hayden was not sure why, but the idea of Simon meeting Miss Sophia Camden sent a frisson of uneasiness through him.

"She has gone to do God's work at the Whitechapel Mission."

Simon's expression turned solemn. "Pious? What a tragedy. Do you think her corruptible?"

"I doubt it."

"Ah, a woman who hasn't succumbed to your charms."

Shifting on the chaise, Hayden cringed. "Do I look fit to charm anyone?"

"Truthfully? No. However, I shall dare you to do so, since you find her so uptight."

"I'm not interested."

"You, not interested in a dare?"

"I've come to the conclusion I abhor dares. The sooner my tart-mouthed nurse leaves my house, the happier I shall be. Now, will you pass me those crutches?"

Simon stood and handed him the crutches. "You need any help?"

"No, I'm going to remain here for a bit." He was sick of lying in bed.

"Then, I shall be shoving off. I might return in a few days, so you can introduce me to your lovely nurse."

"Don't bother. She will be gone shortly." Once again, an odd and irrational feeling of discontent settled over Hayden.

"If you say so. Take care, old boy."

An hour after Simon left the sitting room, Hayden propped the crutches under his arms and hobbled back to the bedchamber. He winced as a stabbing pain shot up his leg. He'd just reached the bed when Mathews entered the room.

The man rushed over to him, his hands fluttering in the air. "Careful, my lord. You might fall."

Hayden narrowed his eyes at the turncoat.

Mathews averted his face. "Surely, you did not expect me to wrestle Miss Camden for your crutches?"

He cocked a brow at the valet.

"I couldn't. She's a woman."

"She's a bloody thorn in my side. That's what she is."

The questioning look in Mathews's eyes clearly betrayed his confusion over the situation. "Is there something else in play here, my lord?"

Hayden grunted an affirmation as he sat on the edge of the mattress.

"Ah, I thought so," the valet said, taking the crutches.

Carefully Hayden swung his legs onto the bed and pulled the counterpane to his waist.

"Might I get you something?"

"No." He wouldn't admit it, but he was feeling bloody tired.

Mathews inclined his head. "I shall leave you so you might rest."

"Has Miss Camden returned yet?" Why he asked he wasn't sure. He should be pleased the woman was gone.

"She has not—" A commotion in the corridor halted the man's reply.

A Saint Bernard the size of a small pony, weighing at least eleven stone, dashed into the room, dragging the butler in its wake. Hawthorne attempted to tighten his hands on the lead as the dog barreled forward.

The animal lifted its head. Hayden recognized the big brown eyes and drool-covered mouth. "Dash it all! What is Lady Olivia doing here?"

A frazzled Hawthorne dug his feet into the thick carpet, halting the dog's progression. "A young urchin left her. I told him you would not want the beast. But he insisted Sir

Harry felt the animal would be good company for you during your confinement."

Bugger it. "Return her to Sir Harry immediately."

"The boy said the gentleman has left town," Hawthorne responded, inching himself away from the animal's salivating mouth and overlong jowls.

Good God, most likely a creditor was on the man's tail. Why he stayed chums with the rascal was beyond him. Harry had few qualities to endear him, unless one had a penchant for gamblers, wastrels, and cads—the man had the illustrious achievement of being all three.

Lady Olivia jerked her head sideways, sending a massive glob of drool onto the butler's perfectly pressed trousers.

Hawthorne groaned. "The boy said the animal must be walked four times a day or she makes a bleedin' mess. Those are the lad's words, not mine, my lord."

The dog jerked forward. A clearly startled Hawthorne released the lead. Lady Olivia barked, and with her tail swishing back and forth in an enthusiastic rhythm, she vaulted upon the bed, and began an affectionate round of face licking, nose nuzzling, and crevice sniffing—all to Hayden's utter distaste.

"Get me my pistol!"

Hawthorne paled. "My lord, you cannot shoot her."

"I'm not going to shoot her. I'm going to bloody well shoot you."

The butler bristled and tipped his long thin nose into the air. "The lad shoved the lead in my hand and took off. H-he just left her. What was I to do?"

Hayden scowled at Hawthorne and then at Lady Olivia. The dog lay on her back. Her tongue lolled out the crook of her mouth as she batted her eyes at him.

Damnation. The deuced dog had always shown a strange attachment to him.

No doubt, Celia would find the animal amusing, but what to do with the beast until she returned was beyond him.

Sophia arrived back at Lord Westfield's residence before three o'clock—in time to bring him his afternoon tea tray. As she neared his room, she paused. The man was snapping orders at someone and cursing like a sailor. Hopefully, it wasn't the new maid. The young girl, fresh from the country, stammered when nervous. Squaring her shoulders, Sophia rushed toward the doorway in hopes of derailing Westfield's tirade.

"Damnation, can't you lie still?" he complained. "Olivia, get your head out from under my nightshirt, and stick your bloody tongue back in your mouth."

Sophia stopped dead in her tracks and eyed the open door ahead. Surely, Westfield was not entertaining a woman with his bedchamber door ajar. She shook her head. She must have misheard.

She stepped over the threshold. Her breath caught in her throat. Westfield nudged at a long body completely snuggled under his bedding.

"You unrepentant bitch. Stop licking my toes!"

Sophia halted with the intention of stepping back out of the room, but Westfield peered up at her.

"I don't know how much Harry paid for her, but the man was a deuced fool. She can't follow the simplest command, and she's as large as a cow." He scooted away from the woman. "She's been here only a few hours, and I've already tired of her."

Sophia stood still, her gaze fixed on the tray she held in her hands. Thomas was correct. The man had no morals whatsoever, dallying with some tart while his door remained open. Worse, he seemed to have no shame with regard to the fact she'd walked in on them.

Westfield's voice broke into her thoughts. "Miss Camden, put the blasted tray down, and tell Hawthorne to get in here. Perhaps he can do something with her."

Sophia's throat constricted. The butler? He wished the butler to have a go with the woman? If this was some indecent ploy to win their dare, he was close to succeeding. She opened her mouth to speak—to tell him what she thought of such moral depravity. However, at that exact moment, Westfield lifted the top edge of his counterpane to glare at his bedmate. "Olivia, stop pawing at me, or I'll have your big hairy bum carted outside."

Sophia had listened to enough of his degradation. The woman, whatever her station in life, deserved more respect than Westfield bestowed on her. She slammed the tray down on the dresser, rattling the china. "You should be ashamed of yourself. I've heard men talk to their horses with more respect."

"I damn well wish it were my horse. Why don't *you* get into bed with her and see how you like it? Better yet, I'll have her sent to your room later, so you can spend the entire night together."

The only thing that would have stopped Sophia from responding would have been a catastrophic event, something along the magnitude of an earthquake or a flood. "Oh, you wicked man. You"—she scraped her mind for a word that would clearly betray her abhorrence—"vile heathen!"

She opened her mouth to continue her fulmination when a long muzzle accompanied by a massive tongue poked itself out of the counterpane at the foot of the bed. Sophia clasped the wool fabric of her bodice and jumped back. "Good heavens, what is that?"

Westfield stared at her as if she were a simpleton. "What

does it look like? It's a bloody dog." His eyebrows pinched together. "Goodness, woman, what did you think?"

"Um . . ." Heat flooded her cheeks.

His dour countenance lightened. His eyes crinkled at the corners and a slow smile spread across his lips. He tipped his head back and burst out laughing. After what seemed like minutes, he swiped at the dampness at the corners of his eyes and sobered his expression.

Folding his arms over his broad chest, he stared intently at her. "Miss Camden, what . . . or should I say *who* did you believe shared my bed?"

Sophia swallowed. "Well, you called her Olivia, and said Harry had foolishly paid too much for her, so naturally I believed . . ." The tips of her ears burned, and she focused on the animal peering at her.

"Yes, do go on," Westfield prompted.

She stepped closer to the bed. "I believe I owe you a grave apology, my lord."

Westfield opened his mouth, and she braced herself for his caustic reproach, but instead he asked in an intrigued voice, "My door is wide open. What manner of man do you believe me to be?"

She gave a weak smile. "Magnanimous, sir."

Westfield grinned. "I've been called many things over the last several years; however, *magnanimous* isn't one of them."

He tugged the blankets off the massive dog. "Lady Olivia, may I introduce you to Miss Sophia Camden?"

The dog, the largest Sophia had ever seen, rolled onto its back and spread its hind legs wide.

His lordship looked utterly disgusted. "No need to curtsey, Miss Camden. As you can plainly see, her ladyship is not a stickler for formality."

"Is she yours?"

"Good God, no. She belongs to a friend. A soon-to-be departed friend, when I get my hands on him."

The dog's long tongue reached out to lick Westfield's toes.

"Lord, help me." He shifted his feet away. "Now, be so kind as to ask Hawthorne to come retrieve her ladyship. He has generously agreed to walk her at least six times a day, though he insists it need only be four."

Chapter Six

The following day, the mantel clock in Hayden's bedchamber chimed three times.

In precisely fifteen minutes, Miss Camden would enter the room with his afternoon tea. The woman was as regimented as a general in the Royal Navy.

A faint tap sounded on the door. It slowly swung inward, and Mathews crossed the threshold like a thief in the night. Hayden noticed the crutches in the valet's hands and smiled. "Where did you find them?"

"She hid them behind a tall cabinet in the laundry room."

The sly vixen. Last night, he'd leaned the crutches against the bedside table and awoken today to find them missing. When he'd asked his nurse where they were, she'd smiled with that wide, sensual mouth of hers.

Hayden swung his legs over the side of the bed and tugged his nightshirt down. It was damn inconvenient wearing the garment. "Where is she?"

Mathews tiptoed to the bed as if expecting Sophia Camden to burst through the door, rip the wooden braces from his hands, and strike the valet over the head with them. "She is conversing with a maid in the kitchen. She should be here shortly."

A laugh escaped Hayden's lips. Perfect. He couldn't wait to see the expression on his pretty nurse's face when she found him up and about again. Balancing himself on his good leg, he tucked the crutches under his arms, and hobbled toward his private sitting room.

He'd reached the doorway when a gasp sounded behind him.

Damn, he wanted to see her expression, but turning around on these blasted crutches was precarious at best. He continued across the room.

"My lord!" There was no mistaking the displeasure in her sharp tone.

Mathews, the coward, squeaked and dashed from the room.

Upon reaching the mahogany desk, Hayden lowered himself into the high-backed chair behind it. He tried to keep his countenance impassive, but the steady throbbing in his leg made it a difficult task.

Hands on her hips, Miss Camden strode toward him. A rosy pink tinged her honey-colored cheeks. She looked lovely when irate. "Do you comprehend the damage you may be causing?"

He pinched the bridge of his nose. She'd look even more attractive if she stood before him gagged. He opened the top drawer of his desk and withdrew some business correspondence that required a reply. "Madam, I have no intention of staying in bed all day."

"You are a most obstinate man."

"Then we are evenly matched, aren't we, my dear?"

The corners of her lips turned up a fraction. "Well, if you insist on this reckless course, at least elevate your leg." She moved to the corner of the room, lifted a small chair, and placed it next to him. "Please, put your leg up on this."

The pain in his thigh was so intense he didn't dare move.

As if sensing his discomfort, she knelt, gently raised his leg, and set it on the upholstered seat. Almost immediately, the throbbing slowed, and all he experienced was the pleasant warmth of her fingers on his calf.

Her head was right below his chin, and the scent of lemon and lavender drifted to his nose. He leaned forward and drew in the enticing fragrance at the exact moment she turned and peered up at him. Only inches separated her mouth from his. Her almond-shaped eyes grew round.

This close, he could see her irises were a few shades lighter than her pupils. A deep, warm chocolate. The urge to brush his fingers over the texture of her silky skin nearly overrode him.

He jerked back.

Bloody hell. She was his adversary. He wanted to win the dare. He wanted her gone. Didn't he?

She scrambled onto her feet, looking as disconcerted as he felt, and tugged at the waistband of her white pinafore. "I brought your afternoon tea. It's in your bedchamber. I shall bring it in here."

As she walked out of the sitting room, he leaned sideways to get a better view of the sway of her hips. He grasped the edge of the desk as he nearly toppled out of his chair. "Damnation, get ahold of yourself, old boy."

Miss Camden stepped back into the room. "Did you ask me something?"

"No," he grumbled.

"Do you wish me to pour?" She set the silver tea service on the desk.

He grunted an affirmation, and watched as her delicate hands lifted the teapot. Her fingers were long and elegant, and he imagined them sliding down his abdomen to his—

"It's hot," she said, jerking him from his naughty daydream. She set the cup and saucer on the corner of his blotter. Her head tipped to the side and she wet her lips. A habit of hers that made the brainless appendage below his waist react. Thankfully, her gaze wasn't on him, but on something on the desk.

She bent closer. "I know that emblem."

He slapped his hand atop the parchment emblazoned with a Hereford bull and the name J. H. MASON scripted beneath it. "Do you mind?"

"I do beg your pardon, my lord. It's just that I see a great deal of crates and barrels burnished with the J. H. Mason mark at the Whitechapel Mission. Do you conduct business with the wholesaler and grocer?"

"What concern is it of yours?"

She pursed her lips. "I daresay it's not. However, Mr. Mason donates a prodigious amount to the charity. And Mrs. Hamblin, the mission's matron, says what he sends is of superior quality, not rancid like most of the other alms they receive."

He swept the correspondence up and folded it.

"Miss Camden, Mason is far from a saint. He buys his goods in quantity, which in turn, allows him to procure them at a better price. Moreover, when he opens a new grocer's shop, he immediately undercuts his competitors. Believe me, a man like Mason doesn't reach the success he has attained without treading ruthlessly upon others. Indeed, if he is in possession of a heart, it is black at best."

She narrowed her eyes. "I beg to differ. Any man who is so generous to the poor and friendless cannot be without merit."

"If you met him, you'd disagree. Now, I have work to do, if you don't mind." He picked up a fresh piece of paper and started writing correspondence to his banker.

"Is there anything else I might do for you before I go?"

Go? His gaze snapped back to her face. "Where? I

hope you're not returning to that hellhole again." His gut tightened.

"Do you mean Whitechapel?"

"Yes."

She smiled, causing those two dimples on her cheeks to make an appearance. "No, I was only going to have a cup of tea in the kitchen."

"Very well, I don't need your coddling." Yet, even as he said it, he had a feeling he'd sit here and wonder when she would return. Sophia evoked an odd dichotomy within him. At times, he wished to wring her slender neck and at other times, when she wasn't about, he experienced a loneliness he couldn't explain.

Sophia strode out of the private sitting room and into Lord Westfield's bedchamber. Her black medical bag sat on a low mahogany dresser, and she rummaged through it. Alice, the chatty maid, was suffering with a terrible toothache.

Ah, here it is. She withdrew a bottle of Dr. Young's Soothing Syrup. Though not a proponent of the tincture, she'd give the maid a *single* dose to alleviate her pain.

She descended the servants' steps to the kitchen. Alice sat at a long table, holding the side of her face. The ginger-haired girl was as pale as a ghost.

"You need to visit a dentist," Sophia said. "I'll give you a spoonful of this to ease your discomfort."

"Thank you, miss."

"Alice, it will only get worse if you ignore it. The tooth might become abscessed. There's a dentist on the Strand. A Dr. Weber. He is most gentle."

The young woman swallowed the syrup and stood. "Mrs. Beecham has already agreed to give me the afternoon off to see a dentist. Thank you, again, miss."

Still clutching her cheek, Alice exited the room.

Sophia poured herself a cup of tea from the porcelain pot on the sideboard. As she sat in the now empty kitchen, she noticed the chef and Elsie, a kitchen maid, in an adjacent room washing root vegetables at an oversize copper sink. The robust Frenchman waved his hands in the air as he spoke to the young girl.

This morning, instead of porridge, Monsieur Laurent had made warm cinnamon rolls and eggs for the staff. He'd acted irate at the additional work involved in preparing such a breakfast, but had smiled repeatedly as the staff *oohed and aahed* as they ate. Obviously, this change from the normal fare was Westfield's doing. His lordship was a bit of an enigma.

After finishing her tea, Sophia made her way upstairs and entered the bedchamber she'd been given: a lovely cream-colored room with a large tester bed with green velvet bedding and a wide mahogany armoire. Not a servant's room, but the closest in proximity to his lordship's apartment across the corridor.

Sophia sat on the edge of the bed and touched her cheek where Lord Westfield's breath had fanned against it, his lips only inches from hers. His blue eyes had stared intensely at her. For a moment, she'd thought he might kiss her. Her heart had fluttered in her chest. Was it all part of his plan to unsettle her? The scoundrel.

A noise drifted up from under the bed, pulling her from her thoughts. She jumped and dashed to the far corner of the room.

Something was under there. She prayed it wasn't a rat. The beasts terrified her. She'd endured them when she'd first returned to London. They had infested her sister Maria's tenement, scurrying about the dark recesses of the squalid room, gnawing in the walls, especially during the night. The recollection dried her mouth.

She reminded herself that she was much larger than any rodent, and one must expect to see rats, especially in a city as crowded as London. Yet, already her palms grew sweaty, and her heart pounded in her chest.

The noise sounded again. Louder.

Sophia lifted her skirts, darted to a small gilded chair, and leapt upon it in a most unladylike manner. The delicate chair creaked, and for a terrifying moment, she feared it would shatter and send her unceremoniously back to the floor.

Another noise filled the quiet room. It didn't sound like vermin, but like a giggling child.

Gathering her skirts high, Sophia stepped off her perch, walked to the bed, and lifted the edge of the counterpane.

A young girl, wearing a white silk half-mask adorned with blue plumage, popped her head out from beneath the bed like a turtle emerging from its shell.

"Why did you jump onto that chair?" the child asked.

Sophia's face warmed. The girl clearly thought her a lunatic.

"Hello," Sophia said, ignoring the question.

The child, who looked to be about seven or eight, crawled out from the darkened space. "You're not a maid. The maids sleep on the fourth floor, and the color of your navy dress is not as ugly as the gray ones they wear."

"Thank you." Sophia took no offense. She'd learned long ago, children were the voice of honesty. She dried her damp palms on her starched apron.

The girl cast her own clothes a dubious glance before she smacked the dust off the skirt of her yellow dress and white stockings, sending a flurry of dust motes into the air.

Sophia smiled and plucked a large dust ball out of the girl's long brown hair and another off the blue plumes darting out from her mask. "Quite a pretty mask you're wearing. Are you to attend a ball this evening?"

"Lawks, no. I found the mask while rummaging through some old trunks in the attic one day. I thought they belonged to my mama, but Mrs. Beecham says they belonged to my grandmama."

This was obviously Westfield's daughter.

"What's your name?" The girl didn't wait for a reply, but continued, "I'm Celia."

"Pleased to make your acquaintance, Celia. I'm Sophia, your father's nurse."

"I thought so. The last nurse was a man. He stayed in this room as well. I wouldn't want to be a nurse." Celia ran her small hand up one of the long feathers and bit her lip. "I don't like blood. I saw lots of blood when my papa was shot."

Who took care of the child? Why hadn't they kept her away from seeing such mayhem? "Where is your governess, Celia?"

"Papa gave her the boot last week. Called her a narrow-minded old biddy."

No wonder Lady Prescott offered such a generous salary; it appeared Westfield went through employees like most people went through coal in January.

"He called her another name too. I didn't know what it meant, and when I asked Aunt Edith, she nearly swooned. Then she took out her Bible and prayed all afternoon. Aunt Edith says I shouldn't eavesdrop. Do you know my aunt Edith?"

"I do," Sophia replied, wondering how the religious Lady Prescott had ended up with such a rascal for a brother, and how he had ended up with such a lovely daughter.

"She and Papa are going to interview for a new governess as soon as he's better. I've been staying at Aunt Edith and Uncle Henry's. But Papa sent a missive saying he wishes me to return home. Aunt Edith doesn't think it wise. She is talking to him right now." Celia frowned.

"You wish to return?"

"Yes, I miss Papa when I'm away." The child bit her lower lip again. "I know I shouldn't be in your room, but when I went to my bedchamber to visit Albert, the little crumb was missing, so I'm searching the house."

"Albert? Is he your cat?"

"No, he's a fancy white mouse."

Mouse? Sophia fisted her hands in her skirts and inched them upward. She didn't care for mice either, though usually they had the decency to scurry away.

"Do you believe him to be in here?"

The child shrugged her narrow shoulders. "He could be anywhere."

"Indeed." Sophia scanned the floor.

The girl's eyes lit up behind her mask. "Would you like to help me find him?"

Sophia suppressed the urge to shudder. "No, my dear, I have to check on your father shortly."

Celia's shoulders slumped. "Papa doesn't like Albert to run willy-nilly about the house." She sighed. "Great-Aunt Hortense gave him to me. Papa was not pleased. He said Albert is a country mouse and would be happier living with Great-Aunt Hortense in Kent."

This tidbit shocked Sophia. She found it difficult to imagine Westfield gently trying to persuade his daughter to return the mouse. She figured him for the type to have one of the maids or footmen just squash the animal with a broom while the child wasn't looking.

Celia pulled off her mask, and Sophia noticed the resemblance between Westfield and his daughter. Except Celia did not possess her father's startling blue eyes. Hers were brown. "I might get a fancy rat instead," Celia said, moving to the door. "They like the city."

Sophia's legs felt weak. "A fancy rat?"

"Yes, Lady Marley has one. She keeps it in a gold birdcage."

Sophia's breath tightened in her chest. "A rat?" she echoed again with more disgust and utter disbelief than she meant to show.

"Yes, I hear the queen has one." The child's voice radiated more than a modicum of excitement.

"I prefer cats myself." Sophia opened the bedchamber door. She didn't elaborate on the fact she had several as a means to control vermin. The child would think her heartless.

As they slipped into the corridor, Celia glanced at her father's closed bedchamber door. Lady Prescott could be heard talking inside the room. "I like cats, but if I got one, I'd definitely have to bring Albert to Great-Aunt Hortense's first."

Celia skipped down the corridor. She placed her hands on her hips. "Albert, you little gadabout, Papa won't be happy if he hears you've taken to roaming around the house." She stopped to peer under a hall table before turning back to Sophia. "I'll bring Albert back after I find him. He likes his tail petted."

Sweat prickled Sophia's palms again. She nodded, but as soon as Celia turned around, Sophia gave an involuntary shudder.

An hour later, when Sophia went to check on Lord Westfield, she found him sitting on the sofa in his private sitting room reading *Beauty and the Beast* to Celia. His lordship wore a sapphire-colored robe of rich velvet with silk lapels over his nightshirt. The child was nestled in the crook of her father's arm while her stockinged feet were propped upon Lady Olivia's back as if the dog were an ottoman.

From the doorway, Sophia surveyed them. The scene emitted peace and contentment. Such a stark contrast to the images she had formed with regard to Westfield and his relationship with the child—especially after Thomas's conversation in the carriage.

But had not Celia's own words implied a loving regard?

"Sophia!" Celia called. "Have you met Lady Olivia?"

The dog lifted its head and excitably slapped its tail against the ottoman Westfield's injured leg rested upon. His lordship lowered the book and narrowed his eyes at the animal.

"I have." Sophia tried not to laugh at the surly expression on Westfield's face.

Celia stroked the dog's back with her small feet. "Isn't she darling?"

Westfield's glower darkened.

"Yes," Sophia replied unable to quell the smile tugging at the corners of her lips.

"I am to remain home tonight," Celia said with exuberance. "And Lady Olivia is to sleep in my room." She turned to her father. "Right, Papa?"

"Only if you wish, dear; otherwise she is going to warm Hawthorne's bed."

Celia giggled. "Oh, Papa, don't be a silly goose."

Sophia blinked. Had Celia just called her father a silly goose, and had Westfield smiled in response?

"Was there something you needed, Miss Camden?" his lordship asked.

"No, I wished to know how you are faring."

He smiled down at his daughter. "Quite well."

"Then I shall leave you both to enjoy your story," she replied.

Westfield started reading to Celia, then glanced up. "Are you fond of books, Miss Camden?"

"Yes, very much so."

He motioned to a row of mahogany bookcases that stretched from the floor to the ceiling. They were crammed with novels, while two more stacks rose from the floor to nearly the height of Celia. The earl was obviously an avid reader. "You are more than welcome to borrow any of the books in this room or the library downstairs, if you wish."

Without waiting for her response, he returned his attention to the child, and began to read again.

"Thank you." Sophia strode toward the bookcases. Her eyes perused the leather bindings, stopping at a familiar brown cover with gold letterings. *Robinson Crusoe.* She blinked away the moisture blurring her vision, and drew the book off the shelf. Grandfather had loved reading this tale to her and her sister, Maria. For a brief moment, she clutched the novel to her chest. Feeling the heat of Westfield's gaze on her, Sophia turned around. He peered at her over the edge of the book he held. Her heart fluttered. Was he looking for a crack in her armor?

"I appreciate the loan of the book, my lord." Sophia moved toward the door.

"No, please stay, Sophia," Celia called out.

"Yes, *Sophia*," Westfield said, his voice as smooth as silk. "Join us."

His lordship's charismatic voice sent a shiver down her spine. His deep blue eyes held hers as he smiled warmly. This was the roué—the man who made the ladies of the *ton* behave so recklessly. Heat coursed through her veins. She prayed she was not blushing like a young schoolgirl.

She should offer an excuse as to why she could not stay. But somehow the words came out differently. "Thank you."

"Sophia," Celia said. "You may sit on the other side of Papa on the sofa."

Next to his lordship? Goodness, no. Westfield's gaze jerked to his daughter. He appeared as startled by the suggestion as she.

"Celia, because I do not wish to crowd your papa's injured leg, I think it best I sit here." Sophia walked to a navy velvet chair that faced them. She sat and opened the thickly bound edition of *Robinson Crusoe*. The leather binding creaked and a musty scent, common in old books, made her nostrils flare.

A soft tap sounded on the open door to the sitting room. The gray-haired housekeeper stood at the threshold. "Excuse me, my lord," Mrs. Beecham said, "but Mr. Talbot is here for Lady Celia's piano lesson."

"Oh, Papa, do I have to have my lesson today? Mr. Talbot smells like dirty socks."

Westfield laughed. "Really?"

Celia nodded. "I wish he smelled like Sophia. She smells nice, doesn't she?"

His lordship peered at Sophia, a twinkle in his eyes. "Indeed, she does. Quite lovely."

A spark of current burst in Sophia's stomach. How silly to allow the scoundrel's flattery to affect her so easily.

Westfield kissed the child's forehead. "Sorry, dear. Today you will have to contend with Mr. Talbot's less-than-gardenlike fragrance."

Celia wrinkled her nose, but slipped off the sofa. She stroked Lady Olivia's head. "Do you wish to come?" she asked the dog.

The Saint Bernard trotted to the door, its tail wagging in an excitable rhythm. Celia's face lit up. "What a smart dog she is."

The smile on Westfield's face faltered. Obviously, the man realized the longer the dog stayed, the more his daughter's attachment would grow.

"I will return after dinner, Papa." Celia darted from the room.

Sophia closed the book and begun to rise from the chair.

"You don't need to rush off." He flashed a boyish smile.

How innocent he looked. Bears looked just as lovable—if one forgot about their claws. Did the man have something up his sleeve? Did he wish to ask her more scandalous questions about anatomy?

She tipped her chin high and sank back onto the thick cushion. "Is there something you want to ask me?"

"Yes."

She braced herself for more of his wickedness.

"Of all the books I possess, I want to know why you chose *Robinson Crusoe*."

The question startled her. Not at all what she'd expected. "It is the same edition my grandfather enjoyed reading."

"Ah, that explains the expression on your face upon seeing it. You may keep it."

"Keep it? Thank you, but I couldn't."

"I have another copy in the library downstairs." As if the matter were settled, he picked up the leather-bound novel lying next to him on the sofa and flipped it open.

"You are too kind."

He nodded, but didn't look up.

As they read, a quiet, companionable silence settled over the room. A comfortable, momentary truce.

The story of the shipwrecked Crusoe caused echoes from the past to drift through Sophia's mind. Grandfather's deep baritone, reading English words in his heavily accented voice, and Maria correcting him when he would occasionally lapse into Italian. The memory tightened her throat. She lifted her gaze from the pages to Grandfather's painting hanging on the wall. How odd that it was here in Lord Westfield's house. Though not Grandfather's largest painting of the River Thames, it was one of his best. He'd painted it standing on the Chelsea Embankment.

"Do you like it?" Westfield asked, peering at the painting.

"Yes, it's lovely."

"It's a Gianni. Very few of his pieces come up for sale. I found this one at a dealer's shop on the Strand. Are you familiar with his work?"

Very. "Yes, I've seen several of his paintings at the National Gallery." She'd bestowed a collection to the museum.

"So you visit museums when not tending to the poor or infirmed?"

"Sometimes."

"What else do you do for entertainment, Sophia? Play whist? Backgammon?" He grinned. "Visit Vinton's gambling hell or dance on the tables at Morley's Music Hall?"

Wanting to shock him, she lied. "The latter, but only on Mondays."

He snorted, and her own laugh bubbled forth.

"Careful, Sophia, your wit is showing." Slowly he lifted his legs onto the sofa and stretched out. He closed his eyes and draped an arm over them.

Sophia's gaze drifted from his bare feet, over his robe and broad shoulders, and to his mouth. Ignoring the fluttering in her belly, she lifted the book and forced herself to read instead of gawk.

With his eyes closed, Hayden listened to Sophia as she softly turned the pages of the book she read. Every once in a while, she would make a small noise. A little sigh that somehow sounded musical.

After several minutes, the sounds ceased, leaving him feeling bereft.

Of course, this fixation with the woman must be due to his interminable boredom. Though he did enjoy their sparring and the way her lovely dark eyes flashed when she grew agitated, along with how easily her cheeks flushed. It had been a long time since he'd associated with a woman who blushed.

Why was she so quiet? He lowered his arm and peered at the chair where she sat. Sophia no longer wore her austere navy dress and starched apron, but a vibrant green gown that clung to her body like a second skin. The low décolletage exposed breasts so tightly corseted they almost spilled out of her bodice. His gaze lifted to her unpinned hair, absent her abominable starched cap. The dark, shiny strands flowed over her shoulders, a magnet to the light streaming through the sitting room windows.

Sophia looked breathtaking.

She stood and drifted across the room as if her feet floated on air. The corners of her wide mouth tipped upward as she surveyed him from beneath the veil of her lowered lashes. Without a word, she lifted a hand to the silk-covered buttons that lined the front of her bodice and started unfastening them.

His mouth grew dry. When was the last time he'd experienced such intense anticipation for the sight of a woman's naked body?

Her bodice fell open to reveal the warm hue of her skin and a black, almost sheer corset. She wore no chemise, and the gauzelike fabric did little to disguise the tawny color of her nipples. He'd seen dancers in the northern district of Paris garbed in such erotic clothing.

The little coquette leaned forward and lightly trailed her fingers over the swell of her breasts.

A quick rush of blood stiffened his already thickened rod.

Straightening, she gave a little wiggle and pushed the gown's shimmering fabric off her hips until it pooled at her feet. She now stood before him wearing a sheer hourglass corset and black gartered silk stockings that encased her long slender legs—legs that seemed to go on forever. His taut bollocks drew almost painfully against his heavy shaft.

She stepped closer to the sofa. So close, he could smell

Chapter Seven

A jarringly unpleasant scream pierced Hayden's ears.

His eyes flew open. Sophia flailed atop him, her face flushed, her expression a mixture of bewilderment and outright anger.

His gaze raked over her body. Where were the over-flowing breasts, the impossibly long legs, and the erotic attire? And why was her horrid hat on a drunken slide over the left side of her face?

Christ almighty! Had he dreamt it all, then pulled her body onto his?

Obviously. What should he do now? Inform her he'd partaken in a lurid fantasy, featuring her as the most willing of coquettes, and then profusely apologize? He should. His actions appalled him. He'd never forced himself on anyone, let alone someone in his employ. Yet, he asked, "Sophia, might I inquire *why* you're lying on me?"

Her mouth fell open. "My lord," she responded, her tone surprisingly calm. "Shouldn't the question be, why is your hand possessively planted on my derrière?"

He peered at his left hand. Indeed, it cupped her bum.

Well, stop gawking and remove it. Now! He slid his

hand off her buttocks. With as much indignation as he could muster he replied, "Goodness, woman, how should I know? I was innocently sleeping and awoke to find you accosting me."

"A-a-accosting you?" she sputtered. "Sir, are you implying *I* leapt on you, then shamelessly placed your hands on my person?"

"Did you?"

"You know I did not." She wiggled her body as though something uncomfortable probed her. Consternation flashed across her face.

Damn and blast. His manhood remained engorged. What was wrong with him?

Sophia blanched and scurried off him as though she sunbathed on a patch of stinging nettles in the nude. She straightened her dress and hat before blowing a midnight-colored tendril off her cheek.

"I believe you were dreaming, and I can only assume what or whom it was about." Her voice had regained its rigid composure.

"Do not fancy it was you."

"I didn't *presume* it was me. I envisioned some full-bosomed tart with a copious amount of air between her ears. In other words, a vacuous nitwit with no better sense than an ant!"

He arched a brow. "She sounds more appealing than an impertinent prude any man of good sensibility would avoid like the bubonic plague."

"Prude? Why, you abominable man." Sophia squared her shoulders, spun away, and stormed toward the door, mumbling about how she'd have to be deficient in the brain to endure him one minute longer.

Is she leaving? Hayden's pulse quickened.

"Are you resigning your post, Sophia? I knew a *mere slip of a woman* like you could never outwit me."

She stopped dead in her tracks and stood still, her back to him. Then, without a word, she exited the room.

Sophia knew she should have headed right for the front door, hailed a hansom cab, and never looked back. Yet she found herself in the kitchen asking the French chef for Westfield's dinner tray.

For a moment, she stared at the freshly prepared pot of coffee and contemplated adding rhubarb root to it. A good purgative that would leave Westfield in discomfort for the duration of the day was what he deserved.

A wave of shame washed over her. Nurses didn't add laxatives to their patients' coffee, no matter how infuriating they were.

She heaved a heavy sigh.

"Is his lordship in zee foul mood?" Monsieur Laurent asked.

"Your question, *monsieur*, implies his lordship has other moods."

The chef guffawed before returning to the task of readying the tray.

Sophia ran a surreptitious hand over her bum. She could still feel where Westfield's large palm had scorched her skin as if cast of iron and as hot as a branding stick. And she most certainly remembered the feel of that hardened *appendage* pressing against her. The man had set every nerve in her body aflame. It had taken tremendous fortitude to act unaffected.

Thank God he'd thought her put off. Better than if he had realized the truth—which was she'd wanted him to kiss her, while her hands had itched to touch him. Well, up until she felt his erection. Then she'd become frightened by the dampness growing between her legs. Prude indeed!

She must be addled. Westfield was nothing but a shameless roué with a wicked mind, a foul mouth, and an overly large male organ between his legs.

He'd probably been dreaming of some young, naïve debutante or thinking about winning that blasted dare. He didn't care one whit about her. A woman would have to be a dolt to want him. Her cheeks warmed, and she glanced at Monsieur Laurent, who stared at her, a smile plastered upon his face as if he could read her mind.

A half hour later, Hayden's mood perked up at the sound of someone moving around in the adjacent room. Had Sophia returned? From where he sat on the sofa in the sitting room, he craned his neck, hoping to get a glimpse of her.

Damnation. Can't see a blasted thing. He grabbed his crutches and hobbled into his bedchamber. The tightness in his chest ricocheted back when Mathews stepped out of the dressing room.

"Good evening, my lord. Is there something you need?"

"Yes, I wish to get dressed. I'm going out." If Sophia had left he would find her and apologize.

The valet gaped. "Miss Camden will not be pleased."

"She's here?"

"Of course. She's in the kitchen."

"Thank God," Hayden mumbled, relief coursing through him.

"What, my lord?"

"Nothing. I—"

Sophia entered the room holding his dinner tray. Ignoring

Hayden, she smiled at the valet and handed him the silver tray. "Mr. Mathews, will you give this to his lordship?"

"Yes, miss."

"Thank you." Without glancing at Hayden, she glided out of the room. Was it his imagination or had the temperature taken an arctic tumble?

Mathews chuckled.

"What do you find so humorous?" Hayden snapped.

"I'm not sure what game you and Miss Camden are engaged in, but I think she is not easily defeated."

The problem was, Hayden wasn't sure he wanted to defeat her. She intrigued him. Baffled him. He rubbed the knot forming in his neck.

"Should I bring the tray into the sitting room?" Mathews asked.

He was bloody tired of being confined to his rooms. He knotted the sash on his robe. "No, I'm going downstairs. To the dining room."

Mathews gasped. "I don't think it wise, sir."

Ignoring the man, Hayden moved through the doorway and down the corridor to the stairs, his crutches thumping against the wooden floor. Mathews followed.

Hayden stared at the long flight of steps. His shoulders tensed. Descending them would be a bit tricky. He motioned the valet to precede him. "Go on, Mathews. I'll be down in a minute." *If I don't break my neck.*

Shaking his head, Mathews carried the tray down the stairs. After the man turned the bend at the first-floor landing and disappeared from sight, Hayden leaned one of the crutches on the wall. It would be wiser to maneuver the steps with one crutch propped under his arm and his free hand grasping the rail.

He took the first step, then the second. By the time he reached the first-floor landing, a stinging warmth seared his injured thigh. He eyed the long upholstered bench built into the wall. Blowing out a heavy breath, he lowered himself onto the cushion, and rubbed his leg.

The clicking of shoes dashing across the tiled floor of the corridor one flight below reached his ears. Someone was running. Sophia. He was going to sack Mathews—the bloody Benedict Arnold.

With her skirts lifted high in her hands, exposing the trim turn of her ankles, Sophia darted up the steps. Her cheeks were high in color. "You foolish man. What are you about?"

"Has anyone ever told you how lovely you look when irate?"

Her blush deepened. "You're impossible." She knelt before him and lifted his robe and nightshirt. Her fingers skimmed up his thigh, causing wicked thoughts to drift in his mind.

"You're lucky you're not bleeding." She stood and scowled at him.

"I'm going to the dining room."

"No, you are not . . ." Suddenly she paled. "Oh, my!" She gave her skirts a violent shake. Then, with her almond eyes as wide as saucers, she frantically swept her hands over the wool of her gown and the skirt of her pinafore, smacking it as though it were on fire.

What in the blazes? He stood and clasped her flailing hands. "Sophia?"

A horrified expression flashed across her face. She scanned the floor and stepped closer to him.

"What did you see?" he asked.

"I believe *Albert* or possibly some c-cousin of his."

"Albert? Celia's mouse?"

She snagged her bottom lip between her teeth and nodded.

How did a little rodent frighten her when she didn't

appear the least bit intimidated by a man such as him? "He scares you?"

She gave an indignant huff. "He climbed up my skirt!"

Stupid mouse. If he were Albert, he would have climbed under her skirt so he might see if her legs were truly as long as they'd appeared in his dream. "He is a very tiny mouse."

"You mock me." Her exotic eyes shone with moisture and her long inky lashes were damp. She blinked, and a lone tear made a slow descent down her flushed right cheek.

He ran his hand down her arm. "Sophia, Albert will not hurt you. Most likely he has already made his way back to Celia's room."

Nodding, she closed her eyes, and two more tears trailed down her face.

He'd never enjoyed seeing those he loved cry, but why the sight of Sophia weeping distressed him, he couldn't say. He wanted to comfort her, to dry her tears, and embrace her while running a soothing hand down her back.

You're a fool, old boy! She'd probably give him a scathing setdown, plant a facer on the bridge of his nose, and storm away, squashing Albert in the process. Especially after his earlier escapade. Yet he could not completely stifle his impulse, and he brushed the moistness away with his thumbs.

Sophia opened her dark, watery eyes and stared at him.

God, she was lovely. Too lovely. "Now, I'm sure Albert has . . ." His voice trailed off as the renegade mouse dashed out from under the bench to the longcase clock in the corner.

She followed the movement of his eyes and turned.

"Sophia," he snapped, drawing her gaze back to his, and then he did the unthinkable—he cupped her face and pressed his lips to hers, for surely it was the only way to distract her.

It was a soft kiss, chaste by his standards, a light brushing of their lips. Nothing more than a prelude, but it engaged him. How strange. He increased the pressure. She stiffened as if she would jerk away, but then her lips moved ever so gently beneath his. He lingered a fraction longer, then pulled back.

He waited for her indignation and her firm right hook, but when her long lashes fluttered open, she said not a word. She looked even more bewildered than he felt. A monumental feat, considering the rapid beat of his heart.

Before he knew what he was about, he cupped the back of her head and drew her lips once more to his.

When Sophia uttered a small gasp, he slipped his tongue into the warmth of her mouth. She tasted like cinnamon. Spicy and sweet.

She made a startled noise—soft and low, an indication of her inexperience. A forgotten feeling heated his insides, leaving him uncomfortable, unsure. He started to pull back, but at that precise moment, she slid her tongue against his. Desire pooled in his belly. He drew her closer, so near he could feel the rise and fall of her breasts against his chest.

Sophia's delicate hands skimmed over his upper arms.

He kissed her cheek, the line of her jaw, and the sensitive place just below her ear. Her head tipped sideways, a silent acquiescence, and he caressed her silky skin with his mouth before he caught her delicate earlobe between his teeth.

"Ah, how lovely you are," he whispered.

Her breathing hitched, she slipped a hand to the back of his neck, and her fingers flexed against his nape as he kissed her lips again.

She'd be ruined if found kissing him. The servants would whisper. Reluctantly he stepped back. Her eyes fluttered open. She stared at him as if she'd just awoken from a dream. How long had it been since a woman gazed at him like this? A woman who didn't understand what lust could do to her, a woman untutored.

"My apologies, Sophia. It appears I'm not prepared to handle a damsel in distress. I wished to distract you, and I took it a bit too far."

Her brows drew together. "Distract me?" She blinked, and then she gave a small laugh.

It wasn't the normal reaction women gave him after he'd thoroughly kissed them, but Sophia was nothing like the women he normally kissed.

"I thank you for the diversion. It was unnecessary, yet interesting." She scanned the floor.

He stared at her. She acted as if they'd shared tea and crumpets. And not even tasty crumpets, but dried, over-cooked crumpets that crumbled in one's hands and tasted only marginally better than sawdust. "That is all you wish to say?"

"Should I say more?" Before he could reply, she added, "Well, if I must, I will say as a distraction, your kisses were adequate, but most uncalled for."

"Adequate?"

She tugged on her pinafore, straightening its waistband, and nodded.

Why, she was the most accursed woman he had ever encountered (excluding Adele, for no one could surpass that madwoman). But Sophia Camden ran a near second. He resisted the urge to drag her onto the long bench and show her just how adequate he could be. Instead, he smiled. "For a woman who was kissed only *adequately*, you made an excessive amount of noise."

She blanched. "Noise?"

"You mewled so loud, I thought I was with a cat."

Her cheeks colored.

"Go get Hawthorne, *Sophia*." He said her Christian name with a low, intimate timbre that emphasized the degree of familiarity they'd attained. "He needs to have a footman capture that wayward mouse, for I do not wish to distract you again. My day is already filled with an excess of tedium."

Her fingers twitched like she itched to slap him, but then she smiled. "Yes, tedium and mediocrity are so hard to endure." And with that said, she spun around and strode down the stairs, holding her skirts off the ground.

Hayden slumped onto the bench. Damnation! Why had he kissed her? Not once, but twice. He raked his fingers through his hair. If he were honest with himself, he'd admit why he'd kissed her the second time. Because during their first kiss, that light brushing of their lips, he'd not thought of his dead wife. And that surpassed his realm of understanding, since after leaving Laura, eight years ago, he'd compared every woman to her.

When he'd kissed Sophia, only the softness of her lips, the scent of her skin, and making love to her consumed him. And he'd not made love since he'd moved to London. No, he engaged in fast and furious copulation that chased away his memories—those demons that controlled his behavior. But with Sophia, he'd felt no frenzied need, just a peaceful feeling of completeness. And after he'd relinquished her lips and gazed into her eyes, he'd known he would kiss her again because once the contact had been broken, he'd grown bereft and more alone than ever. Until he kissed her once more and became lost in her taste and scent and found something akin to solace.

Chapter Eight

Sophia signed her name to the bottom of her letter to Mrs. Nettles. Great-Uncle Charles's housekeeper had shown her kindness when she'd lived with him, and she and the woman corresponded often. Whereas her contact with Great-Uncle was minimal, though he did send the occasional summons demanding she return home and cease her folly to become a physician.

Every so often, he sent a gift. Parasols with terse notes to stay out of the sun. Bottles of Lawson's Facial Bleaching Cream—a caustic mixture of arsenic and lead. Presents that were cruel, more than kind.

She'd lived under Great-Uncle's roof for nine years, but he remained a stranger to her. He'd rarely conversed with either her or her sister, Maria, unless he'd wished to disparage them or their mother, or take a leather strap to their knuckles until he drew blood.

Her headstrong sister, angered by their circumstances, tried to punish him the only way she'd known how, by eloping with a man she knew he'd not approve of. A gardener.

Maria's actions only reaffirmed Charles's opinion that their mother's foreign blood rendered them common. And what had her sister gained? A tombstone at Kensal Green, along with poor little Georgiana, who now lay in the plot next to her mother.

Sophia blinked away her tears. Thinking of them made her melancholy. She'd raised her niece after Maria's death, but failed to keep the child safe. Perhaps if she'd known about infections then, Georgiana would be alive and well.

A soft knock sounded on Sophia's bedchamber door. She folded the letter and slipped it into her pocket. "Yes, come in."

Alice entered. "Miss, his lordship is asking for you."

She should have realized Westfield would not allow her to play the coward and hide today. She'd avoided him last night. Only checked on him once and not conversed while she'd examined his wound.

"Did you bring him his breakfast tray, Alice?"

"Nearly dropped it, I did, when he demanded to know where you were. Sounded as angry as a gent who's had his pockets pinched. He's downstairs. Wishes you to meet him in the morning room."

So, the silly man had ventured down the steps again. Infuriating scoundrel.

Alice walked over to the mahogany dresser and sniffed at a bar of scented soap. "It's got lavender in it, right, miss?"

"You may have it."

The maid's eyes grew round. "Truly?"

"Yes." The least she could do, having subjected the poor girl to an irate Westfield.

Smiling, Alice took another audible whiff before she slipped the soap into the front pocket of her white apron. "Thank you."

Sophia opened the large armoire and removed her navy wool cape.

"You going out, miss?" Disbelief heightened the younger woman's voice.

Sophia nodded and slipped the garment over her shoulders. "I wish to take the air."

"But his lordship?"

"He'll have to wait."

Alice gaped. "Aren't you frightened of him?"

Yes, but not in the way Alice thought. Sophia feared she'd make a complete cake of herself where Westfield was concerned. She touched her lips and remembered the press of his warm mouth caressing hers. He was more than adequate at distraction. A few minutes longer and she might have begged him to relieve the desire growing within her. Worse, she'd dreamt of him last night. His mouth on hers. His hands skimming up her body.

What was wrong with her? She'd conducted the whole of her life properly. When younger, she'd wished to make her parents and grandfather proud. In Northumberland, she'd wanted to disabuse Great-Uncle Charles of his opinion of her limited worth. And here, in London, she'd garnered a modicum of respect for her abilities and intelligence while living a quiet, respectable life. Nevertheless, she appeared capable of tossing it all aside to experience a bit of wickedness with a rogue.

She touched her earlobe where Westfield had nibbled it. She would have sworn he'd whispered, *"How lovely you are."*

A jolt of pleasure shot through her. How silly to be so easily flattered. The man held a title. He would not want her for anything more than a dalliance.

"Miss?"

"I'm sorry, Alice. No, he doesn't frighten me," she lied. "He is a man, nothing more, and I have another position should he decide to dismiss me." Doubtful he would. He was determined to win the dare. "I apologize for asking you to bring him his breakfast."

Alice giggled. "I didn't mind. I think he's the handsomest gentleman I ever seen. And those broad shoulders." The maid appeared wistful and ready to swoon.

An odd feeling settled in the pit of Sophia's stomach. Did Westfield mingle inappropriately with all his female employees? "Alice, he doesn't . . ."

"Doesn't what?" Two red flags suddenly colored the maid's fair cheeks. "Oh, no, miss!" Alice shook her head. "He don't dally with the staff. Not his lordship. One of the downstairs maids kept batting her lashes at him. Sent her packing, he did. And Mrs. Beecham sets the girls straight right away, she does."

Sophia released a taut breath and opened the door. So he'd told her the truth. He'd meant nothing more than to distract her.

Oh, she was such a nitwit!

An hour later, Hayden tried not to scowl as Sophia entered the morning room with Lady Olivia trailing her as if she held a ham bone before the dog's snout.

He set the morning paper onto the round dining table and peered at the wall clock. Damn, how dare she disregard his authority and take such an inordinate amount of time. "Why didn't *you* bring my breakfast?"

She motioned to the crutches leaning behind his chair. "I have told you, gallivanting about will only delay your healing."

"We appear to be having two separate conversations, Sophia."

The room grew quiet. Lady Olivia whimpered, did an about-face, and bounded from the room, her tail drooping between her hind legs. Sophia raised her shapely eyebrows—a silent insinuation that seemed to say even the dog doesn't wish to be here. He motioned to the chair to his right.

The stubborn woman didn't budge. Was she so averse to conversing with him? "Sophia, *please* be seated."

With innate grace, she sat and primly folded her hands in her lap.

He cleared his throat. "I apologize for my earlier transgressions."

Her lashes lowered a fraction. "I apologize, as well. I behaved in a most unprofessional manner. Really beyond the pale. I beg your forgiveness."

Forgiveness? If she only knew how he'd enjoyed the encounter.

As if she intended on standing, she shifted in the chair.

Was she leaving already? Holding up a staying hand, he asked, "Are you going upstairs to pen another letter?"

Every day, without fail, she wrote a missive while she sat in the corner of his bedchamber. "I thought you would feel more comfortable penning it here, so I had a writing slope brought in."

"I have already sent Dr. Trimble a note this morning."

"Ah, so it is Trimble with whom you correspond?" He fought the urge to snarl at the mention of the physician's name.

"I keep him abreast of how you are faring. My missives consist of the visual appearance of your injury, along with notes on the amount of discomfort you are feeling, and your progression toward healing. Initially I reported on your temperament, but I have forgone that part of the report."

"And why is that?"

"You are always of the same temperament in the mornings."

"Are you implying I am anything but charming when I awake?"

"Certainly not." Her dark eyes smiled, and she snagged her bottom lip between her teeth like a child caught lying to an elder. As if realizing it, she soothed the bruised skin with the tip of her tongue, glistening the plump surface.

Their earlier kiss flashed in his mind's eye. He recalled the slide of Sophia's tongue sensuously stroking his and the taste of her cinnamon warmth. His manhood grew heavy.

Damnation. The woman was a minion sent by Satan to plague him. He tensed, and the muscles in his neck bunched painfully. He craned his head sideways and lifted a hand to knead the knot.

"Are you experiencing discomfort?" She stood.

"No, it's nothing."

"If you'll allow me, I believe I can help alleviate your pain."

He wanted to laugh. She certainly could.

"I used to massage my grandfather's back." She moved behind him and set the heels of her palms into his shoulders. "You're tense. Relax."

Relax? His manhood was hard, and he was fantasizing about making love to her on the table. He needed a distraction. "Tell me about your childhood."

Her warm fingers trailed soothing touches over his neck and shoulders. "Surely, you do not wish me to bore you?"

"Sophia, you have a tedious propensity to answer a question with one of your own."

"I had a pleasant childhood."

Something about the tone of her voice said differently.

"Was the work your grandfather performed laborious?" He didn't believe so. The way she carried herself didn't reflect an impoverished upbringing, but she'd been brought low if now required to tend to louts like him and runny-nosed children.

"No." She didn't elaborate.

For several glorious minutes, her deft hands meticulously worked over every inch of his shoulder and neck muscles until his pain vanished.

"Better?" she asked.

"Yes, much." He fought the urge to reach out and pull her down onto his lap and taste her mouth again. *Idiot.*

"I have a salve I could apply if you wish?"

He cringed. His nanny had had a penchant for salves. Ointments with the consistency of cow dung that hadn't smelled much better. He shook his head, his gaze on those lovely long fingers. Did she massage Trimble's neck? A nerve in Hayden's jaw twitched.

"Papa!" Celia burst through the doorway with Lady Olivia. "It's snowing." She ran to the bank of windows, and both she and the dog peered outside. Lady Olivia's tail wagged enthusiastically, and her panting breath clouded the panes of glass.

Giggling, Celia nudged the dog's massive nose away, and mopped the sleeve of her lavender-colored dress against the glass. "Come look, Sophia! They are the largest snowflakes I've ever seen and falling so fast the ground is all but covered."

Sophia looked at Hayden.

"By all means," he said, motioning to the windows.

With exuberant strides, Sophia crossed the room. It was impossible to miss the earnest smile she gave Celia, or how Sophia's face lit up when she gazed outside.

"Can I go out and play in it?" Celia ran over to him. When he didn't immediately respond, she pressed her small hands together as if praying.

He placed a palm on his robe where it covered his injured thigh. "I can't walk in it, but perhaps we can convince your aunt Edith to take you for a carriage ride."

She frowned. "No, Papa, Aunt Edith told me she is to visit Lady Marley today."

Sophia was still gazing out the window. "Sophia, are you partial to snow?" he asked.

"I am," she replied.

Before Hayden could utter another word, Celia ran to her. "Would you care to go ramble about in it?"

"If your father approves, I would be delighted."

Celia didn't wait for his response, but grabbed Sophia's hand and pulled her toward the door. "Of course he approves."

Smiling, Sophia glanced over her shoulder at him.

He mouthed the words, *Thank you*.

At the doorway, Celia came to an abrupt stop. "Do you have a muff, Sophia?"

"No. But my gloves shall be fine."

"I think I saw one in Grandmama's trunk in the attic."

Hayden cringed. Though Celia was fascinated with the musty items in the attic, he doubted Sophia would wish to don them. "Dear, I'm sure Sophia's gloves will do nicely."

The child nibbled on the corner of her lower lip. "Papa," she said, her voice low, "why are none of Mama's trunks in the attic?"

His heart skipped a beat. How could he tell Celia her mama had never set foot in this house? No, that wasn't true. Hard to forget how she'd called here after his father's funeral. How he'd refused to see her, and then left for the Continent.

What a fool he'd been.

If only she'd brought Celia with her. If he'd seen the child's face and her resemblance to his family . . . *Ifs*. His past remained full of ifs and second guesses. He blinked at the sudden sting in his eyes.

"Papa?" the child prompted, drawing him from his thoughts.

"Celia," Sophia said as if she knew the child might be hurt by the truth, "I'd love to wear your grandmama's muff. But we should get it now, for if we dawdle the snow may stop, and we will not get to taste the flakes as they fall."

The pensive look on Celia's face vanished. "Taste the flakes?"

"Have you never opened your mouth to let the flakes land upon your tongue?"

"No, but I would like to. We shall see you later, Papa. We must hurry, if we are to taste the falling snow!"

On the fourth floor, Celia dashed to a door adjacent to the maids' quarters and opened it. "This is the way to the attic."

Sophia surveyed the dim and narrow stairs. The speed of her heart escalated. She didn't care to venture any place rodents favored nesting. At least, Albert was back in Celia's room.

"There are lots of treasures up here," Celia said, smiling over her shoulder as she climbed the steps.

Not wishing to disappoint the child, Sophia took a deep breath, lifted her hem, and followed. In the attic three oversize dormers stood watch over Brook Street. Their glass cast wide slashing bands of sunlight across most of the contents and the rough honey-colored beams and floor.

Celia skipped toward several wooden trunks and knelt on a tattered linen pillow that rested on the floor near the smallest one. "These are my grandmama's. I'm sure I saw a muff in here."

Heart still beating fast, Sophia scanned the floor as she moved to stand next to the trunk.

Celia unlatched the brass lock and eagerly flipped open the lid, revealing a myriad of feathered and beribboned fripperies. As Celia eagerly tossed items to and fro, Sophia looked around the space. Besides the trunks, there was also a pair of ornate boulle tables with intricate marquetry and a gold rococo mirror adorned with ornate shells, its reflective surface marred by a thick skin of dust. Near the corner were several paintings tossed about. The fronts of their canvases faced the wall.

A bolt of anger shot through her. Paintings were the sweat and blood of the artist. Something to be cherished, and if not to one's liking, they were to be passed on to someone who could appreciate them—not left in such uncharitable surroundings.

With hesitant steps, Sophia walked over to them. She flipped the first canvas around—a painting of Westfield in his youth, his eyes downcast as he peered at a hound. She examined it further. No, the breeches and intricately tied cravat dated the boy to an earlier time.

"That's my grandpapa," Celia said, standing, a fur muff held in her hands. "He resembles Papa, doesn't he?"

"Yes," Sophia replied.

"All those paintings are of him." Celia motioned to them with a sweep of her hand.

Sophia reached forward to turn the next portrait around, but stopped when she caught sight of a massive gilded frame leaning in the corner, nearly indiscernible in the shadows.

The canvas was torn. No, not torn, but slashed as if someone had purposely destroyed it.

Celia stepped next to her. "It used to hang in Papa's study above the mantel."

Sophia ran her hand over the shredded canvas. The old earl's face was unrecognizable as it hung in tattered strips from the carved frame. This was no accident. Someone had been angry. Enraged. "What happened?" she asked, turning to Celia.

As if transfixed, Celia stared at the painting. Then she lifted the muff. "Here, I found it. This should keep your hands warm." She stepped toward the stairs.

Sophia stared at the tattered portrait a moment longer before following Celia.

The child stepped onto the first tread and glanced back. "Papa did it." Absently Celia ran her hand over the muff. "He had just brought me here to live in this house. He was yelling, and I came downstairs and saw him in the study. When Mrs. Beecham saw me, she brought me back to the nursery. Told me not to be frightened. She said my papa was a good man and he'd be right as ninepence in the morning." She took a deep breath. "He doesn't know I saw him." She nibbled on the nail of her index finger. "You won't tell him I remember?"

What had the old earl done to cause his son to be so enraged? Sophia placed a hand on the girl's shoulder. "No, Celia, I would not tell him unless you wished it. And I am sorry I asked about the painting. It wasn't my place to do so."

Celia looked at her. Then, as children are apt to do, she appeared to forget what they'd been discussing, and she raced down the stairs, calling back, "We should hurry."

With a grunt of disgust, Hayden tossed the latest edition of the *Morning Post* atop the slew of other dailies and periodicals strewn across the table in the morning room. It appeared the public had not yet lost its taste for tawdry details about his shooting. He was still front-page news in both the *Times* and the *Illustrated London News*, while *Punch* featured a less than favorable cartoon, portraying him as a wolfish caricature being shot by a caped woman who looked like an innocent rendition of a nursery rhyme character.

Adele innocent? What a bloody joke. On their last assignation, the hellcat had produced a set of handcuffs and a whip she wished to use on him. He'd snatched the leather strap from her hand, opened the window, and flung it out, sending her into a tizzy.

Outraged, she'd come after him hissing and clawing and drawing blood. Before he'd known what he was about, he grabbed the handcuffs from her, tossed her on the bed, and shackled one of her wrists to the headboard. By the time he'd finished, Adele had been purring and rubbing herself against him like an alley cat stroking a fishmonger's leg. But instead of giving her the rutting she'd desired, he'd slipped from the bed, tossed her the key, and told her it was over between them.

As he reached the door, Adele's amorous mood had turned caustic, and she'd suggested he perform several physically impossible acts upon himself.

Footsteps pulled him from his thoughts.

"Is there anything you require?" Hawthorne asked, stepping into the room.

Hayden gathered the newspapers up and handed them to the butler. "Yes, toss these in the grate." He didn't wish either Celia or Sophia to see the caricature.

As Hawthorne rolled up each newspaper and set them on the hot coals, Hayden pondered why Sophia's good opinion mattered. Taking a deep breath, he braced a hand on the table and stood. He grabbed his crutches and hobbled out of the room.

He entered his ground-floor study and slumped into the large leather chair behind the desk. The sound of laughter and barking drifted through the windows. What in blazes were Sophia and Celia up to in the garden?

The sounds quieted.

"Hawthorne!"

The butler appeared in the doorway. "Yes?"

With his chin, Hayden motioned to the window. "What's going on out there?"

"It is snowing, my lord."

"Good God, man, I'm not blind. What I wish to know is what are Lady Celia and Miss Camden doing?"

Hawthorne moved to the windows. The joyous sound of laughter returned. The butler smiled. "I believe they are making snow angels."

"Snow angels?"

"You are not familiar with them?" Hawthorne's tone implied one who lacked such knowledge lived a deprived life.

Hayden gritted his teeth and held his tongue.

The butler scratched the back of his head. "It's when one lies on the snow and . . ." He flapped his arms by his sides.

The man looked mad. Hayden frowned.

"You see," Hawthorne continued, "when you move your arms against the snow it looks like an angel's wings." The man grinned as if pleased with his explanation.

After lifting himself up onto his crutches, Hayden moved to the window. Both Celia and Sophia were lying on their backs in the snow, waving their arms back and forth as insanely as Hawthorne had.

They stood, and he noted the angel-like impression they'd made in the light snow. Celia's cheeks glowed and utter jubilance radiated across her young face. Laughing gaily, she grabbed Sophia's hands and spun her in a circle while the dog barked at them.

Sophia's hat fell, and her long, heavy hair tumbled loose to sail in the air behind her. Hawthorne moved to stand next to him. As the butler gazed outside an expression of infatuation flickered across his face.

"Hawthorne, stop drooling. You look like an overheated dog."

"I do not drool, my lord." Hawthorne stiffened, grabbed the edge of his waistcoat, and tugged it down.

Hayden stared at Celia. How happy she looked. Damnation, he needed to find her a new governess, someone like Sophia. He shook his head. When had Sophia Camden turned from adversary and imposition to something cherished—something he wanted?

At that moment, Sophia turned to the window as if she sensed he watched her. She shaded her eyes with her hand and smiled.

His heart skipped a beat.

He turned away. She was not for him. She was naïve and proper, while he was soiled and debauched.

Like the last few mornings, Hayden awoke expecting to see Sophia's delicate face peering at him. He glanced about his bedchamber. Where was she?

Not wishing to analyze his disappointment, he shoved it aside and rubbed at the coarse morning bristle on his jaw. He reached for his crutches and blinked at the empty space.

Hell and fire, she'd absconded with them *again*. He eyed the bathing room door.

You can make it, old boy. He stood and braced his weight on the bedpost, then waited for the stinging sensation to ease.

A soft tap sounded on the bedroom door and it swung inward. Sophia entered the dim room, her body illuminated by the subtle shaft of light dancing across the threshold from the corridor. She cast the bed a glance, took one more step, and froze. As if her eyes deceived her, she stared at the empty bed. Her piercing gaze shifted to him and her delicate hands fisted into tight little knots. She closed the distance between them.

Sophia was tall for a woman, a good five foot six, but

he towered over her by at least seven inches. Both his height and the breadth of his shoulders intimidated many, and more than once, he'd used them to his advantage. He shifted forward. So close, his nightshirt and legs touched her skirts. She tipped her head back and squared her shoulders.

He should have realized she'd not cower to him, not his Sophia.

His Sophia? How odd to think of her that way.

"Why you foolish, foolish man. You are intent on sabotaging your recovery. I want you in that bed. Now."

Even though he tried not to smile, the corners of his lips inched upward.

As though realizing how the words might be misconstrued, her eyes widened. She opened her mouth.

He leaned down.

Her mouth snapped shut.

"Do you, Sophia?" he whispered in her ear. "Want me in bed? How forward you are when we are alone." The scent of her skin and the memory of their kiss caused an unwanted reaction. With a grimace, he straightened. He played a dangerous game with her, and neither of them would be the victor if he took it too far.

"You know I was not propositioning you, my lord. Now please return to your bed before you do irreparable damage to your leg."

He glanced at the bathroom and contemplated defying her.

"I wouldn't suggest you try it," she said, as if reading his thoughts.

"Do you think you could stop me?"

She bit her lower lip. Hayden's body tensed as he waited for the inevitable flick of her tongue over her bottom lip.

"Don't," he said, his voice low, nearly ominous to his own ears.

Her delicate eyebrows lifted. "Don't try to stop you?"

No, don't lick your . . .

As if on cue, her tongue darted out to glisten the plump surface. His bollocks tightened. Didn't she realize there were women who invited salacious behavior with that movement?

"Out of my way, Sophia." His voice sounded angry. He was angry. Angry she held the power to turn him into a green lad. Angry that upon awakening the first thing he'd wanted to see was her face. And furious that at this moment, he wanted nothing more than to pick her up, toss her on his bed, and tutor her with his lips, his hands, and his cock. He was a reprobate, and it disgusted him.

He let go of the bedpost to step around her.

She quickly shifted, blocking his path.

"Damnation, woman, move out of my way!"

Her chin notched up another inch. "I will not."

"Sophia, I'm warning you."

"Someone, my lord, must save you from your foolish—*owf.*" The air swooshed out of her lungs as he bent down, wrapped his hands around her thighs, and tossed her over his shoulder.

"Put me down!"

"I'm going to use the bathing room, and it appears you are to accompany me."

"Damn you, Westfield."

"Such language, my dear," he chastised. A sharp pain raced down his injured leg, and he stumbled as he walked.

Sophia gave a small shriek and knotted her hands in his nightshirt. Her fingers digging into his skin distracted him from the throbbing in his thigh. He set his palm on her lovely bum to steady her. "Don't worry, I won't drop you."

Sophia slapped his back. "I insist you put me down."

"If you insist." He swung her upright and deposited her

into the massive tub. She grabbed the edge of the vessel and begun to lift herself up.

"I wouldn't advise that," he warned, moving to stand before the sink.

From the corner of his eye, he watched her toss her tumbling hair out of her face and sit up. He began to hike his nightshirt up.

"Oh, goodness!" She slid back down. "You are beyond reproach."

He tossed his nightshirt atop her head.

She gasped. "Are you naked?"

"No, not quite," he replied, wrapping a towel around his waist. With his back to her, he brushed his teeth and watched her reflection in the mirror.

Sophia brazenly lifted the edge of the garment and peeked at him. She appeared to take great interest in his backside. He flexed his muscles. She angled her head first to the left, then the right.

He chuckled.

Her gaze shot up to meet his in the mirror. Her cheeks turned bright red. She wrapped her fingers around the edge of the tub and began to rise.

As if the devil prodded him, Hayden placed his hands on the towel as though about to remove it.

"Oh my." Biting her bottom lip, she pinched her eyes closed and slid back down in the tub. "You horrid man. Are you naked?"

He wasn't but he didn't wish to reveal that. He wanted her to stay in the room and converse with him. He wanted to find out more about her. "Look and you will see."

"I will not." She made an exasperated noise.

"Tell me, Sophia, how old are you?"

She huffed out a breath. "Twenty-four." Her words resonated against the walls of the tub.

"And what has brought you so low you must attend a man such as me?"

"A moment of madness."

He grinned. "It's obvious you were raised by a family of means. I would say your speech indicates here in London, though occasionally you inject a word or two which confirms you lived in the North Country. Does your family still reside there?"

"I do not wish to converse with you, my lord."

Laughing, he sharpened his razor against a leather strop.

"Are you shaving?"

"Hmm," he replied.

After several minutes she said, "Your leg must be throbbing."

He splashed water onto his face. "No, I'm doing miraculously well."

She gave a disbelieving snort.

He soaped up a facecloth and washed his upper arms. He was tired of sponge bathing. He'd give nearly everything he owned to take a bath, especially if he could convince Sophia to wash his back. After tossing the cloth into the sink, he walked over to Sophia lying in the tub. A droplet of water dripped off his chest to land on her face.

Without opening her eyes, she rubbed the back of her fingers over her cheek. "Are you dressed now?"

"As I said, you only have to look to find out."

"Wicked man."

Ignoring the pain in his thigh, he squatted by the edge, folded his arms over the tub's rim, and stared down at her. How lovely she looked. Dark wisps of her silky hair had sailed free of their rigid constraints to stand in stark relief against the tub's copper lining. A vision of her lying naked in the tub, warm crystalline water glistening upon her skin, caressing the tips of her breasts—

"Without the crutches, standing for any length of time is not wise," she said, disrupting his lurid thoughts. She jabbed a loose tendril back into her chignon.

He reached down. His fingers itched to unpin the rest of her shiny dark hair and remove the abominable cap that clung to it. He pulled his hand back and stood. "Sophia, I wish to bathe."

"No, I must be adamant. You cannot wet your wound."

"I could sling my leg over the edge of the tub. You could assist me as you did that tot you took care of. What was his name? Ah, yes, little Edward Shore."

She sighed. "Edward is a child."

"But if my memory serves me correctly you claimed him my contemporary."

"Oh, you confounded man. You know he is a far cry from your contemporary." She slowly opened one eye, then the other. A breath eased out from between her pretty lips as her gaze settled on the towel wrapped about his waist.

He placed a hand to his chest. "You have restored my wounded vanity." He reached for her hand to assist her up.

She smacked it away. "May I assume you're done with this tomfoolery and will return to your bed?"

"Yes." He reached for her hand again.

"I do not wish for your assistance."

He stepped back, leaned against the wall, and folded his arms across his chest.

Sophia had nearly righted herself when her right shoe caught on his nightshirt. Her foot slipped, and she toppled backward with a heavy *thud*.

Chapter Nine

A sound reminiscent of an approaching train filled Sophia's ears. The noise grew louder, culminating in a roar. It receded, leaving a voice floating above, muffled as if captured in a bottle. As though someone tipped the bottle, several words spilled forth. *Lord. Benevolent. Father.*

A prayer? Was that Westfield's voice? Westfield praying seemed as unlikely as snow in summer.

"Sophia?" The voice, though gentle, grew more insistent. So did the hand tapping at her face. "Sophia?"

She opened her eyes, and Westfield's face slowly came into focus.

"Thank God." He set his forehead to hers, pulled back, and stared at her.

She was dreaming again. This one appeared more depraved than the last, for she was lying in Westfield's bed, and he sat on its edge leaning over her, nearly naked. She reached out, touched his sensual mouth. The warmth of his breath heated her cold fingers.

He folded her hand in his and pressed his lips to her knuckles. "You mustn't move." He glanced over his shoulder. "Mathews!" He turned back. Deep lines furrowed his brow. "Do you know who I am?"

Of course she did. This was her dream, but he was so high-handed, he was taking over.

"You've taken a tumble. Do you remember?"

Tumble? She cupped the back of her head and winced. It throbbed as if a blacksmith with an arm of steel had mistaken her skull for his anvil. She glanced around the bedchamber, then at the towel wrapped precariously about Westfield's lean waist.

This was not a dream!

"Sophia, you should have let me assist you out of the tub."

By thunder, the tub! She remembered now. She pulled her hand from his, fisted her fingers, and hit his naked chest.

"I deserve that and more. Now"—he lightly touched the back of her head—"you're in need of some ice for that goose egg." He glanced over his shoulder again. "God knows where Mathews is." He cupped her face and stroked her cheeks with his thumbs.

His intimate touch and near nakedness caused a warmth all over her body. Frightened by her reaction, she braced herself on her elbow. "I must get up."

He forced her shoulders back into the mattress. "No, you must—"

A gasp from the doorway cut Westfield's words short. "My lord," Mathews said breathlessly. "What do you think you are doing undressed? You know Miss Camden will not attend you in such a state of dishabille."

Mathews stepped fully into the room. His eyes widened upon seeing her, and he rushed to the bed. "Oh, my. Oh, my!" He cast his employer a belligerent look. "Have you struck her?"

Westfield rolled his eyes heavenward. "Miss Camden is injured. I've not beaten her. Now take several deep breaths and go get some ice and send for Dr. Thomas Trimble."

Mathews spun on his heel and dashed from the room.

Sophia pushed herself up again.

"Lie still, love." Westfield pressed her back down, then turned up the gas lamp on the bedside table. The sudden brightness caused her to squint and a tear spilled from her eye. Westfield's gaze seemed to follow the drop as it progressed down her cheek. He swallowed, and she realized he was not as callous as he wished her to believe.

He ran the pad of his thumb lightly over the moisture. "Sophia," he said softly, his blue eyes intense. "If you wish to gather your belongings and leave, I will consider our dare and subsequent wager null and void."

He was giving her an out. She could go and not owe him a forfeit. The thought of curling up in her own bed tempted her, but she didn't wish to leave. She needed to prove her competence and mettle and win Westfield's support for reforming medical licensure.

What rot! She knew her reluctance to leave had more to do with the complex man before her—the man whose proximity caused her lungs to tighten.

"I'm going to complete the ten days and win," she said. "Do you wish to concede?"

The pad of his thumb slid down her cheek to touch her lower lip. "No."

He was toying with her. Her heart raced in her chest. "I really must get up."

"I shall carry you to your room." His hand fell away, and his body shifted closer.

"No." She placed her palm over his chest to push him away. His skin was warm. Her hands flexed against firm muscle.

"Sophia, you're not capable of standing. And I doubt Dr. Trimble would be enamored with the idea of tending to both of us in the same bed, though if you insist I will oblige you."

She opened her mouth, intent on saying something, anything that would make him move away from her. His hand eased beneath her shoulders and the hard pectoral muscles contracted under her palm. She closed her eyes, searched her mind for a distraction, but even the *thump, thump, thump* still beating against her skull appeared unable to sway her wayward thoughts.

"Are you about to swoon?" he asked, pulling her tighter to him.

She opened her eyes. He was so close his breath caressed her face. She couldn't pull her gaze away from his sensual mouth. "No," she finally replied.

"Sophia, I fear I might need to distract you once more." His fingers stroked her neck.

Distract her? Did he mean kiss her? That idea frightened her more than the relentless throbbing in her head, yet she closed her eyes.

Westfield's lips touched hers. He coaxed her mouth open and deepened the kiss.

Molten heat pooled in her belly. She lifted her other hand to his chest and ran her fingers over the coarse hair, each wisp a reminder of his maleness—of the differences between their bodies. She slipped her hands to his back, pressed her breasts closer, desiring, needing the contact.

His hand shifted to her collar, and his nimble fingers undid the first few buttons lining the front of her dress. He ran his thumb over her throat and the indentation above her collarbone while his tongue continued to tangle with hers.

He stilled and pulled back. "Mathews is coming."

A second later, the valet barreled into the room, and Westfield lifted his deft fingers to refasten her buttons.

"No, no, no, my lord," Mathews exclaimed. "She is a gently bred woman. Not some strumpet."

"Do not get your peacock feathers in a twist," Westfield replied, his voice so cool it sent a shiver down her back.

"Miss Camden felt faint. I thought some air upon her skin would alleviate her need to swoon. Have you sent for Dr. Trimble?"

"Yes, someone was dispatched to fetch him, a maid is coming with ice, and that strapping footman, Peter, is on his way up to carry Miss Camden to her bedchamber. He shall be here any minute." He darted into the dressing room.

The urgency in Mathews's voice lifted the fog clouding Sophia's mind, and she pushed Westfield's hands away from her buttons so she could complete the task. Mathews returned with a green velvet and damask robe clutched in his hand.

Westfield stood and slipped the garment on.

Peter entered the bedchamber. The young footman's mouth dropped open when his gaze settled on her lying in the bed.

"Don't stand about gawking, Peter," Westfield snapped. "My leg is bloody well killing me. And Mathews has greatly inconvenienced me by placing Miss Camden in my bed after she took a tumble. Please take her to her room. My breakfast has been detained long enough."

My heavens, he was good! The conviction in his voice had her almost believing Mathews had placed her in the bed, but her lips still tingled from Westfield's kiss, and she was sure his hands had left indelible marks on her skin.

A pale-faced Peter rushed forward.

"I can walk," she hastily said.

"No," Westfield replied firmly. "You will allow Peter to carry you. No, never mind. I'll do it."

Mathews and Peter stared at each other before returning their gazes to her.

Heat singed her cheeks. "No, you mustn't . . . your leg."

Ignoring her warning, he lifted her, and cradled her

against his chest as he carried her. The warmth of his body filtered through her clothes, heating her skin.

"I'll open Miss Camden's bedchamber door," Mathews said, rushing before them as they entered the corridor.

In her room, Westfield set her down on the bed. For several heartbeats, their gazes locked. He lifted her hand and held her fingers for a moment. She had the strangest feeling he wished to say something, but he turned and strode from the room, limping ever so slightly.

A half hour later, Thomas entered the room.

Sophia shifted uncomfortably in the large bed.

Her dear friend's jaw visibly clenched as he placed his black medical bag on a chair. "What in God's name did *he* do to you?"

He'd be livid if he knew the truth.

"I slipped while in Westfield's bathing room."

He arched a dark eyebrow. "Sophia, both of us know you are not prone to clumsiness, and I can tell when you are being purposely vague."

When she didn't respond, he let out a weighted breath and took her right hand in his. "I very much regret you coming here."

"I'm fine, Thomas."

He released her hand. "Yes, I can see that," he quipped, taking her chin between his thumb and forefinger and angling her head toward the light. "After I examine you, we can leave. Lady Prescott can bloody well find someone else to tend to her brother."

Thomas never used profanity in front of her, and the vehemence in his voice startled her. "I wish to stay."

Lines creased the smooth skin on his forehead. "Why?"

"Because Lady Prescott asked me to come here, and Westfield's sister has been a great benefactress to many of the charities we both hold dear. Has she not promised to hold a ball to help garner more donations for the new hospital's building fund?"

"Yes, but I do not believe it prudent for you to stay here, no matter how much she and Westfield donate."

"Westfield? I was not aware his lordship had made a contribution."

"Yes, a substantial amount. Now, if you don't mind, I'll have one of the maids pack your belongings so we can leave. Or we can have them sent over to your residence later."

"Thomas," she said in a firm voice, "I regard you as my dearest friend, but I stayed in London to gain my independence. To make my own decisions."

"Of course. I do not wish to overstep. . . ." He raked his fingers through his brown hair. "But I feel responsible for you being here, especially if it is because you don't wish to upset Lady Prescott."

"I came here of my own accord. You most certainly didn't force the position upon me. I feel well enough to get up and resume my job."

"As your physician, I insist you stay in bed for the remainder of the day. I will inform Westfield that you must not return to duty until tomorrow. Can we at least agree on this?"

She saluted. "Yes, Thomas."

He squeezed her hand. "Are you sure I can't persuade you to leave with me now?"

Westfield's kiss flashed before her mind's eye. "I wish to stay."

In the gloom, Hayden leaned back against his headboard and took another sip of whisky. He stared at his bedchamber door. Throughout the day, he'd listened to members of his staff entering and departing Sophia's room across the corridor. They'd trotted in and out as if she offered tea and biscuits and a Punch and Judy show. Even Celia had begged him to allow her to visit Sophia. "Only for a few minutes," he'd said. "She needs to rest."

Mathews had informed him that the household staff was fond of Sophia. During her stay here, she'd supplied Laurent with a salve to help heal a burn on the chef's hand, a tincture to ease Alice's toothache, and made a warm poultice for Mrs. Beecham's sore back.

But now that darkness consumed the sky, they'd all taken to their beds, leaving the house still. Over the last several years, he'd come to despise the quiet quality of night when his mind was free to wander. Normally during the small hours, he avoided solitude, knowing his thoughts would center on Laura and all his deceased wife had endured. Yet, at this moment, his mind focused on Sophia.

He took another sip of whisky. An irate Dr. Trimble had confronted him this morning. The good doctor had slammed his medical bag down on a chair. The man was known for his imperturbable demeanor. Trimble's actions spoke loud and clear. He carried a torch for his little protégée. Hayden's hand tightened against his glass. What was their relationship? Did she return the doctor's sentiment?

Hayden reached under his pillow and pulled out Sophia's cap. He'd found it in his bed. Bringing it to his nose, he drew in the scent of lavender and lemon.

With a derisive shake of his head, he shoved it under his pillow and glared at the half-empty bottle of whisky. He'd indulged in enough liquor to tranquilize a small elephant, yet surprisingly, and inexcusably, he found no respite from his guilt or his thoughts. The sound of Sophia's head hitting the tub continued to replay itself in his mind. Utter terror had besieged him upon hearing it. Unease lingered in him still.

An inexplicable, burning need to confirm her well-being

assailed him. He threw his bedding aside, swung his feet onto the floor, and cringed as a bolt of pain shot through his thigh. It hadn't been wise to carry Sophia to her room. He'd known his stitches had ripped open when he'd lifted her from the tub, but the thought of Peter carrying her agitated him.

As he stood, he ran his palm over his thigh. Trimble had stitched the torn skin closed again. The sawbones had done a brilliant job. The stabbing pain was subsiding. He took a step and the room tilted. Apparently, he'd given the doctor too much credit and the liquor not enough.

He listed toward his dressing room. Inside, he turned up the gaslight. There, between two tall armoires, stood the brass stand that held his assortment of walking sticks. Bracing a stiff arm on the first armoire, he removed his gold-knobbed stick, a gift from Celia, given to him on his twenty-seventh birthday. Of course, he had Edith to thank for its simple elegance. Celia, if left to her own accord, would have wanted a handle much more ornate, possibly a bear's head with sapphire eyes or a serpent. Both would be fine for a night at the theater, but for ambulatory needs, the gold-knobbed stick would serve him well.

He grabbed the handle firmly with his left hand, braced his weight on the walking stick, and hobbled out of his room. He tottered toward Sophia's bedchamber door. Was she well? When was the last time someone checked on her?

He opened the door and stepped inside.

Chapter Ten

The coals in the grate and a low-burning lamp cast weak light over Sophia's bedchamber. From the doorway, Hayden stared at her slight frame cocooned beneath the bedding.

As he moved closer, the thick carpet muffled his walking stick. He peered down at her slumbering form. Her countenance appeared serene. The taut breath held in his lungs eased out between his teeth as relief coursed through him.

"Sophia, I'm so dreadfully sorry," he said under his breath.

For several heartbeats, he stared at the way her normally constrained hair flowed like dark waves of silk over the white pillowcase. He reached out to touch a lock, then yanked his hand back. This was so wrong.

She's fine. Now get the hell out of here. He hobbled to the door. A few feet from it, the walking stick tangled with the leg of a chair. He tumbled to the floor and landed with a *bang*.

Bugger it! He rolled onto his back and braced himself on his forearms.

Sophia bolted upright, clutching her blankets to her bosom.

"Is-is someone in here?" she asked, her voice an uncertain whisper.

Ignoring the pain, Hayden froze. From where he lay, he watched her survey the room. Thankfully, her gaze didn't dip to him sprawled on the floor. Sighing, she tossed the covers down and slid off the bed.

Hayden sucked in a breath. She wore a cream-colored nightgown of finely spun silk and lace. His gaze traveled down her lithe silhouette to survey how the fabric clung to every turn of her body before ending to expose the swell of shapely calves and finely turned ankles.

Well, he'd be damned. He'd envisioned Sophia, more than once, asleep in her bed, but she'd always donned a woolen nightgown with buttons nearly up to her nose, not some gossamer garment.

She padded toward the fire with her arms wrapped about her waist. At the hearth, she stirred the coals with a brass poker and inched her toes closer to the warmth.

The light from the fire and the lamp on the mantel cast a glow through the thin material revealing the shape of her long, slender legs and their juncture. His mouth grew dry. He should remain quiet, but his damnable conscience forced her name from his lips. "Sophia."

With a gasp, she spun around and lifted the poker menacingly in the air.

He cleared his throat. "Don't be frightened."

"My lord, is that you?"

Indeed, are there any other restless souls in this residence besides me? "Yes."

Hesitantly she moved toward him and without the glow of the fire directly behind her, the outline of her naked body beneath her nightgown faded.

"What are you doing in here?"

She must think him a lecher. "If I told you I sleepwalk would you believe me?"

A long moment passed. "No."

"Would you believe when sleep evades me I come in here and lie in this very spot?" He tapped the carpet below him for emphasis while he inwardly chastised such a half-witted tale.

She uttered a short sound that imparted her disbelief in his inane explanation.

"You doubt me?" Forced indignation tinged the timbre of his voice.

"I do."

He heaved a heavy breath. "Do you know, Sophia, intelligent women can be such a bother."

Leaning forward she peered at him. "Are you drunk, my lord?"

Slightly sodden, but not inebriated enough not to know he shouldn't be in here. However, he seized the excuse like a hawk upon a field mouse. "Yes, utterly soused." For emphasis, he grinned like a buffoon.

"Ah, I see," she said quietly.

"Sophia, unless you intend to skewer me, I would appreciate you lowering the poker."

She glanced at the tool she held in the air and pursed her lips. "I don't know if I should."

"Skewer me or put it down?"

"Both."

"Yes, I understand how you might conclude I have entered your room with some nefarious intent, but if that had been my plan, wouldn't I have climbed into your bed instead of taken residence on the floor?"

Pressing her teeth into her bottom lip, she stared at him, then lowered the poker and walked back to the mantel. The closer she moved to the fire, the more her silken gown turned diaphanous.

"Sophia, will you please find *something* to cover yourself?"

She spun back toward him, her head tipped to the side. She glanced down at herself. Her sleepy eyes flashed wide. "Oh!" She cupped her hands over her breasts.

His cock hardened. He groaned. "Good God, woman, don't stand there doing that."

On quick feet, she padded to the bed and slipped on a cotton robe. "You shouldn't be in here."

She was right, but in his defense, he'd not expected her to be wearing little more than a veil. He shifted onto his knees and braced his weight on the chair.

Pulling the wrapper tightly about her, Sophia knelt next to him and picked up his walking stick. "At least you had enough sense not to gad about unassisted."

The lemony scent of her hair along with the lavender on her skin filled his nose. He swallowed. Dangerous to be in here when he wanted to pull her close and breathe in her fragrance. He reached out to take the walking stick from her.

She tucked it behind her back. "I do not think you are thoroughly intoxicated, my lord."

"If I say I'm in my cups, I am."

"At the mission, I see many women and even children who are bitten by drink. You may have indulged, but you're not exhibiting the symptoms of someone who is truly drunk. Your speech is not slurred and . . ." She looked pointedly at him balanced on his knees. "Your equilibrium seems intact, though obviously faulted."

He thrust out his hand. "Give me my walking stick."

"Perhaps you wished to assure yourself I was fine?"

He gave a derisive snort. "That conk to your head has scrambled your logic."

"Has it?" She settled her bum onto the heels of her feet. The perceptive minx had the audacity to smile.

"What is so humorous?"

"I know the truth, my lord."

"And what truth do you think you have happened upon?" he asked.

"That you are *much more* disposed to thoughtfulness than you wish most to believe."

Thoughtfulness? He wanted to laugh, for at this moment he wished for nothing more than to press her onto her back, settle himself between her thighs, and take her right here on the rug. What would she bloody well think of that? "Do you really believe you've got me figured out?"

She nodded.

He inched closer and drew a finger slowly over the seam of her full lips. Her dark, long-lashed eyes grew round. "Tell me, Sophia, do you truly wish to know what is going through my mind?"

Sophia studied Westfield's heated blue gaze. Desire warmed her skin. Obviously, she'd relinquished her sanity. She should be scrambling to her feet as any sensible woman would do. Yet she lingered as little jolts of electricity exploded within her stomach.

What was wrong with her? There was little time to ponder her own convoluted mind, for without further warning, Westfield seized her upper arms and dragged her body close to his. His face was taut, and for a moment, she was unsure of his intent. He slipped a hand to the small of her back and drew her mouth and body to his. The movement seemed almost violent, as if fueled by anger, but when his lips covered hers, they were gentle.

With a soft moan, she released the walking stick. It toppled to the floor, and its gold head hit the thick carpet with a muffled *thump*. She wrapped her arms around him, allowed her hands to glide over his white nightshirt and the corded muscles of his back.

Their bodies moved, shifted. Suddenly she lay on her back, and his tongue invaded her mouth. The sparks in her belly grew, traveled through her veins, leaving a nervous, yet exhilarating sensation in their path.

Threading her fingers through his hair, she cupped the back of his head and slid her tongue against his. He made a husky sound, while one of his large hands slid to her breast. She arched against the pressure—the heat of his palm. She couldn't seem to get close enough to douse the fiery need within her.

Westfield released her mouth, trailed kisses over her cheek, and down her neck to the ridge of her collarbone. His mouth replaced his hand to capture her breast through the thin fabric of her nightgown, teasing her nipple until it turned pebble hard. With his eyes locked on hers, he breathed on the dampened cloth.

Her lips parted, and she arched up again, silently begging him to continue his wickedness. His lashes lowered and slowly, as if he wished to torment her, he drew his tongue over her other peaked tip.

He peered up at her. "I won't do anything you don't wish, Sophia. You have only to say the word *no*, and I shall stop."

Though raspy, his voice possessed a soothing tone. It made her feel safe, but it was an illusion, a wistful dream, conjured in her own mind and solidified by his skilled touch.

She opened her mouth, intent on telling him they had gone too far, but before she uttered a word, he ran his tongue over the shell of her ear and whispered, "Ah, Sophia, how beautiful you are. Remarkable in every way."

Did he realize what those words did to her? How they spoke to some deep craving within her—some need born from the echo of her great-uncle's cruelty, his disdain. She turned her face and set her mouth to Westfield's.

She wasn't sure how long they kissed. Minutes were seconds. Seconds were hours. It seemed impossible to measure time. His hand slid over the swell of her hip to settle on her left thigh. His fingers flexed. Cool air danced across her lower legs as he drew her hem up, inch by inch, as though he realized the touch of the silky fabric, traveling up her skin, heightened her desire, adding another layer of intrinsic pleasure. His hand shifted to her inner thigh. His palm and the pads of his fingers danced lightly over her skin, a soft sway like the gentlest of breezes that scatters gooseflesh over one's skin. His hand slid—cupped her most private spot where dampness grew.

The noise he made sounded almost feral in its rough tone. It should have frightened her, but she'd crossed a point where fear heightened pleasure, and pleasure seemed absolute. His touch felt good, better than any touch she'd experienced. An ache for more grew within her. She let her thighs relax—an invitation for him to increase his exploration. He drew his finger over the seam of her nether lips while his tongue filled her mouth. She felt wicked and lost in the tumultuous sensations, the maelstrom of desire.

Then the warmth evaporated. Dispersed like a flash of lightning in the sky. Cold air flowed over her dampened skin.

Her eyes fluttered open. Westfield stared at her, his chest heaving, his face shadowed. He jerked back. His taut expression turned the heat coursing through her to ice. She shivered.

With terse movements, he tugged her nightgown down over her legs and pulled her wrapper about her. He leaned on the small chair, grabbed his walking stick, and scrambled to his feet.

Dumbfounded, she watched him move to the door and

set his hand on the knob. "Westfield?" The rasp of his name was barely audible to her own ears, but he turned and glanced down at her.

"You asked why I came into your bedchamber, Sophia. By now it should be exceedingly obvious. I wished to seduce you." He took a heavy breath. "However, I am a man who is enormously fond of a challenge, and this seems all too easy."

She covered her mouth with her hand, but it didn't eradicate the sound of her gasp. She turned her face away and willed her tears not to flow.

The door opened, and then clicked shut.

His vile words spun in her head, and the more she absorbed them, the more her body trembled. A sob caught in her throat. He had played her for a fool, and she had let him. She curled into a tight ball on the floor and wrapped her arms about her knees. Tears blurred her vision, and then spilled forth with a nearly forgotten vengeance.

Hayden slammed the back of his head against his door. Had he ever wanted a woman so desperately? Yes, a long time ago, but he had turned his back on Laura and only added to her heartache.

Sophia deserved someone better. A man who would whisper words of love to her while he took her innocence. Someone who would cherish her forever and offer her fidelity and marriage. Someone who would protect her. Someone besides himself. Better to hurt her now. Better to show her what kind of man she dealt with.

He shouldn't have touched her, but her scent had filled his nose and he'd forgotten propriety and almost let his desire ruin her.

"I am a man who is enormously fond of a challenge, and this seems all too easy." His unforgivable words

echoed in his head. Sophia would be gone in the morning. He was sure of it. Just as he was sure it was for the best.

His gaze settled on the bottle of whisky. He hobbled to the bed, picked it up, and took a long swig, hoping this time it would numb his brain. He sat on the edge of the bed and brought the bottle to his mouth again and again until it was dry. Then he fell back against the mattress and prayed sleep would overtake him.

Hayden stretched out over the blanket he'd placed atop a grassy patch of land adjacent to a small shimmering lake. Sophia lay beside him, her delicate hand clasped within his as they surveyed a squadron of geese rippling the water's still surface.

He turned to his side to kiss her, but she vanished, and in her place stood a wayward gosling which seemed to have taken offense to his presence.

Squawking, the bird pecked insistently at his right arm. He shook the waterfowl's beak loose and scanned the edge of the lake. Sophia remained nowhere in sight, and the bird's cries intensified, causing his head to pound.

"Wake up, Papa!" Celia's voice snapped from somewhere in the distance.

With great difficulty, not to mention a good deal of pain, Hayden opened one heavy-lidded eye. Celia stood by his bedside. He placed his hand on his pounding head, opened his other eye, and forced a weak smile. He tipped his head sideways and surveyed the empty whisky bottle that mocked him from the bedside table.

"Celia?" His voice reverberated loudly between his ears as though his head mimicked a great empty tower which amplified sounds to astronomic proportions. He closed his eyes and prayed the echo would cease before his head split open.

Celia pinched his arm.

Oh God, he was dying, and the child pounded the nails into his coffin with just two tiny fingers. He forced his eyes open again. "Yes, dear." He swallowed the bitter taste coating his parched mouth.

"She is gone, Papa!"

Her voice pummeled his ears, and he winced. "Let us play a game, Celia. See who can whisper the softest. The winner shall decide what dessert Chef will prepare today. Now repeat what you said, but remember the game."

If Celia had meant to whisper, she failed terribly. "Sophia is gone, Papa!" She dashed away the tears on her face.

Comprehension settled in his pickled brain. Hayden sat up so abruptly he feared his head would roll off his shoulders and topple to the floor. "Gone?" he repeated, forgetting his own game and setting off the reverberations again. "Where?" Then it all came flooding back to him like a deluge on the lowlands.

"I-I don't know." Her narrow shoulders sagged. "I overheard Mathews and Hawthorne talking."

The emptiness in his dream returned. Gone. He had expected nothing less. It was for the best, for if Sophia had stayed he'd have begged her to forgive him, and ended up wanting her even more than he did now. And she deserved far better than him.

"My lord."

He looked up at Mathews's scowling face. "When did she leave?" Hayden asked.

Mathews walked over to the windows and drew the curtains open. The room filled with cruel light. Hayden squinted against the shafts cutting through the glass.

"Left near seven this morning." Mathews strode to the side of the bed and removed a note from his inside breast pocket.

Hayden thrust out his hand.

Mathews shot him a disdainful look. "It is for Lady Celia," he said, handing it to her.

Celia studied the paper in her hand. "Did you sack her, Papa?"

Hayden's muscles tensed. No, he had done something much worse. "Do you wish me to read the letter to you or would you prefer to read it yourself?"

She rubbed her fingers over the slightly felted parchment before handing it to him.

He patted the mattress next to him, and Celia climbed atop the bed. Snuggling herself under the bedding, she peered expectantly at him.

He unfolded the note as though it was a public decree declaring him a grievous fiend. However, the short missive, directed solely at Celia, didn't mention his name, not once. He cleared his throat. Then read aloud.

Dearest Celia,

I'm sorry, but I had to leave sooner than expected. I wanted you to know I shall always remember, with great fondness, the fun we had making snow angels. I wish you health, happiness, and much success in your life. Such a special girl deserves nothing less.

Fondest regards,
Sophia Camden

Feeling an overpowering wish to smash something, combined with a great deal of self-disgust, Hayden resisted the urge to crumble the paper held taut in his hand. Instead, he focused his attention on Celia's solemn, upturned face. "I'm sorry, Celia, but Sophia couldn't stay forever. There are those who need her care more than I."

Without a word, Celia tucked her face into the crook of his arm and chest.

He ran his hand down her back and glanced at Mathews. The man eyed him with an ungracious and accusing expression etched upon his face. "Mathews, please have two breakfast trays brought to my room. Celia and I shall be spending the day together."

After taking the omnibus to Oxford Circus, it took Sophia a mere fifteen minutes, walking at a brisk pace, to reach Thomas's Harley Street residence.

When the housekeeper opened the large oak door, the pungent smell of freshly brewed coffee spilled forward as if under the guidance of an easterly gale.

"Good morning, Mrs. Morehouse. A beautiful day, isn't it?" Sophia asked, feigning cheerfulness.

The slender, gray-haired woman eyed her critically before giving a resounding *humph*. Then without a word, she dipped her right index finger into her mouth, leaned forward, and raised said finger into the crisp morning air. "'Tis going to rain, and you without an umbrella."

"Really?" Sophia glanced over her shoulder at the startling blue sky.

The elder woman pursed her lips as a clap of thunder exploded in the distance. It probably would rain. Sophia should know better than to doubt the woman. The old crow was like a walking barometer with the uncanny ability to predict precipitation with nothing more than her confounded finger.

"Is Dr. Trimble in his office?" Sophia inquired, stepping fully into the black-and-white-tiled entry hall and unbuttoning her coat.

Mrs. Morehouse nodded. "On his third cup of coffee." The lines framing the housekeeper's pencil-thin lips deepened. "I guess you'll be wanting a cup as well?"

Sophia hung her coat and hat on the hall tree and smoothed the skirts of her serviceable navy dress. Whatever the housekeeper lacked in personality, she made up for with her coffee. And since Thomas couldn't make it through the day without drinking pots of the stuff, it explained why he'd never dismissed the cantankerous woman.

"It does smell wonderful."

"Aye," Mrs. Morehouse replied, turning and heading toward the kitchen.

After making her way down the corridor, Sophia rapped softly on Thomas's office door.

"Come in." His brisk tone indicated he didn't welcome the intrusion.

Sophia opened the door.

Thomas, dressed in his shirtsleeves, bounced up from his chair, his somber expression replaced with one of unabashed pleasure. "Sophia."

She crossed the room, and Thomas warmly grasped her hands within his.

"I was just contemplating what time I should return to Westfield's today to check on you, and here you are." His right hand reached out to touch the lump on the back of her head. He frowned and motioned to one of the sturdy wooden chairs facing his large oak desk. "You are well?"

"Splendid. And I'm ready to return to work." The coiling in her stomach twisted tighter as she sat. She had always felt so comfortable around Thomas; nevertheless, she did not relish his inquiring why she'd changed her mind about attending Westfield.

His eyebrows rose. "You are returning to work today?"

Dipping her chin, she tugged off her gloves. "You were right, Thomas. Westfield has recovered sufficiently. I'm sure the danger of infection has all but passed."

Thomas settled against the back of his leather chair and

pressed his steepled fingers to his lips. "Did you examine him this morning?"

"No, I left early."

He nodded again and lowered his fingers. "Words cannot express my pleasure. You have been dearly missed here."

"How kind of you to say so."

"It's not kindness. It's the truth."

She glanced down at her gloves. She'd kept her tears at bay all morning, but they suddenly threatened like dark, ominous clouds.

"Sophia, has something upset you?"

Luckily, the appearance of the housekeeper, bearing a tray, saved her from having to reply.

She forced a smile. "Thank you, Mrs. Morehouse."

Without expression, the housekeeper set the tray, laden with a barrel-shaped mug of steaming coffee, a linen-lined basket with currant rolls, and a small porcelain fruit dish with raspberry jam, on the table adjacent to Sophia's chair. "There's a Mrs. Barnes asking for you, Miss Camden."

Sophia tapped her chin. "Mrs. Barnes?"

The woman nodded. "Says she knows you from the Eastern Dispensary."

"Oh, yes. Please tell her I'll be there shortly."

As the housekeeper exited the room, Sophia picked up the hot cup of coffee and took a sip. She peered over its rim. Thomas still stared at her. She lowered the mug. "Do you remember Mrs. Barnes?"

"Your reticence in answering my question only confirms something has distressed you. That scoundrel didn't . . . He didn't offend you, did he?"

She couldn't tell him how foolish she'd been. "Of course not. *Really*, Thomas." She waved a dismissive hand. "Now,

I guess I should go and see what has brought Mrs. Barnes here today."

"Sophia?"

"Yes." She stood and placed the cup on the tray. The sting of tears pressed on her eyes.

Thomas slammed his hands down on his desk. "What did that blackguard do?"

She shook her head. "Nothing. I am fatigued, that's all."

He opened his mouth, and then pinched it closed.

"I am pleased to be back." She moved to the door. With her hand on the handle, she turned back to him. "Thank you."

"For what?"

"For not questioning me more, and for promising me you will not have an inquisition with Lord Westfield."

"I have made no such promise."

"But you will, won't you?"

An uncomfortable silence filled the room. "Of course," he said at last. "If that is what you wish."

She nodded and stepped from the office, anxious for an end to the conversation.

Chapter Eleven

Hayden glanced up from his desk as Hawthorne entered the study with a calling card centered on a silver salver.

"A Mr. Ambrus Varga is here to see you, my lord."

"Send him in." Hayden tossed aside the large stack of unanswered mail that had accumulated in the three weeks since Sophia left. He pinched the bridge of his nose and surveyed the ledgers and monthly reports scattered about the desk like inconsequential rubbish. If he didn't settle his mind on his business dealings, he'd soon find his finances in a shambles.

Varga stepped into the room. Time had taken its toll on the Hungarian over the last couple of years. The lines on the older man's face appeared etched in stone and his long moustache and muttonchops were now gray. Nevertheless, he was still the best private investigator London had to offer.

Hayden motioned toward one of the chairs facing the desk. What perversity had caused him to hire the man in the first place? And more importantly, what did he hope to accomplish? "So, tell me what you have learned." He leaned against the back of his chair and stretched out his legs.

"Very little, as of yet, m'lord."

"What do you have so far?"

Varga reached into his breast pocket and extracted a small journal bound in black leather. "Miss Camden resides in Chelsea. A Cheyne Walk residence."

"A suite of rooms?"

"No, a private residence."

"A private residence?" he echoed.

"Yes, she employs a housekeeper and several other servants, but only the housekeeper lives in."

Hayden eyed the decanter of brandy on the sideboard. Too early to fortify himself with liquor, yet he might be tempted to drink a glass after hearing the answer to his next question. "Who holds the lease and pays the staff?" Fearing he'd hear Trimble's name, the muscles in the back of his neck tensed.

"It's hers, m'lord. Lock, stock, and barrel. Moved there nearly three years ago."

It was obvious Sophia had been raised in a well-to-do home. He'd thought her brought low by financial hardship or some bitter twist of fate, but she was a woman of means.

Varga's next sentence severed his thoughts. "Had a baby with her when she moved in."

He sat forward and set his forearms on the desk. "A child?" His voice betrayed his disbelief.

"Her neighbors are rather closed-mouthed, but one of their maids passed on that tidbit. Looked like her, the servant said. A girl."

Hayden would have sworn the ground beneath him shifted. A child. He found it hard to fathom. Yet, this would explain a great deal. Why she seemed removed from the society she'd been born into. "You said had. Where is the child now?"

Varga tugged on the left side of his long moustache. "The maid said the baby died, near two years past."

Died. The word echoed in Hayden's head. His heart

grew heavy as he recalled how Sophia had bonded with Celia in such a short time. How had she coped with the loss of her own child? "Go on," he prompted.

The man closed the journal. "That's all I have for now. I'll start searching the parish records tomorrow. See what else I can find."

"I'll expect a full dossier delivered to my residence next week."

"Some of them parish records are in disorder, m'lord. It could take—"

Hayden raised a silencing hand. "Patience is a virtue I lack." Standing, he shook the man's hand, forcing an end to their conversation.

Varga nodded. "I'll be in touch, m'lord."

After the man exited the room, Hayden braced his palms on the desk and stared blindly down upon its surface. Sophia had borne a daughter. He wasn't the type to make moral judgments, not after the life he'd led, but the information shocked him. She'd seemed so inexperienced when he'd kissed her.

He swept his hand across the desk. The ledgers toppled to the floor and correspondence flew in the air.

Why was he angry? Was it because some bastard had gotten her enceinte, then possibly abandoned her? Or simply the fact that she'd endured the pain of losing a child?

He sat and surveyed the mess he'd created. He doubted he'd muster even a small semblance of concentration tonight. He glanced at the brass clock perched on the desk. Simon and several chums were gathering at the Coat of Arms Pub. He stood. He'd not intended on going, but he needed a distraction. No, he needed to get drunk.

The scent of strong spirits and tobacco permeated the pub. Hayden tipped his glass to his lips and took a heavy sip of whisky. The numbness engulfing him relented to the scorching burn of alcohol trailing down his throat.

He set the near empty glass on the table and cradled it between his hands. The amber liquid pooling in the bottom absorbed the hue of the darkened wood beneath it before catching the glow of the gaslights above. The color reminded him of Sophia's dark tear-filled eyes.

Hayden drew the glass back to his mouth and drained it dry. He surveyed the men seated at his table conversing amiably. He'd not listened to a single word they'd said over the last half hour. He'd come here to forget, yet he'd need several more drinks if he were to find any measure of solace from the single-mindedness of his thoughts. Restlessly he looked around the taproom for the serving girl.

"Westfield!" Someone hailed above the din of the crowded room.

He glanced up to see George Boswitch standing by the pub's etched glass doors waving his hat in the air. The redheaded young man, an heir apparent fresh from Yorkshire, had relentlessly tried to ingratiate himself into their merry band of revelers since gaining admission to one of the clubs they all subscribed to.

Hayden acknowledged him with a quick nod. However, he refrained from inviting Boswitch to join them. The lad was ingenuous and truly out of place with their iniquitous group.

Had he ever been so callow?

Yes, how could he forget the youthful, reckless antics Simon and he had engaged in? He recalled the first time they'd taken the rail into London from Eton. They'd ventured deep into the seedier enclaves and sampled everything from fish at Three Tuns Tavern to loose women in a dirty dockside inn. They'd stumbled out of that less-than-fine establishment three sheets to the wind.

They returned to school thinking themselves worldly

swells, the best of young fellows, who'd had a stunner of a time. Until Simon realized he'd not only brought back some titillating memories, but a severe case of nits in a most unfortunate place, while Hayden had spent the whole of the next day casting up his accounts. They'd been fortunate. They could have returned with the dreaded French disease or been beaten senseless by hooligans while swaying drunkenly down the streets of Wapping.

Without further deliberation, he lifted his hand and motioned Boswitch to their table. The young man eagerly made his way through the heavy throng of patrons and the thick smoke that turned the stagnant air into a cloudy shroud.

Simon, seated directly to his right, peered at him. "Hayden, you cannot be seriously considering initiating that pup into our fold?"

"I remember our exploits when younger. We could have used a benefactor to steer us in the right direction. You haven't forgotten our visit to Wapping?"

"Christ, how could I forget? Had my bollocks swathed in mercury ointment and Persian powder till they turned nearly purple and the bloody itching drove me mad." Simon shifted uncomfortably in his chair.

"Then we should take pity on the lad, for I fear his eagerness may bring him more trouble than he may wish."

"I don't doubt that, but what are we to do with him? He's barely out of his nappies, and I could swear he's got some wet nurse's milk dried up on his chin."

"He's older than we were when we went to the East End, and those are whiskers on his chin."

Simon peered at the approaching man. "Oh, I say, that's just sad."

"Better he get his tutoring where the girls are clean. Why don't you do me a favor and take him to Madame

Trumann's. You're always touting that establishment's ample endowments."

Simon's face puckered. "I'd probably have to burp him after he's finished with one of Trumann's girls." His friend gave him a contemplative look. "I know you're not fond of brothels, old chum, but I think one of Trumann's pretty little birds would do you a world of good. Why don't you accompany us?"

"I should head home. Edith and I are to interview for Celia's governess tomorrow." He shoved his chair back, tossed several bills onto the table, and stood. "I bid you all a most pleasant night."

A riotous protest arose from those seated at the table.

"Damn and blast, Westfield. You off so soon?" Edmond Wright boomed.

He nodded.

"Lady Randall is having a small, exclusive gathering tomorrow, Westfield," Julian Caruthers added with a wink. "Know she'd be tickled pink if you were to attend."

Westfield had partaken in most of Lady Randall's exclusive parties. They started at her terrace in Belgravia and ended at her estate in Kent. They lasted well over a week and were full of dissipation. A month ago, he would have joined the revelry, yet today his stomach soured at the thought. With a grimace, he ran his hand over his thigh. "I think I shall have to forgo the festivities, Caruthers. Though do give Lady Randall my regard."

"Aye, still not up to snuff?" Alasdair McGrath asked with a plaintive expression.

Picking up his walking stick, Hayden feigned a look of resigned sorrow, and a commiserative murmur arose from the group.

He turned from the table to see Boswitch staring at him as if he were a paragon. Poor misguided lad. "Boswitch, my good man, take my seat." He motioned to his vacated chair. "I need to be shoving off."

Boswitch gave the group a wide smile. "W-well thank you, Westfield."

Westfield thumped Simon on his shoulder, then bracing his weight on his walking stick, he walked to the door. Had he done Boswitch a favor or a disservice leaving him with that group of reprobates? Well, for all Simon's indifference, he could be trusted.

As soon as he stepped out onto Maddox Street, his coach appeared. He opened the carriage door and extracted his heavy wool overcoat and top hat. "I wish to walk, Evans." He closed the door and stepped back.

"Walk, m'lord?" The coachman stared pointedly at Hayden's leg and walking stick. "Do you wish me to follow you?"

"No, drive on."

Evans hesitated, then tipping his hat, he drew the horses into a trot. The carriage faded into the fog and darkness.

Hayden slipped his overcoat on and took a long draught of cool air into his lungs. Hopefully, it would clear his mind or at least numb it.

By the time he'd reached Brook Street, the night air and solitude had done little to alleviate his tenacious thoughts of Sophia. He wondered what she was doing at this moment or whether Trimble was with her. The latter possibility seemed to incinerate good judgment, and before he knew what he was about, he hailed a passing hackney and gave the driver Sophia's Chelsea address.

From inside the carriage, Hayden stared at the four-story brick home with flower boxes overflowing with dark boughs of evergreens. Even with the mist swirling off the Thames, hovering around its façade, Sophia's residence looked warm and inviting—a beckoning light upon his dark soul.

Through the fanlight above the front door, a dim light radiated from the rear of the house. His gaze lifted to the first floor; it was dark. However, the windows on the second floor glowed with a soft light. Was that Sophia's private suite of rooms? The thought of them suddenly darkening lodged an uncomfortable weight in his gut. He'd intended to only drive by and get a glimpse of her residence, but the cozy outside beckoned him and his desire edged him forward. He stepped from the hackney. With hurried hands, he reached for his billfold and paid the driver.

The clopping of the horses' hooves had all but faded by the time he swung open the ornate metal gate and moved up the flagstone pathway. The need to see Sophia overwhelmed him. His feet moved as if pulled by gravity. It was lunacy calling on her at this hour—madness to call on her at all. But he'd not turn back.

He had won their wager. Sophia owed him recompense, and he finally knew what he wanted.

Her.

Chapter Twelve

The soles of Mrs. MacLean's shoes landed heavily on the treads as the housekeeper trudged up the stairs. The woman's grumbling grew louder as she moved toward Sophia's bedchamber.

Sophia straightened in her chair and set her open book on her lap. The composition titled *The Perfect Rose* had arrived in today's post. Another hateful gift from Great-Uncle Charles. A book that touted not only what features constituted the ideal English woman—a bow-shaped mouth, a heart-shaped face—but also implied a woman was flawed if she possessed any opinions at all. She should have burned it. Not read a stitch of it.

Mrs. MacLean entered the room and pursed her lips. "If ye be asking me 'tis too late to be receiving a gentleman caller."

A jolt of apprehension flooded Sophia's belly. She snapped her book closed. "A *gentleman* caller?"

"Aye," the elder woman replied, peering at the crisp white calling card held in her hand. "'Tis Lord Westfield. An' he don't look nothing like that caricature I seen of him in *Punch*. No, indeed. The man looks twice as menacing.

A right buirdly gent. Noot like most of them pasty-faced nobs one's apt to see west of Charing Cross."

Sophia's heartbeat escalated, and the odd sensation pooling in her belly exploded sending hot rivulets over her nerves. "Westfield," she said his name—two distinct syllables, the latter drowned under the thudding of her heart echoing in her ears.

"Yes, an' insisting on seeing ye."

With trembling fingers, Sophia placed the book on the side table and stood. Wringing her hands, she paced the room. She stopped and spun back toward the housekeeper. "Mrs. MacLean, please send him away. Tell him . . . tell him I've retired for the night." The shrill tone in her voice echoed in the bedchamber.

The housekeeper tapped her foot on the floor and gave an exaggerated sigh. "I tried, miss, but he's a plucky gent that don't seem accustomed to being turned away."

Indeed, Westfield was used to getting his way; he'd most likely remain ensconced in her entry hall until she received him. She let go of the death grip her hands were placing upon each other and took a deep breath.

"Show him to the drawing room," she replied, mustering her courage.

What did he want? Rubbing her moist palms over the folds of her gold and red gown, she resumed pacing. She moved to the doorway and peered into the dim corridor. She could slip down the back staircase and out the rear of the house.

No, she would not be intimidated. Squaring her shoulders, she walked to the stairway and descended the steps. By the time she reached the drawing room, her heart was racing in her chest again. She took several calming breaths and opened the double doors.

Westfield leaned casually against the window frame, his gaze directed out the panes of glass. She knew the view across the street was nearly unperceivable. The air drifting off the Thames had thickened and settled over the embankment like a vaporous cloak.

He was impeccably dressed in a crisp white shirt, dark silver ascot, and waistcoat. His navy frock coat molded itself to his broad shoulders, and gray trousers encased his long legs. He looked every inch the gentleman. She nearly laughed aloud at the stream of her thoughts. It would be unwise to let the cut of Westfield's bespoke garments fool her. He was a man to be wary of, especially where her pride and heart were concerned.

He pushed his tall form away from the window's casings and turned to her. Her stomach clenched. His blue eyes were shadowed, and there was a weariness to his normally handsome visage.

She stifled the foolish urge to rush forward. *You must act indifferent, you silly goose.* She stepped into the room and closed the doors to hinder Mrs. MacLean's prying ears.

"Lord Westfield," she said coolly, "to what do I owe the honor of your visit?" The steady tone of her voice pleased her.

His gaze raked over her, and she looked down at the gold and red gown she wore with its simple soft flowing skirt and square neckline. Self-consciously she lifted a hand to the exposed skin above the décolletage.

Many of the artists who resided in Chelsea donned aesthetic clothing and no corsets, but Westfield would think her Bohemian. Dash it all, she'd let the man touch her intimately. Of course he thought her Bohemian. She lowered her hand and returned his bold gaze. Thankfully, she hadn't unpinned the chignon at her nape.

"You look well, Sophia," he said, breaking the silence.

His deep masculine voice felt like a tangible force caressing her skin. She took a slow breath, tried to regulate the elevated beating of her heart. "Thank you, my lord."

The silence in the room grew.

"Sophia, are you going to offer me a seat, so I may rest my weary leg?"

She wished to refuse his request; nevertheless, she motioned to the pair of chintz-covered chairs set before the hearth.

With a congenial nod, he strode across the room. An occasional hitch marred his stride. Yet otherwise, his gait was smooth for a man who'd suffered an injury such as he had. She bit back the temptation to tell him he should be using a cane, but then she noticed the familiar, elegant gold-knobbed walking stick propped against the wainscoting near the window.

He stood waiting for her, and reluctantly she moved toward the other chair. A flutter besieged her stomach with each step that brought her closer to him. She'd not forgotten how his mouth and hands had stroked her skin or the feel of his hard body, and certainly not how she'd welcomed his touch.

After she sat, he folded his tall form into the opposite chair. Casually reclining against its upholstered back, Westfield steepled his hands, pressed his index fingers to his lips, and looked at her.

Under his intense scrutiny, the fluttering in her stomach turned tempestuous. "My lord, it is—"

"Hayden."

"What?"

"I wish you to call me Hayden."

Not likely! "It is rather late, *my lord*. May I ask the reason for your visit?"

He leaned forward and braced his forearms on his knees. So close she could smell the faint scent of his shaving soap, along with the smell of tobacco drifting off his clothes. "I have finally decided what my recompense should be for winning our little game."

"*Your* recompense!" She sprung to her feet.

Westfield quickly followed suit, standing, and closing the short gap between them. He peered down at her. "A dare was placed between us, Sophia, along with a wager. As the victor I'm due a forfeit."

She wanted to step back, but she was pinned between his tall body and the chair behind her. "You told me I could leave and consider our dare and that silly wager null and void."

The corners of his mouth lifted into an uneven smile. "I did. However, if my memory serves me clearly, you stated you did not wish to end either. In fact, you told me, quite adamantly, you intended to win. But since you left, you lost."

How could he hold her to that, especially after what had transpired between them? "You sent me a check in care of Dr. Trimble's residence," she replied as though such a fact offered absolution.

"Yes, which you've yet to cash."

How could she? She'd not won the staggering amount he'd sent her. Accepting it would have made her feel dirty, so she'd burned it. And the money Lady Prescott paid her, she'd given to Thomas for his hospital fund. She crossed her arms over her chest and glared at him. "You cannot be serious about this."

"Quite."

"And what recompense do I owe you? Shall I return the wages your sister paid me, grovel at your feet, or hail you superior?"

Sophia awaited his answer, but abruptly he moved toward the double doors. She stared at his back in confusion. Was he leaving? She wasn't sure whether to feel relieved or once again offended.

He flung the doors open. Mrs. MacLean jumped back with a squeal that rivaled a scavenging hog.

"Madam," he snapped. "I suggest you retire to your room."

The housekeeper momentarily froze, then fled down the corridor.

Westfield slammed the doors closed.

Sophia stood motionless as he stalked back toward her. With his hands on her upper arms, he pulled her close. "No, Sophia, I don't want your deuced wages or you groveling at my feet. A night in your bed should suffice."

Her knees weakened, and for a brief moment, she appreciated he held her. But indignation quickly overpowered shock. She tipped her chin in the air. "Over my dead body."

He grinned. "My dear, contrary to any rumors you may have heard, I assure you I am not so depraved."

"Lord Westfield, you are mad if you believe I will consent—"

His large hands cupped her face, and his lips covered hers. She opened her mouth, intent on rebuking him, but he deepened the kiss, caressed her tongue with his own, withdrew, only to plunge hungrily again. The rhythmic, primal sensation felt tantamount to a heady drug.

He stepped closer, pressed his hard body intimately against hers. Sinful heat radiated from him, warming her skin. Almost light-headed, she slipped her arms around his neck and returned his kiss.

His hold relaxed, one hand shifted to tangle in her hair, the other fell to her waist. "How I want you," he whispered into her ear, his voice raspy and intense. He nibbled at her neck before returning for another deep kiss.

The foolish, imprudent part of her wanted him, as well, but she couldn't stop the echo of her inner voice reminding her of his cruel words and the humiliation they brought about. *A minute or two more*, the rash side of her urged, *then step out of his embrace and ask him to leave with the same indifference he showed you.*

Cold air brushing over her spine interrupted her thoughts. Hayden had skillfully unfastened the buttons on the back of her gown. If she didn't pull back, she'd tangle herself in a web spun by her own recklessness. She turned her mouth away and set her hands against his chest.

"Please don't pull away, Sophia. Those dreadful things I said . . ." He briefly glanced away and mumbled a curse. "I didn't mean them. The truth is you awaken emotions I believed long dead. I am an imperfect man, and God knows you deserve someone better."

Startled, she peered into his eyes. They looked tired. She placed her hands against his cheeks and touched her thumbs to the dark smears under them. "I don't know when you're lying to me or offering the truth."

"You wish to hear the truth?" He gave a bitter bark of laughter. "I have spent the last three weeks with one foot in purgatory and the other slipping off stable ground." He brushed the back of his fingers against her cheek. "I think of you constantly and accomplish little."

He appeared sincere, and she had already lost her heart to him. *Don't be rash,* a voice warned, but instead of heeding it, she perched on her toes and pressed her lips to his.

With a deep, guttural sound, he cradled the back of her head and kissed her again. Within minutes, her gown pooled on the floor, and Hayden's coat and tie draped a chair. She tugged at the buttons of his waistcoat. That fervent need to press her skin to his consumed her. He shrugged the garment off his shoulders, and then his fingers were on the small satin ties that held her white chemise closed. The thin material fell open, exposing her breasts.

With lowered lashes, she glanced at his face. He was looking at her as though he'd never seen a woman before.

Her face warmed. Self-consciously she pulled the material closed.

Gently he pulled her hands away. The fabric fell open again. Leaning forward, he whispered, "Forgive me for staring, but you are not only a remarkably intelligent woman, but beautiful."

How did he know that at this moment, after Great-Uncle Charles's thoughtless book on the perfect English rose, she desperately needed to hear such words? To feel desirable. Wanted.

His hand captured the weight of her breast. Her already budding nipple hardened against his palm. He lowered his mouth and trailed a slow path to the breast he held. His tongue darted out, teased the tip.

She hadn't thought he could drive her madder with want, but the sensations from his wet mouth and tongue, along with the slight abrasion from his shaven chin, heightened her desire. It was impossible to stifle the little sound that escaped her throat. By the time he pulled away, she was panting.

"Will you allow me to make love to you, Sophia? Not because of some blasted dare, but because you wish to."

The thought of their bodies tangled together, their mouths on each other's skin, inflamed her. She buried her face into the folds of his white shirt, breathed in his scent. "Yes," she mumbled against the cloth.

Without another word, he swept her up, cradled her in his arms, and moved to the settee. Abruptly he stopped. "Where is your bedchamber?"

"The second floor, but I can walk. Your leg—"

"It feels fine," he responded dismissively.

As they ascended the stairs, Hayden kept glancing at her. Her expression most likely conveyed her apprehension. This was insanity. Once again, she had let his touch and his words play havoc with her judicious mind. Could she do this—take carnal pleasure with a man who was not her husband? A month ago, she would have laughed at such an outlandish thought, but now . . .

At the second-floor landing, he turned toward her room where light still shone from within. He crossed the threshold and with his foot nudged the door closed. The four-poster bed loomed. Fear and anticipation fought for control as Hayden carried her toward it.

As if sensing her doubt, he laid her down and turned the gas lamp low, leaving the room bathed in a subtle glow. Setting a knee on the bed, he braced himself over her and covered her mouth with his. He shifted back. "Are you sure?"

No. Yes. This surpassed recklessness, but his kiss and touch left an ache that needed to be soothed. She nodded.

His sensuous lips turned upward. He slipped his braces off his shoulders and tugged his shirttails free. In one swift motion, he drew the crisp shirt over his head, causing his pectoral muscles to bunch reflexively.

Her mouth grew dry. He was magnificent. Her fingers twitched. She wanted to touch him—this man with a body so different from her own, a man hard in places where she felt soft.

He tossed his shirt onto her favorite chair. The sight of the garments touching the flowered surface evoked a sense of intimacy—an intimacy shared by husbands and wives, and yes, lovers.

His gaze never left her as he kicked off his shoes, unfastened his trousers, and slipped them off. As he removed his socks and drawers, his forearms flexed. Swallowing, she forced her gaze lower. His penis looked hard and thick, nothing like the flaccid illustrations in Thomas's medical books. She understood the mechanics of coupling. Knew a man needed to become firm to make the whole process work, but never had she imagined it would become so large that the veins would strain against the taut skin.

Hayden moved to the edge of the bed, took her hands in his, and pulled her to her knees. He kissed her long and deep while he lifted the hem of her chemise. He broke the kiss and drew the garment over her head. The warmth on her face spread to the tips of her ears.

"How beautiful," he said, sliding his large palms over her shoulders, arms, the tips of her fingers. His hands lifted to her hair, extracted the pins that held her chignon. The long mass tumbled down her back—swayed against her bare skin. He wrapped his hand in it, tipped her head back, and then capturing her mouth, he lowered them both to the bed.

For long, splendid minutes, he lay next to her merely kissing her. Then his nimble fingers drew off her remaining garments. His hands moved over her, exploring, shaping, feeling. Her skin grew hot. She ached for something more, an unknown entity—primal, yet natural. She shifted closer.

The tips of his fingers grazed her skin, a featherlight touch. Too soft. A torment. She felt him smile against her neck. He comprehended what he did to her. Knew it was not enough. She bit her lip, forced herself not to beg him to increase the pressure, but she couldn't stop her body from arching, pleading.

In answer, he rolled her nipple between the pads of his thumb and forefinger. It should have caused pain, but it satisfied, drew her closer to the elusiveness she sought. He lowered his mouth to her breast, sucked one, then the other. She tangled her hands in his silky hair and held him to her.

His hand skated over her abdomen to settle between her legs. Her body quivered. He slid his palm against her feminine skin, now dampened by her own uncontrolled yearning. He took possession of her mouth while his fingers stroked her. At the exact moment he deepened the kiss, he slid a finger into her. She pressed her heels into the mattress and lifted her hips.

Wanton. Yes, she felt wanton, and close to bursting from her own heated skin. She wished for more—for Hayden to bury himself in her, to join with her, to satisfy the overwhelming need that clawed for release. But instead, he made his way down her body nipping and kissing. His mouth moved past her navel and dipped between her legs.

Oh, heavens! What was he about? She tried to shift away.

But he held her hips and peered up at her. She stilled, suddenly wanting to experience what his heated gaze promised. His tongue delved where his fingers had been. Every nerve in her body centered in that spot he touched. An unexplored, foreign sensation threatened to overwhelm her. "No," she said, scrubbing her head back and forth over her pillow.

"Hmm, but you taste so lovely," he said, his breath, little puffs against her damp skin.

"Please." To her own ears, the single word sounded like a plea for the continuation of his sensual ministrations, but he heeded her former word and pressed kisses against her inner thigh before he shifted and braced himself above her.

She reached out, tentatively wrapped her hand around his hard manhood. The texture was smooth and silky; it defied its appearance. Fascinated she ran her fingers up, then down its length, stroking him.

He made a noise, low, animalistic in its timbre, and threw his head back. When he glanced back at her, his eyes appeared nearly black. Air swished between his teeth. He shifted, settled between her legs, and pulled her hand away. With one quick thrust, he buried himself in her.

Sophia flinched and dug her nails into his shoulders.

She had counseled women on the discomfort associated with the tearing of the hymen, yet she'd not really known what to expect. It had not been too painful. He stilled for a second, drew back, and looked at her, his expression puzzled.

Her stomach fluttered. She must seem gauche, awkward. He opened his mouth, but she laced her hands around his neck and brought his lips down to hers. With a groan, he started moving within her, partially withdrawing, only to plunge again. An exquisite sensation that coalesced pain and pleasure until only the latter survived.

The rhythm of his movements grew stronger, deeper. She wrapped her legs around his hips. Her body clawed at the growing sensations as if it realized something fantastical lay just out of reach. She wanted to ask him to explain what was happening, but instead she arched up, demanded it not elude her. The fine edge of his teeth grazed her neck before his tongue soothed the scraped skin.

She closed her eyes and centered her mind on the pleasure building within her, drawing her closer to the edge of something—a culmination. Then it overtook her. Her legs quivered and hot rivulets of pleasure shot through her body. She floated in a cloud of sated weightlessness.

Hayden's voice drew her back. "Ah, Sophia, your climax humbles me."

He thrust forward, once, twice. His breath ragged, he thrust again, tensed, and the sinew on his neck tightened as he held himself deep within her and shuddered. He kissed the top of her head and rolled to his side, taking her with him. He remained inside her and she could feel herself pulsating around him. She buried her face against his chest, listened to the heavy strumming of his heart, and drifted off to sleep.

* * *

Hayden brushed his hand over Sophia's silky hair. She slept soundly, her head upon his chest and one small hand curved around his forearm. The even rhythm of her breathing marked the inevitable passage of time. He wanted nothing more than to stay cloistered in her bedchamber for a few days while the world slipped by.

If he'd meant to purge himself of his desire for Sophia, he'd failed miserably. When he was with her, the past and his guilt over what had happened to Laura drifted deeper into the recesses of his mind.

Edith was right. His wife's death had tossed him in a dark hole of regret and self-destruction. He'd given up on himself and happiness, but the woman lying beside him made him believe there could be more to his future than regret. She made him want to be a better man.

He flattened his palm against the smooth plane of her belly. He always took precautions, usually more than one. Yet he'd been reckless. The fortitude to withdraw had deserted him, making him wonder if he'd come here to allay his baser instincts or to bind her to him.

Perhaps he didn't wish to lose the peaceful calm he experienced when beside her. Did that equate to love? Or self-preservation? He wasn't sure.

So where did that leave him? Did he wish her to be his mistress? That offer would likely be met with a firm slap across his face. Which left only one other option.

Marriage.

But would she accept his proposal?

Damnation, he was a member of the peerage. An earl. Though admittedly, one with a sullied reputation. Yet he had a feeling she wouldn't care a jot about his title.

So what offer would he make? One might turn her away from him, and the other would bind them for life. And both possibilities were scary as hell.

Chapter Thirteen

Sophia awoke bathed in warmth like a cat stretched languidly across a sunny windowsill. A strange experience, for she knew the wind pummeling the façade of her house carried the dampness of the Thames and a bitter chill. She glanced at the front windows. Moonlight seeped around the curtains, infusing the room in a subtle blue light.

The longcase clock struck five times, resonating through the house. Hayden should leave soon. Mrs. MacLean rose early, and the dailies would arrive in a few hours. Every cell in her brain told her she should wake him. Nevertheless, she pulled the quilt over her bare shoulders and nestled deeper into the crook between Hayden's arm and chest, closer to the glorious heat his body offered.

"Sophia?"

Hayden's deep voice rumbled beneath her ear. A shiver of awareness shot through her. He must have perceived the frisson, for his left hand, splayed on her lower back, pressed her tightly toward him as though he wished to warm her skin with his own.

She peered up at him. He looked magnificent, even with his hair tousled as if he'd ridden a fast mount through a turbulent gale.

Had she done that to him? Yes, she remembered running her fingers through the thick mass. "Good morning." She feigned a sense of ease.

He flashed a devilish grin. "How lovely you look upon awakening."

She probably resembled the doxies she'd seen in Whitechapel, the ones with red whisker abrasions on their faces.

God, what have I done? A vision of herself with her legs wrapped around him assailed her. She had behaved like a wanton, acting far beyond the realm of anything imaginable, all because his blue eyes had begged, and her heart—her foolish heart—wanted him.

For the first time in her life, she comprehended why many of the women who sought guidance at the mission acted so recklessly. Desire and lust, the touch of a tongue, the stroke of a finger, all conspired with the heart to overpower rational thought.

She should prompt him to leave. It would not be prudent to let anyone see Hayden leaving her house. It would herald her ruination as clearly as a town crier's proclamation.

"You should be going. Mrs. MacLean is an early riser."

"I shall speak to her. I assure you she will not say a word to anyone." He stroked his hand up and down her back.

If he spoke to her housekeeper again, Sophia feared the elderly woman might suffer some malady of the body or mind—possibly both. "Mrs. MacLean will not gossip."

His hand stilled and one dark eyebrow edged upward. "Sophia, the woman had the audacity to eavesdrop."

"She's tended to me since I was twelve. She will chastise me as though I am still of that age, but nothing more."

Hayden flashed an expression of disbelief but didn't argue the point. Neither did he appear ready to leave. She reached out and turned the bedside lamp higher. "I ran into Lady Prescott the other day. Your sister said she is to help you interview governesses today, several young women from Queen's College. She is excited over the candidates."

He didn't respond.

"Hayden?"

"Just a bit longer." His hand resumed the gentle sweep across her back.

"You realize," she said softly, "though Chelsea may be far more liberal than Mayfair, I cannot have the *wicked* Earl of Westfield seen leaving my house at the crack of dawn."

"Wicked? I don't believe anyone has ever had the temerity to call me that to my face."

A smile tugged at her lips. "No, I presume they wouldn't." She ran her fingers through the dark wisps of hair that dusted his chest.

He gave her a wry grin and rolled her onto her back. "I think I should stay and teach you deportment, my dear Miss Camden."

"*You* teach me deportment?"

He favored her with another arrogant lift of his brow.

"I fancy you've taught me quite enough." She gave him a slight push with her hands in an effort to prompt him off the bed. A futile attempt.

"On the contrary." He drew the quilt off their bodies. "I wish to teach you a great deal more." He slowly traced a finger lightly over her waist, causing her to laugh.

He grinned. "Ah, you are ticklish."

"No, I'm not." She sobered her expression and tried not to squirm beneath his touch.

His fingers circled her navel. The sight of his large hand touching her caused a warm yearning to grow.

His hand moved lower.

Her heart beat faster.

Lower.

Her mouth grew dry.

He froze. She followed his gaze to a light smear of

blood on her left inner thigh. His brows furrowed as if he'd not expected to see the proof of her lost innocence.

Her cheeks warmed, and she quickly tugged at the blanket to cover her body. "Did you believe me anything but chaste?" she asked, her voice hollow.

He closed his eyes briefly. "I thought you'd had a child. A daughter."

Is that what he thought? Her throat clogged. She swallowed the thickness. He'd been misinformed. Oh, how foolish she was.

After gathering the quilt around her naked body, she slipped from the bed and padded across the room to the large oak dresser. She didn't know why she felt irate. What had she expected of him? They lived in different worlds. Nevertheless, she'd wanted him to realize what she'd given up, yet he thought her a fallen woman.

She opened the top drawer, pulled out a small flannel cloth, and slammed the drawer closed. She spun around to face him. "Is that why you bedded me, Lord Westfield?" Her stomach pitched and rolled. "Did you think me a whore who bestows her favors with ease?" She didn't wait for his reply, but squared her shoulders and moved toward the bathing room.

Hayden leapt from the bed and reached for her.

With little forethought, she let go of the quilt and shoved him. Hard. A nerve twitched in his taut jaw, but otherwise he didn't move.

"Do not put words in my mouth, Sophia. I said I thought you'd had a child, nothing more."

She turned away from his steely gaze and searched the shadows of the room. "Your information is faulty. I have never borne a child or shared the intimacy of my bed."

He took a deep, audible breath. "Look at me."

She kept her face averted, not wishing to reveal the tears threatening to stream down her cheeks.

"Sophia, please."

She peered at him. The hard glint in his eyes softened.

"I should not have come here last night. I should never . . . Damnation, you're trembling." He swept up the quilt, draped it over her shoulders, and held it closed. "When I entered you, I thought my information flawed. But you said nothing." He raked a hand through his hair. "I wish you to know I do not go around defiling virgins."

"Ah, such noble restraint."

His nostrils flared. "I was misinformed. Perhaps I realized it—refused to grasp the facts—to admit what I had done. I took your silence and used it to ease my conscience. Allowed myself to believe only what I wished, not what I *knew*." His fingers traced the line of her jaw. "Sophia, we both wanted this, and somehow I think it was inevitable—a beginning." He pulled her back into his embrace.

She stood still, absorbed his words. They implied a future, but what it entailed she didn't know.

"Tell me about the child?"

She hesitated. "Her name was Georgiana. She was vibrant and lovely, and she was my sister's child. My niece."

"And she lived here with you?"

"My sister, Maria, died after giving birth. Puerperal sepsis."

His brow furrowed.

"Childbed fever."

His arms tightened around her. "I'm sorry. What of the child's father?"

How did she explain why Maria married Samuel? That love had not factored into the equation. That her sister had married a man beneath her station to anger Great-Uncle Charles. Samuel was Maria's pawn, and in turn, she his. "Her husband abandoned her before Georgiana's birth."

Talking about Maria and Georgiana always made her melancholy—amplified her loneliness. She pressed her nose closer to Hayden's skin, seeking its soothing scent. "She didn't have our guardian's blessing to marry, so she ran away with Samuel to Scotland. Her letters to me were always brief until the last one, when she asked me to come to London. To Spitalfields."

"Spitalfields?" His tone reflected his awareness of the destitution the rookery contained.

"Maria and Samuel had come to London to meet with Father's solicitor about her inheritance. The money should have lasted them several years, but it ran like water through Samuel's fingers, and when it was gone, so was he. My sister was left not only destitute but shamed and pregnant."

She thought of grandfather's landscape hanging above the mantel in her morning room. Maria had never realized how valuable their grandfather's paintings had become. "I arrived five days after Georgiana's birth, and three days later Maria died." She swiped at an errant tear.

Hayden stroked his hand up and down her back, soothing her inner turmoil, buoying her courage to continue. "Maria and I grew up here, in Chelsea, with our parents and grandfather. After we were orphaned we went to Northumberland to live with our paternal great-uncle. I bought this house a few years ago, hoping to give Georgiana the life Maria and I had known here." Her chest tightened. "I failed. Georgiana died only a year after her mother."

"Sophia, I'm sorry, but surely it was not your fault."

She tipped her face to his. Her tears blurred his handsome visage. "Thomas said infection caused the fever that took Georgiana."

"Trimble was your niece's physician?"

"Not at first. But when she took a turn for the worse, I went to his Harley Street home in the middle of the night. After he saw how distressed I was, he came here to examine her." She dashed her fingers across her cheeks to remove the tears streaming down her face. "If only I had brought her to Thomas initially, perhaps . . ." A sob caught in her throat.

With his fingers entwined with hers, Hayden pulled her toward the bed. He sat, leaned against the headboard, and settled her on his lap.

She couldn't stop the tears. She wept for both the loss of her sister and niece, and, if she were honest, for giving her virginity to a man with a reputation for womanizing. A rogue who'd never once said he loved her.

Sophia awoke, feeling the press of Hayden's lips upon her own.

"Sophia, I must go. It will be light soon."

Dazed, she looked at him. He sat on the edge of the bed, fully dressed. Had she cried herself to sleep?

He cupped her face. "As you are aware, I shall be interviewing candidates for Celia's governess throughout the day, so I won't be able to get away. But I wish to talk to you. Will you call on me?"

She wrapped the quilt tighter around her naked body. "We do not need to talk, my lord. What happened—"

He placed a finger to her lips. "If you call me *my lord* one more time, I'm going to renew our acquaintance by crawling back into your bed. Now, say you will come."

She nodded.

"Good." He kissed her again, a long and sensuous kiss, and then he strode from the room, leaving it once again cold.

Late that afternoon, as Sophia approached the front door of Hayden's town house, the sweet aroma of almond macarons wafted delicately to her nostrils. She leaned over the wrought iron rail and peered down the stairwell to the steam-covered windows of the basement kitchen.

Someone mopped a sleeve across the moist glass. The servants' entrance flew open to reveal Alice and Elsie standing shoulder to shoulder over the wide threshold. "Miss Camden," Alice called, beckoning her with an enthusiastic wave.

Sophia swung open the gate and made her way down the stairs. She entered the warm, humid room, and Monsieur Laurent glanced up from the dough he aggressively kneaded.

"*Bonjour*, Mademoiselle Camden." The Frenchman flashed a generous smile. "What 'as brought you 'ere?"

What, indeed? Her first thought was lunacy, but then her mind visualized Hayden's kisses as he made love to her. The truth was too scandalous to voice.

"The wonderful aroma of your macarons. I smelled their divine scent all the way in Chelsea."

"*Mais oui*," he replied arrogantly. "I was famous for my sweets in Paris. Zee people would flock to my patisserie on Rue Royale just to get zee whiff of them." After dusting the flour off his hands, he pointed to the pastries with a pudgy finger. "*Vas-y!* Sit. Sit. You must try zem."

Elsie's and Alice's eyes grew wide, and Sophia realized the magnitude of honor the chef bestowed on her. "I would be pleased."

Beaming like a man whose wife has just given birth to a set of healthy male twins, he motioned her to sit at the massive wooden table that dominated the room. "Elsie," he boomed, "get mademoiselle a dish of macarons and a cup of tea."

As the kitchen maid scurried off, Sophia slipped onto one of the chairs that surrounded the servants' table.

The chef plunged his thick fingers back into the dough and without looking up asked, "Are you 'ere just to sample my pastries, mademoiselle, or do you wish to call on 'is lordship?"

Thankfully, his keen eyes were not upon her, for something in his tone made her cheeks heat. "Y-yes, though I'm sure his lordship is progressing splendidly, I wish to confirm it. One can never be too careful where health is concerned."

"Ah, he's faring rather well, if you ask me," Alice mumbled as she folded a pile of starched napkins.

Sophia's gaze swung to the maid.

With an impish smile, Alice hurried to the table and slipped into the chair directly across from Sophia. She glanced surreptitiously over her shoulder. "The master was out all night. With a woman, no doubt." Her voice sounded like an odd dichotomy of both titillation and prudishness.

The tips of Sophia's ears burned. Monsieur Laurent's astute gaze settled on her. A smile teased the corners of his lips, and she thought he winked. She mumbled a thank-you to Elsie when the maid placed a steaming cup of tea and a dish laden with pastries in front of Sophia.

Elsie made a tsking noise. "Alice, you best be mindin' your tongue. If Mrs. Beecham hears you stirring scandal broth you'll find your bum out on the curb without a letter of reference."

"What did I say?" Alice asked.

Elsie grinned. "Wot don't she say? Right, Miss Camden?"

Sophia smiled before she nibbled on one of the meringue treats. They tasted superb, but the dryness in her mouth made her feel as if she tried to swallow overly salted kipper.

She'd never been a competent liar. She took a sip of her tea to alleviate her parched mouth. "*Délicieux, monsieur,*" she said, trying to sound lighthearted. "*Merci.*"

"*Avec plaisir.*" He glanced at Alice and Elsie and heaved a heavy sigh. "You both may have one as well, but quickly before Beecham sees." Both women's countenances lit up as they rushed to the tray.

"*Seulement un.*" He held up his floured index finger. "Only one."

Alice and Elsie chatted amiably, but Sophia only half-heartedly listened, her mind still contemplating whether Monsieur Laurent had winked at her or whether it had been a figment of her guilty conscience.

Chapter Fourteen

"I believe Miss Appleton's qualifications are superior," Edith said cheerfully. "She is the best candidate we have spoken to so far."

Hayden raked a hand through his hair. He and Edith had been interviewing for Celia's governess, cloistered in his study throughout most of the day. The dark mahogany paneling was closing in on him.

"Are we in agreement, Hayden?"

He drummed a quick staccato with his fingers on the desk while glaring at the door beyond his sister's shoulder.

Edith twisted around in her chair, following his gaze, then turned back to him. She pursed her lips. "Hayden, do you hear me?"

Where was Sophia? Had she decided not to come? Did she regret last night? His gut clenched.

"Hayden?" Edith repeated.

"Yes?"

Edith made a disgruntled noise.

"Forgive me, Edith. What?"

"Miss Appleton, dear. What did you think of her?"

Appleton? Ah, yes, the one fluent in a multitude of languages. He recalled her florid, pinched face and ginger hair. She reminded him of a Derbyshire Redcap hen who was quick to peck. "I found her unsuitable. Too stern. I fear she'd stifle any creativity Celia might exhibit."

Edith tapped a finger to her chin and nodded. "Yes. Yes, a bit austere for Celia."

A bit? Miss Appleton appeared so inflexible, he'd feared she would splinter when she'd sat. He opened his mouth to reply, but a knock on the door halted his words.

Sophia. He sprung from his chair, sending several sheets of paper skittering to the floor. "Come in."

Hawthorne entered. "Lord Adler is here and wishes to know if you are in, my lord."

Hayden collapsed back into his seat. "Tell him Lady Prescott and I have not completed the interviews for Celia's governess."

"But surely you can spare your oldest and dearest chum a moment?" a deep voice said only seconds before the man himself appeared.

Edith cast Adler a disapproving glower. His sister didn't approve of Hayden's friendship with his closest chum. She'd thought Simon a bad influence ever since a school prank at Eton, which involved their housemaster, two flaming burlap bags of horse manure, and a large pail of water.

"Lady Prescott," Simon said amiably, "how wonderful to see your smiling face."

"Adler," she said, wrinkling her nose. "Hayden, the next candidate is not due for another half hour. I will be in the nursery taking tea and visiting with Celia should you need me." She stood and exited the room as though the air within had become unpleasant.

"As always, Lady Prescott, a grand pleasure to see you again," Simon called after her. "Why, Hayden, I believe your sister is coming around splendidly. I think she actually smiled at me today." Grinning, he unbuttoned his coat and sat in the chair Edith had vacated. "Well, old boy, you won't believe whom I saw this morning."

Hayden leaned back in his chair and arched an eyebrow.

"You, arriving home before cockcrow by way of hackney."

Hayden forced his expression to remain complacent. "I've heard that men who repeatedly engage in tipping the muffs of whores are destined to become blind. Alas, Simon, your sexual deviances have taken a toll upon you. You are mistaken. I assure you I retired early last night."

Simon laughed. "My eyesight is flawless, and as far as my deviances, I have yet to tip a buttered bun. Beyond the pale even for me." Bracing his hands behind his head, Simon stretched out his legs. "I shall not dispute your claim to having retired early; I only wish to know with whom?"

Hayden scowled. He'd not reveal where he'd been. Avoiding the question he asked, "What reason did you have for being on Brook Street so bloody early?"

"I returned that pup Boswitch to his suite at Claridge's. You do recall that fine establishment is located up the road?"

God, he'd forgotten about Boswitch. "You returned him safe and sound?"

"Yes, and grinning like a fox that's just raided a hen-house. Now back to you, my friend." Simon tapped a finger to his lips. "Let's see who might have caught your fancy. . . . Ah, that flower seller down at Drury Lane. I hear she carries a knife in her boot, and once attempted to carve her initials into a thief's hand when he tried to pilfer a bouquet of violets. Definitely your type of woman."

Hayden took a deep breath. Simon would never let him live down his foolish decision to engage in a dalliance with Adele. The muscles in Hayden's back knotted. Sophia's small, delicate hands would know how to ease the tightness, and her lovely smile would relieve the heaviness in his soul. He rolled his shoulders. Where was she?

A half hour after entering the kitchen, Sophia made her way up the servants' stairs, wondering, with each step she took, whether she should turn and run. She'd spent the whole of her life living properly, and now she was what?

A wanton?

Indeed.

Upon reaching the ground floor, she peered down the long central corridor. Surely, she couldn't wander about looking for Hayden like some trollop in search of her next romp. She glanced toward the entryway, hoping to espy Hawthorne. She needed the butler to announce her. She took a silent step down the hall and froze when masculine voices drifted from Hayden's study.

"By God, I've got it!" an unfamiliar voice exclaimed, sounding exceedingly pleased with himself. "I know who it was. You sly rascal! Mark me a fool for not figuring it out sooner. That nurse, Miss Camden. You bedded her, didn't you? Why you unscrupulous roué, I knew you couldn't resist *my dare*, especially when it entailed such an exotic bird."

Dare? The word echoed in Sophia's head like a perverse taunt.

Oh God, what have I done? She clasped her hand over her mouth and stepped backward until the wall pressed against her shoulders. Hayden's voice clamored to the foreground of her mind. *"It would be a grave error on your part, Miss Camden, to dare me. I have a terrible weakness for them."*

"I told you, Simon. I have no interest in the woman," Hayden snapped, pulling her back to his conversation.

"Yes. Yes, I know. What was it you said about her? Ah,

I remember. Stick your tongue in her mouth and you'll find yourself mute." The man laughed.

The vile words and the pounding of her heart filled her ears. She grabbed the handrail. As she descended the steps, they waved oddly, rising and falling as though she'd inhaled some noxious gas that caused one to hallucinate. She nearly stumbled. Tightening her hand around the rail, she slowed her pace, and tried to master some semblance of gentility and grace. As she entered the kitchen, Alice glanced up from the napkins she folded.

"Miss Camden?" The maid's expression reflected her puzzlement at Sophia's quick return.

She forced herself to smile at Alice, then Elsie, who was polishing a soup tureen. "His lordship is presently engaged. He no longer requires my *services*." How she spoke without babbling like a lunatic was beyond her. Thank God, the intuitive Monsieur Laurent was not about.

Alice grinned. "Did you see Lord Adler? I saw his carriage pull up a short time ago. He's a fine-looking gent even with that scar on his face."

"I think his scar makes him look like a pirate," Elsie added.

Lord Adler? So that was who'd dared Hayden. The man's scandalous reputation made him the perfect cohort for Westfield. They were both immoral rakehells. What had she been thinking to allow such a man in her bed?

"No, I didn't," Sophia replied, then hastily said her good-byes.

Outside dark clouds hovered. Had the weather turned, or had she been blind to the gray sky? She tipped her head downward and shielded her face from the badgering wind chafing at her skin. Tears rolled down her cheeks. What a senseless woman she was to even contemplate a member of the peerage might want to court her.

Great-Uncle Charles's voice echoed in her head. *"Silly*

girl, your desire to work only confirms you are not worthy of a gentleman of means or good sensibility. Why would a man want you when he could choose a woman who knows her place in society? A proper English miss."

She swiped at the tears trailing down her cheek and wished she'd never laid eyes on Lord Hayden Westfield. She squared her shoulders. She wouldn't cry over him. She'd forget his wicked touch, false words, and never speak his Christian name again. Westfield was nothing more than an unscrupulous rogue and manipulator who couldn't be trusted.

A thunderclap split open the sky, punctuating her pronouncement as if it were God's own decree.

Hayden gritted his teeth. *Damnation.* Did Simon truly think him capable of bedding Sophia for the sake of winning a dare? God, he'd sunk low, but not that low. "I told you I had no interest in your dare."

Simon chuckled.

"What do you find so humorous?"

"Wright has an opera singer for a mistress, McGrath a dancer, and you wish to have a nurse. I can completely understand. A savior to have around if you find yourself at the wrong end of a pistol again."

"I don't wish her to be my mistress." He realized he desired something more permanent. "Now, if you'll excuse me, I've got several more candidates to interview."

Simon grinned, but didn't shift from his recumbent position. "Well, old chum, if you're not interested in the woman, perhaps I should lure her away from Trimble's employ. I have a position I'd like to hire her for." Simon winked. "Several new positions, if she's limber enough."

Hayden would have sworn someone threw pitch in his eyes, for the room turned dark. When his vision cleared,

Simon lay sprawled on the carpet, and Hayden stood over him, fist clenched.

A grin spread across Simon's face. "Ah, you wish for a bout, do you?" Standing, the man shrugged out of his coat.

Simon, like himself, had always enjoyed a good bare-knuckled brawl more than those tedious rounds of boxing where one was held to the Queensberry rules. They'd not engaged each other in fisticuffs since boyhood. But Sophia had not shown up and he felt like hitting something, and his friend appeared as anxious. Hayden tossed his coat to the floor and rolled up his sleeves.

They circled each other. A right undercut to Simon's chin sent the man stumbling back against a tall bookcase. Several tomes fell to the floor with a heavy *thud*. The man's grin widened, and he loosened his neckcloth.

Hayden motioned him closer with his hands. "Come on, let's see what you've got—"

A left jab to Hayden's jaw halted his sentence. His head twisted, straining his neck's muscles. Flashes of light danced before his eyes. Christ, the southpaw had the best left he'd ever had the misfortune to come across. But it didn't douse the fire burning in Hayden's belly.

He hit Simon with a solid blow to his face; his friend's head jerked backward. But if he thought that would end the fight, he was mistaken. The man counterpunched him soundly in the gut. Hayden's breath exploded from his lungs. Undeterred, he delivered a jab to Simon's jaw.

Simon shook his head as though trying to clear his vision, then stepped closer and drew back his fist.

A feminine scream pierced the air.

They froze.

Hayden turned toward the sound.

Edith stood at the study's threshold, her complexion wan, her eyes as round as a full moon. "I cannot believe such behavior. You two act no better than thugs. You're foolish sods." Edith tossed them both a scowl, gathered her skirts, and flounced from the room, slamming the door in her wake.

Both he and Simon stood staring at the door, mouths gaping.

Hayden rubbed his hand across his tender jaw and contemplated Simon's superior left jab, his saintly sister's use of such a vulgar word, and his own burst of anger. In retrospect, it had been utterly foolish to drag his oldest friend out of his chair and plant a facer on him like a raving madman.

"I didn't know your sister had such an extensive vocabulary," Simon finally said, falling into a chair, his breath sawing in and out of his lungs.

"Nor did I." Hayden leaned against the edge of the desk and scrubbed a hand through his tousled hair.

Gingerly Simon ran his forefinger and thumb over the bridge of his nose. "Hayden, don't you realize I was baiting you? I'm quite aware you are taken with your little nurse, though I never realized to what extent."

After scooping up his discarded coat, Hayden jammed his arms through the sleeves. "Is it that obvious?"

"Blatantly. You've been exceedingly morose since she left."

Hayden sat in his chair, reached into the carved wooden box on the desk, and extracted a cigar. He tossed it to Simon and opened his mouth, intent on apologizing, but Simon raised his hand.

"No need, old fellow. I enjoyed that immensely." Standing, Simon clamped the cigar between his teeth. "In fact, I think I'll head down to Clapton's Boxing Club and find myself a sparring partner." He picked up his discarded clothes. "If you truly haven't seen Miss Camden since she left your employ, Hayden, I suggest you call upon her soon."

Yes, if she didn't show up, he would go to her Chelsea residence this evening after interviewing for Celia's governess. He shook his head, tried to silence the voice that kept whispering, *She's not coming. Only a fool would marry a man branded such a heartless rogue.*

And Sophia was far from a fool.

As dusk settled, Hayden walked Edith to her awaiting carriage.

"So, do you have a favorite candidate for Celia's governess?" Edith asked. Light from a streetlamp illuminated her face.

No, not a single one had impressed him. He wished he could've asked Sophia her opinion, but she'd not shown up. He grimaced.

"Is your leg hurting you, dear?"

He smoothed out his expression and tried to concentrate on the matter at hand. "No. Perhaps we should interview another round of candidates."

"More?" Edith sighed. "It feels as if we interviewed an army of them today."

None right for the position. Too rigid. Too stern-faced. Too . . . Oh, blast it, who was he kidding? The problem was none of them made him think of Sophia—her caring nature, quick wit, her smile.

"If you insist, I'll set up more interviews," Edith said.

"Thank you." He kissed her cheek.

Edith climbed inside and Hayden closed the carriage door. "Drive on," he told the coachman.

The man tipped his hat, and the carriage moved up the dim street.

Hayden hobbled back into his residence. Hawthorne

stood in the entry hall. "Your dinner will be ready shortly, my lord."

He had no time for eating. He intended to call on Sophia. "Have my carriage sent around."

A short time later, Hayden found himself staring disbelievingly at Sophia's housekeeper as she informed him her mistress didn't wish to see him.

She'd had a change of heart. He'd known it was possible. The life he'd led since returning to London after Celia's birth made him a sad prospect for a husband. But he needed to speak with Sophia. He wouldn't admit the truth about Celia's parentage—he couldn't cast that shame on the child—but perhaps if Sophia were in the room, he could convince her of his feelings.

He brushed past the housekeeper and walked to the steps. "Tell your mistress I'm waiting for her." He spoke loud, hoping if Sophia skulked at the top of the stairs she'd realize he wouldn't leave until they spoke.

Mrs. MacLean twisted her hands in her white apron. "I believe Dr. Trimble will be asking for her hand in marriage."

The thought of her with any other man made his jaw clench. He narrowed his eyes at the harridan.

The woman stepped back. "Dr. Trimble cherishes her. He'll give her a family she will be able to love and care for." She tipped her chin up. "What will happen to her when ye tire of her?"

"Is that what you think, Mrs. MacLean, that my intentions are not honorable?" Hard to blame the woman for thinking otherwise. The gossip columns tossed his name around like a shuttlecock during a badminton game.

"Are they?" She didn't wait for his response. "Milord, I've known the lass a long while. She has a pure heart. Better than most, but 'tis fragile. She has lost everyone she's ever loved. After her niece died, she suffered a dire case of the blue devils. Aye, the good doctor saved her, he did. Told her he needed her help with his patients. He's not only good to her. He's good *for* her."

Silently Hayden damned the old witch to hell. She didn't fight fair. Somehow, she comprehended his fears. Knew he was haunted over having failed Laura and worried he'd fail Sophia as well, yet he'd not leave until he spoke with her. He opened the double doors and stepped inside the drawing room.

As if he was a recalcitrant puppy fond of piddling on the carpet, Mrs. MacLean followed him into the room.

"Tell her if she doesn't come down here, I shall go up," he said.

The woman's eyes grew round. She darted out of the room and up the stairs. Her feet moved up the treads at a speed which seemed to defy her advanced years.

The sound of footfalls descending the stairs perked up his ears.

He took a deep breath, shoved his hands in his pockets, and then took them out.

Sophia stepped into the room. Unlike last night, she was dressed in one of her serviceable navy gowns, her hair pinned into a tight chignon, and her expression as tight as a clergyman's giving a eulogy.

"Sophia."

"Lord Westfield."

So she would not call him by his given name. Yes, he was right. She'd had a change of heart. Everything in her demeanor conveyed that.

He swallowed the hard lump in his throat. "May we speak?"

"It appears I have little choice in the matter." She glanced at the housekeeper, now standing at the threshold, and the woman moved away from the doorway. "I would offer you a seat, but I'm rather tired, my lord, so I hope our conversation will be brief."

He stepped toward her.

She held up her hands. "You should pat yourself on the back. You really are quite adept at winning. Did you add a wager on this dare as well? Tell me, my lord, what value did you place on my virginity? A shilling? Five pounds? A bottle of wine?"

The muscles in his shoulders tightened. "You believe I bet someone I could *bed* you?"

"Lord Simon Adler, to be specific."

"The devil take him. Did he tell you that?"

"No, I overheard you, so please do not deny it."

"Overheard?"

"When I called on you today."

"You called at my residence? Hawthorne never informed me."

"He didn't see me. I came up the servants' stairs from the kitchen. That's when I heard you and your *vile* friend talking about his dare to bed me."

"Believe me when I say, I didn't accept Lord Adler's foolish dare. Do you really have such a low opinion of me?"

Her hesitation, along with the way she averted her gaze, answered the question. Her eyes centered on him again. "I believe you are a master manipulator who clearly knows what to say to achieve what you want."

Good Lord, she thought him no better than a snake in the grass. He'd earned his reputation with his fast and scandalous life, but he'd thought . . . What had he thought? That she'd seen through all of his tomfoolery? Thought him someone worthy of her tender companionship? Her love?

Obviously not. He should go. The housekeeper was right. Trimble would give Sophia a stable life with a man she could trust. She deserved that and more.

"Since you have me all figured out, we have little to discuss." He walked to the door. "Good night, Sophia."

Chapter Fifteen

Beads of sweat prickled on Sophia's forehead. Kneeling, she grasped the wooden edge of the commode with white-knuckled fingers and squeezed her eyes closed. She stiffened her jaw and fought her stomach's churning rebellion.

All in vain. A second later, she heaved her breakfast into the porcelain bowl. She drew the back of a hand over her mouth and moved to the sink. A splash of water on her face cooled her heated skin while brushing her teeth obliterated the vile taste that coated her tongue.

She glanced at her pallid reflection in the mirror. Too pale. She was also . . .

Don't say it. If you do, you shall find yourself a weeping mess, and Thomas will be here shortly. She pinched her eyelids closed, waited until the burning desire to cry subsided. She spun away from the looking glass and stepped into her bedchamber.

"Miss!" Mrs. MacLean tapped on the door and without waiting for a reply flung it open. "Dr. Trimble is here and looking rather fit, if I may be bold enough to say—"

The housekeeper stopped her chattering and blinked.

"Aye, ye poor lass. Been sick again, have ye?" With her apron bunched in her hand, Mrs. MacLean rushed forward and blotted Sophia's damp brow. The elder woman shook her head. "Ye are normally so hale. Haven't seen ye with a case of the collywobbles since ye were a young lass. I'll make a mixture of . . ." Mrs. MacLean's voice faded, her eyes grew wide, and she clutched her dress at her bosom. "Saints preserve."

Ignoring the woman's gaping mouth, Sophia moved to the armoire, removed her pale blue paletot, and slipped it on. "A touch of gastritis. I must have eaten something disagreeable."

"Oh, lassie dear. 'Tis the second time in less than a week ye retched yer morning meal." The woman ticked off her fingers and counted. "Seven weeks since you let that blackguard into your bed, and I'm thinking he left more than his calling card."

Dashing an errant tear off her cheek, Sophia sat on the bed and stared down at her lap.

"Miss—"

The sound of someone clearing his throat halted the housekeeper's words. Thomas stood in the doorway. "I know it's in exceedingly poor taste to enter a woman's bedchamber uninvited but . . ." He looked pointedly at her. "You are usually so punctual. I thought there was a problem. I called up. Neither of you answered."

Standing, Sophia glanced at him. Had he heard? She toyed with the tasseled fringe edging the bottom of her coat. "Sorry, Thomas, I'm ready." She forced a small smile. "Did I mention how pleased I am you've asked me to accompany you to Mr. Philips's architectural office? I'm sure the exterior perspectives of the new hospital will be fascinating."

He stared at her, but said not a word.

She pressed her palms to her cheeks. *I must look dreadful.*

Thomas stepped fully into the room. "Mrs. MacLean, would you be kind enough to give Sophia and me a few minutes alone?"

The woman appeared hesitant, but exited the bedchamber.

Tears pressed the backs of Sophia's eyes, and she moved to the window. Several pedestrians walked along the embankment. Her gaze shifted to a shiny black carriage slowly moving past Thomas's equipage. How many times had she seen that grand equipage rolling by her house and both hoped and dreaded it was Westfield? How foolish.

"Thomas," she said, not turning around, "shouldn't we talk on the way? I'm sure you do not wish to be late for your meeting."

He moved to stand behind her and placed his hands on her upper arms. "I care a great deal for you."

He watched her reflection in the glass. She ducked her head.

"Sophia."

A sob caught in her throat. He was going to propose—try to save her from her own folly. She couldn't marry him. He deserved a woman who would love him unconditionally, and she had given her heart foolishly away, only to have it stomped on.

"I'm with child," she blurted out.

He turned her so she faced him. "I am aware of your condition."

Ashamed, she dropped her gaze to one of the brass buttons on his wool overcoat. "You heard Mrs. MacLean?"

"You wound my physician's pride. Like you, I'm aware of the signs of morning sickness. I take it Westfield is the father?"

She nodded.

"I know several ways I could kill the man and not even leave a mark. An injection into his carotid artery of—"

"Thomas, don't joke."

"I'm not joking." A lethal tone edged his voice.

"He didn't force me." She dashed at a tear. "You must think me both shameless and half-witted."

"No, I think Lady Prescott sent a lamb to the slaughter." He withdrew a handkerchief from his inside breast pocket and dabbed at her cheeks.

"I . . . we . . . just once."

"You are an educated woman. You know it only takes once." His voice sounded free of condescension, but she sensed the anger it contained.

She refrained from telling him that her education had been lacking. No book or person had ever informed her how overpowering desire could be or how rash one became under its spell, especially when stronger emotions gripped one's heart.

He placed his fingers under her chin and tipped her gaze up to his. "Sophia, will you marry me?"

She swallowed. "I cannot. You deserve better than a soiled, foolish woman."

"I believe we could build a life together and be happier than most. I will be a good husband. And despite what I feel about Westfield, I'll love the child as if it were my own. I give you my word on that."

She placed her forehead against his chest and Thomas wrapped his arms around her.

"You do not have to accompany me to Mr. Philips's office. You should rest. I'll pick you up tomorrow evening for the hospital's fundraiser, and you can give me your answer then."

Her heart thumped against her ribs. Over the last several days, she'd completely forgotten about Lady Prescott's ball to benefit the hospital's building fund. She could not attend. She would not risk seeing Westfield. She shook her head. "I cannot go!" Her voice came out shrill.

"Westfield does not attend such functions." He kissed her forehead. "Rest. I will see you tomorrow evening." He had just reached the threshold when he turned around. "Have you told him?"

Nausea rolled in her stomach. Tell Westfield his dalliance had created a child? He would not care. He'd been as reckless as she. He probably had an army of bastards throughout Britain. "He isn't interested in me or the baby, Thomas. I believe he was bored, and I was nothing more than a game. A distraction to relieve his ennui."

Disgust twisted Thomas's handsome visage. "Then he doesn't deserve either of you, and you will both be better off without him."

Edith had been adamant Hayden attend her benefit ball. He, on the other hand, had been adamant he would not. Yet here he stood in his sister's entry hall, wondering whether he'd come to appease Edith or for another reason.

He'd arrived well past the hour of being fashionably late, hoping the crowd would have thinned. However, the cacophony of laughter and raised voices floating down the circular staircase, along with the carriage-lined street, informed him he should have delayed even longer. He handed his formal cape to one of the footmen and moved across the patterned marble floor.

Strange, he'd not seen Sophia in weeks, yet he sensed her presence as if the air that touched her skin had gained a tangible force. An unwelcome vision of her twirling about in Trimble's arms to the strains of a Viennese waltz flashed through his mind.

He should leave—haul himself to the Continent to call upon that German physician he'd read about in the newspaper. The one who studied the human brain. What was his name? Wundt. Yes, Wilhelm Wundt. The man would proclaim him a helpless sod. He spun around to snatch his cape back from the footman.

"Ah, Hayden, so good to see you," a familiar voice called.

He forced himself to turn around. Hiding his agitation, he shook his brother-in-law's hand.

"Edith had resigned herself to the fact you wouldn't attend. She'll be exceedingly pleased."

"Henry, I was just leaving." He withdrew a bank draft from the inside pocket of his formal evening coat. "Will you give Edith this along with my felicitations? Her gala appears a success."

His brother-in-law unfolded the check. "Ah, generous as always."

He may not care for Dr. Trimble personally, but the hospital the doctor was building in the East End would be a godsend and an economic boon for the residents who lived near.

"Did you say you were leaving? It appears you have just arrived." Henry clapped a firm hand onto Hayden's shoulder. "You know Edith will be devastated if you don't say hello before dashing off." Henry handed the check back to him. "Why don't you give this to her yourself?"

Even though Thomas had assured Sophia that Westfield wouldn't attend Lady Prescott's fundraiser, apprehension fluttered in her stomach. A murmur arose from the crowd, and the fine hairs dusting the nape of her neck prickled. She glanced about the ballroom. Her eyes homed in on the tall, dark-haired gentleman slicing through the throng as if it were an inconsequential field of grain and he a sickle-wielding farmhand.

By the time Westfield emerged from the swarm of brightly colored silk and dark formal attire, her heart thundered in her chest. Without a hitch to his step, he moved to the perimeter of the room, no more than ten yards from where she stood conversing with Thomas and the elderly Lord Pendleton, a supporter of the new hospital.

Westfield wore a black tailcoat precisely cut and taut across his broad shoulders. She knew, firsthand, it was not padding that enhanced his physique. There was no denying his raw magnetism. Her palm settled over her abdomen. Certainly, *she* couldn't deny that. She wanted to scurry from the room, return to the solitude of her Chelsea residence, but her feet seemed rooted to the floor.

With a formidable expression on his handsome face, Westfield surveyed the guests. A group of gentlemen moved toward him. He cocked a brow at them, and their progression ceased. It was like watching a white-breasted raptor tossed into a cage of doves.

A moment later, Lady Prescott stood beside him. His stern expression evaporated as he kissed his sister's hand before surreptitiously pressing a piece of paper into her fingers. Her ladyship unfolded the paper and smiled brightly. To Westfield's obvious chagrin, she kissed his cheek. A donation? Yes, and sizeable judging by her ladyship's exuberance.

Westfield and his sister talked alone for several minutes until a few braver members of the assemblage joined them. He appeared unengaged in the conversation as he scanned the crowd as if searching for someone. If she had to endure watching him dallying with some other woman, Sophia might shatter into a million insignificant pieces.

He turned his head in her direction and their gazes met.

Immediately the bright colors and people within the ballroom faded to muted shades of gray and brown as if an artist took sepia to them, forcing them into the background to leave Westfield standing alone in the massive room.

"Do you not agree, Sophia?" Thomas asked.

Startled, she looked back at Thomas and Lord Pendleton. They awaited her response. She wasn't sure what Thomas had said. However, they rarely disagreed. "Of course," she replied.

Pendleton nodded in concurrence, and the discussion between the two gentlemen moved along at a rapid clip.

Sophia's gaze swung back to Westfield.

He was gone.

She scanned the room. He stood a few yards away, moving toward her. Her stomach lurched. Surely, he didn't intend to engage her in conversation.

A petite woman placed a halting hand on Westfield's upper arm. The blond-haired woman with her bow-shaped mouth and skin the color of fine bone china carried herself with the air of blue-blooded superiority. Her eyes were an extraordinary green. Their color, along with their shape, reminded Sophia of the archangel cats she'd seen exhibited at the Crystal Palace.

The beauty slid her fingers to Westfield's chest. The touch spoke of familiarity.

Lovers? Of course. Sophia placed a palm to her abdomen. How inconsequential she'd been.

Westfield whispered something into the woman's ear.

The woman laughed.

Sophia looked away. She didn't want to witness their amorous play. She tried to become engaged in Thomas and Lord Pendleton's conversation, but morbid curiosity drew her gaze back to Westfield.

With taut features, he stared at the blonde, then motioned to his brother-in-law, Lord Prescott, or the man standing next to him. She'd seen the other gentleman before. He was a patient of Thomas's. He had something to do with the Home Office or Scotland Yard. Yes. Sir Edmund Henderson, the commissioner of Scotland Yard.

Westfield and the woman drew several people's attention. He flashed them an amiable smile, but when his attention returned to the green-eyed woman, his own eyes were like shards of steel. If the lady was a lover, she had fallen out of favor. He stepped away, but the woman's fingers clasped possessively onto his forearm. He removed her hand from his sleeve and strode away.

He stared at Sophia—moved toward her. She controlled the desire to grab the skirts of her gown and flee. It would draw too much attention if she ran. She glanced back at Thomas and Lord Pendleton, now engaged in an animated conversation about politics and the general election. Her hands trembled. Wrapping one around the other, she steadied them. She needed to excuse herself—walk calmly from the ballroom and gather her faculties. She waited for a lull in their conversation, tried to resist the urge to interrupt them, but in the end, she did so anyway. "Excuse me, gentlemen."

Thomas smiled, and then a shadow cut across his face. His gaze shifted to someone who stood directly behind her.

Westfield. She knew it without turning around—the warmth of his body singed her back, and his clean, masculine scent drifted in the air.

"Well, Westfield." The elderly Pendleton lifted his pince-nez to his nose. "Fancy seeing you here. I do say you cut a fine dash for a man who's recently had the lead picked out of him."

Westfield moved to stand next to her and gave Pendleton a wry smile. He shifted closer, and his arm brushed against her skin, sending a wave of awareness through her body.

"Miss Camden, I hope the evening finds you well," he said, practically ignoring the two gentlemen.

His deep voice set her further on edge.

Stay calm.

With a slight inclination of her head, she replied, "Quite well, Lord Westfield." Her voice sounded steady, even though her chest felt as though a ham-fingered physician percussed it.

"Gentlemen," Thomas said, "I think you'll have to excuse Miss Camden and me. I believe the musicians are about to start another set, and she has graciously promised me a dance."

"Of course," Pendleton responded.

As Thomas took her elbow to usher her toward the dance floor, Westfield stepped into their path. "Miss Camden, may I have the honor of the next set?"

Goodness, no. She didn't want him to hold her—to experience the desire his proximity always evoked.

Thomas's jaw visibly clenched. He opened his mouth, then glanced at Pendleton before returning his gaze to Westfield. "My lord, as your physician, I must advise you against dancing. You do not wish to impair your recovery."

Westfield smiled at Thomas, but the expression lacked any warmth. "Ah, Trimble, as always you are the voice of reason." He held her gaze. "Miss Camden, I fear I must retract my offer. My physician feels it unwise." He paused. "Will you honor me with a stroll in the conservatory instead? My sister tells me she has added some remarkable new rose specimens that I am most eager to see."

What poppycock! He most likely wished for another meaningless assignation. She wanted to refuse his invitation, but Pendleton's rapt attention centered on them. "I would be honored, my lord," she replied, and walked away.

Chapter Sixteen

Hayden knew Sophia's words proclaiming she'd be honored to take a stroll with him were a bold-faced lie. She'd forced a smile, looking like a woman condemned to the gallows.

His gaze followed her and Trimble moving across the dance floor. He unclenched his hand and glanced around the ballroom. Where the hell was Adele? Her appearance had startled him. When had she returned from the Continent? Damn her brother to hell. Lord Kent had promised his sister would never return to England.

The madwoman had acted as if nothing were wrong between them. As though she'd never *shot* him. He'd wanted to drag her from the ballroom by the scruff of her neck, but he'd not wished to embarrass Edith in front of her guests.

Instead, he'd pointed out Commissioner Henderson. Told Adele the fellow was a nice enough chap if one stayed on the right side of the law. Then threatened if she didn't leave Great Britain, he'd have her carted off to a tidy little cell.

He scanned the perimeter of the ballroom. It appeared she'd left. Tomorrow, he'd send a note to Lord Kent, demanding he send his lunatic sister away again or commit her to an asylum, or he'd reveal the truth about who'd shot him.

"Did you say Edith has several new species of roses, Westfield?" Pendleton asked, breaking into Hayden's thoughts.

He turned to the man.

Pendleton twisted his moustache. "My wife fancies herself an expert on the subject. Only last week, she went to Surrey to visit a conservatory the Royal Horticultural Society is working on." He gave a shrug. "I don't see what all the bloody fuss is about. But I shall tell Henrietta, so she can accompany you and Miss Camden."

He tried not to scowl at the man. He didn't wish Pendleton's harpy wife tagging along, especially since he had no intention of going to the conservatory. No, he wished to show Sophia something else.

"I wouldn't suggest you tell her, Pendleton, for you shall have to accompany her since these are no ordinary roses, but *Rosa carniverosa*."

"*Rosa carniverosa*?" Pendleton echoed.

"Carnivorous."

Pendleton's brows twisted in consternation before he let loose a thunderous laugh. "Why, you sly devil, Westfield." He waggled a crooked finger at him. "I may not know a dashed thing about roses, but I damn well know there's no such thing as carnivorous ones, or I'd have bought them for Henrietta years ago."

The man reached up and slapped him conspiratorially on the shoulder. "You just want to be alone when you take Miss Camden for a stroll. Don't fret. I won't tell Henrietta a thing about your sister's new roses, if indeed they exist. I may be old, but I've not yet forgotten what it was like to be in love."

Pendleton spoke plainly, a trait Hayden *usually* admired in him, but not today. "Pendleton, I advise you to stop imbibing that Russian vodka you're so fond of. That liquor is addling your brain."

"I don't think so. I saw the way you looked at her. Can't blame you, though. She's lovely."

Hayden tried to ignore the man, but he prattled on endlessly. He shot Pendleton one of his bollocks-withering scowls, but since the man had known him since Hayden wore short trousers, it seemed to have no effect.

The music stopped, and Sophia and Trimble moved off the dance floor.

"Excuse me, Pendleton." Hayden strode up to Sophia. Trimble looked ready to throw a right hook at him. He savored the thought of going toe-to-toe with the man, but Edith would never forgive him. He leaned forward. "We're garnering an excessive amount of attention, Trimble. Wouldn't look good if she cut me. The gossips would wonder why."

Trimble flashed a clearly forced smile and relinquished her arm.

Sophia set her hand on his sleeve, and they strode to the perimeter of the room where the crowd thinned.

"I do not wish to accompany you to the conservatory," Sophia whispered. "If you have something you wish to say to me, please do so here."

He gazed into angry, dark eyes. Sophia regretted their night together, but he remembered her soft sighs and how responsive she'd been. "Is it me you fear, Sophia, or yourself?" He found it difficult to soften the sharp edge of his tone.

She harrumphed, but her cheeks reddened. "The only reason I do not wish to leave the ballroom is because our departure will cause gossip."

A footman passed with a tray of champagne flutes. Sophia stopped and took a glass. Slowly she drew the cut crystal to her lips and sipped. "Do you always draw so much attention?" With her drink, she motioned to a gaggle of young women.

He glanced at them and they tittered.

"Why don't you ask one of those debutantes, or all of them, to accompany you to the conservatory? They appear willing enough."

He smiled, his heart lightened by her jealous tone. He let his gaze travel over the length of her body. She wore an elaborate gown of yellow silk and chiffon, ornamented with delicate embroidery at the waist and above the tasseled hem of her overskirt.

She blushed.

"You look lovely, Sophia."

She glowered at him.

"Smile, my sweet, or the presumption will be made we are having a tiff."

The edges of her mouth lifted slightly upward.

He took the crystal flute from her hand and placed it on one of the large circular tables set around the perimeter of the room. "You've stalled long enough." He grasped her elbow and moved them toward one of the large, ornately plastered archways that exited the ballroom.

"Don't you dare drag me out of here," she hissed.

"Do you really wish to dare me again, Sophia? You know I can't resist them."

She sucked in an audible breath. "How do you sleep at night?"

Feeling less generous to her indifference, he responded, "You tell me, Sophia. How do I sleep at night? Or were we too preoccupied that night in your bedchamber to ever sleep?"

She tried to pull her elbow away.

He tightened his hold. "You'll draw attention to us if you storm away. So think well and good before you do so."

She relaxed her stance.

"Now, there is something I wish you to see." They moved through one of the arches, and he maneuvered her behind a pair of velvet draperies into a small windowless alcove lit by a gas sconce. The light cast a soft glow over a life-size statue of a naked woman with a hand lying provocatively upon her breast and a snake slithering up her leg.

Sophia turned a puzzled expression toward him.

"Edith fears some of her guests might be offended, so it is draped off when she entertains. It is one of my brother-in-law's acquisitions. Prescott purchased it before he and Edith married."

"Quite lovely, but if you think it will ignite my baser desires, you are mistaken. I will not—"

He pressed a finger to her warm lips. "I thought you would wish to see the statue because it is one of the few your grandfather did." Varga's dossier had revealed a great deal, not only who her grandfather was but her great-uncle as well.

Her eyes widened. "Nonno's?"

"Yes. Why didn't you tell me Gianni was your grandfather?"

"What purpose would it have served?" She ran a hand over the perfectly honed marble. "Grandfather told me he had done two statues when a young man, but I had not expected anything so large. So exquisite. Do you think Lord Prescott would consider selling it?"

He smiled. "Are you considering displaying it in your entry hall or next to your chintz chairs?"

"No, I'd like to see it displayed in a museum. I have loaned most of my grandfather's paintings to various museums."

Her palm stilled over the thigh of the statue, and he placed his fingers atop hers.

She pulled her hand away. "I thank you for showing the

statue to me, but we should return to the ballroom. I'm sure our absence has been noted."

"You give us too much importance."

"Not us, my lord, *you*."

He stepped closer, drew in her familiar lavender and lemon essence. "Sophia . . ." He stilled. Someone approached. With a tilt of his head, he motioned to the heavy drapery and placed his index finger to his lips.

The footfalls on the hard marble floor grew louder—nearer. A woman giggled and a gentleman laughed.

He maneuvered Sophia against the wall, shielded her body with his, obscuring her identity. The heat from her skin enticed him. He shifted closer.

Scowling, she forced her hands between them and pressed against his chest.

"Have I mentioned how fond I am of you touching me?" he whispered.

She narrowed her eyes.

The sound of the footsteps halted outside the alcove, and the drapery parted.

"Forgive me, my dear," he murmured, extinguishing the light and covering her mouth with his.

The moment the silky texture of her lips touched his, he was lost to the hunger that had clawed at him like some insistent beast over the last several weeks. With a groan, he deepened the kiss and tasted the champagne that lingered on her tongue.

For several heated seconds, Sophia didn't respond, but then she made a small, almost helpless sound, and her tongue moved against his. She might not want him, but her body did.

"Deuced inconvenient," the man outside the curtain grumbled. "Someone's already in there, Gladys."

The curtain fell back into place and brushed against his legs. The couple retreated. Their footsteps faded. He should pull away, relinquish his hold, but instead he nibbled the soft skin of her neck and took satisfaction in her little gasps.

"No. Please," she said, her breaths coming fast. "You told me once if I said no you would stop. I'm saying no. I wish you to stop."

She sounded close to tears. He pulled away.

"Thomas has asked me to marry him. And I cannot do this to him."

He stepped back. The curtain brushed against his legs, letting in a small beam of light. Her face was downcast. "Do you love him?"

She glanced up. "Yes."

She didn't hesitate, only affirmed her attachment. He resisted the urge to shake her. Ask how she could give him her virginity when she cared for Trimble, but he'd no right to make moral judgments. "Then I wish you the best." He lifted his fingers wanting to touch her face. He let his hand fall to his side, then pivoted on his heel, and strode away.

What else was there to say? If he needed confirmation, he had it. She wanted to marry Trimble. His gut tensed.

She most likely knew what the denizens of London whispered—that he'd abandoned his wife only months after Celia's birth. That he was a scoundrel and a rogue. He couldn't reveal the truth about Celia's real father, erase the reputation he'd earned, nor change his past, but he *would* be a better man moving forward. A better, less scandalous father to Celia. Someone she'd be proud to call Papa.

Hayden disappeared through the velvet curtains. The material swayed back and forth, and Sophia stared at the cloth, forcing herself not to run after him. She slumped against the wall and cupped her face with her hands.

She'd wanted to tell him about the child growing within her. But Westfield didn't want a wife, only someone to warm his bed. He seduced women, used them, and then discarded them. She'd seen his disgust for the highborn woman in the ballroom. *I will not end up like her, begging for his favors.*

Yet, for a moment, he'd looked vulnerable.

How foolish! She couldn't trust such a seasoned rogue. She slammed her open palm against the wall and absorbed the pain on her skin. She glanced at the statue and placed her stinging hand on the cool marble.

Nonno, what have I done?

Thomas expected an answer from her today, but she'd have to put him off, answer him another day. She couldn't accept his marriage proposal. She loved Thomas, but not the way a wife should. She loved him as one loved a brother. And Thomas deserved so much more.

Perhaps she'd go to Italy. She had family there.

She sat on the statue's platform and wished the ground would open up and absorb her.

Chapter Seventeen

Sophia glanced at the watch dangling from the bodice of her navy dress. Four o'clock and she still had several patients to examine. Normally by this time, she and Thomas would have finished attending the women and children at the Whitechapel Mission's infirmary, but an emergency had called Thomas to the hospital's operating theater.

Her thoughts shifted to Thomas's coachman. Upon their arrival, she'd asked Angus if he wished to come inside, but he'd declined, refusing to leave the equipage unattended in the side alley. The poor man—doubtful he'd anticipated such a long wait in the cold.

Tucking a stray lock into her chignon, she slipped from the examining room and into the anteroom. The mission's stony-faced matron, who sat at a desk speaking to an elderly woman, glanced at Sophia over the rims of her wire-framed spectacles.

"I shall return shortly, Mrs. Hamblin."

The matron acknowledged her with a curt nod before returning her scrutiny to the gray-haired woman.

As Sophia moved through the narrow room, she surveyed the other weary faces that crowded the small space. Her gaze settled on a young mother who cradled a toddler.

The poor woman's left eye was contused and her bottom lip swollen. The bruises weren't new. The skin was already mottled and yellowed, giving her a jaundiced appearance. Sophia's ire rose. Never would she become immune to seeing such depravity.

She stepped out of the room and moved down the long corridor. The aroma of baking bread drifted from the kitchen, along with the voices of the cook and her assistant squabbling over the din of clanking pots and pans. Sophia's stomach growled. She'd eaten a light breakfast consisting of dried biscuits and tea, hoping to avoid the retching that had plagued her five days ago.

Nearing the alley door, she sidestepped the prodigious number of crates and railroad barrels bearing the name J. H. Mason. As she moved past a crate, she ran her fingers over the burnished marking of a Hereford bull that branded the wooden slats. She didn't care what Westfield said about the wholesaler. Here, in this place, Mason was a godsend.

She swung the door open. Angus, who leaned against Thomas's carriage, jerked his head up from the newspaper he read. He tipped his hat off his brow and gave her a broad smile. His warm breath sent puffs of white into the chilly air. "Ready to leave, miss?"

"Do forgive me, Angus, but it's taking a bit longer without Dr. Trimble."

"'Tis no problem," he responded with his unfaltering smile.

She pulled out several coins from her skirt pocket and pressed them into his hand. "You must be famished." She gestured up the alley to Whitechapel Road. "There are several taverns to the west. Why don't you get yourself something to eat? I shan't need you for at least another hour. Possibly two."

The coachman glanced at the coins.

"If you don't go, I shall feel dreadful," she added.

He slipped the money into his coat pocket. "If ye insist, miss."

"I do," she said, ignoring the low rumble of her own indignant stomach.

An hour later, Sophia sighed as the last patient, the woman she'd seen talking with Mrs. Hamblin, exited the examining room. The poor, malnourished creature had taken to visiting the gin palaces and drinking her meals instead of eating them.

Sophia picked up the weekly report book and jotted some additional notes regarding two little boys, brothers who'd come to the mission yesterday with what appeared to be a case of croup. She'd instructed Mrs. Hamblin to separate them from the other children and to place several pots of steaming water in their room. However, she wanted it noted that if either boy's breathing became distressed or if the coloring around their noses, mouths, or fingernails turned bluish, they were to be conveyed to Royal Hospital, posthaste.

The matron entered the room. Sophia handed her the report and buckled her medical bag closed. "Mrs. Hamblin, have you ever met J. H. Mason?"

The woman glanced up from the report she perused and shook her head.

"So he has never visited the mission?" Sophia slipped her wool cape from the wall hook and draped it over her shoulders.

"No, Lady Prescott serves as intermediary."

How interesting.

Sophia acknowledged Mrs. Hamblin's words of thanks and left the room. As she once again passed the alms from J. H. Mason, her mind reverted to the papers she'd seen on Westfield's desk, the ones with the grocer's marking printed on them. Was Westfield responsible for Mason's donations? Did he pay the man to donate them? Doubtful, given his complete disinterest in the mission. She opened the side door to stare into the murky alley now cast in shadows. Angus had yet to return.

"Penny for the poor, mum?"

Startled, Sophia stepped back. A man dressed in tattered clothes, a ragged derby atop his downcast head, moved out of the shadows, his open palm extended. The bedraggled soul appeared crippled. His left foot dragged behind him as though weighted by chains.

She set her medical bag down and hesitantly stepped toward him—fearful of the rats that lingered in the alley. "Sir," she said, reaching into her pocket for some coins, "there is a Benevolent Friends Society—"

Her voice froze as the man wrenched her arm behind her back and placed a knife to her neck.

"Scream an' I'll slit yer gullet," he rasped, straightening, exposing his full height.

Heart thundering in her chest, Sophia placed a hand to her abdomen. "I shan't scream. I've only a few coins, but you are welcome to them."

He gave a low, bitter laugh. She couldn't see his face, but the smell of decay drifted from his mouth. "Yer worth more than a few paltry coins."

With her arm still twisted behind her back, he propelled her into the depth of the alley. At the end of the constricted space, they stepped into one of the narrow routes that weaved behind the buildings. Her panic soared—pinnacled. The farther the man forced her into the rookery's belly, the more difficult it would be to extract herself. Almost paralyzing fear welled up inside her. Yet the knife at her throat kept her moving. Whenever they passed another pedestrian in the stygian path, he slipped the knife under her cape and pressed it against the nubs of her spine.

Twice she tried to speak to him, and twice he applied

more pressure to her arm until she feared he'd dislocate her shoulder. They turned so many times she became disoriented, but then she saw the spire of Christ Church Spitalfields under the rising moon. They were near where her sister had lived. They finally emerged onto a lane lined with tenements more dilapidated than Maria's had been.

Something brushed against her feet and squeaked. Rats! The hammering in her chest filled her ears with a steady *swish, swish, swish*. "How much money do you want to let me go?"

"Quiet," he hissed, pressing the blade closer to her throat as they stepped under an arch into a dark warren.

A sharp, intense pain lanced her skin and a trickle of blood wove a path down her neck. She fought the urge to scream.

The clanking of keys resonated in the thick, dull air, only a moment before the man thrust her against the surface of a wooden door covered with blistered green paint. With his body pressed to her back, he lowered the knife and slipped a key into the lock.

Fearful this might be her last chance to escape, she jabbed her elbow backward and into the man's rounded belly.

Air exploded from his lungs. He folded in two.

As she dashed by him, the brute's large hand clamped around her throat like a vice. She tried to scream, but she couldn't even breathe as darkness swallowed her.

Hayden leaned back in his chair and propped his booted feet on the corner of his desk. He tossed a financial report on his blotter and closed his eyes. Sophia's delicate face floated in his mind's eye. Thoughts of her had plagued him throughout the day, and now they appeared determined to haunt his evening. He could almost smell her alluring lavender scent, lingering in his house.

With a disgruntled snort, he surveyed the stack of unfinished work before him. Once again, he'd sat at his desk all day and accomplished little.

Footfalls neared his study, along with Hawthorne's indignant protestations and a man's raised voice. Hayden swung his feet to the floor, leaned forward, and unlocked the bottom drawer of the desk. He extracted his pistol. He'd just cocked the hammer when the door burst open to reveal Thomas Trimble.

With a curse, Hayden lowered the gun pointed at the doctor looming in the doorway.

A flustered Hawthorne stood behind him. The butler ran his fingers over his brow. "My Lord, Dr.—"

Raising his hand, Hayden silenced him. "That will be all, Hawthorne. Thank you."

Trimble stepped into the room and slammed the door closed. He moved to the desk.

"You trying to get your bloody bollocks shot off, man?" Hayden returned the gun to the drawer before propping his feet back on the desk.

The doctor braced his hands on the mahogany surface and leaned forward. "Where is she?"

Did he mean Sophia? Christ, did he truly think if she were here, he'd be sitting at his desk? "To whom do you refer?"

Trimble lifted his right hand and pounded it on the blotter. The swift shot of air sent several sheets of paper skittering to the floor. "You wretch! You damn well know I'm referring to Sophia! Where is she?"

Hayden glanced at the papers on the rug and restrained his rising ire. "If you have lost your pretty little assistant, you won't find her here."

The red color singeing Trimble's cheeks drained away leaving a sallow cast to his skin. "God, as much as I despise you and what you've done, I bloody well wish she was."

"Perhaps she's cried off." The possibility lightened Hayden's mood.

"She's gone missing." Trimble raked a hand through his hair. "Went to Whitechapel—"

Hayden sprung to his feet and wrapped his fingers around Trimble's lapels, cutting off the doctor's words. "Tell me you weren't fool enough to let her go to the *Chapel* alone?"

Trimble flung Hayden's grasp off, but the indignation etched upon the doctor's face faded. "My coachman accompanied her, but she's vanished."

Hayden barely heard Trimble's words as he grabbed his pistol and headed out his residence, into the doctor's waiting carriage.

As Hayden and Trimble made their way to Whitechapel, a haunting tension cloaked them. It didn't help that the farther they delved into the East End, London's perpetual fog thickened into a dark, almost reddish winter blanket of grime and cloying stench. Hayden stared at Sophia's *intended*.

"Though you have not asked," Trimble said, breaking the quiet void, "I feel honor bound to inform you I have told Sophia that if we marry I will raise the child with as much devotion as I would my own flesh and blood."

"Damnation, Trimble, what are you prattling about, I . . ." Hayden's words trailed off. For several seconds, he believed he'd not be able to speak above the roaring in his head or see past the black marring his vision. "Sophia is with child?" He heard the question spoken aloud, and though it was his voice, it sounded soft, like an echo from his past—the voice of a naïve twenty-one-year-old scholar who had favored quiet nights reading *The Bard* and soft-spoken conversations on philosophy. A man who'd believed love conquered all—a fool's voice.

When the blackness faded from his vision, he was pleased to notice the color in Trimble's face had drained away. He didn't wish to be the only one too exposed.

"I thought she'd told you. She said you had no interest in the child."

Sophia carries my baby. A mixture of elation and anger rushed through him. How could she not tell him? He knew the answer: his wicked reputation, along with the man sitting across from him. Why marry a rogue when you can marry a saint, and Sophia had admitted her love for the physician.

Leaning forward, he forced his clenching fist to relax. "You understand what this means, Trimble?" His tone, once again, sounded firm and unwavering. The voice of a man who brooked no opposition—a man few trifled with. "No man, no matter how saintly, will raise my child as his own, unless he's willing to put me six feet under."

A nerve ticked at Trimble's jaw. "What will you do, Westfield? Set her up in some pretty house where she can raise your bastard while scorned by society?"

"I advise you to use the word *bastard* with prudence."

"You'll marry her?" Trimble's voice betrayed disbelief.

"As soon as we find her."

The brakes ground against the wheels and the equipage stuttered to a stop before the mission. Hayden flung the door open and jumped to the pavement. He scowled at the coachman descending his perch. "Where did you wait for her?"

"Here, me laird," the man said, motioning to the alley as he unfastened the lamps off the conveyance.

Hayden and Trimble both took a lantern, and the three men moved down the dark passage.

Angus pointed to the side door. "Aye, she was to come out here, but all I found was her bag."

Hayden scanned the draped windows of the brick mission. He turned and studied the adjacent building. Its dark, uncloaked windows looked like black, lifeless eyes staring down upon them, except for one window above the ground floor where the subtle glow of light emanated. He turned to Trimble. “What’s this building used for?”

“A warehouse, but it’s been empty these last five months.”

“Someone’s up there.” Hayden pointed at the window.

Trimble looked up. “A squatter most likely.”

All three men moved to the warehouse’s chained and padlocked side door. For once, Trimble and he were of a like mind, for they simultaneously slammed a booted foot into the wood. It splintered like the hull of a rotted ship, sending shards of beetle-eaten wood into the air.

As they slipped into the dark and dank warehouse, Hayden pulled out his pistol. He glanced at Trimble. The man extracted a knife from his right boot. The knife possessed a jagged, lethal edge, more suited for a fishmonger or cutthroat than a revered physician and surgeon.

They crossed the uneven floor—made of nothing more than rough-hewn planks set atop dirt. Hayden held the lantern aloft. A back window stood ajar, and several rats scurried for the shadows. Damnation, if Sophia were here, she would be terrified.

The floorboards above them squeaked, and all three men strode to the narrow stairs that ran along the back of the building. They crept up the rickety treads to a long corridor with a handful of rooms to the left. Holding his lantern high, Hayden nodded to the doorway where they’d seen the light. They entered the room to find a woman cowering in the corner. She held an infant wrapped in a ragged quilt.

“I ’aven’t taken nofin,” she said, pressing the child to her bosom.

Tucking his pistol into the waist of his trousers, Hayden glanced about. Bloody hell, there was nothing to take. The room stood barren, except for a pallet, some tattered bedding, and a candle that sent as much smoke into the room as light.

"Are you alone?" Hayden asked. The woman nodded, and his glimmer of hope faded.

"Me husband was 'ere, but 'e left several days ago and 'asn't come back."

Westfield pointed to the window. "Did you hear anything out there today?"

"Nofin. I swear I didn't see nofin."

An interesting and telling reply, since he hadn't asked what she'd seen. He stepped closer to her. "I think you *did*."

"No," she replied, staring at her feet while she shuffled them.

He withdrew his billfold and removed several banknotes. "Are you sure?"

She wet her dry, cracked lips. "I did see sumpin."

"Yes?" he prompted.

"I seen a lady come out of that buildin'." She turned toward the window and pointed at the mission. "There was a man in the alley and when she went to give 'im sumpin, 'e grabbed 'er."

Hayden cursed.

The baby in the woman's arms fussed, and she patted the child's back. "If she's dead it isn't me fault. For wot could I do?"

"Did you know the man?" he asked anxiously, trying not to ponder her words or the helplessness tightening his stomach into knots.

She shook her head and shuffled her feet again.

Hayden withdrew several more banknotes. "Think."

"I may 'ave seen him before."

"Where?" Both he and Trimble asked simultaneously.

She eyed the money. "I don't want no trouble."

"Just tell me where he lives," Hayden said. "That's all."

"Nasty piece o'work. No better than a cutthroat." She glanced at the money again. "'e lives on Little Marlie Row. Number Five. Right 'cross from McCarthy's lodging house."

"Christ," Trimble muttered.

Hayden turned to him. "You know the street?"

The doctor nodded. "Not fit for the devil."

Hayden thrust the banknotes into the woman's hand. "I suggest, madam, you use this to find you and your child suitable lodging and food."

"I gots to wait for me Billy. 'e'll be back soon."

He and Trimble glanced at each other as they sped to the door. He didn't have time to argue with the woman, but he doubted *Billy* intended on returning, especially if he'd left both her and the child unattended in such a wretched place.

When Sophia came to, she found herself in complete darkness, lying on a mattress infused with the stench of sweat and urine. Her jaw tensed, and her abdomen constricted. Sitting up, she pressed a fisted hand to her mouth and willed herself not to toss up what little vestige of food her stomach contained.

Nearly unbearable fear clutched at her as she patted the mattress and searched for its edge. Her hand glided over the frayed cording that bordered the top of the pallet and traveled down. The tick lay directly on the planks of the floor. She scrambled to her feet.

The room appeared devoid of windows. With her hands outstretched, she moved in the darkness until her fingers touched a cold wall. An unbidden thought drifted into her mind. There were probably rats burrowing in the walls searching for warmth. She snatched her hands back and frantically wiped them against her skirts. She took several slow breaths, forced her fear not to overtake her. Tentatively she lifted her fingers back to the surface and made her way around the perimeter, searching for a means of escape.

The thin layer of grime that covered the walls slid against her fingertips. She ran her hands farther to the right and touched the casings of a doorway. Relief washed over her as she grasped a cold metal knob. She turned the door handle.

Locked. Her elation faded.

Why had the man taken her? There were villains who abducted women and children and took them to brothels that catered to men with a taste for depravity. A chill ran down her spine. She pulled her cape tightly about her. She hiked up her skirts, squatted, and then got on her hands and knees to crawl around. Perhaps there was something lying on the floor she could use as a weapon.

Her fingers had just touched the edge of the mattress when footsteps sounded someone's approach. A yellow shaft of light seeped under the door, lifting the pall that cloaked the room in total darkness.

For a moment, there was an eerie, almost oppressive quiet. Even her breathing seemed to cease. The sound of metal scraping against metal shattered the void, and the door swung open.

The large whiskered man from the alley stood at the threshold, a candle in his hand. His dark eyes looked like two black pits in his gaunt face. Without a word, he shoved the candle into a tarnished sconce that hung above the doorway. Its cracked globe caused odd, jagged shafts of light to skitter across the grimy walls in muted relief.

Heart pounding against her ribs, she scrambled to her feet. “What do you intend to do with me?”

He laughed, exposing black teeth, and kicked the door closed. It slammed against the jamb causing the candle in the sconce to perch forward like a drunken bird in a glass cage. Rubbing his hands together like a starved man about to feast on a hearty meal, he stepped toward her.

She realized his intent. Corrosive bile burned her esophagus. She clasped a hand to her throat.

His smile broadened. “Bet ye never had a real man,” he said with a salacious sneer, stroking a firm hand up and down the bulge in front of his trousers.

She balled her hands as self-preservation took hold. Her fingernails dug painfully into her palms.

The wretch moved closer. The pungency of his breath and the potent odor of sweat, clinging to his body like a shroud, drifted forward. Her nausea intensified. She stepped back against the cold wall.

His large hands reached out and grabbed her shoulders to drag her body against him. He inhaled audibly. “Ye smell clean.”

He pinned her to the wall while he tugged up her skirts. Before she could scream, his mouth came down on hers, fierce and hard, bruising her lips against her teeth. She tried to twist her face and body away. A futile effort.

His mouth moved across her cheek. His coarse beard chafed her skin. “Keep fightin’ me, me little bird,” he whispered. “I likes it when a woman ’as a bit of fire in ’er belly.” He reached under her cape and tore her bodice. Cool air washed over her neck and upper chest. His damp breath panted against the swell of her corseted breasts. Her mind went numb, disembodied, as though she were a spectator to all that unfolded. He tugged at her corset, and with one last gasp of sanity, she rammed her palm into his nose.

He stumbled back, cupping his face.

She dashed toward the door. His hand reached out and snagged her wrist. "Ye bitch!" He flung her around to face him, and struck her cheek, knocking her to the floor. Flashes of light interspersed with dark colorless voids. They danced before her eyes while the metallic tang of blood filled her mouth.

"I'll teach ye good and right, I will!" He lunged atop her and dragged up her skirts.

Terrified, she pounded her fists against his shoulders, chest, and head.

"Stupid wench!" He struck her face again, hard. Not once, but twice with his open palm.

Her head rolled back against the floor. Her mind teetered on the brink of darkness. The man's ranting came to her as if she lay submerged under the churning of a rough and angry sea.

Little Marlie Row could only be entered by an archway too narrow for even a dogcart. Hayden's stomach clenched as he and Trimble disembarked the carriage. The poorest denizens of the East End lived in these dirty warrens. Some so desperate, they'd do nearly anything to put food in their bellies, including attacking and robbing a woman.

But the blackguard had taken Sophia with him, and only one thought crossed Hayden's mind as to why a man would do such a thing.

Bile traveled up his throat. He quickly unlatched a carriage lamp.

"There's a police station not far from here on Leman Street," Trimble said to the coachman. "Get a constable."

They raced under the arch and scanned the addresses.

Number Five was a decrepit tenement that looked abandoned. The few windows that graced the façade were missing panes of glass.

Hayden turned the handle. The unlocked door opened, and the stench of sewage greeted him.

"I'll check the ground floor," Trimble said, hastening down the corridor, holding his lantern high.

With a nod, Hayden charged up the steps. The winding stairway was so tight, his shoulders brushed against the grimy walls, slowing him down. As he reached the first landing, a *thud* rattled the floor above.

A woman's cry pierced the cloying air, followed by an oppressive quiet.

Heart pounding a steady tattoo, he bolted up another flight.

As he moved down the narrow corridor, his gaze shot to the end of the hall. Weak light shone under a door.

Three strides brought him there. He set his lamp down and shouldered the door open. It banged against the wall.

A hulking man lay atop Sophia's still body. Startled, the miscreant turned and peered over his shoulder.

Sophia's slim body suddenly moved, and she rammed her knee up, hitting the scum between the legs.

The man howled in pain and collapsed onto her.

"Bastard," Hayden hissed through clenched teeth. He grabbed the man by the scruff of his coat, dragged him off her, and smashed his fist into the groaning man's face.

Unconscious, the miscreant hit the wall and slid to the floor. Hayden knelt beside Sophia and slipped an arm beneath her shoulders.

"No!" She reached out, raking her fingernails down the left side of Hayden's face.

Pain seared his cheek. "Sophia, it's Hayden—" His voice broke as a wave of emotion crashed upon him.

Dazed eyes stared at him. "Hayden?" she rasped, her voice barely audible.

"Yes." His trembling hand traveled up and down her body, examining every inch, before settling on her abdomen. "Did he hurt you?" An inane question, since the dim light revealed her red cheek and blood seeping from the corner of her mouth. But she knew him, and that was a good sign.

"No. I-I'm fine."

"Did he . . . ?" Fear knotted his gut as he tried to force the words out. "Violate you?"

"No." Her eyes drifted closed.

Hands shaking, Hayden peeled off his overcoat, wrapped it around Sophia, and scooped her up.

Trimble stepped over the threshold. The doctor raised his lantern, lifted Sophia's eyelids, and seemed to study her pupils. "I need to examine her."

"We'll return to my residence." Hayden pulled Sophia's limp body tighter to him.

"Your residence?" Trimble echoed, his voice betraying disbelief.

"I meant what I said, Trimble. I'll wed Sophia by week's end, if not tomorrow." Whether Sophia liked it or not, she was about to become his wife. She might love her sainted Dr. Trimble, but he couldn't allow her to marry the man. Not now. Not while she carried his child. There would be no turning back for either of them.

Angus and two constables rushed into the room.

Hayden snapped several orders at the policemen.

One of the constables set his hands on his hips. "Wait a minute, sir. I need specifics as to what happened here before I arrest the man."

Angus leaned over and whispered in the policeman's ear.

The constable visibly swallowed. "Yes, *my lord*. I'll send

Chapter Eighteen

As Hayden descended the stairs of his town house, the front door burst open. He'd known the missive he sent to Edith would have her rushing to his residence posthaste. Nevertheless, he'd not expected her to arrive only minutes after receiving it.

His sister, normally the picture of propriety and a person of sound judgment, looked in a state of dishabille. Instead of donning one of her fitted gowns, she wore her woolen coat over her wrapper and nightgown. And if that wasn't laughable enough, one side of her hair was pinned up while the other hung about her shoulders in disarray.

"Where is he?" she demanded, glaring at Hawthorne.

Hawthorne's stoic countenance faltered. "A-ah, Lady Prescott."

"Edith," Hayden said, taking the last steps.

She spun around.

"I was expecting you. Please join me for breakfast?" He motioned to the center corridor.

"Heaven knows I couldn't eat a thing! And what has happened to your face? You look like you were in a brawl with a cat."

He briefly touched the scratches Sophia made on his cheek, then, with a gentle hand on the small of Edith's back, Hayden prompted her forward, ignoring her question.

Once in the dining room, he dismissed the footman who stood by the sideboard, picked up a plate, and turned to his sister, who paced the floor like a parading Grenadier Guard.

"Sit, Edith. I shall bring you something to eat."

She withdrew his missive from her coat pocket. "Have you taken up opium smoking, or have you just taken leave of your senses?"

Having filled the dish with an assortment of foods, including a poached egg, several sausages, and a scone with a large dollop of clotted cream and strawberry jam—Edith's favorite—he turned a discerning eye toward her. "At least I had the decency to dress this morning."

"Dress?" She heaved an explosive breath. "How could I do so after being set upon with a missive stating you are to be married? Tomorrow!" She shook the paper violently in the air, emphasizing her distaste at its contents.

He peered at Edith's shoes. She wore open-toed slippers with three-inch heels and a flurry of feathers embellishing the leather band that ran above her instep. They resembled something a cancan dancer would don in one of the seedier music halls in Paris. Risqué by most standards, especially Edith's. His lips twitched.

"You might have donned decent shoes before you rushed over to offer me congratulations. Aren't your feet cold in those things?"

Her pale cheeks colored before she cast an angry glower upon him. "Whom, may I ask, are you to wed? I can think of no one. . . ." Her hand fluttered to her bosom. "Do not tell me it's that lunatic Adele Fontaine."

"You truly do think me mad."

She sighed and slumped into the closest chair.

Hayden placed the dish laden with food before Edith and poured her a cup of tea. "Sophia and I are to be married."

"Sophia?" Edith repeated. She blinked. "Sophia Camden? You cannot be serious."

A nerve in his jaw twitched. He'd thought Edith would be the one person who would not question him. The one person who would offer support, as she'd done when he'd announced his intent to marry Laura. He poured himself a cup of black coffee.

"Have you become snobbish, Edith, or is it me you do not approve of?" He leaned back against the marble-topped sideboard and took a sip of the warm brew.

"You know, well and good, I'm not a prig. But people will talk, and what they will say will be spiteful. They will wonder what transpired in this house while she resided under your roof. They will call her an upstart. They will say you have married beneath yourself. Again." Edith cupped a hand over her mouth.

"Was that what you truly thought, Edith? That Laura was beneath us. How can you even think that after what Father did?"

"Hayden, I didn't say I agreed with what had been said. Nor what will be said, only there are those who will take great pleasure in showing Sophia only a modicum of civility."

He took another sip of his coffee. "Then you should be relieved to learn Sophia is not only a competent assistant to Trimble, but the great-niece of Charles Camden. In fact, she is his only living relation."

Her brow furrowed.

"You do not recognize the name?"

Edith shook her head. "No."

"The man supplies most of the coal to Manchester, to its factories, and to the London and North Western Railway."

Edith's eyes grew round. She opened her mouth to speak, but Hayden held up his hand. "She is also Vincente Gianni's granddaughter."

Her mouth fell open. "The painter?"

"The one and only."

"Oh," she replied, her startled expression deepening.

"Her great-uncle's fortune, in and of itself, shall keep tongues from wagging. I do not doubt she'll be accepted into the finest drawing rooms."

"I see," she said. "I wish to know when this came about. You seemed barely civil to her, yet now you are to be married and in such haste." She drew in a sharp breath. "Hayden, you didn't . . . ?"

"Force myself upon her? Does the blood coursing through my veins predispose me to acts of a heinous nature? If it does, my dear sister, I must remind you it courses through your body as well."

"I know you would never force yourself upon a woman. I just thought perhaps you had, well, seduced the poor girl."

"I hardly think a woman of twenty-four is a girl."

"No, certainly not. But she is not, shall we say, as experienced as the women you usually consort with."

"You have always been the wisest bird in the flock, my dear."

"Oh, Hayden, not while she was under your roof. Under your protection."

Uneasiness settled in his stomach. He *had* seduced Sophia, but he'd feel no shame. No, he'd try to set things right. He would be a good husband. Faithful. Devoted. And God knew he'd love the child. Sophia's and his. He would make his family proud and protect them. "I grow tired of this conversation." He straightened and placed his coffee down. "The wedding is at eleven tomorrow. The guest list shall be short. Only you, Henry, Celia, and anyone Sophia wishes to invite."

"What of our family? Surely, you mean to include at least Great-Aunt Hortense?"

He considered telling Edith what had happened to Sophia and the bruises that marred her face. He would tell her later. "If Sophia wants we will have some grand event later."

"But Hayden—"

"The matter is settled. Eat your food, dear. I need to go shopping. I have a wedding ring to purchase."

Sophia awoke in a lovely bedchamber decorated with a yellow damask counterpane and flowery primrose chintz curtains. The mahogany furnishings were sturdy but distinctly feminine with soft edges and delicate carvings of roses and leaves. Even the four-poster in which she lay had intricately carved buds and flowers in full bloom.

Where was she? She lifted the bedding to toss it off. A memory blossomed in her foggy head of Hayden cradling her in his arms.

Was she at his town house? She glanced around again. Yes, and this bedchamber—with its exquisite furnishings—belonged to the lady of the house. The room that adjoined his. She'd seen it once when a maid had left the door open while cleaning it.

The man was scandalous. Outrageous enough he'd brought her here, but to place her in this bedchamber was beyond the pale. And what did it mean?

She settled back into the feathery pillows. The scent of Hayden's shaving soap drifted to her nose, along with a faint remembrance of him lying in this bed, his arms wrapped around her, telling her she should have told him about the baby. She set her fingers to her temple. *A fragment of a dream? Yes, what else?* The image resurfaced—clearer this time. She shook her head, and another vision shifted to the forefront, this one of Thomas spooning a sedative into her mouth. No doubt, the tincture lingered, clouding her perception.

A knock sounded on the door. Dressed only in her shift, she tugged the counterpane up to her neck. "Yes, come in."

Alice entered the room with a scuttle of coal. The tension in Sophia's body eased. Yet, instead of greeting her in her usual, animated voice, the young maid acted anxious and uncomfortable. She bobbed a quick curtsey. "I'm to tend to the fire, miss, I mean, my lady."

My lady? Sophia wondered what Hayden's servants had concluded by him having brought her here, instead of her own residence. They probably knew more about what was going on than she did.

"What is being said belowstairs, Alice?"

"It isn't my place to say," she replied, squatting before the grate.

The maid had always been so forthright, but the walls separating their classes now stood erect. "Won't you tell me?"

The young woman glanced over her shoulder. "I don't wish to lose my job."

"You know I wouldn't jeopardize your employment by repeating anything you say."

Alice nibbled on her bottom lip.

"Or anything you have said in the past," Sophia added quickly.

A sheepish expression settled over the servant's countenance. "I knew you were different. A right proper miss who could speak French and all, but never in my life would I have guessed you a great heiress or that you would be marrying his lordship."

With a gasp, Sophia sat up straight. "Is that what they're saying?"

Alice's head bobbed. "Yes. I heard your great-uncle owns half them collieries up north and your grandfather was a famous painter, and that his lordship is to marry you tomorrow."

The room spun. Sophia leaned back. "Tomorrow?"

"Yes, miss. A vicar was here talking with his lordship." Alice stepped closer and spoke low as if the walls could hear. "And it's said his lordship's sister called upon him early this morning wearing nothing but her unmentionables. Her ladyship always resembles a fashion plate, so I thinks Peter, I mean the person who told me, was tugging my leg."

Sophia hoped so, for the implication reflected Lady Prescott found the idea of a marriage between Sophia and Hayden distasteful. She probably wished her brother to marry a young blue-blooded debutante.

"And Chef is in a tizzy. Says he absolutely cannot make a wedding cake in so short a time, nor the wedding breakfast. Keeps saying *merde* this and *merde* that. Elsie thinks *merde* means mother. I never heard a grown man call for his mother so much in all my life." Alice took a deep breath. "And there's a florist in the blue drawing room, filling his lordship's fancy Sevres vases, you know the ones Mrs. Beecham won't let me touch, with more flowers than I ever seen in my whole life."

Another memory slipped back into place, this one of Hayden telling Thomas that he would marry Sophia because of the baby. She touched the side of her bruised face.

It was starting to throb, as was her head. Whatever medicine Thomas had given her was wearing off.

"Does it hurt terribly?" Alice asked anxiously.

"No, not really," she lied. "Though I must look a fright."

The young woman hesitated, and then shook her head. "It isn't so bad. Is it true his lordship and the doctor saved you from some depraved cutthroat while you were down in Whitechapel doing God's work?"

Goodness, it appeared Hayden had not only told them she was an heiress, but an angel of mercy.

Someone knocked lightly on the adjoining door, and Alice jumped and scurried back to the hearth.

Sophia's heart raced in her chest. "Yes?"

The door opened and Hayden entered. As always, the sight of him made her stomach flutter. "Ah, you are awake. How are . . ." He paused and glanced at Alice, who frantically filled the grate.

The maid stood, bobbed a quick curtsey, and made her way to the door.

"Thank you," Sophia called out as the young woman fled.

Hayden moved to the bed. "You look well."

"I fear you are myopic," she replied, cupping her sore cheek, knowing it must be discolored.

He sat on the edge of the mattress. "Is the pain excruciating? Should I send for a physician?"

"No, I shall be fine."

"Sophia, I have obtained a special license."

"It's not necessary."

One slashing eyebrow rose, and his large palm slid over her abdomen. "Do you carry *my* child?"

She briefly lowered her lashes, momentarily avoiding his direct gaze. "Yes."

A nerve in his jaw twitched. "You should have told me."

"I didn't think you'd care."

Anger filled his eyes. "You are mistaken. Tell me, Sophia. Would you have accepted a marriage proposal from me, if I'd asked before you heard me and Lord Adler talking?"

Yes. Perhaps. She wasn't sure anymore. "I don't know."

The weight of his hand on her abdomen grew, reaffirming possessiveness. "Well, now we have no choice. We will marry tomorrow. If we wait there will be no way to escape the gossip. As it is, the tabbies will feast on our infant's early arrival."

"If we marry by special license they will gossip anyway."

He intertwined his fingers with hers. "Perhaps they will say we were so taken with each other we couldn't wait to be wed."

Love hadn't bound them, but if she didn't marry, she'd be cast out of polite society.

"It's irrelevant at this point," he continued. The warmth of his touch slipped away. "If you believe I'll allow Trimble to raise my child, dear, you are mistaken." There was a hard, ruthless edge to his voice and shards of steel in his blue eyes.

"I wasn't going to marry Thomas."

His eyes widened. "You said you love him."

"I do. Just not the way a wife should. He is my closest friend."

"*Just* friends?"

"Yes."

A brief grin touched his lips before his dark expression returned. "I will not allow my child to be born out of wedlock."

She didn't want that either, but she needed to ask. "So we are to marry, even though there is no love? To forget what brought us to this cusp?" Several beats of her heart passed as she awaited his reply.

He slid his thumb over her lower lip. “Many marriages are based on less than what we share.”

The seductive timbre of his low voice made her stomach tumble. Her cheeks grew hot, yet it was not the answer she hoped for. “But that is not love, is it?”

“Love can grow. Hopefully, for both of us. For now we must consider the child.” He stood. “Tomorrow, Sophia.” His voice held a note of finality.

Chapter Nineteen

The following afternoon, Hayden held back a groan as Edith sat next to Sophia on the settee in his drawing room. His new wife looked exhausted. Were his sister and Henry ever going to leave?

It had been thoughtless of him to insist they wed today. Though in his defense, he'd not realized Reverend Moseley would try to compensate for all the years Hayden had not attended services by reciting every psalm and prayer the vicar knew. Or that his crazy French chef would serve twelve courses. Even now, the recollection boiled his blood. During the ninth, he'd contemplated going to the kitchen to strangle the man.

To Sophia's credit, she'd not complained, though she'd looked ready to flee throughout the near endless ceremony. By the time the reverend pronounced them man and wife, her face was deathly pale, even with the cosmetics she'd worn to hide her discolored skin. She'd looked no better during the wedding breakfast.

Understandable, after she'd overheard his conversation with Simon. And most likely her housekeeper and Trimble had given Sophia a list of all the reasons she shouldn't wed him. Marrying a man with a reputation as a heartless husband and philanderer would unsettle even the most hardened woman.

The sound of his brother-in-law clearing his throat interrupted his thoughts. He turned to see Henry staring at him.

"Ah, distracted by your beautiful bride." Henry smiled and patted him on the shoulder. "I was just saying that Huntington, Cartel, and I are to breakfast at the Reform Club tomorrow morning to discuss the railway system, though I doubt you will attend."

Hayden made a noncommittal noise and motioned to his sister. "Doesn't Edith look tired?"

Henry glanced at his wife. "No, she looks love . . ." His voice trailed off and he grinned. "Ah, yes, quite wan." He peered about. "Where is Celia? I'm sure Edith would love to have her visit for a few days?"

At that moment, a smiling Celia entered the room with Mrs. Beecham trailing behind her. The child held several small cake boxes decorated with ribbons. She rushed over to him. "Papa, Mrs. Beecham says I'm to give these to Aunt Edith and Uncle Henry."

"More cake?" Henry patted his rounded belly. "I shall be too fat to fit through my front door."

Giggling, Celia handed him a box. "It's not to eat now, Uncle Henry. You are to take it home."

"Thank you, dear. Aunt Edith and I would be pleased if you would stay with us for a bit."

Celia's shoulders drooped. She glanced at Sophia. Yesterday, the news of the impending nuptials had set Celia's spirits high, and she'd asked to visit with Sophia. Afterward the child asked what caused the bruises on Sophia's face. Not wishing to frighten her, he'd told her Sophia had fallen while descending a carriage.

"Sophia does appear tired, Papa. I think I should go so she can rest."

Hayden ran his hand down Celia's long brown hair. Such an astute child, too wise for her years. Experiencing a pang of guilt over the life he'd led, for the things she'd seen, he squatted and took her small hands in his. "Have I told you how lucky I am to have you in my life?"

She smiled, causing two dimples to appear on her face. "Yes, Papa. Many times."

From where Hayden stood in the shadows, he surveyed Sophia's supine form nestled in her bed. She looked so peaceful and innocent in sleep.

He hadn't intended on visiting her bedchamber tonight. He was not so callous or unaware she was not only physically exhausted, but also mentally drained. Yet here he stood like some forlorn lover. Did he hope an epiphany would enlighten him as to why he'd wished to marry Sophia even before he'd learned about the baby?

Eyes still closed, she made a soft, feminine mewl, stretched her arm above her head, and rolled onto her side. She now faced him. The tips of her fingers traced her collarbone just above the neckline of her chemise.

Hayden swallowed. Such a simple movement shouldn't cause a base reaction, yet his manhood thickened. He took a deep, silent breath and pushed away from the wall. He glanced at the open doorway that joined their bedchambers, and though his mind told him to move toward it, his legs brought him to the edge of the bed.

He reached out and softly cupped the turn of her warm cheek. Her skin was now absent the cosmetics that had made her bruising almost invisible during the ceremony. Now the bluish shadow on her face was a blatant reminder of what had transpired.

Did all women contend with the violent depravity of men? Or just those whom he . . . What? *Loved?* The word reverberated in his head. His stomach knotted. Could a man find such an emotion twice? He'd not thought it possible.

The feelings that blossomed between him and Laura had been borne over time. They'd known each other since childhood. Emotions between them had grown until he could call it nothing less than love. Yet with Sophia, he felt caught in a maelstrom—something he couldn't fully grasp or possibly didn't wish to acknowledge.

Sophia gave a slight smile and turned her face into his palm as if she sought his warmth and comfort. His turbulent thoughts scattered. Would she have done so if she were awake? What did she think of him? He'd asked himself that exact question throughout their wedding ceremony.

One thing he knew, whether she wished to admit it or not, she'd found pleasure and release in his arms. They had that, if nothing else. He pulled back his hand.

Will I be a better husband this time? Will I be able to protect her?

As if he'd spoken his tumultuous questions aloud, her dark lashes fluttered open. She peered at him, her gaze unfocused and confused in the gloom lessened by only the orange glow radiating from the hearth and a low-burning lamp.

"Go back to sleep," he whispered.

"Sleep?" She lifted her head. "Oh," she uttered, seeming to recall her surroundings and the events of the day. Bracing herself on an elbow, she peered at the mantel where a Meissen clock decorated with pastel flowers and cherubs stood. After rubbing her eyes, she stared at it again. "What time is it?"

Like her, he was unable to discern the time from this distance. He reached for his fob watch. His fingers brushed against velvet. He'd forgotten he'd removed not only his watch, but his morning coat, waistcoat, and tie. He wore a navy velvet robe atop his open-collared shirt and trousers. He stepped toward the clock. "A little past nine," he replied, returning to the bedside.

Pink colored her cheeks. "I'm sorry. I didn't mean to nap so long."

Did she think him a tyrant, here to demand his conjugal rights? He opened his mouth, wishing to alleviate her fears, but the warmth of her touch on his hand halted his words.

"Have you dined?" she asked.

She'd eaten little during their wedding breakfast. "Not yet, but Chef has already prepared dinner. I'll have your meal sent up to your room."

"Will you join me?" She sat up. She wore only a white chemise, and her dusky nipples pressed against the material.

The blasted appendage south of his navel took note. "I shall be honored. Do you wish Chef to include something special?"

She tucked a loose raven tendril behind her ear. "Some toast and a bit of fresh fruit, if that would be fine."

"Of course."

Poor Laurent would be disappointed. Mathews had informed Hayden the Frenchman was ecstatic there was to be someone in the household who would appreciate his mastery of *high art*. Yet here Sophia asked for nothing more than toast and fruit, while his kitchen overflowed with every herb and French sauce known to humanity.

After tugging on the bellpull, Hayden set a gateleg table between the yellow-and-white-striped chairs that graced the fireplace, turned up the two gas lamps on the mantel, and stirred the coals. It resembled a cozy dining nook in a quaint country inn. He smiled to himself.

Someone tapped on the door and Hayden opened it.

Uttering a startled squeak, Alice curtsied.

"Please inform Hawthorne her ladyship and I will dine

in her bedchamber tonight. Make sure he is aware we wish for a light dinner that includes fruit and toast."

"Yes, my lord." She curtsied, once, twice, then raced down the corridor.

Within an astoundingly short time, an inundating flux of female servants, led by Mrs. Beecham, entered the room. They paraded through the door with a bevy of rolling carts, loaded with domed dishes and platters that clanked and clattered as they made the transition from the wooden floors to the thick Aubusson carpet.

The maids, many of whom were awkward at best—having been hired from his sister's various charities—appeared to have found their footings. They avoided any mishaps and filed out until only Mrs. Beecham remained. The housekeeper snapped a starched cloth above the table. It floated downward, a pristine cloud of white that obliterated the dark wood. Then she quickly set the table, placed a vase of roses in its center, and inquired whether they wished a footman to serve.

"We shall be fine, Mrs. Beecham. That will be all."

The door clicked closed. Sophia sported two bright spots of color on her cheeks, while she clutched the counterpane to a point just below her chin.

"I wish I had been dressed," she said, her voice a whisper.

With her tousled hair, she looked tumbled senseless. "You look lovely." They were not false words. She looked not only ravished, but also ravishing.

She flashed a dubious expression and slipped from the bed. "I should get dressed."

Hayden noticed her shiver as the cold air in the room touched her warm body. He removed his robe and draped it over her shoulders. "That should do."

Dark, exotic eyes peered up at him.

"Thank you." She slipped her arms through the sleeves.

They were so long they swallowed up her small hands. He reached down and folded the material up. "Warmer?"

She nodded.

He pulled the chair out for her, and she sat. One by one, he lifted the silver domes off the serving dishes. His chef had suffocated nearly every morsel with some elaborate sauce. Hayden frowned at a bowl of creamed spinach, a platter of asparagus with orange puree, and a dish of stuffed mushrooms with béchamel. He removed another lid to reveal several slices of toasted baguette accompanied by a bowl of raspberry preserves.

At the sound of Sophia's small sigh, he glanced at her.

"Laurent must have thought simple toast a sacrilege to his French fare." He placed the platter next to her, then surveying the assortment of dishes, he extracted a compotier and placed it adjacent to the platter of baguettes. He lifted its lid, revealing a mélange of sliced fruit, whole berries, and a large dollop of crème suffocating it. With a deep breath, he tried to regulate his anger.

"He's an extraordinary chef," Sophia said as if trying to defuse his displeasure. "I'm sure he would impress even the most discriminating. Do you entertain a great deal?"

Though not adverse to small gatherings attended by his closest friends and business acquaintances, lately he'd grown tired of crowded balls where the air became thick and cloying with heavily perfumed men and women. Hopefully, Sophia held little fondness for such social gatherings. She probably didn't care for them; otherwise, she wouldn't have hidden her identity.

"Not often," he replied. "Though sometimes my business dealings require small dinner parties. I prefer simple, intimate gatherings."

An expression of relief flashed across her face.

"I asked since you do not appear overly enamored with

Monsieur Laurent's culinary skills. I thought you might have employed him because you favor entertaining."

Sophia was correct on one count—he was a man of simple taste when it came to food. A thick slice of beef with lightly salted potatoes and braised vegetables suited him fine, especially when accompanied by a superb glass of wine. In truth, Laurent's culinary skill had little to do with the reason he'd employed the chef. No, he'd hired Laurent away from Lord Hamby after hearing the pig had forced himself on one of his defenseless maids again—who like the others had run back to her family in the country. Angered, Hayden had offered the chef an exorbitant salary.

Nevertheless, after learning that Hamby, the lecher, had nearly suffered a coronary thrombosis upon hearing of his prized chef's defection, Hayden thought the salary of little consequence. "Perhaps I hired him so I could be the envy of others."

She laughed—a light tinkling sound that infused the air with warmth. Smiling, she tipped her head to the side and studied him. "I do not believe you give a fig what others think. No, you hired him for some other reason, though I am baffled as to what that reason could be."

"You are astute, Sophia." He returned his attention to the serving dishes, and tried not to scowl at the béarnaise sauce drizzled over the châteaubriand. He took a piece and some sautéed potatoes garnished with fresh parsley.

"Are you going to divulge the truth or shall I start guessing?" Her voice sounded light, playful.

"His last employer, Lord Hamby, thought Laurent his greatest acquisition. I hired him because it gave me immeasurable pleasure to deprive him of Laurent's services."

Her smile and the sparkle in her eyes faded. "I see."

His admission of vindictiveness seemed to cast a pall over them, and they ate in silence. Sophia ladled a few pieces of fruit into her patterned bowl. She spooned a couple raspberries into her mouth, but her appetite appeared diminished.

He drew in a deep breath. Over the last eight years, the good opinion of others had mattered little to him, but he didn't wish Sophia to think it merely an act of spite. Leaning against the back of his chair, he set his utensils down. "I stole Hamby's beloved chef because the man uses his wealth and power in a way no man should. He's a lecher who takes pleasure in abusing the women employed in his household."

"Oh," she said softly. "Oh!" she repeated, grasping his meaning. "How horrid."

He picked up his wineglass.

"Hayden?"

He didn't believe she'd used his given name more than a handful of times since he'd brought her here. The sound of it on her lips, in such an intimate place, pleased him, brought him back to that night in her bed. "Yes?"

"Thank you." She glanced down at the table, ran her hand over the tablecloth. "Not only for hiring Monsieur Laurent out from Lord Hamby but for confiding in me." She picked up the serving spoon and filled her bowl with fruit.

They ate in companionable silence. He tipped his wineglass to his lips and peered at her over its rim. Her fruit bowl was empty, except for one plump strawberry with its stem still attached. She picked up the berry, removed the hull, and took a bite. Her full lips glistened with the juices, and the smallest dollop of crème, no larger than a teardrop, punctuated the bow of her upper lip.

Hayden placed his glass back on the table. He couldn't draw his gaze away from her mouth and the single drop of crème. He shifted uncomfortably in his seat.

Sophia examined the half-eaten fruit she held before

surveying the compote. "Forgive me. I've eaten all the strawberries. Do you wish to finish this one?" She outstretched her hand, offered him the sweet remnant held between her fingers.

His gaze fell to the berry and the translucent juices running down her index finger.

Sophia's cheeks colored and she began to pull her hand back. "How foolish of me. Of course you don't wish to eat a bitten—"

He caught her wrist, brought her fingers to his lips, and took the strawberry. After swallowing, he drew her index finger into his mouth and suckled it before slowly releasing it. "Hmm, sweet." His thumb glided over the thin skin of her inner wrist.

Wide-eyed, his innocent wife stared at him for a long moment, and then she ran her tongue over her upper lip, erased the small white teardrop of crème, and drew it into her mouth.

His cock jumped to attention. Damnation, the seducer was once again the seduced. Best to leave before he let his desires override him—before all his good intentions evaporated. Sophia needed to rest. He released her, pushed his chair back, and tossed his linen napkin on the table as he stood. "I think I should retire. Good night, Sophia."

He'd nearly reached the door when her voice halted him. "Are you leaving me for some assignation?"

Hayden swung back around. "What?"

She stood. "Do you have a mistress?" She wrapped her arms around her slender waist. "Are you running off to see her?"

He'd not bedded a single woman since her. "Is that what you think? I'm impatient to get to some clandestine meeting with a lover on my wedding night?" She really did think him a rutting dog.

Since the dissolution of his marriage, he'd slept with only one woman whose taste lingered on his tongue, who consumed his thoughts, and she stood before him. Anger, desire, resentment all coursed through him—a volatile mixture. He strode toward her.

Her eyes widened, and she stepped back until her bare heels collided with the skirting board. He pressed his palms flat on the wall, caged her in. "I've never kept a mistress. I've had liaisons, mostly brief and loveless, not to mention sordid."

She gasped. "So you are leaving me for some meaningless assignation?"

"The only assignation I have engaged in as of late has been conducted with a dark-eyed temptress."

She notched her chin up an inch. "I don't wish to hear about her."

"Ah, but I think you should."

"A gentleman would never speak of such things. I won't listen." She slammed her palms against his chest.

He laced his fingers with hers and gently pinned them to the wall above her head. "I suggest you do." He stepped close—let her feel the hardness beneath his trousers. "Just the thought of her leaves me . . . shall we say wanting."

"You are wicked," she said.

"So they say, and yet you allowed me into your bed. Perhaps you're a little wicked as well." She narrowed her eyes, and he believed that if he didn't hold her hands, she would have struck him. "But I digress. Let me finish telling you about my temptress. I shall start with her eyes. They are lovely, dusted with long lashes nearly as dark as her lemon-scented hair. And her skin . . ." He let go of one of her hands and ran the backs of his fingers over her neck and collarbone. "It looks kissed by the sun's warmth."

Her eyes misted and a tear trailed down her cheek.

He pressed his lips to her skin to absorb the moisture. "And her tears are sweet, absent the salt they should contain." Hayden released her other hand, slipped his arm about her waist. "Do you understand?" he asked softly, his anger fading into a warm pool of desire.

She tipped her head to the side and moistened her lower lip. "You lust for *this woman*?"

"Yes, more than any other. To the point of distraction."

Sophia stared at him, then she stood on her toes, and pressed her lips to his.

He touched her face, mindful of her bruised cheek, and returned her kiss. He held back his desire to taste her, to take the kiss to a new level. *Gentle. Be gentle,* a voice in his head advised.

She moaned.

His tentative hold slipped. He coaxed her lips open, dipped his tongue into her mouth. She tasted like sun-warmed fruit. He slipped a hand beneath the open robe to capture the weight of her breast in his palm.

The coiled longing he'd held in check over the last several weeks unraveled. He untied the satin ribbon of her chemise, parted the material, and kissed her neck and collarbone before running his tongue over her nipples. He lifted her legs, drew them around his hips, and pressed his manhood against her. He rocked, insinuating himself closer.

Her legs parted wider.

Eager, he unfastened the top button of his trousers.

He froze.

What in God's name was wrong with him? Sophia offered him a chaste kiss, and here he was grinding himself into her, preparing to take her right here, pressed against the wall. Had he forgotten she was pregnant? Or that some ham-fisted animal had assaulted her? Biting back a groan, he set his forehead to the cool plastered wall.

Sophia clung to him—quiet, except for the heavy cadence of her breathing which entwined with his. Slowly he set her down. Her respiration remained labored. His unchecked desire probably frightened her. She needed to rest, and he needed a cold bath or a dunk in the Thames, possibly both.

He swept her into his arms, carried her to the bed, and laid her down. Her dark hair spilled against the white sheets. Quickly he drew the disheveled blankets up to her chin.

"You should rest." He kissed her forehead and left through the door that connected this bedchamber to his before he changed his mind.

Chapter Twenty

Sophia stared at Hayden as he strode into his bedchamber and closed the door behind him. She sat up. What in heaven's name just happened? The man had kissed her and pressed himself sensuously against her body until she feared she might melt from the heat growing within her.

How could he leave her in such a state? Curse him!

She slipped off the mattress and marched to the door. As she clasped the brass handle, Mathews's voice drifted through the wood.

Well, she very well couldn't demand an explanation with the valet in the room. With an unladylike utterance, she stormed away from the door and crawled back between the sheets.

A half hour later, the voices faded, along with her anger and heated skin. She tossed restlessly about, pulled Hayden's robe around her, and buried her nose in the cloth to draw in his spicy scent.

Doubtful after what had brought them to this marriage, that Hayden and she would ever have the relationship her mother and father had shared, a union based on mutual adoration for each other. But for the sake of their child and Celia, this marriage needed to work, no matter its inauspicious conception. He'd spoken of the possibility that in time they might love each other. If she made him content would he stay with her, not stray? She darted back to the connecting door, placed her ear on the hard surface, and listened.

Silence.

Inhaling a deep, fortifying breath, she opened the door, only to collide with a wall of cold air and darkness. Her gaze veered to the fireplace grate. The normal glow from the coals was absent. Why was the fire not banked?

"Hayden?" she whispered, moving to the massive four-poster bed that the gloom had all but swallowed. She peered at her husband. His hair was sopping wet and he wore no nightshirt. She sucked in a mouthful of cold air. "What in God's name?" she exclaimed.

Hayden's eyes opened. He blinked. "Are you an illusion? If not, please go away."

"You're going to catch a deadly chill. Have you gone mad?" She stepped to the side of the bed and turned up the gas lamp on the night table.

"By God, you're not a dream." He bolted upright and narrowed his eyes at her.

"You're shivering."

"Yes, well, that is what happens when one bathes in cold water." He gritted his chattering teeth.

"Why would you do such a harebrained thing?"

He mumbled. She could have sworn he counted to ten under his breath. "Sophia. Go to bed."

"Are you delirious from the cold?" She leaned forward and set her hand to his forehead.

The noise he uttered sounded a bit like a growl. The type a stray dog makes when a stranger approaches.

"If you are not warmed you might catch pneumonia." She lifted the bedding and froze. He wore not a stitch of clothing. She remembered the heat of his naked skin against hers. Her mouth grew dry. She shrugged out of his robe and pressed her knee to the mattress.

His gaze widened. "What are you doing?"

"I read an article about two Russian explorers lost in the wilds of Siberia. They survived by bundling together."

"We are not in Siberia."

"I cannot imagine it feels any colder than this room." She climbed into the bed and slid next to him.

"Out," he snapped, lifting the blankets up while he motioned for her to leave.

Ignoring him, she leaned over his body and began rubbing his shoulders. His cool skin warmed under her palms. Her own body heated. She peered at him through lowered lashes while she slid a hand down his abdomen. Desire exploded low in her belly.

He closed his eyes and made a sound as though in pain. "Sophia, either you are the most naïve woman in all of Great Britain or you're trying to seduce me."

Indeed. The more she touched him, the more she wanted to explore every inch of his skin—to have him do the same to her. Her face warmed. She averted her gaze. "I am, but it appears I'm inept."

"Good God, woman, if this is inept, you might have me weeping when you are more skilled. If you are doing this out of some misguided sense of—"

She pressed a finger to his lips. "Why did you kiss me, then leave?"

"You have been through so very much. I thought you should sleep."

"I don't wish to. I feel . . . restless."

He took a deep, audible breath like he fought some internal struggle, and she knew he intended to send her away. "Sophia—"

"You do realize we can . . . That the baby is not harmed if we . . ." The heat on her cheeks traveled to her ears.

"I do, but you should sleep."

She snuggled closer, slid her hand lower on his abdomen, and trailed a finger over the narrow path of hair below his navel.

His eyes drifted closed. When he opened them she could see the desire in their blue depth. "For someone inexperienced with seduction, you are doing a remarkable job. If you continue to torment me, dear wife, there will be no turning back. I might want you all night. Not once, but several times. Do you understand?"

She swallowed. Her body felt molten—more aroused than she thought possible. The place between her legs grew wet. She gave a quick nod of her head.

He set his hands on her thighs and slid her body atop him so she straddled his hips. His firm manhood pressed against the dampness between her legs. Awareness, desire, and need shot through her. She rocked forward, wishing he was inside her.

He groaned and slipped his hands up her thighs, dragging the cloth of her chemise upward. He stilled and held her gaze. "Undress for me, Sophia. Lift your undergarment over your head."

A shiver of unease raced up her spine. For several long seconds, she stared at him, fighting her discomfort, then she drew the fabric up and tossed the garment aside. She would have thought it impossible, but his manhood grew firmer beneath her. Gooseflesh scattered over her arms.

"We're going to take this slow." He twined a hand over her nape, drew her mouth to his, and deepened the kiss.

She loved when he kissed her like this—when his tongue tangled with hers, over and over until her body grew limp. He flipped her onto her back and lay beside her.

His hands explored her, sliding across her abdomen, her hips, until his fingers drifted into the curls at the apex of her legs. Closing her eyes, she savored his touch while he caressed and stroked her. One finger, then another, he slipped into her as his teasing tongue lapped at her breasts, turning the buds hard.

Warmth traveled through her. Could one die from such wicked pleasure? She skimmed her hand from his shoulder to his ribs, down the slightly rippled plane of his abdomen, and curled her fingers around his manhood.

He sucked in an audible breath.

She slid her hand up his silky length, then back downward. Gripping him tighter, she hastened her strokes.

A groan escaped him. He wrapped his fingers around hers. "Slow." He chuckled. "Or it shall be over much too quickly. Yes. Yes, like that." His breathing grew heavy. He pulled her hand away, and set his palm on her inner thigh.

"Hayden?" She arched her hips upward—her body's silent plea for him to fill the void he'd skillfully created.

"Spread your legs, love," his raspy voice commanded.

She did so, and he settled himself between her thighs. Slowly he buried himself in her heightened flesh. He moved, a rhythm that brought him deeper within her after each thrust.

Her body clenched around him. Her breathing ratcheted upward. She teetered on the edge, nearly there. He pulled back, plunged deeper, withdrew, and filled her again, eliciting exquisite pressure. Once, twice, a dozen times. The nerves in her body gathered. A pulse beat where he joined her, and she splintered at the exact moment his face grew taut and he drove so deep she believed they momentarily became one.

His warm body collapsed onto her. Mumbling an apology, he rolled off and tucked her into the crook of his arm. Their heavy breathing echoed in the still room.

Every nerve within her hummed. Contented, she shifted closer and listened to Hayden's strong heartbeat.

As her sated body and mind settled back on reality, worry eclipsed her contentment. Was she a fool to try to make Hayden love her by sharing his bed? Though the physical pleasure seemed immeasurable, coupling wasn't love, and desire could wane. Sophia reflected on what Thomas had revealed about Hayden's first marriage. A union based on an unplanned pregnancy—like her own. And, in the end, Hayden had walked away. She bit her lower lip. Was trying to hold on to Hayden like trying to grasp air in one's hand? An unattainable feat? Perhaps it would be wiser to harden her heart toward him, not give it away so freely. That way, the pain wouldn't be so severe, if he ended up leaving her.

She needed to remember, no matter what he said, that history had a habit of repeating itself. She thought of her family—all gone. She didn't wish to lose another person she loved. No, it was better not to love Hayden. Better to guard her heart, save her love for the child growing in her.

After all, if the past were anything to go by, it would be just the two of them soon enough.

Hayden scanned the stack of mail readied for the morning post. He'd breezed through several weeks of correspondence in a remarkably short time, buoyed by a nearly forgotten sense of contentment. He skimmed over the last letter he'd written, and, with a slashing stroke, signed his name to it.

Lawrence Bishop was an art dealer with connections in every major city. Varga's dossier on Sophia had revealed she'd sold three of her grandfather's paintings to purchase her Chelsea residence.

How strange Hayden had bought one of them. The art dealer would know who'd purchased the other two. If he didn't, the monetary gains he offered Bishop would set the bloodhound within the man to ground. Hayden smiled as he anticipated Sophia's expression when he bestowed them on her. They would make a wonderful gift for his new bride.

He stuffed his business ledgers inside the top drawer of his desk and locked it. He stood, slipped the key under the inkpot, and strode to the stairs. Was Sophia still asleep? He'd made love to her not once, but twice during the night, and he feared, if he hadn't vacated the room early this morning, he would have awakened her again.

At this rate, she'd be with child every year. He'd always wanted a large family. Before he'd married Laura, they'd talked about filling the rafters with their brood, yet it was not in the devil's plans.

A sick feeling settled in his stomach. He was not the same naïve young man who'd married at twenty-one. Now he knew about deceit and hate, and that life was unpredictable and contentment sometimes fleeting.

In bed Sophia and he shared a passion, but now he needed to make her love him—trust him again. Not with words, but with actions. If he could do that, he might have a second chance at happiness. A chance to have all he'd dreamed of. A thread of guilt weaved through him, for there was no second chance for Laura.

Did he deserve to be content?

No, but Sophia did.

He took the steps three at a time, inching the door open and slipping inside the room.

The morning sun highlighted the empty bed. Rubbing the back of his neck, Hayden eyed the door to the adjoining bedchamber. He strode to it and turned the handle.

Locked.

"Sophia, may I come in?"

"I'm dressing."

He grinned. "I could help."

"I assure you that isn't necessary."

The cool tone of her voice dissolved his smile. What had happened since last night?

His chest tightened. He blindly peered at the sculpted carpet beneath his bare feet while remembering the panicked expression on Sophia's face when he'd slipped the diamond and sapphire ring on her finger during the ceremony. Hayden understood her trepidation. They'd say she married a scoundrel. A man who wouldn't be faithful. A bargain she couldn't win. But he'd prove them wrong.

But he couldn't prove himself to her, if she built a wall between them. He knocked on the door again.

The soft patter of feet approached on the other side. The lock snicked and Sophia opened the door. She wore a simple day dress in light blue. Her long dark hair trailed over her shoulders. He recalled how the silken mass had cascaded about his chest and shoulders last night, cocooning him in her clean lemony scent like a sensory aphrodisiac.

Face unreadable, she walked over to the dressing table and started pinning up her hair.

"Why are you up so early?" he asked, stepping into the room.

"I am an early riser. You?"

Was she upset she'd awoken to find him gone? "I let my business dealings fall to the wayside. I needed to tend to them."

Apprehension flashed across her face. "Hayden, I wish you to know my great-uncle does not condone my desire to work. He does not support me monetarily or emotionally in my endeavors." She took a deep breath. "My inheritance from my father is not paltry, but modest, and I have no grand dowry. And most of my grandfather's paintings are on loan to museums where I can visit them. They have sentimental value, and I do not want to part with them. Though I live a comfortable life, I am not some heiress if that is what you believe."

Most of the women who courted his attention knew he could buy them whatever their hearts desired. It seemed unfathomable that Sophia knew nothing of his wealth. His breweries could barely keep up with the production demanded of them, and the whisky distillery Simon, James Huntington, and he owned turned a substantial profit. "Do you think I care whether you are wealthy?"

"I'm not sure."

"Sophia, I assure you, your great-uncle's wealth does not interest me." He drew in a deep breath and glanced around the room. "I shall have your things moved into my bedchamber."

Her eyes widened. A small lump moved in her slender throat. "My numerous house calls to Thomas's wealthy patients have made me aware that many husbands and wives who are members of the nobility do not share the intimacy of a bedchamber. They have separate rooms. They only share it to . . ." Her cheeks turned pink. "I-I thought we would do the same."

A nerve twitched in his jaw. He paced to the window and pivoted around. "From now on you are to share my bed."

She nervously wrung her hands. "I think it would be best if we had separate sleeping quarters."

"There will be only one bed in this marriage, Sophia," he repeated. "Now, if you will excuse me."

"Are you going out?"

No, he needed to distance himself from her. He wanted her again—the touch of her silky skin against his, the sound of her little gasps, the scent of her aroused body filling his nose. But he needed to take this slow and win not only his wife's body but her love and good regard. "I intend to take a bath."

A cold one. In fact, he might spend the rest of his life bathing in water as frigid as the River Thames if he couldn't win Sophia's heart.

Chapter Twenty-One

Sophia smiled as Hayden draped her navy cape over her shoulders. His hand lingered a fraction longer than necessary on her neck, causing warmth to flood her body.

How could she make herself immune to someone whose every simple touch made her desire him?

The physical attraction wasn't the only obstacle making it difficult to harden her heart against her husband. The first two weeks of her marriage had contained unexpected, yet pleasant revelations. Her suspicions that Hayden partook in a great deal of business proved true. He attended numerous meetings at both his residence and about town, dispelling the notion he was a man of leisure. Yesterday alone, he'd engaged in two meetings in his study. One in the morning with two Algerian gentlemen and another immediately after with a Lord James Huntington.

Even more startling—he'd dined at home every night, and during the evenings they retired to the drawing room where they read, played cards and chess, or simply conversed. Now they were to take Celia on an open carriage ride to Richmond equipped with warm lap rugs, a heater for their feet, and a hamper from Fortnum and Mason filled with savory and sweet treats.

His behavior implied he wished their marriage to work, but an uneasiness simmered right below the surface within her. She couldn't dispel her fear. Hayden had left his first wife. Abandoned her only months after Celia's birth. Would it happen again? Would he bore of her and seek the companionship of his dissolute friends—members of the privileged class? Was it only a matter of time?

"Papa, do say Lady Olivia can accompany us to Richmond. Please!" Celia said, drawing Sophia from her thoughts.

Hayden frowned at the dog sitting before him in the entry hall, while Celia held her breath in anticipation of her father's reply.

"Yes," Sophia said. "Lady Olivia may join us."

Celia stretched her hands in the air and danced on the tips of her toes while the dog's tail tapped a rapid staccato on the marble floor. Hayden's daughter grabbed the dog's lead, and Hawthorne opened the door to assist the child into the waiting carriage.

Hayden arched a dark eyebrow.

Was he vexed?

"You, my dear wife, are raining anarchy upon my household." His lips twitched and he proffered his arm.

"Admit it." She placed her hand on his sleeve. "You are fond of Lady Olivia."

He made a noncommittal grunt, but a smile lightened his eyes. "Come, my dear, your chariot awaits. Along with one anxious child and an overgrown beast whom I shall instruct to sit on your lap."

Once they crossed the bridge and were well into the open spaces of Richmond, they stopped to lower the top of the landau. The cool winter air, along with the excitement of the journey, heightened the color of Celia's cheeks.

"Look," the child exclaimed, pointing at the red brick

wall ahead that encompassed Richmond Park. "Papa, do you think we will see any deer today?"

"I expect we shall."

Celia slipped her hands back into her muff and swung her legs back and forth.

While they traveled through the park, enjoying their hamper full of treats, Sophia listened to Hayden talk with Celia about the red deer and wildlife in the park. No matter what one thought about him, Hayden loved his daughter and was a good father.

After a leisurely drive through the park, they headed back to Mayfair. Halfway home, Celia's heavy-lidded eyes fluttered closed and her hand, stroking the dog, stilled.

Hayden pulled a green woolen blanket out from under the seat and draped it across Celia before patting the dog's head and feeding it a whole meat tart.

Sophia laughed softly. "It is obvious you care for that dog."

"Rubbish."

"You adore her."

Grinning, he slipped his glove off, curled his hand around her nape, and brushed his lips against hers. "Later tonight, I'm going to teach you to behave and show more deference to your husband and not argue with him."

Images of Hayden and her lying in bed, him buried deep within her, flashed in her mind. Trying to ignore them and the anticipation that grew within her, she shot her husband what she hoped looked like a scolding, disinterested expression.

His gaze dropped to her breasts. The layers of her clothing hid her hardened nipples, but somehow he knew. Knew her body craved his touch.

She recalled the first three nights of their marriage when she'd stubbornly ignored his mandate that she share his chamber. He'd entered her room and carried her into his bedroom and whispered seductively his one-bed rule.

Some nights he'd make love to her, other nights simply hold her in his arms. That seemed even worse—more intimate. She could understand his physical need for release, but the embracing made guarding her heart so much more difficult. It made her believe they could have a life together until they were old and gray, and that loving him wouldn't leave her vulnerable.

Hayden settled against the squabs and draped his arm over her shoulders.

Trying to ignore the undeniable pleasure his touch gave her, she motioned to the dog. "Celia has become attached to Lady Olivia. She will be heartbroken when your friend returns to London and wishes to retrieve her."

"I'm in custody of several of the man's gambling markers. His debts are the reason he left town. So the matter has been settled in a manner agreeable to both of us. We are now the proud owners of one overgrown, quite costly, salivating Saint Bernard."

"Does Celia know?"

"No, I thought we might tie a bow on Lady Olivia and tell her tonight."

"Celia will be ecstatic." Sophia patted the dog's head, just as thrilled with the news.

The carriage pulled up before their town house. Hayden lifted his slumbering daughter and moved to the front door. Lady Olivia followed him like a shadow. He turned and narrowed his eyes at the dog.

Another soft laugh bubbled up Sophia's throat. "You fed her a meat pie," she whispered. "She might follow you for the rest of the day, if not into next week. She might even wish to sleep with you again."

He leaned close. "Only one lady sleeps in my bed, and that is you, my dear wife."

If only I could believe that would always be true.

Hawthorne greeted them at the door. The butler looked perturbed. "My lord, a Mr. Charles Camden is here. The gentleman claims to be related to her ladyship. I told him you were out, but he insisted on waiting."

Sophia's heart skipped a beat. *Great-Uncle Charles? Here?*

Hayden turned to her. "How lovely, dear. Your great-uncle has come to visit."

She forced a smile, wishing her enthusiasm for their guest matched her husband's. "Where is he, Hawthorne?"

"In the blue drawing room, madam," the butler replied.

A slumbering Celia shifted in Hayden's arms. "I shall lay Celia down and join you shortly. I look forward to meeting your great-uncle."

As Sophia made her way up the stairs to the blue drawing room, she wiped her damp palms on her skirt. The man never visited London. Why was he here?

At the entrance to the room, she took a deep breath, opened the door, and stepped inside.

Great-Uncle Charles stood by the mantel. As usual, he wore a severe black suit, white shirt, and black cravat that looked plucked from a century ago. Though his hair was gray, his posture was still brittle and unbending. He peered at her with those cold steely gray eyes of his.

"Great-Uncle Charles, how are you?" She brushed a kiss on his cheek.

His nose twitched as if she carried the stench of the Thames on her body. "Sophia, I see you have not used the bleaching cream I sent. You're still as dark as a gypsy. You were always a stubborn child."

She fought the urge to tug the cuffs of her sleeves lower. Instead, she squared her shoulders. "Might I ask what has brought you to London?"

"I came to see you. I hear you have married. Thank

goodness you have given up your foolish whim to become a doctor."

"I must correct you, sir. I still hope to be a physician one day."

His pale face grew mottled. "It is ridiculous."

"Why?"

"Child, it is an unseemly profession for a woman, especially one married to a nobleman."

So that was why he was here. She'd done what he'd asked her father to do. Married nobility. And in her great-uncle's eyes, a scandalous earl was better than no earl at all.

"I believe my husband will support me."

"Then he hasn't given you his permission to continue with this folly?"

She swallowed. No, they hadn't broached the subject. But surely . . .

"Tell me, Sophia, how did you manage to marry an earl? Is he hard up for money? Is he expecting a dowry?"

Once again, he made her feel unworthy of anyone's love or good regard. She wanted to tell him to go, but instead she remained silent. He would find out about the child she carried in time; then his comments would become even more caustic, even more demeaning.

He waved a hand in the air as if it was of no importance. "However it came about, you are now a member of the nobility. A countess does not tend to the sick. You have gone against my advice and society's expectations of proper behavior for a woman, but now you must conform and act accordingly. I do not wish you to draw more shame on this family than you already have."

"I will not give up my dream to be a physician."

As Hayden approached the blue drawing room he grinned. Today had gone well. He believed he'd come a bit closer to winning Sophia's heart. She'd smiled freely at times and when he'd told her about the dog, she'd looked like she wanted to not only kiss the Saint Bernard but him as well. And now her great-uncle was here. How pleased his wife must be to have her only living relative in Town.

"My lord," Hawthorne said.

Hayden pivoted. "Yes?"

"I have instructed Mrs. Beecham to have one of the maids prepare the green bedchamber, should her ladyship's uncle be staying."

"Ah, splendid." He clapped the butler on the shoulder. "Bang-up job you're doing, old boy."

The butler blinked. His bony cheeks reddened. "Why . . . why thank you, my lord."

"I'm in a fine mood, Hawthorne. Give the staff a raise in their wages."

Hawthorne's eyes widened. "But they received their yearly increase only last month."

"Did they?"

"Indeed, sir."

"Give them another. And don't forget yourself."

The man smiled showing a large amount of teeth. "If that is what you wish, my lord."

"I do. Have you instructed someone to bring refreshments to my wife and her great-uncle?"

"Alice should be here any minute with the tray."

"Very good," Hayden said.

As Hawthorne strolled away, Hayden could have sworn the stoic butler whistled an Irish jig.

The sound of Sophia's great-uncle inside the drawing room drew Hayden's attention.

"You must follow society's rules," Camden's snide voice said. "You are a silly, stupid, strong-willed girl with no sense of propriety. I hope your new husband puts you in your place!"

Hayden fisted his hand. How dare he disparage Sophia? She was beyond intelligent. *I'll strangle the man. Then kill him. Then strangle him again.* And what did he mean by "put her in her place"? Did he mean strike her? Did he believe a man should control a woman with his fists? He flung the door open.

The thin, gray-haired coot turned and smiled at him.

Sophia's earlier lighthearted expression no longer remained. Her whole body radiated discomfort. But he would take care of that. No one would hurt his wife, with words or actions, if he could stop them.

"Sophia," her great-uncle said in that superior voice of his. "Aren't you going to introduce his lordship to me?"

"Hayden, this is my great-uncle Charles Camden. Uncle Charles, my husband, Lord Hayden Westfield."

He strode over to Charles Camden and extended his hand.

Smiling, the old bugger shook it.

Returning the man's pleasant expression, Hayden squeezed the man's fingers so tight, he thought he might snap one of the coot's bones.

The smile faded from Camden's lips. He paled.

"Pleasure to meet you, Camden. What brings you to our fair city?" *A death wish?* He released the man's hand.

Camden visibly swallowed. "My niece, of course. I haven't seen her in a terribly long time."

The rattling of the tea tray being rolled into the room drew everyone's attention. Alice set the silver tray on the ottoman.

"Thank you, Alice," Sophia said.

The maid curtsied and left.

Camden frowned. "Sophia, you should never smile at a servant or thank them. It gives them a sense of complacency."

Hayden fought the urge to open the window and toss the

windbag out and onto his head. “My staff is quite fond of *Lady Westfield*.”

The old man tipped his nose up. “But don’t you think, Lord Westfield, servants must be made to feel their employment is precarious at best?”

“I believe whatever rapport my lady wife decides is best.” Hayden reached for her hand, brought her fingers to his lips, and kissed them.

Sophia blinked.

The old man visibly bristled.

“Please, sit, sir.” Sophia motioned to a chair as she sat. “You take your tea with milk, if I recall.”

The curmudgeon sat and nodded.

After pouring the tea, Sophia added a smidgen of milk.

“Too much!” Camden snapped.

Hayden growled.

The man looked at him as did Sophia.

Hayden coughed. “Forgive me, I fear I have something in my throat.”

“Tea, Hayden?” Sophia asked.

“Thank you, but no, dearest.”

Without pouring herself a cup, Sophia leaned back, shoulders ramrod straight as though she feared if she didn’t the man would crack a ruler over her knuckles.

Had he struck her when she was a child? *The bastard!*

“I wonder, Westfield, if we might talk in private about Sophia’s dowry.”

His wife’s puzzled gaze jerked to the old man. She stood. “I shall leave you both to your discussion.”

Hayden rose, showing proper respect. The old man remained seated.

“Great-Uncle,” Sophia said, “you are more than welcome to stay with us while in London.”

The man finally stood and set his cup down. "I would be delighted."

As soon as Sophia walked out of the room, Hayden set a heavy hand on Camden's shoulder. "Listen here, you old goat, you can keep your bloody dowry."

Camden's eyes bulged. "W-what?"

"You heard me. And don't you ever call my wife stupid."

"I-I didn't."

"You did. And if it ever happens again, I will take the most inordinate pleasure in trying to ruin you. Do I make myself clear?"

The man pulled a handkerchief from his pocket and dabbed at his shimmering brow.

"Now," Hayden continued, "you are going to give your apologies to my wife and inform her you are leaving Town. Tell her pressing business has called you back to Northumberland. And if you ever come here again, I will feed you to my dog."

As if on cue, Lady Olivia bounded into the room, saliva dripping from her long jowls.

Camden's Adam's apple bobbed.

"Now get out," Hayden said, his voice low and threatening.

The man dashed out the door and hastened down the stairs.

Hayden followed him, biting back the desire to kick the man in the arse.

Sophia stood in the entry hall. "Are you already finished?"

"Yes, but sadly your great-uncle has realized he must return home," Hayden said.

A quick smile flashed across Sophia's face, so brief it seemed like an illusion. "I'm so sorry you cannot stay with us, sir. Are you unwell? You look rather pale."

"N-no, I'm fine. I have business up north."

Hayden opened the door. "A pleasure meeting you, Camden."

Sophia pressed a kiss to the old goat's cheek. "Godspeed."

The man stepped out, looking as if he'd just survived a train wreck.

Hayden closed the door.

"I didn't know I had a dowry," Sophia said. "Great-Uncle never mentioned it. I hope it was of an agreeable amount."

"Yes, Camden and I struck a bargain I'm quite pleased with."

She fiddled with her sleeve.

"Tell me, Sophia, are you upset your great-uncle had to leave?" He entwined his fingers with hers, stilling her hand.

"Truthfully, no."

"Was he cruel to you growing up?"

"He was indifferent more than anything else." She looked at him carefully. "You sent him away, didn't you? Tell me why, Hayden."

"I didn't like his tie."

"That's silly.

"Nor his shirt. And I think he has wooden teeth."

"No, he doesn't. Please tell me the truth."

"Because, my dear wife, I shall always protect you." He pulled her into his embrace.

She said not a word, but wrapped her hands around his waist as if he were the most important thing in the world to her. And he believed he might have finally knocked a few more bricks loose from the wall she was trying to erect between them. Perhaps even toppled it to the ground.

The following morning, Hayden returned from an early meeting to find Sophia standing before the cheval glass, garbed in one of the navy dresses and white aprons she'd worn while attending him.

From the doorway, he watched her pin her winged cap to her hair.

"Sophia?"

She spun around. "Oh, you gave me a fright," she admitted, slipping a pin into her hair.

"May I inquire where you are off to?"

A weak smile briefly touched her lips. "I have been negligent in my duties. Fortunately, Thomas is a very understanding employer."

"Sophia, you must realize you do not have to work."

Her smile broadened. "Ah, yes, I forgot, I'm an heiress of considerable magnitude."

"No," he said stiffly, "because you are a countess married to a man of great wealth."

Her head tipped to the side, and she stared at him. "Am I? Then I shall feel no shame in telling you that I shall not receive a stitch of monetary compensation. Today Thomas and I are volunteering at the Whitechapel Mission. At the dispensary."

The image of her battered, lying in that squalid room, that wretch trying to violate her, seized his mind. A knot tightened his stomach. He shook the image away.

Sophia turned back to the mirror.

He moved to stand behind her and watched her reflection in the glass. "Have you forgotten what happened the last time you were there?"

"I doubt I shall ever forget. But it's unlikely to happen again. And I shall be with Thomas this time."

"That fact does not ease my mind."

She slipped another hairpin into her chignon and turned back to him. "Thomas is a good man, Hayden, and he needs assistance at the dispensary."

"Then I shall hire someone to assist him. Someone who is not with child. I forbid you to go."

The color drained from her face, and the hairpins held in her hand fell to the floor. "You cannot do that!"

"Sadly, my dear, I can." After what had transpired at the mission, how could she not understand how one's life could change in the blink of an eye? How easily a man could overpower her in the rookeries. Not wanting to hear her protestations, he moved to the door.

"Hayden, I *am* going to the mission whether you approve or not."

His heart skipped a beat. He couldn't protect her there. "Do not defy me, Sophia."

"Why are you acting this way?"

He couldn't tell her. Could not admit the fear that came over him when he thought someone might hurt her like his father had hurt Laura. "I shall be back shortly. If I return to find you have accompanied Trimble, I shall go to that godforsaken cesspit and carry you back home, if I must."

Sophia paced the drawing room floor. Hayden had left over an hour ago. Even though she'd changed and sent Thomas a note explaining she'd not be able to assist him today, she now toyed with the idea of defying her husband and going to the mission.

Yes, she would go. The devil with Hayden. She strode toward the double doors. Without warning, one of them swung open.

"Hello, dear," Edith said cheerfully, stepping into the room. Edith's effervescent expression faded. She rushed forward. "Sophia, you look agitated."

She forced a smile. "Do I? It's nothing."

"Dearest, you are not some simpering miss. If you are upset, I know it is not because of some nonsense." Edith adjusted the bustle of her navy day dress and sat on the blue damask covered settee. She patted the spot adjacent to her. "Sit, dear. Tell me what has vexed you so." She smiled encouragingly. "Please, we are sisters now."

Sophia dearly wished to confide in Edith. Her sister-in-law's earnest voice comforted, while her brown eyes held a nearly palpable kindness. Sophia sat and folded her hands in her lap. "I . . ." She paused, for the words drifting about in her head scattered like dry leaves caught in an autumn breeze.

Where do I begin? "Hayden has forbidden me to accompany Dr. Trimble to the Whitechapel Mission."

Edith placed her hand on Sophia's. "He is concerned about your safety."

"I realize I should not have approached that man in the alley." Her voice shook with self-recrimination. "But I shall not be so careless again."

"I'm sure you won't, but I think it is my brother's love for you that makes him act like this."

Startled, Sophia glanced up. "Love for me?"

"Yes, I saw the way he watched you during the wedding ceremony. He cares deeply for you. Can you not see it in his eyes?"

Could she? There were times when she believed Hayden's gazes reflected something greater than lust. And when he touched her—yes, when he touched her, she thought his hands communicated an emotion so deep within his soul that perhaps he was not aware of it.

The second morning after their nuptials flashed in her mind. Nauseous, she'd hastily vacated their bed to make her way to the bathroom. As she'd knelt before the water closet, she'd been startled by the feel of Hayden's hand gently soothing her back while she retched helplessly into the enamel bowl. When she'd finished, he'd tenderly swept her into his arms and carried her back to their bed.

He'd spent the next quarter hour patting her face with a damp cloth. She'd told herself his concern was for the child she carried, but the gentleness of his touch and the look in his eyes left her unsure. And then there was yesterday when he'd sensed how uncomfortable Great-Uncle Charles made her feel and sent him away.

"Wouldn't a man who loves me say so?"

"At one time, I believed my brother's speech too lucid and his countenance too transparent. However, his candor has faded with maturity and with what our . . ." Edith waved her hand in the air. "It is not always easy for a man to communicate his feelings. Most men are frugal creatures when it comes to divulging sentiment. Or perhaps, he doesn't even realize what he feels. Or is frightened of the emotion."

She couldn't imagine Hayden being frightened of anything.

The door burst open, and an exuberant Celia rushed in with a pair of ice skates.

"Sophia, can we go to Hyde Park to glide upon the ice?"

A line marred Edith's forehead. "I believe the authorities have closed the Serpentine to skaters."

Celia's expression crumbled.

Sophia glanced at the clock on the mantel. By the time she dressed and made it to the mission, Thomas might have finished seeing to the women and children there. She would take Celia skating instead. But when Hayden returned, she would speak with him. "We could venture to St. James," she said to Celia.

The child's countenance brightened. "I shall get my woolens." She dashed from the room.

Edith turned a concerned look to her, and Sophia couldn't help noticing the glance Edith cast at Sophia's abdomen. "There will be a monstrous crush, and the ice turns the children quite rambunctious. Are you certain you should attend?"

Sophia had wondered if Edith knew the true reason for Sophia and Hayden's rushed nuptials. It appeared she did, yet her voice held no censure, only concern. She gave her sister-in-law a reassuring smile. "I shall be fine. Would you care to join us?"

"No, dear, I'm expected elsewhere." Edith rubbed Sophia's forearm. "Be patient with Hayden. He is only trying to protect you. He will come around. I promise."

They had skated for over an hour when a tall, well-dressed gentleman moving toward a hirer of skates caught Sophia's attention. The man's height and broad shoulders looked familiar.

Hayden? No, it couldn't be.

Several young, boisterous boys appeared next to her and Celia. Sophia tightened her grasp on the child's hand, pulling her tighter to her side. After the boys passed, she peered at the bank. The gentleman was gone. She'd been mistaken. She couldn't envision Hayden hiring skates and taking to the ice.

"Are you tired, dearest?" Sophia asked Celia.

Celia shook her head emphatically. "No, do say we can stay a bit longer."

"Of course," she replied, slowing their pace as they neared three young women skating with their arms linked together. As they maneuvered around them, a hand pressed gently on Sophia's back.

"May I join you?" a deep, familiar voice asked.

"Papa," Celia squealed. "Have you come to skate with us?"

"How could any man resist such enchanting partners?" He winked at Celia before he smiled at Sophia.

How charming he can be at times. Sophia averted her face. She would not let his smile relinquish her anger over his earlier mandate.

"Papa, hold our hands." Celia unlocked her fingers from Sophia's.

He clasped their hands and turned his attention to his daughter. "I was watching you. You're doing splendidly."

Celia's eyes grew bright. "Do you truly think so?"

"Indeed," he replied, his tone firm with conviction.

The child's smile broadened, and she appeared more confident as she placed one foot before the other and glided next to her father.

Hayden chatted amiably with Celia. When he conversed with his daughter, his emotions were transparent. He adored her. Could this attentive man have walked away from both wife and child? When she considered his devotion to Celia, it seemed impossible he could have forsaken her. What had transpired between him and his first wife?

Hayden stroking his thumb over her gloved palm interrupted her meandering mind. Such a simple touch should have felt innocent; however, it was like a provocative caress, mimicking his finger stroking her in a much more intimate spot. She attempted to ignore him, to let her indifference convey her anger, yet she couldn't stop her awareness of him from overtaking her body.

He leaned close. His warm breath brushed against her cold cheek. "Do you know, Sophia, there is little gratification in arguing, but reconciliation can be rather pleasurable."

She wished to utter some cutting remark, something that would disabuse his notion she'd be easily placated. "I am vexed with you." A mild rebuke compared to the one she'd envisioned making. But Edith's words, along with time and his touch, dulled her anger.

"Then, I shall have to be diligent in seeking forgiveness." A low and seductive timbre edged his voice.

A frisson chased down her spine. She knew exactly what method he'd take to dissolve her anger. Did other husbands engage in such licentious acts with their wives? Did they use their mouths and tongues to make them quiver? Did other wives enjoy it so much? Her cheeks warmed, and she was relieved when Celia tugged on his arm, and he turned his perceptive blue eyes away from her.

"Papa, my toes feel like someone is pricking them with a thousand needles."

"Ah, I know the cure for such an ailment," he replied. "Hot chocolate and a warm fire."

Celia giggled. "No, I think it might take more than that. I believe I shall need some spiced gingerbread as well."

"Really? I must say, I've never heard of such a remedy." He turned to Sophia. "Madam, you are skilled in such matters. Are you aware of such a cure?"

Celia's large brown eyes implored, and Sophia couldn't help her lips from turning upward. "Yes, spiced gingerbread is a practical restorative. I have seen it prescribed numerous times."

They skated to the bank and removed their skates. In the carriage, Hayden settled next to Sophia on the plush cushion and flashed another grin as the carriage journeyed to Brook Street.

Her stomach fluttered, and she silently cursed her husband's ability to make her desire him by offering little more than a smile. He slid closer and draped his arm over the back of the seat, while his muscular thigh pressed against her leg.

Did he disconcert her on purpose? Yes. The master manipulator. The seducer.

She would not be controlled. She'd moved out from under her great-uncle's thumb to gain her independence. Hayden would not steal that away from her. She fought the urge to ram her elbow into his stomach; instead, she narrowed her eyes.

His grin broadened, and he turned to his daughter. "Let's see what we can do to warm your toes." He leaned forward and slipped off the child's half boots. With his large hands he rubbed at Celia's feet, occasionally tickling her toes, causing her to wiggle and laugh. "Better?" he asked.

"Yes, Papa." Celia yawned and rubbed at her eyes.

After tying Celia's shoes back on, Hayden moved to the seat opposite Sophia.

What was he about?

"Are your toes cold, as well, Sophia?"

Before she could answer, he reached down, lifted her left foot, and slipped off her shoe. A mischievous sparkle lit his eyes. His gaze never left her face as he skimmed his warm palm up the back of her calf.

Sparks traveled up her leg.

Wicked man.

The carriage slowed, and the brakes squeaked.

Home. Thank God. A minute more of his hands on my skin and I might beg him to forgive me. What madness. A person should not possess such power over another's body. She snatched her shoe off the seat, and, ignoring her husband, jerked it on, anxious to be away from his intense gaze and disconcerting touch.

An hour later, Sophia peered at the slumbering child sitting next to her on the settee. It had taken only three pieces of gingerbread, a half cup of hot chocolate, and the heat from the fire in the morning room to put Celia to sleep.

Only a few minutes earlier, Celia had been chattering away, asking when they could return to St. James, but now, her head rested firmly against Sophia's arm, her breathing deep and even.

Hayden, who stirred the coals in the grate, turned around. "Is she sleeping?" he whispered.

Sophia nodded. "The fresh air and the exercise have worn her out."

He carefully lifted Celia into his arms and retreated through the open doorway, his broad shoulders swallowing up the space before he passed through it.

She took another sip of her hot chocolate, now tepid. Placing the cup and saucer upon the teacart, she stood, then walked to the windows overlooking the back gardens.

Two birds fluttered around the bare branches of a birch before settling themselves atop the boxwood hedge that circled a tall lotus fountain, now void of water. How lovely this garden would be in the spring.

Sophia moved to the hearth and inched her stockinged feet toward the warm grate. She didn't appreciate Hayden's autocratic manner, but she realized his concerns were valid. Not that she believed someone would accost her again, but there was always the danger of contagions when one treated the infirmed.

She set her hand on her stomach. She loved this baby—their baby, and she'd not place it in danger.

A movement caught her attention. She peered at the doorway. Hayden leaned against the jamb, watching her. "You look miles away."

"Do I?"

"Hmm." He kneaded the back of his neck. "I'm sorry, Sophia. I shouldn't have demanded you heed me this morning, but your intention to go to Whitechapel startled me."

"Why?"

"It can be a dangerous place."

She didn't want to agree with him, but he was correct.

"Were you sincere about your offer to employ someone to assist Dr. Trimble?"

"Of course."

"Then I have decided I shall not return to the mission until after our child is born." She squared her shoulders, unsure how he would take her next words. "Though I still intend to become a physician." She held her breath.

He nodded, closed the door, and locked it.

Sophia felt like a hare under the gaze of a hungry fox. Did he wish to make love to her in this room? Anxious energy exploded in her belly.

"Celia will sleep a good while," he said, seeming to read her thoughts. He closed the distance between them with the light-footed grace of a cat.

"Do you wish to play cards, or do you have business to attend to?" she asked, taking a single step back.

"I have canceled all my appointments today, and I fear a game of cards holds little appeal at the moment." He slipped his coat off and tossed it over a chair, then pulled her close.

My goodness, there was no denying his intentions. His erection pressed against her. She contemplated pulling away and retaining her anger, but Edith's words echoed in her head. *"My brother loves you. Can you not see it in his eyes?"* Would she see what Edith spoke of in this room where no shadows lingered?

"Do you know I burn for you the moment we're apart?" His voice sounded low and raspy.

Her body warmed. Hayden swept her into his arms, set her on the hearthrug, and lay beside her. Propping himself up on an elbow, he leaned over her. His eyes were intense, dark.

She tangled her fingers in his hair and drew his lips to hers.

With a groan, Hayden slipped his tongue into her mouth while his nimble fingers made quick work of the buttons lining her jacket and dress.

She had removed her corset before she'd left to ice skate, not wishing to feel its restraining form.

He lifted his head. "Ah, Sophia, you are shockingly improper at times."

Her cheeks warmed.

He set his hands on the collar of her chemise and tore the thin fabric wide open.

She gasped. "Hayden," she chastised, even though his actions heightened her spiraling desire.

"Ah, I must atone for my haste." He released the rent cloth, cupped the bottom of her breast, and captured a nipple in his mouth.

She lowered her lashes—watched his tongue and mouth against her skin. The edge of his teeth softly scraped the sensitized bud. Excitement exploded in her belly, settling liquid heat in the most intimate and private area of her anatomy. A soft moan escaped her lips.

He stroked her nipples, soothing them with his warm tongue. He held her gaze. "Do you want me to make love to you, Sophia? Do you need me as much as I need you?"

Need? Did he mean in a carnal way or something less tangent, but ultimately stronger? Though not sure which question he asked, she knew the answer to both. She couldn't guard her heart against him. Not when he already possessed it. "Yes," she whispered, her voice throaty. Impatiently she tugged her skirts upward.

He reached for the buttons of his trousers. His hard flesh sprung forth, and he slowly sheathed himself into her welcoming body.

Chapter Twenty-Two

"I can't wait to read it," Celia said, a week later, standing in Hatchards.

Sophia returned the child's exuberant smile. The display of Walter Crane's latest illustrated book, *The Frog Prince*, had immediately caught Celia's eye when they'd entered the bookshop. Now she radiated pleasure, bobbing up and down on her toes as the clerk wrapped up the book.

"Shall we go to Madelyn's Tea House for some hot chocolate and sweet buns?" Sophia asked as they exited the shop.

Celia's eyes widened, and she nodded. As they made their way up Piccadilly, the child sang in a low voice, *"Hot cross buns. One a penny, two a penny—"* She abruptly stopped and pointed. "Look!"

A large gray Shire, nearly twenty hands, moved up the street, pulling a green dray. The cart looked heavy, better suited to being drawn by two. However, the white-stockinged horse made easy work of it.

Tugging Sophia behind her, Celia moved to the curb. "Isn't it the biggest, prettiest horse you've ever seen?"

"Quite so."

The carman, who sat on a high perch, tipped his cap at

the pedestrians gathering to gawk. A swarm of excited children jostled both Sophia and Celia before knocking Celia's hat into the street.

"My hat!"

Sophia glanced at the dray. The horse was a short distance away, but the hat lay close, well within reach. "I'll get it." Releasing Celia's hand, Sophia crouched down, outstretched her arm, and twined her fingers around the velvet rim.

A violent blow struck Sophia's back. The air exploded from her lungs. Her gloved hands skidded across the pavement as she flew into the street. Pain, like hot ash, seared her palms.

The metallic screech of the dray's brakes rent the air, along with Celia's scream. Saucer-sized hooves approached. Sophia covered her head with her arms. The Shire's iron shoes hit the pavement. The sound exploded in her ears. Dirt sprayed and prickled her exposed skin like sand-sized hail.

The heavy clopping receded—moved past. Her tense body sagged. The dray's wheel stood only inches from her. The air held tight in her lungs hissed out between her teeth.

Strong hands were on her, lifting, cradling her against a broad chest. She stared into a set of brown eyes, nearly as dark as her own.

"I hope you are not injured, Lady Westfield," the gentleman said, setting her feet to the ground. He clamped her upper arms, steadying her.

Though his voice sounded as smooth as honed marble, it sent an odd quiver of recollection up her spine. Sophia stiffened. Lord Simon Adler. The man she'd seen entering Hayden's home weeks ago. The same man who'd dared Hayden to sleep with her. Her already rolling stomach spun.

"S-Sophia, Uncle Simon!" Celia darted toward them.

Lord Adler released Sophia and effortlessly lifted Celia into his arms.

With watery eyes, Celia stared at Sophia. "I-I thought y-you were going to be trampled." Her voice broke on a sob.

"Shhh, Celia, all is well," Lord Adler murmured, cupping the back of the child's head and pressing her face to his shoulder.

Sophia tugged off her rent gloves. Her palms were abraded and small grains of dirt embedded her skin. She rubbed the grit off before running a reassuring hand down Celia's back. "I am fine, dear." Closing her eyes briefly, Sophia tried to gather her bearings. She set a hand over her abdomen, thankful the baby was still small and her hands took the brunt of her fall.

"Lady Westfield, are you going to be ill?" Lord Adler's voice radiated what sounded like genuine concern.

Before she could reply, the dray's driver appeared next to her. The man stared anxiously at her, his cap crushed between thick fingers. "Ye 'urt, mum?"

"No. I thank you for your concern and of course your skilled driving."

The man's chest expanded. "Me Finn's a great big beast, but 'e's as gentle as a new puss. Wouldn't've 'armed you for the world."

"You own the horse and dray?" Lord Adler asked.

"Aye, I do," the carman replied.

His lordship withdrew a card from his breast pocket and gave it to the man. "Come see me if you're ever in want of employment."

The man's eyes widened. "Yes, m'lord. Thank you."

Adler arched a brow, clearly dismissing the man. He shot the same haughty expression at the crowd, and they dispersed.

"I do not believe we have ever been introduced, Lady

Westfield. I'm Simon Adler. Your husband and I are old chums."

Sophia avoided his gaze by straightening her clothing. "Yes, my lord. I'm aware of that." She could not contain the brisk edge in her voice.

When she glanced up, he gave her a broad smile, quite different from the roguish one he'd flashed at her outside Hayden's house. This one seemed more honest, reaching his eyes. She had a feeling he didn't offer it too freely.

"I'd be honored if you'd allow me to accompany you and Celia home."

"I thank you, my lord, but it is unnecessary." She reached out to take Celia from him.

The smile on his face faltered. "I assure you, madam, Hayden would expect nothing less from me."

Even before Hayden's town carriage made a complete stop in front of his residence, he noted the indolent figure leaning against one of the columns of his portico. Simon Adler took a long draw on his cigarette before releasing a swirl of gray smoke into the cold air.

"Simon," Hayden said, stepping down from his equipage. What the deuce was the man doing standing outside instead of before a warm hearth?

"Remarkable woman, your wife." Simon flashed the lackadaisical grin he'd perfected. The one that made strangers think him benign.

Hayden rolled his shoulders. He would trust his friend with his own life, but he didn't favor the incorrigible bounder sniffing around Sophia's ankles.

Grinning, Simon dropped his cigarette and ground it beneath his shoe. "Relax, old boy. I enjoy having my bollocks attached to me."

Hayden motioned toward the door.

With a small shake of his head, Simon withdrew his pocket watch. "Don't have the time. Already dreadfully late for an appointment, but we need to have a chat."

His friend's tone caused the hairs on the back of Hayden's neck to stand.

"I happened upon Lady Westfield and Celia today while on Piccadilly." He paused. "Your lovely bride appeared to have stumbled and was nearly trampled by the hooves of a great big beast."

Heart beating fast, Hayden leapt the few steps to his door. "Is she hurt?"

Simon clapped a hand on his shoulder. "A bit frayed, but seriously hurt . . . no."

Hayden reached for the door handle.

"Hayden," Simon said, halting his progression. "I don't believe it was an accident."

Dread rolled in his stomach. "What do you mean?"

"There was a crowd gathered to watch a large Shire. People were moving toward the curb. Someone screamed. When I looked, I saw a lad moving quickly away from the commotion. His head was down and he wore a cap, but he glanced up—mind you it was only a second, but I'd swear it was no lad at all, but Adele Fontaine."

A cold chill flooded Hayden's body. "Kent told me he sent her away again."

"I might be mistaken." Simon rubbed his jaw. "It was only a glance, but I thought it best to tell you."

"Thank you." Hayden rushed into his foyer and shrugged himself free of his heavy overcoat. A stoic Hawthorne entered the hall, and Hayden shoved the garment into the butler's hands. "Where are my wife and daughter?"

"In your bathing room, my lord."

Taking the treads three at a time, he darted up the stairs. He stepped into his bedchamber. Celia's laugh echoed off the tiled walls of the adjacent room. The joyous sound eased the hard metal bands compressing his chest.

He entered to find Celia sitting in a bubble-filled tub, white suds piled atop her head, chin, and cheeks.

"Papa, look at me! I'm Father Christmas."

"My goodness," he replied, forcing the edges of his lips to turn up, "if you aren't his spitting image."

Giggling, Celia scooped up more bubbles and patted them onto her cheeks, thickening her faux beard.

Hayden's gaze shifted to Sophia, seated on the fringed ottoman that usually resided in his dressing room. Lady Olivia lay sprawled by Sophia's feet. The dog thumped her tail excitedly, while Sophia gave a clearly hesitant smile before starting to rise.

He stepped forward and offered his hand to assist her. She winced when he tightened his fingers and pulled her upward. He turned her palm upward and surveyed the angry red skin. He swallowed. Guilt clogged his throat. He contained the urge to slam his fist into the wall, wanting, almost needing, a tangible pain that would exceed hers.

"You heard?" she asked, her voice soft.

He took a calming breath. "Yes." He examined her other hand.

"I'm so dreadfully sorry, Hayden. Truly, I do not know what happened, but I swear I shall be more careful when I accompany Celia about."

God almighty, she thought him angry with her when it was *he* who should be horsewhipped. He pulled her to him, slipped his hand between their bodies, and touched her belly. "The baby?" he inquired sotto voce.

"My hands took the brunt of the fall. The baby is fine and Celia as well."

"Celia? She fell too?"

"No, but she was quite distraught. There was a crowd and . . . Oh, I don't know. It all happened so fast."

His gaze shifted to Celia splashing about in the tub. She looked well—better than well. He pulled his wife tighter to him, wishing to feel her heartbeat, needing its rhythmic reassurance. He should tell her what Simon told him, but he didn't wish to frighten her, and it still remained possible his friend was mistaken. He'd find out more first—confirm Adele was in Town.

"Papa, are you going to kiss Sophia?"

"Do you think it would be terribly improper of me to do so, Celia?" he asked, his eyes still on his wife.

When Celia didn't answer, he glanced at the child. She pulled on her foam-covered chin like some wizened old scholar. "I have seen Aunt Edith kiss Uncle Henry." Her eyes sparkled mischievously. "Especially when she thinks I'm not about." Celia placed her small, wet hands over her eyes. "Go on, Papa. I shan't peek."

Hayden tipped Sophia's face to his and touched his lips to hers—first gently, then with an intensity he couldn't subdue.

Celia chuckled.

He stepped back.

The child's hands still covered her eyes. However, one iris peered at them from beneath splayed fingers.

How content Celia was, even after the events of the day. Sophia made Celia happy. And whether he deserved it or not, his wife made him happy. When he'd thought her hurt, he'd feared his heart would stop. Whether he wished to admit it or not, he realized how deeply he loved his wife.

Was it all about to slip away as it had eight years ago? His stomach clenched. No, if what Simon said was true, he'd find Adele and set everything to rights. He would not allow anyone to harm his family. He'd failed Laura, but he would not fail Sophia.

"If you'll excuse me, Sophia, Celia. I have business to attend to. I'll be back shortly."

He found Hawthorne in the entry hall. "Tell Evans to bring the carriage around."

A few minutes later, Hayden hammered the brass knocker at Lord Kent's Curzon Street residence.

The sour-faced butler opened the door. "See here—" The man's reprimand died in the air, and he audibly gulped. "Lord Westfield."

So the butler remembered him. How could he forget? The last time he called here, he'd left Kent's sister, Adele, screaming and screeching like the bedlamite she was after he'd broken the relationship off.

"Where is she?" Hayden snapped, stepping into the white-tiled entry hall.

"She's not here. If you wish to leave your card, I shall make sure Mrs. Fontaine receives it when she returns from holiday."

Westfield narrowed his eyes.

"Really, my lord." The butler took several precarious steps back, and then straightened his form.

"Billows, what the devil is all this raucous about?" Halfway up the central corridor, Lord Kent poked his balding head out of a doorway. "Oh heavens!" Kent disappeared back into the room.

Hayden stalked past the butler. He stepped into Kent's study to find the man pouring himself a glass of whisky with an unsteady hand. The baron glanced up, his face a pasty shade of white.

"Where's Adele?"

"Westfield, I-I assure you she is not here. After your last letter informing me she approached you at Lord Prescott's, I took her to Dover myself and w-w-watched her and Finnegan, the new man I hired to take care of her, board the ship. I swear, I've not seen h-hide nor hair of her since. And if she'd run away Finnegan would have sent w-w-word."

Kent's propensity to stammer always took a turn for the worse when the man became nervous. If he was hiding his sister, he damn well better be terrified.

"Someone thought they saw her on Piccadilly."

Kent's pale complexion turned sallow. "Impossible."

Hayden stepped closer. "Damn you, Kent, if you're lying to me."

Whisky sloshed on Kent's sleeve and his overly large Adam's apple bobbed convulsively. "I am not. I do not wish her here anymore than you do, Westfield. I would have committed her years ago if not for the scandal."

"If you hear from her, I want to be the first to know. Or so help me . . ."

"Of course. I have been the recipient of Adele's cruelty since we were children. There is no love between us. In truth, I believed myself rid of her when she married Fontaine, but the bloody bastard had to go and die."

That statement set off an alarm in Hayden's head. Fontaine, a French diplomat, had drowned while on holiday with Adele on some remote island.

A bead of sweat trickled down Hayden's back. He rushed out of Kent's house.

"Evans," he called to his coachman. "The Bacchus Club."

The servant's eyes grew round at the mention of the private club that catered to men and women with fetishes.

"Damnation," he snapped, agitated by the censure in the coachman's countenance. "Just take me there, fast." Hopefully, Simon was mistaken and Adele remained on the Continent, but in case he was right, Hayden needed to visit Adele's haunts.

If she wasn't there, he'd head to the Sade Club, where flagellation and rough play were in favor, and tonight, after Sophia went to bed, he'd delve into the seedier parts of London and scour every opium smoking room he could find.

A disturbing thought bubbled up in his mind like noxious gas from a cesspit. Beckett—the man who'd attacked Sophia in Whitechapel—could he have been Adele's lackey? No, the idea seemed too preposterous to give credence. Nevertheless, first thing tomorrow, he'd go to Newgate Prison and question the man. And by God, he'd have the truth.

Chapter Twenty-Three

Sophia tried not to tap her foot or smooth the tablecloth before her. She'd done both a dozen times as she and Celia sat at the dining table waiting for Hayden to return home.

Celia fidgeted with one of her spoons and restlessly kicked at the leg of the chair next to hers. Surely, not fair to make the child wait to eat dinner.

She turned to Hawthorne. "Will you start serving, please?"

"I'm sure his lordship will be here shortly," the butler replied.

Celia's stomach rumbled.

"I believe we are past the point of waiting. There seems to be a hungry beast in Lady Celia's stomach."

Celia giggled.

The butler nodded, and within ten minutes, an army of footmen entered the room carrying silver serving dishes.

As they ate, Sophia continued to glance at the door. Unease crept up her spine. Had Hayden forgotten they were to eat an early dinner, so they could attend a play at Royal Albert Hall—their first *public* venue together?

"Papa promised to read *Alice's Adventures in Wonderland* to me before you and he went out tonight."

Sophia pushed her bowl of raspberries away and stood. "If you wish, I will read it to you."

"Do you know how to do all the voices?" Celia asked.

"The voices?"

"Yes, the Queen of Hearts and the March Hare?"

"I can try." Sophia took Celia's hand and led her up the stairs to the nursery.

After Celia washed and slipped on her nightgown, they settled on the bed, and Sophia read. Near the end of the book, she glanced up from the page.

Hayden stood in the doorway. A raw tension emanated from him. He looked as tightly wound as a boxed devil about to spring. Did he blame her for her earlier mishap? Or, like Great-Uncle Charles, did he now think her clumsy and less refined than the women in his social circle? Or did he fear, as she did, she'd become a magnet for mayhem?

"Papa!" Celia exclaimed as he stepped fully into the bedchamber. "Where have you been? You promised to read to me before you and Sophia went out."

His gaze slid to Sophia's face, and a sharp pain lanced her heart. He'd clearly forgotten their plans.

"I'm sorry, Celia," he said. "A business meeting kept me longer than expected."

A lie. She'd checked his appointment book earlier, and he'd cleared his schedule.

"That's fine, Papa. Sophia does the Queen of Hearts's voice even better than you."

The tautness edging his face eased a little. "Ah, does she now?" He set his hand on Sophia's shoulder and gave it a slight squeeze before taking the book from her. "How are you feeling, Sophia?"

"I am well."

"You look exhausted. Why don't you retire early? I shall finish the book."

She gave Celia a kiss and headed for the door.

"Sophia," he called after her.

She turned back.

"I'm sorry we missed the play."

Are you? She wanted to ask, but she would not do so in front of Celia. She acknowledged his apology with a brief nod and left the room.

In their bedchamber, Sophia dressed for bed, then paced the floor. She would confront him. Ask him why he'd not accompanied her to the theater. Was he ashamed of her because she wasn't a member of the nobility?

An hour passed.

Sophia slipped her wrapper over her nightgown and went to the nursery. Celia slept soundly.

She ventured downstairs. Light streamed from beneath Hayden's study door. Stiffening her spine, she stepped into the room.

Not here.

"He's gone out, madam," Hawthorne said, striding toward her.

Where did a man go at night? Was he out with his rakehell friends? Up to no good? She pulled her robe tighter around her body.

"Thank you, Hawthorne." She dashed back upstairs and crawled between the bedding. Arms folded across her chest, she leaned against the headboard. When her husband returned, she would ask him where he'd gone off to.

Sophia awoke to a cold, empty bed. Rolling onto her back, she slipped her hands over her abdomen.

Curse Hayden for making her love him. And curse

him for lying. Business meeting her foot. What had she expected from such a man? God knew what time he'd returned home last night. She'd fallen asleep before she could confront him.

Thomas's words about how Hayden abandoned his first wife only weeks after Celia's birth and acted the rogue drifted through her mind. Was history now repeating itself? Well, she wouldn't play the martyr, if he'd gone back to his wicked ways. She would return to Chelsea. Mrs. MacLean and the dailies, tasked with boxing and packing her belongings, were still there. When they were finished, Hayden had offered them employment, even Mrs. MacLean. She would send a note, telling them to unpack everything. She'd return to her home on Cheyne Walk.

Celia's sweet face floated in her mind's eye. What would she say to the child? She'd be no better than Hayden, giving love then snatching it away. Sophia curled her fingers against her palms until her nails bit into her still raw skin. Her conscience would not permit her to abandon the child. And though Hayden left Laura after Celia's birth, Sophia believed he would not allow her to leave with his unborn baby, perhaps his heir. She would move into the bedchamber next door. She'd been a fool to trust him—to give him her heart.

After completing her toilette, Sophia descended the stairs, ready to confront Hayden. She noticed the tightness on Hawthorne's face as he stood in the entry hall. His expression, along with the fact she'd awoken to the solitude of an empty bed, told her Hayden had once again vanished.

"He has gone out?" She forced her voice to remain even.

"Yes, madam. He left a note." He handed her a sealed missive.

She stared at the dark strokes that spelled out her name before inquiring about Celia's whereabouts.

Hawthorne's somber expression lightened. "She went to the kitchen, not fifteen minutes ago. She wished to know if Monsieur Laurent would bake Lady Olivia some dog biscuits."

"Oh, my," Sophia gasped, wondering how the Frenchman would take to such a degrading request.

"My thoughts, exactly," Hawthorne responded. "But there was no dissuading her."

With the missive still clutched in her hand, Sophia gathered up the sides of her skirts and hastily made her way belowstairs.

She breathed a sigh of relief at the sight that greeted her.

Celia knelt on one of the chairs that surrounded the massive wooden table, pouring water from a small ironware pitcher onto a floury mixture, while the chef graced her with a benevolent smile.

"Just a little more, *ma petite*," he instructed Celia as he enthusiastically kneaded the wet and dry ingredients together.

Celia nodded.

"Zees biscuits were a favorite of Emperor Napoleon zee third's basset hounds," the Frenchman announced proudly.

Celia peered up at him, her eyes wide with unabashed pleasure. "Do you think the royal chef makes these biscuits for the queen's dogs?"

He clucked his tongue, the sound distinct and crisp. "I am zee only one who knows zis recipe."

She beamed. "Lady Olivia is most fortunate, Monsieur Laurent." The chef's chest seemed to expand with each word the child spoke. Obviously, Celia had discerned flattery was the key to the man's heart.

Unnoticed, Sophia turned and made her way back up the servants' stairway. She slipped into Hayden's study, opened the envelope, and read her husband's bold hand.

Sophia,

I have an early meeting. I ask that you remain home today. I shall endeavor to return as early as possible.

Your devoted husband,
Hayden

Devoted husband. Ha! She crumbled the missive with hands that shook. Why in heaven's name should she wait about while he was . . . was . . . ? She moved to the fireplace and tossed the note atop the cooling gray ash dotted with flecks of orange embers. Smoke darkened its crisp edges before it burst to flame.

Seething, she stalked to the desk, intent on writing a scathing retort. She pulled on the center drawer, only to find it locked.

Her eyes surveyed the mahogany surface before settling on the French inlaid desk tray. She lifted the inkwell, revealing a key. "Too obvious, Hayden." She slipped it into the keyhole of the center drawer. The lock gave a soft *click*.

Sophia sat and opened the drawer. An assortment of neatly placed ledgers stared up at her. She slammed the door closed, then unlocked the top right drawer and opened it. A crisp stack of parchment embossed with Hayden's noble emblem and bound with elaborate ribbon lay in it. She lifted it and peered beneath, hoping to find plain stationery, but instead she found a small navy journal with gold-embossed lettering. HAYDEN JAMES MILTON, VISCOUNT MASON.

She stared at it. Hayden's journal. The lesser title dated it to an earlier time.

Mason? The familiarity of the name hit her as soundly as if someone had conked her on the head rattling her brain into sensibility. If she inverted the initials it would read J. H. Mason—the wholesaler and the mission's most generous benefactor. Could it be?

After placing the journal on the desk, she reopened the center drawer. She pulled the ledgers out and read them. Wincombe Manor, Westfield Hall, River Spey Distillery, Magniess Brewery.

Magniess Brewery? Did Hayden own Magniess Brewery? The writing was unfamiliar, yet the bold notations scratched into the margins were his.

How inane he must have thought her when she'd questioned if he teetered near financial straits. Pubs across Great Britain and beyond sold Magniess Ale. It shipped as far as Africa.

She looked at the next ledger. J. H. Mason. Her heartbeat escalated as she opened it and flipped through the pages containing her husband's writing in the notations. She closed it and ran her fingers over its leather binding. Why had he acted with such disdain toward Mason, when it appeared they were one and the same person?

Was Edith responsible for the donations? Had she coerced Hayden into giving them?

Her mind still dancing about, Sophia looked down at the near empty drawer. A small leather hinged case peered up at her. Slowly she lifted it. Her already tumultuous stomach leapt as she opened it, exposing a gold-framed miniature portrait of a woman one could only describe as breathtaking. Sophia's finger traced the filigreed edge of the frame, while she studied the woman's flaxen hair, blue eyes, and her pink bow-shaped mouth.

Sophia touched her own wide mouth, so different from the subject's delicate one. Great-Uncle Charles would have deemed the young woman the perfect example of English beauty.

Bang! The front door slammed, rattling the sturdy walls of the ground floor.

Hayden?

Of course. No one else would have the audacity to shut the door with such violence. Sophia quickly returned the portrait and ledgers, slid the drawers shut, and locked them. She placed the key beneath the inkwell.

Footfalls approached. She stepped around the desk and froze when the glint from the golden letters of Hayden's journal brazenly reflected the light from the desk lamp. Heart pounding, she turned her back to the door and slipped the little navy book into the side pocket of her skirt.

The study door swung open.

Sophia spun around.

Hayden entered the room, his expression dark and ominous.

Chapter Twenty-Four

Hayden stepped into his study and froze at the sight of Sophia standing before his desk. He forced a smile. Difficult to do, since his visit to Newgate had offered no answers.

After arriving at the gaol, the warder informed him that yesterday Beckett attacked a guard in the exercise yard. For his imprudence, the man received a severe flogging. Too severe. This morning Beckett's body lay cold and hard. A day ago, the miscreant's demise would have pleased him, but not now, not when he sought answers.

"Sophia?"

She stepped away from the desk. "Hawthorne gave me your note. I slipped in here to read it."

The paleness of Sophia's cheeks unsettled him. "Are you unwell?"

"No, you startled me."

He nodded and closed the door. For a moment, he could do nothing more than drink her in. The thought of holding her lightened his dark mood.

"Might I ask where you went so early this morning?" She smoothed a hand down her blue day dress.

Best to tell her the truth. And what would that be? That

he'd gone to the prison to ask the man who'd abducted Sophia if Adele Fontaine hired him. That the deranged woman, an ex-lover of his, might have pushed Sophia in front of the carriage on Piccadilly. That Adele was the same lunatic who'd shot him.

He'd found no proof Adele hid in Town, and Kent was adamant his sister remained on the Continent under the watchful eye of Finnegan. Simon was probably mistaken. But to ensure Sophia's safety, Hayden had hired Varga to help him locate Adele and keep surveillance on Hayden's residence. Right now, the investigator's men guarded both the front and rear of the house. Sophia was safe as long as she remained home. He'd not frighten her unnecessarily. "A business meeting."

"Another meeting? So early?" She frowned.

"Hmmm," he mumbled, drawing her into his arms, shaping his mouth to hers, and silencing her questions that made him feel no better than a lying slug. He noted her resistance, an unmistakable tautness in her body.

Was she still angry he'd forgotten their engagement yesterday? Yes, of course. He would make it up to her. Take her to every bloody play London offered, if she desired. But first, he needed to confirm Adele's whereabouts.

"You have reason to be angry with me," he whispered, trailing kisses down her neck while his hands traveled over her waist and hips. He touched something hard in her pocket—a small book.

Abruptly she took a step back. "Why would you think me displeased?" The clipped tone of her voice belied the calm expression on her face.

"I acted thoughtlessly yesterday. I should have sent word that my meeting would detain me, not only for dinner but for most of the evening."

"And last night?"

Blast it all. He should have made sure she'd fallen asleep before going out to search Adele's haunts again.

"Hayden?" She crossed her arms over her chest.

Damnation, he could not continue lying to her. Secrets had destroyed his first marriage. He'd not allow them to destroy this one. "Sophia, I need to tell you something."

As if weak, she grasped the back of a chair. Her knuckles turned white and the color drained from her face.

His gut clenched. Holding her waist, he steadied her. "Are you going to faint? Is it the baby?"

"No, I-I didn't sleep well . . . that's all. What do you wish to tell me?"

He should wait one more day to tell her what Simon thought he saw. Sophia looked too pale. His mother had miscarried two children. No, he would not terrify her when she appeared so fragile. He would protect her. "We'll talk later."

"If you have something you wish to say, Hayden, please do so now."

"It can wait. You should lie down."

"No, I have agreed to accompany Edith on a few calls. She wishes society to see her acceptance of me."

Hayden strode to the stand-mounted globe and slowly spun it. He couldn't allow her to gallivant about with Edith, not when even the slightest possibility remained Adele had tried to harm her. "I have cleared my schedule. I thought you and I might spend the day together. Please send Edith your regrets."

"But I have already told Edith I would go."

He walked to his desk and snatched up his pen. "If you won't write her, I shall, dear."

"First you tell me I cannot got to Whitechapel. Now you insist I not accompany Edith." With a disgruntled noise, she pivoted and headed to the door.

Better she be agitated with him and safe. He moved to

stand before her. A nearly palpable anger radiated from her, warming her skin, filling his nostrils with her lavender scent. "I wish you to remain home and rest because you are pale. I am concerned about you."

She averted her gaze.

"Look at me," he whispered. When she didn't comply, he embraced her, nibbled the sensitive skin of her neck while he captured the weight of her breast and drew his thumb over its peak. Her nipple hardened into a sweet bud. She may be vexed, but her body was not immune to his touch.

"Please, let me go."

Reluctantly he released her.

She turned away and left the room. He took a step to go after her, but Hawthorne appeared in the doorway. "Mr. Ambrus Varga is here, my lord."

Hayden raked a hand through his hair. "Send him in."

The butler nodded.

"Hawthorne," he called after the man. "Should my wife ask for her carriage to be harnessed, inform her the axle is in need of repair."

"Yes, my lord."

Hayden walked around his desk and sat.

The private investigator's normally unfathomable expression conveyed apprehension as he entered the room. "I've been unable to gather any information on Mrs. Fontaine's whereabouts, m'lord."

"Then what the bloody hell are you doing here, man?" Hayden gritted his teeth.

Varga combed his fingers through his left muttonchop. "I wished to make you aware I've sent several men to the ports, most to Dover, to scour passenger lists and check hotel registries, and a man to Calais to confirm Mrs. Fontaine is still in the French city with her caretaker."

"If you haven't done so, I want continuous surveillance outside her brother's residence."

"Already done, m'lord. I shall keep you updated." The man moved to the door.

Hayden scrubbed a hand over his jaw. "Varga."

The investigator pivoted on his heels. "Yes, m'lord."

"What's the name of your man stationed in front of my house?"

"Dillard, m'lord."

"Proficient with a pistol?"

"Of course. Dillard is one of my best men, as is Higgins, who is guarding the rear of the residence."

"Good. I'm starting to think Lord Adler was mistaken, but my mind is eased knowing they are here."

"Understandable, m'lord. Understandable. Your wife is well protected under the watchful eye of my men."

Hayden sighed. Sophia talked amiably to Celia as they completed their luncheon. His wife had spoken barely three words to him, and if looks were lethal, he'd be lying in a silk-lined box.

He couldn't blame her. No doubt, she thought him a dictator. But she remained safe, and for that he would not regret his imperious decision. He would spend the day with her and hopefully make her forget her anger. Hayden reached across the white tablecloth and captured her hand in his.

She shot him another malignant glare. Then, discreet as a vicar eyeing a woman's diddeys, she lowered their hands below the table and attempted to disengage them with several futile tugs.

Celia scraped the last remaining bit of blancmange from her custard cup and spooned the dessert into her mouth.

"Papa," she said, folding her hands before her, "may I be excused? Ginger and I are to play a rousing game of cards after we work on my sums."

The only Ginger he knew worked as a chambermaid. He arched an eyebrow at Sophia.

"I hope you don't mind, *my lord*," Sophia said. "I asked Ginger to spend time with Celia today. You have yet to hire a governess."

Hayden could practically taste the censure and condemnation in her voice.

"I did not believe you would find it objectionable," she continued, "since Ginger is in possession of a pleasant disposition and reads exceedingly well."

He glanced at Celia's expectant face. "Go on, dear."

"Thank you, Papa." Celia pushed back her chair and darted out of the room.

The sweet expression on Sophia's face evaporated. "I thought I wouldn't be home today and when Celia is left alone, she is bored witless. I know Mrs. Beecham would gladly look after her; nevertheless the woman lacks sufficient time to give Celia the attention she should receive." She sighed. "I greatly fear Celia will be married before *you* engage a new governess."

Hayden peered at the footman who stood silently by the sideboard. "Peter, you may be excused."

Wide-eyed, Sophia's gaze swung to the retreating servant. Apparently, she'd forgotten his presence.

"Shrewishness does not become you, Sophia."

"It does not," she readily agreed, "but neither does bullying and autocracy become you, *my lord*."

He ignored her repeated use of *my lord* as if he were no better than something one found pickled in a laboratory jar. "You shall be pleased to know, *my sweet*, that I narrowed the candidates for governess down to three. The final interviews should have taken place the day after we married. I delayed them. I wanted you and Celia to become better acquainted. I hoped you would take part in the final interview and gauge which candidate would suit Celia best. I happen to value your judicious opinion in this matter, above my own."

Only the momentary lapse in her taut expression betrayed her surprise, but she said nothing more than a mumbled "thank you," while staring at her uneaten blancmange.

Hayden frowned. He knew the custard to be a favorite of hers, reminding her of the cooked cream, flavored with hazelnut, she'd told him she'd eaten as a child.

The sound of Sophia's chair sliding back drew him out of his thoughts.

"Now, if you will excuse me." She tugged her hand free. "I have pressing matters to attend to—such as staring at the walls while drumming my fingers restlessly upon some polished surface."

He was tempted to carry his incensed wife upstairs and suggest an altogether different activity she could put her restless fingers to. But since he didn't relish looking like he'd tangled with an angry feline, he'd wait until her anger cooled.

A half hour later, Hayden strode to the morning room. He rubbed the tight muscles in his neck. One of Sophia's massages would relieve the tension, but she might just strangle him instead. Releasing a heavy breath, he stepped into the room. Sophia sat by the fire, her hands placed protectively over her abdomen. Her face remained pale.

The contents of his luncheon churned in his stomach. "Sophia?"

She glanced up at him, then redirected her gaze to the hearth.

He placed his hand over hers where it rested on her belly. "Sophia, would you like your feet rubbed?"

"No."

"Anything else rubbed?" He winked.

Her almond eyes grew round. She looked at him as if he'd sprouted two heads and asked her to parade down the street naked. Definitely not the reaction he wanted.

A tap on the door drew his attention. "Yes, come in."

Hawthorne entered the room. "Reverend Mosely is here and wishing to speak with you, my lord."

What the deuce does that windbag want? "Send him away."

Sophia arched a brow at him.

Hayden sighed. "Never mind, show him to the drawing room." Leaning close, Hayden brushed his hand over Sophia's arm. "After Mosely leaves, if your color has returned, I will take you to Edith's."

Her eyes widened. "To call on her friends?"

"Perhaps you can do that another time." Hayden bent down and gave her a long kiss. "I shall be quick."

Sophia slipped out of the morning room and into Hayden's study. Though she'd not read Hayden's journal it burned in her pocket like a devil's temptation. Best to lock it away. Thank goodness, the gabby Reverend Mosely would distract her husband long enough for her to return it.

She withdrew the diary. Voices in the corridor moved closer—Hawthorne's and a member of the staff. Were they looking for her? She fumbled with the little book, hastily tried to shove it back into her pocket. It snagged on the material and tumbled to the floor. Hawthorne paused outside the door. She clasped her hands together, waited for him to knock, but the voices receded.

Exhaling sharply, she crouched to pick up the journal, which had landed with the front cover open, revealing an inscription. Not written in Hayden's hand, but a swirling feminine script.

To my beloved Hayden, on this our wedding day. I give you not only my undying love, but this journal, so you may record your thoughts as we pass the days of our lives together.

Your ever affectionate and loving wife,
Laura

Startled by the potency of the woman's words—the evidence of her fidelity and love—Sophia stared at the exquisite writing until the letters blurred beneath a veil of tears.

Laura had loved him. Dearly, and he'd abandoned her. How could he have cast her aside and so callously flaunted his infidelities? His actions spoke of cruelness.

She drew her fingers over the blue satin ribbon that marked a page. She opened the book, expecting the journal to be blank. However, the parchment was not a sea of white.

September 27, 1867

Tonight as I write in this book, my heart is full, for today I felt life stirring in Laura's womb. How can I express the emotions that besiege a humble man during something so profound? Eloquence escapes me, for my love for my wife and my contentment eclipse even the power of the written word.

The tears pooling in Sophia's eyes overflowed.

He had returned Laura's regard. Loved her.

A tear splashed onto the bottom of the page. It spread, darkening the parched surface like a droplet of India ink.

She snapped the book closed, feeling like an intruder—an emotional voyeur, glimpsing something too private. With haste, borne on the breath of guilt and shame, she removed the key, slipped the diary back under the stationery, locking it away.

As she made her way upstairs, she found it difficult not to ponder either Hayden's or Laura's written words. What had happened to their love? And if he was capable of abandoning Laura, when he'd loved her so dearly, where did that leave Sophia?

Outside the drawing room, she listened to Reverend Mosely. It sounded as if the man was giving a Sunday sermon.

Releasing a heavy sigh, she made her way to their bedchamber. Sophia swung her wool cape over her shoulders before dashing down the stairs.

"Are you going out, my lady?" Hawthorne inquired.

Whether Hayden wished it or not, she intended to go to Edith's residence. Not to accompany her on any social calls, but to see if her sister-in-law would help her understand the past and the enigmatic man, now her husband.

"Yes, I'm going to call on Lady Prescott. After Reverend Mosely leaves, please inform his lordship where I've gone."

The butler's normally stoic countenance softened. "I am sorry, my lady, his lordship told me your carriage is in need of repairs."

"I shall walk." She inched her gloves over her abraded palms and stepped out of the house. A stocky man, dressed in a gray sack suit, casually leaned against a lamppost, a newspaper tucked beneath his arm. His posture stiffened upon seeing her. For a moment, she believed he waited for her, but he gave his newspaper a perfunctory shake and lifted it before his face.

A mere twenty minutes later, Sophia arrived at Edith's residence and the butler showed her to the drawing room.

"Sophia, I'm delighted to see you are well," Edith said, sitting next to Sophia on the gold settee. "Hayden's note worried me." Her sister-in-law's visage turned contemplative, and her smile wavered. "Though, I must say, you do look wan, dear. We should make our calls another day."

Sophia released a taut breath. "Yes, that would be best."

A maid entered the room, placed a tea service before Edith, and left.

"Edith, I hate to impose upon you, but—"

"Dear, you could never impose."

Sophia hoped her sister-in-law would retain that sentiment after she inquired into Hayden's past. "I wish to ask you about several things."

"Yes, dear." Edith leaned over the tea tray to pour.

Fearful she'd lose her courage, Sophia barreled forward. "I wish to know what happened between Hayden and his first wife, Laura. What caused their estrangement?"

The delicate cup and saucer in Edith's hand rattled, and she placed them back upon the tray. "Has someone said something?"

Sophia shook her head. "No. I shall be honest with you, as I hope you will be with me. I found an old journal belonging to Hayden. A gift to him from Laura." She twisted her hands together. "There was an inscription from Laura. She clearly loved him. I know I should not have read any of it, but . . ." Sophia averted her gaze. "I opened the journal to the marked page."

"Oh, Sophia." A gentle trace of censure infused Edith's voice.

"I know it is no excuse, but I thought the pages would

be blank. I found it difficult to envision Hayden keeping a diary." She ran her fingers over the napkin on her lap. "I read only one entry, nothing more. I know that does not absolve me."

"And you were surprised by what you read?"

"Yes. I believed the marriage loveless. I heard Hayden came to Town only weeks after Celia's birth. That he took lovers. That he was less than discreet."

Edith's face flushed. "It's best you ask Hayden these questions. It is not my place—"

"Do you truly believe he would answer them?"

"Perhaps."

Sophia thought of the ledger proving Hayden owned J. H. Mason. "Why? Because he is so forthright or because you have the false illusion he loves me?"

"He does love you."

"Edith, this morning, Hayden forbade me to accompany you. He said it was because I looked pale, but I don't think that was it. Then later, he mentioned he'd take me to visit you, but still reiterated he didn't wish me to pay any calls. Do you think he is embarrassed because I'm not a member of the nobility?"

"Phfft. Surely, you don't believe that. Laura wasn't a member."

"Yes, and we know what happened there."

Edith shook her head adamantly. "That was not the cause. It's quite complicated, my dear. And since I am sworn to secrecy, I cannot reveal the whole sordid affair. Go home. Talk to Hayden." Edith curled her fingers around Sophia's hand. "He has taken his vows seriously. If he hears of your concern, he might reveal what transpired."

She wasn't quite sure what Edith spoke of, but the woman's eyes turned teary. "I will, Edith. Thank you."

Her sister-in-law hugged her, and Sophia took her leave.

Making her way down Upper Brook Street, Sophia

pulled her cape tighter about her neck to ward off the cold winter air. What was the secret Edith spoke of? When she arrived home, she would ask Hayden. It would be terribly uncomfortable, but Edith was right, she needed to know.

She stopped at an intersection as a carriage took the turn. Restlessly she glanced about at the other pedestrians strolling up the street and those waiting for the carriage to pass. A little girl and her nursemaid stood behind her. The child cradled a bisque doll. With a whimsical smile, the child lifted the toy toward Sophia.

The nursemaid pressed the doll back against the child's chest. "Leave the lady alone, Doris, she's not interested."

The child's lower lip protruded.

Sophia smiled at the girl. "But such a lovely doll begs to be admired."

The nursemaid sniffled, and Sophia glanced at her. But it was not the woman's sour expression that caught her attention, but the man standing behind her. The same man she'd observed outside Hayden's town house, the one dressed in a sack suit and holding a newspaper. Their eyes met, and he averted his gaze.

An uneasy sensation crawled up her spine. Without waiting for the carriage to clear the corner, she dashed behind it and crossed the street. Behind her, the little girl began to cry, and the nursemaid exclaimed, "You deuced brute. Look what you've gone and done!"

Sophia peered over her shoulder. The vexed woman stood in front of the man, hands braced on her hips, while the poor child wept as she stared down at her doll lying by her feet. Red-faced, the man started to push past the nursemaid, but the woman angrily grabbed his sleeve.

Seizing the opportunity, Sophia hastily made her way down the street. Near the entrance to a mews, a closed carriage pulled up beside her.

The equipage's door opened. A fair woman, garbed in a silk day dress that matched the vibrant green color of her eyes, smiled. "Lady Westfield."

The appearance of someone who knew her, most likely one of Thomas's patients, eased her growing apprehension.

The woman arched a brow. "You don't remember me, do you?"

"No, I'm sorry. You look familiar, but I can't place where we met," Sophia replied, casting a glance up the street to the man. Having extracted himself from the irate nursemaid, he moved toward her.

"I'm a dear friend of Hayden's." The green-eyed woman's attention shifted to the man. She opened the carriage door wider. "May I offer you a lift?"

Even from this distance, Sophia discerned the dark expression on the man's face as he shoved through the pedestrians. She climbed in, and the woman rapped on the roof.

"What is coming to the world when a lady cannot walk about without being accosted by some ruffian?" The woman motioned to the fellow now shouting for them to halt. "You don't know him, do you?"

"No. I fear he was following me."

The woman tugged the back shade down. "He's most likely a reporter. The scandal sheets plague poor Hayden to death."

"I had not thought of that. You must be right." Relief settled over Sophia, and she studied the woman seated across from her. The hem of the woman's costly gown appeared dirty and her foot tapped nervously on the floor. "I'm sorry," Sophia said. "You have me at a disadvantage. You are?"

"Adele, dear. Mrs. Adele Fontaine."

Chapter Twenty-Five

A nerve ticked in Hayden's jaw. He glanced at the mantel clock. Dash it all, Reverend Moseley had talked nonstop for over an hour.

Impatient to return to Sophia, Hayden pushed himself out of his chair. "Sounds feasible, Mosely. I'm more than willing to help fund the restoration of the bell tower."

The clergyman blinked. "But I haven't given you all the specifics."

If he let the man continue rambling they might be here until midnight. "No need, sir. You've convinced me already. I'll send a check tomorrow."

Mosely stood. "Will I see you and your lovely wife at Sunday services this week?"

At this point, he'd promise the man anything to get him to leave. "Indeed."

The reverend smiled.

In the entry hall, Hayden jerked the front door open.

Setting his bowler hat on his head, the clergyman stepped out and into his carriage. As Hayden closed the door, he noticed the man tasked with guarding the front of the town house running up the pavement, huffing and puffing. Dillard braced his hands on his knees and tried to catch his breath.

Good Lord, had the man seen Adele? The muscles in Hayden's back knotted. "Did you see her?"

Dillard's mottled face paled. "You mean she hasn't returned?"

"What the hell are you talking about?" he demanded, talking above the sudden hammering in his chest.

"Your wife, my lord. Lady Westfield . . ."

As Dillard spoke, the pounding in Hayden's chest grew, resonating until it filled his ears, obliterating bits and pieces of the man's words. But he heard: "Upper Brook Street," "carriage," "hard to see, but the woman looked like the picture of Mrs. Fontaine."

Christ! Adele has Sophia.

With no time to wait for his carriage to be harnessed, Hayden ran down the street, searching for a hackney. Finding one, he leapt into it. "Curzon Street," Hayden shouted. "Fast!"

He closed his eyes and prayed that when he opened them, he would find himself in bed, Sophia beside him. But the carriage's swaying obliterated hope that this was a dream. No, he'd stepped into a nightmare of his own making. He should have stayed with Sophia. Never left her side. Leaning forward, he braced his face in his hands, and listened to the sound of thundering hooves, the jangling of the harnesses, and the cabby's voice urging the horses to a faster pace. He needed something to focus upon, something to stop the fear within him from festering—rendering him useless.

"Stop here!" he shouted as the carriage neared Lord Kent's residence. Hayden jumped out. "Wait," he said to the driver.

Hayden pounded on the front door. As it opened, he pushed it inward. Caught off balance, the butler stumbled backward. Hayden stormed down the hall and into Kent's study.

Adele's brother, seated behind his desk, jumped to his feet.

"I must warn you, Kent, I'm a hair's breadth away from madness. Have you seen your sister?"

"No." Kent gave a nervous shake of his head.

Hayden grabbed a piece of paper off the man's desk and slammed it in front of him. "I want a list of every bloody piece of property you own. Start with London first, work your way outward."

"Westfield, I tell you m-my sister wouldn't take lodging at any of them."

He stepped forward and slammed his fisted hand on the man's desk.

Swallowing, Kent grabbed his pen and frantically jotted addresses down. When done, he handed Hayden the paper.

Damnation, the man was a bloody slumlord, no better than Crossingham or any of the other men who housed the poor in substandard ratholes.

He noted the Little Marlie Row address halfway down the list, the same address where he and Trimble had found Sophia, where that monster Beckett had taken her. His breath seized in his lungs.

He jabbed his finger at the paper. "This is yours?" he asked, his voice raw, incredulous.

Kent stared at where he pointed, and then shook his head. "No, I shouldn't have written that one. Sold it a couple of months ago to a chap called—"

"Beckett?"

Kent's eyes grew wide. "Y-yes. How'd you know?"

"Does Adele know him?"

"I don't believe so. The man's a c-common thug. Deals in opium down in Spitalfields and Whitechapel."

Uttering a curse, Hayden raced from the room.

As the hackney made its way to the East End, dread filled Hayden's mind drawing him near the edge of hopelessness.

Please, God, let Sophia be safe.

As soon as Adele Fontaine's carriage turned away from Brook Street, Sophia realized something was amiss. "Madam, I . . ."

Grinning, Adele withdrew a pistol from beneath her skirts.

Sophia's heart pounded in her chest. "I don't understand."

"No?" Adele's green eyes narrowed. "He doesn't love you."

Suddenly, Sophia recalled where she'd seen Adele. Edith's fundraiser. The woman Hayden had appeared displeased to see.

Adele smiled. Then, as though delighted with some humorous joke, she giggled and burst into euphoric laughter. "I know why Hayden didn't tell the police I shot him. My buffoon of a brother said it was because Hayden didn't want the incident played out in the newspapers, but the truth is Hayden loves me. I'm sure he didn't want me sent away."

A chill ran up Sophia's spine. This woman had shot Hayden. Adele Fontaine was mad. Sophia peered out the side window. They were in the East End, traveling on Whitechapel High Street.

The woman's laughter ceased. The carriage interior grew quiet. A fine sheen of perspiration grew on Adele's creamy skin and the pistol began to tremble. Adele made a noise like a wounded animal and pressed a palm to her stomach while beads of sweat trickled down the side of the woman's pale face.

"Mrs. Fontaine, you are not well. Will you allow my employer, Dr. Trimble, to examine you? He could give you something to alleviate your obvious distress."

The morose expression on Adele's face cleared, and she gave another discordant laugh. "You'd favor that, wouldn't you? If you think I'll be locked away in some asylum run by religious zealots and moral reformers, it is you who is insane. Bad enough my brother hired that Mr. Finnegan to watch me. I don't need a caretaker, and Finnegan learned that the hard way. He won't be bothering anyone else. Ever."

My God . . . "Did you—"

"Be quiet!" Adele rubbed her temple. "My head is pounding and your voice nauseates me. How poor Hayden tolerates it is beyond me."

"I—"

Adele leaned forward and pressed the pistol to Sophia's chest. "One more word from you and I shall immediately do Hayden the favor of disposing of you."

The carriage rocked to a stop and swayed as the driver jumped down from his perch. The door opened, and Sophia recognized the archway that led to Little Marlie Row. She swallowed the thickness in her throat. So her abduction had not been some random twist of fate. Adele had orchestrated it.

"Out," the woman snapped.

After descending the carriage, Adele jabbed the muzzle into Sophia's back, and they moved toward the entrance.

When Beckett had forced her in there, the gloom of evening had marred the complete bleakness and dissolution of the narrow street. But she recalled the unworldly stench oozing from the brick arch, proclaiming it one of London's portals to hell, if not hell itself.

A young boy, in tattered clothing, ran up to them and held out his dirty palm. "Penny, mum?"

Adele's wet breath puffed against Sophia's neck. "I'd

shoot the child just as easily as spit on him, so I advise you not to say a word to anyone."

Even though the air was cold and damp, sweat trickled down Sophia's spine. She shook her head at the child and continued walking.

"You know where we are going, don't you?"

Sophia nodded and walked toward the green blistered door of Number Five.

Once inside, they moved into a room on the second floor. Sophia cast a quick look at the lone window in the bleak space. Fighting the nausea threatening to overwhelm her, she strode to the windowed wall.

The unhinged woman's bizarre behavior suddenly intensified. She ranted unintelligibly and paced. With her back pressed against the wall, Sophia slid closer to the window. She froze as Adele ceased her manic movements to cast a contemptuous look at her.

Sophia tried to hold her expression unfathomable. The woman appeared to garner a great deal of malicious pleasure whenever Sophia showed fear. Adele moved to the only table in the sparsely furnished room and lifted one of the amber bottles marked CHLORODYNE. The vessels of opium elixir appeared empty. Nevertheless, every few minutes Adele picked one up, brought it to her lips, and then slammed it down. Without warning, Adele hurled a bottle. It ricocheted off the wall, nearly hitting Sophia before it skittered across the floor.

Don't react. Don't react. She prayed the woman wouldn't notice her knees shook or that she used the wall for support.

Bang. A noise like the front door crashing inward echoed from downstairs.

Adele spun toward the sound.

"Adele, are you here?" Hayden called out, a frantic tone in his voice.

"Yes, I'm here!" Adele rushed to the room's threshold.

"Hayden, you aren't angry, are you? Of course not. I know you don't love her!" She turned to Sophia, triumph burning in her eyes.

Fast footfalls raced up the stairs. Hayden came into view at the end of the long corridor. Her husband, usually so in control, looked as pale as a marble statue.

"Let her go, Adele. Then you and I can go to France together. Wouldn't you like that?" With a discreet tip of his hand, he motioned Sophia to the window.

Sophia nodded and inched closer to the glass panes. A lean-to abutted the back of the building, its roof no more than three feet below the sill.

"Paris?" Adele stared at him.

"Yes." He took a single step forward.

"If she's dead, you can marry me." Adele turned and aimed the gun at Sophia.

"Adele!" Hayden screamed, drawing her attention back to him. "You are angry at me, not her. If you wish to shoot someone, shoot me."

Shoot him? Sophia's heart raced. "No," she cried out.

"Shut up." Adele lifted the gun and pointed it at Hayden. "You love her?"

"No, never." Hayden crept closer to Adele with each syllable he spoke. "Just you. Come to me."

The gun in Adele's hand wavered.

Quietly Sophia opened the sash and flung first one leg, then the other out the window. Hands gripping the sill, she lowered herself onto the structure below. She couldn't leave Hayden with Adele. The lunatic had shot him once, she would do it again. If she called to Adele—got her to come to the window, Hayden could seize the madwoman from behind.

With her body pressed flat against the building, Sophia stepped down the incline. "Adele," she screamed.

"You bitch, get back here!" Footfalls moved toward the

window. Adele leaned out, her pale face crimson with rage as she shook the gun wildly in the air. Grabbing the casing with her free hand, the madwoman knelt on the sill and leveled the pistol at Sophia.

"No!" Hayden's frantic voice and hurried footsteps boomed from inside the room.

As though unaware of her precarious position, Adele released the casing to glance over her own shoulder. She pitched forward, headfirst. A shrill cry rent the air, silenced when the woman's head hit the roof with a sickening *thud*.

With the gun still clasped in her hand, Adele's body slid down the roof, stopping mere inches from Sophia's feet. Sophia knew the vacant look of death, but somehow Adele's lifeless green eyes accused as they stared up at her. With a sob, Sophia pressed her face against the rough brick of the building.

"Sophia!"

Through her tears, she peered at Hayden crawling out the window.

"Don't move!" he said.

"I couldn't even if I wished to."

With a hand on the tenement, Hayden made his way down the slope toward her. As soon as he reached her, he pulled her to him, and pressed his lips to hers.

Chapter Twenty-Six

Sophia parted the curtains and peered out the window onto Brook Street. Only one carriage remained. The others had driven away to be swallowed by the fog and darkness.

The front door of their residence opened, spilling light upon the black uniforms and solemn faces of the policemen who stood on the pavement below.

"Get on with it, men! About your business," an authoritative voice commanded.

The men dispersed.

Sophia recognized the voice of Edmund Henderson, the Commissioner of Police. He, along with a Detective Williams, had questioned her in the drawing room while Hayden had paced, stopping occasionally to glare at one or both men.

Neither Henderson nor Williams had been oblivious to the dark expressions cast at them, and when Hayden insisted she retire before they questioned him, they'd said not a word.

She watched the commissioner climb into the carriage while her mind turned over everything Hayden had disclosed during the ride home from Whitechapel. He'd told her about Adele—his affair with the woman and his shooting, then revealed Lord Simon Adler's observation on Piccadilly. Explained why he'd been so adamant she not leave their residence, and told her about Varga and the man who had followed her. He had even revealed he'd been trying to confirm Adele's whereabouts the night they were to attend the theater.

The horses' hooves echoing in the still air drew her attention back to the carriage as it vanished into the thick night. She let the curtain fall and surveyed the feminine room with its yellow décor. She'd not slept in this bedchamber in weeks.

The door connecting this room to the one she and Hayden shared flew open. Hayden stood at the threshold, dressed in shirtsleeves, the top buttons unfastened and the sleeves rolled up.

His gaze drifted downward, over her unbound hair trailing over her shoulders to her bare toes peeking beneath the hem of her cream-colored nightgown. Briefly his eyes closed and a visible tremor escaped his body.

What had he thought when he'd entered their bedchamber and not found her there? Had he believed she'd taken the time afforded her to slip away from this house and him? She had only come in here to peer out the front window, hoping most of the policemen had left.

His eyes shifted to the bed, and she knew he wondered if she intended to sleep in here instead of with him. Earlier today that had been her plan. Not now. Her stomach churned as she remembered him telling Adele to shoot him. He'd been willing to give up his life for her and their child.

"Sophia, you must be weary. Why aren't you asleep?"

She'd been waiting for him. Their empty bed held little appeal. She needed the contact of his warm body, the scent of his skin, and the soothing cadence of his breathing weaving gently in and out of his lungs to ease her tattered nerves.

He moved across the room and took her hands in his. His expression grew intense and his touch firm, as though he feared she would disintegrate if he relinquished his hold. During the carriage ride home, he'd pulled her atop his lap, held her tightly, and begged her forgiveness.

"Do you wish me to read to you?" With his chin, he gestured to a book set on the windowsill.

"That's Thomas's new book, *Lectures on Germ Theory and Treatments for Specific Abscesses*."

He grimaced. "I should retrieve something more conducive to lulling one to sleep."

Without responding, she stepped closer and rested the side of her face against his chest. She needed to listen to the rhythmic beating of his heart.

He embraced her.

She took a deep breath. "You haven't asked me why I called on your sister."

The palm of his hand moved in little circles over the small of her back. "I presumed you went to show me you wouldn't be dictated to."

She pressed her nose into his shirt and breathed in his familiar scent. "No, I went because I wished to ask Edith some questions about your past."

His hand stilled.

"She believed you should be the one to answer them. Would you be forthright with me, Hayden? Would you answer my questions?"

Silence filled the air. "Yes, of course."

"Are you the proprietor of J. H. Mason?"

"Yes."

"And who is responsible for the donations?"

He pulled back, but she caught the front of his shirt and held tight.

His nostrils flared. "I am."

"And that is a secret because?"

"Because it is no one's business."

"Forgive me, I thought we had gained some sort of understanding." She released his shirt, stepped back, and twisted her wedding ring about her finger.

He took a deep breath, shattering the silence that hung between them like a physical wall. He placed his hand under her chin and tipped her face up to his. "I beg your forgiveness. As my wife, you have every right to know I am responsible for the alms. Though, I do not wish it common knowledge."

"No, of course not. Such knowledge might shatter the image of indifference you have arduously cultivated, even with me."

He gave a humorless smile. "Yes, in truth I'm a prince among men. Isn't that what you were thinking after I allowed this to happen? I should have told you what Simon revealed to me, but I did not wish to upset you. I wanted to protect you."

"I am stronger than you think, Hayden."

"You are. But this morning you looked so pale. Too pale. And you are with child. I didn't wish to frighten you."

"I was confused by your behavior. The lies. Your mandates."

He took her hand and set her palm to his heart. "Sophia, do you feel that?"

His heart beat strong, the tempo elevated. She nodded.

"That's what happens when I ponder what could have befallen you today."

"Because of the child I carry?"

"Not just the child, Sophia. When I thought I might lose you, my world felt as if it was crumbling at my feet." He framed her face between his palms. "I realized how much I love you."

His admission startled her—words she had longed to hear. Tears pricked her eyes. She wanted to say, *I love you as well.* But what did his avowal, his affirmation mean? He'd divulged his love to Laura, then forsaken her. She wanted to ask him about Laura, but right now she felt too raw. Adele's face kept flashing in her mind. She pressed her body to his, just wanting to feel—to forget today.

"Show me," she whispered. "Show me you love me."

Gently he swung her up into his arms and carried her to their bedchamber. He set her down on her feet, and his nimble fingers moved over the tiny pearl buttons that lined the bodice of her silk nightgown. The fabric gaped, exposing her breasts.

The hunger in his eyes excited her and quickened the rhythm of her heart.

"You take my breath away." His voice sounded low and raspy.

She brushed the fabric off her shoulders. The nightgown slithered over her arms and hips to pool on the floor like a silken cloud.

Hayden reached out. One finger traced the length of her arm. His light touch nothing more than a whisper of breath against her skin. It inflamed her desire, a tease that stroked anticipation, but did not feed it.

Eager to touch him, she unfastened the remaining buttons of his shirt, and he tossed the garment to the floor. The desire to taste him overtook her, and she pressed her open mouth against his chest, let her tongue absorb the salt lingering on his warm skin, while her nose drew in his masculine essence. She wished to flood her senses, to forget the memory of Adele's dead eyes.

A primal hunger she could not contain took hold. She bit Hayden gently on the shoulder as her hand slid over the front of his trousers. A shudder shot through him. Where her assertiveness came from, she did not know, but it pleased her. She desired control—something she'd little of during the day. She reached lower, cupped him more firmly.

He unbuttoned his trousers and slid her fingers against his arousal. She filled her greedy hand with his flesh. His breath hitched. He jerked back, shed his remaining clothes, and pulled her body to him. Soft and supple skin collided with hard muscle while his mouth covered hers.

She wrapped her arms around his neck and parted her lips, begging him to deepen the kiss. His tongue slid into her mouth, a movement that seemed as frenzied as hers, like a man deprived of a woman's touch and sensual contact all his life. His palms glided over her skin, a possessive caress. They smoothed over the curve of her hips to capture her bum. He lifted her up, and she wrapped her legs about his naked hips as he kissed her deeply, roughly.

Movement assailed her, and the next thing she knew she sat perched on the edge of the high bed, her legs still wrapped about him. She ran her hands over his broad chest and taut abdomen before twining her fingers around his jutting manhood.

Indrawn air hissed through his clenched teeth as she slid her hand over his silken skin. He tipped his head back, and his nostrils flared. When he looked back, his blue eyes appeared as dark as her own.

He pressed her shoulders into the soft mattress, forcing her to release him. And with his feet still planted on the floor, he leaned over her and retook her lips. His hands cupped her breasts to shape them to his palms.

She moaned, wanting more.

His mouth moved to her breasts, one, then the other, and she tangled her fingers in his hair. The sharp edge of his teeth scrapped at her nipples. The rough sensation and pleasure entwined into something deeper.

"Yes, yes." Her voice sounded husky, foreign. She arched up, her body pleaded, reiterating her spoken word.

His tongue soothed her skin. Closing her eyes, she focused her senses on his touch, the sensation of his warm mouth, loving her body—drawing her closer to that explosion of nerves and energy—the ultimate physical climax.

His hands skimmed over her thighs. He unwrapped her feet from his back and placed her heels on the edge of the bed. The height of the bed seemed perfect, and she knew his intent.

She reached above her head, knotted her hands in the counterpane. His countenance darkened. A few weeks ago, such an intense expression would have frightened her, but now it only heightened her base desires. He shifted, moved closer, spreading her legs wider.

He clamped his hands on her hips, pulled her to the edge of the bed, and entered her. A slow, exquisite slide of skin against skin until her welcoming body completely sheathed his hard flesh. His thumb stroked her swollen nub as he pulled back and entered her over and over again until nothing but an anxious tension and exquisite pleasure thrummed in her body.

Their eyes locked. "I love you," he said again.

His words were the catalyst—the toppling force. She climaxed so forcefully her thighs quivered as they clamped against his hips, holding him to her. His eyes closed. His face grew taut, and she knew he followed her into the abyss of physical pleasure.

Through the thick fog, Sophia ran up Little Marlie Row. The narrow housing swayed back and forth as though susceptible to the whim of the wind. Something brushed her feet, and she stopped to glance down. Rats, hundreds of rats, scurried about the street. She turned, intent on running, but a clawlike hand caught her arm. She swung around and stared straight at the angry, demonic countenance of Adele Fontaine. Her green irises had an unearthly glow and her skin was black.

Sophia's eyes flew open.

With her heart pounding in her chest, she scanned the dim bedchamber lit only by the gentle kiss of gray sunlight peeking shyly over the horizon.

She shifted in bed. Hayden slept soundly beside her, his arm draped over her naked waist. *A nightmare, nothing more*, she reaffirmed, soothing her overwrought nerves.

Exhaling a taut breath, she placed her hand over Hayden's forearm. The knowledge he lay beside her quieted the beating of her heart to a normal cadence, and Adele's image drifted away, evaporated, the way images in one's dreams are apt to do upon awakening.

She snuggled closer to the solidity and warmth of his body, not daring to shut her eyes, fearing Adele's face would resurface. Yet when her heavy eyelids finally drifted closed, it was not Adele's face she remembered, but the miniature portrait in Hayden's desk, the one with the beautiful blond woman. The image appeared clear and detailed as if Sophia held the painted ivory within her hands. Had the artist embellished the woman's beauty or the blue of her eyes, painted with barely diluted cerulean pigment?

Sophia's lashes drifted open, and she stared at the shadows on the ceiling.

Who was she? His mother? No, the style of the clothing did not speak of several decades past.

A lover? Probable, but who had captured him so completely that he kept her miniature secreted away in the top drawer of his desk when she'd not seen even a single painting or photograph of Laura?

Was it Laura?

No, the woman had blue eyes like Hayden's eyes. And Celia's brown eyes must have come from her mother.

A cousin?

What a fanciful thought.

Sophia slipped out of the warm bed, pulled her dressing gown on, and walked downstairs. She paused at the doorway to Hayden's study.

Turn around, an inner voice urged. Her legs were not in accord with her mind. She opened the door, made her way to the desk, and lit the small lamp set atop it. After removing the key from under the inkwell, she unlocked the top drawer and withdrew the miniature from its case. For a long minute, she studied the lovely woman in the painting. Then with great care, she removed the frame's backing, hoping the miniaturist had inscribed not only his name, but noted the subject's identity as well.

He had.

Laura Milton

By Reginald Easton

With unsteady legs, she lowered herself to the edge of Hayden's chair.

Laura?

With trembling fingers, Sophia reattached the backing and turned it around. Deep blue eyes peered at her. It didn't make sense. She'd read Francis Talbot's paper on heredity. He'd written about traits. The odds of two blue-eyed parents giving birth to a child with brown eyes was rare.

Edith had spoken of some secret. An uncomfortable

chill spread down Sophia's back as if a cold finger from the grave traced her spine.

Laura, tell me you didn't betray him.

Sophia leaned back against the chair.

"I'm being foolish," she mumbled.

Yet it would explain why he'd abandoned both wife and child. But Celia's resemblance to him could not be discounted. Her smile, the shape of her mouth, even the angles of her face. And her brown eyes mirrored Edith's eyes.

Sophia peered at the landscape above the mantel. Celia's voice echoed in her head as she spoke of the damaged portrait of Hayden's father in the attic. *"It used to hang above the mantel in Papa's study. Papa did it. I remember."*

"Oh, merciful God."

Grabbing the desk lamp, Sophia slipped the miniature into the pocket of her dressing gown and made her way upstairs.

By the time she reached the attic steps, an oppressive weight consumed her chest. The thought taking root, nourishing itself in her mind, seemed too heinous to fathom.

With the lamp clasped in one hand and her hem lifted in the other, she nervously scanned the narrow stairs. A dark spot on one of the treads seemed to shift and then scurry into the shadows. Sophia stepped back. Panic took hold, increasing the rhythm of her heart while beads of sweat prickled her back.

For a moment, she believed her fear of vermin would render her incapable of moving forward. She stared at the now empty tread and fought the urge to turn and flee.

You can do this. Taking deep breaths, she concentrated on the air moving in and out of her lungs as she stepped forward and took the first step and each subsequent step until she reached the top.

The cool air of the attic chilled her damp skin. The

subtle light floating through the dormers illuminated the portraits. They seemed miles away, yet she knew it only a short distance. Anxiously she swept the lamp in a large arc over the wide floorboards. Then taking several more steadying breaths, she made her way to the paintings.

She set the lamp on the floor, pulled her dressing gown about her legs, and squatted before the paintings. She glanced at the tattered portrait of Hayden's father, leaning in the corner.

The anger raging through Hayden when he'd destroyed it seemed palpable. She flipped over the first painting—the one of Hayden's father with his hound. Once again, the resemblance between father and son amazed her. The old earl's gaze was downcast, making it impossible to discern the color of his eyes. She moved the painting aside and turned the next one over.

She inhaled a jagged breath. Brown eyes caught the light of the lamp. Eyes that resembled both Celia's and Edith's eyes. Forgetting her fears, she knelt on the floor and extracted Laura's miniature. She gazed at the beautiful woman portrayed within.

Did you betray him with his father? Were you so cruel?

A shadow cast a dark pall over the floorboards, and Sophia's head shot up.

Hayden, clothed in his green dressing robe, stood looking at her, his large body stifling the morning light, working its way through one of the dormers. His gaze shifted from his father's portrait, illuminated by the lamp like an actor in an Athenian tragedy, to the miniature she held.

"Aren't you a clever one?" His voice sounded cold, dangerously detached.

If she had needed confirmation, she had it.

Celia was not his daughter. She was his sister.

The charged silence was broken by the sound of feet

shuffling up the stairs. "Who's up there?" Mrs. Beecham called out impatiently as she stepped fully into the attic.

Hayden shot a thunderous glare toward the housekeeper.

"Oh, my lord, m-my lady," the elder woman stuttered as she gave an awkward bob of her head.

Sophia glanced down, not wishing the woman to see the tears pooling in her eyes. Hayden's shadow shifted and moved like a specter across the floorboards. When she peered up, he was making his way down the stairs.

Sophia hastily slipped the miniature into her pocket and scrambled to her feet. Mrs. Beecham's gaze appeared frozen on the illuminated portrait of the old earl.

"Was the very devil he was," Mrs. Beecham whispered, a quiver lending unsteadiness to her low voice. "Didn't care a farthing who 'e 'urt."

Obviously, the image, created with oil and pigment, distressed the housekeeper, so much so that her speech became less cultured, belying her humble origins. "I remember . . ." Her voice trailed off and she wrapped her arms about herself as if attempting to protect her body from an unwelcome memory.

Sophia cupped her mouth. The haunted look in the woman's eyes . . . her posture. Sophia had seen women at the mission with that scathed look. She'd known the cause, examined the bruises on their throats, arms, inner thighs. Women who'd been violated. The old earl had either coerced or raped Mrs. Beecham, and Sophia feared it the latter.

Sophia turned to the tattered painting.

Laura? Had it been an act of mutual congress or . . . ? Oh God, had Hayden's father been a monster?

She studied Mrs. Beecham's trembling form and knew the answer.

Sophia did not realize she'd gasped until the woman

stepped toward her. "Forgive me, my lady," the housekeeper implored. "I forgot myself. I beg your pardon." Her expression crumbled. She appeared ready to weep. "Forgive me."

Sophia closed the distance between them. She folded Mrs. Beecham's chilled fingers within her clammy hands.

"Don't," she said firmly. "Don't apologize." Sophia took a deep breath. She needed to speak with Hayden. She needed him to know she understood some of his past—what motivated his tight rein on her, his fears, even the anger she sensed within him. Retrieving the lamp, she motioned the housekeeper to precede her down the stairs.

"Mrs. Beecham, I wish those portraits packed away. Crated and nailed shut."

"Yes, madam, I'll see to it myself."

"No," Sophia said, not wishing the woman to have to look at them again. "Tell Hawthorne I wish one of the footmen tasked with the job."

An expression of relief flashed across the housekeeper's face, and she nodded.

Sophia opened the bedchamber door to find Hayden standing before a low dresser, his palms braced on the wood surface, his back to her. Without a word, she stepped behind him and slipped her arms about his waist. She set her cheek against his shoulder. His breath shifted in and out of his lungs, strong enough to stoke the flames of a blacksmith's forge.

After his breathing calmed, he spoke. "When Celia was born, I thought myself the most blessed of men. Laura appeared well and Celia looked round and pink. So beautiful. Yet I feared . . ." He paused, took a deep breath. "You see, I believed her arrival premature. Laura and I had been married only seven months. Contrary to what you may believe, I am not in the habit of despoiling virgins, even those I wish to marry. I did not realize Laura was not chaste on our wedding night. I was a man of little experience."

She tightened her hold on him.

"After Celia's birth, while Laura slept, I spoke privately with the doctor. I needed confirmation Celia would not suffer any complications due to her early birth. The doctor assured me Celia was not premature. To the contrary, he said her wrinkled skin indicated she was overdue. 'Stayed in the oven a bit too long,' he said. 'Just stay in the country a few weeks and no one will be the wiser.'"

Sophia pressed her face tighter to his back as tears welled up in her eyes.

"I had the oddest urge to strangle the man when he winked at me. Bloody fool didn't comprehend he'd just informed me Celia was not my daughter. I tried to discard his words as the ramblings of an old country doctor, but Celia was so robust."

"A week later, I asked Laura who fathered Celia. She would not tell me. Three weeks later, with betrayal gnawing at me like some insidious disease, I left for London. I'm sure you've heard I did not live a virtuous life. A man fueled by what he conceives as betrayal has a panache for revenge. I flaunted my infidelities. I chose women specifically from my own social stratum, a stratum Laura was not part of. She had privately humiliated me, but I wished for something grander for her. A public crucifixion that clearly stated my indifference."

"You were distressed," Sophia whispered.

He swung around abruptly, and she stumbled backward. He grabbed her shoulders and steadied her. His fingers bit into her skin. "You don't understand."

She feared she did. She looked at his eyes—sharp with

pain. “Then tell me,” she implored, hoping a catharsis would ease his anguish.

He closed his eyes, and when he opened them, dampness wet the corners. “I abandoned her when she was guilty of nothing. Nothing,” he repeated, his voice raspy. “If you think Laura would have willingly slept with that sod who called himself my father, you are mistaken. I defied him by asking a woman below my station to wed me, and the bastard unleashed his anger on her.” Hayden swallowed. “He forced himself on her.”

Sophia took a steadying breath and pressed a hand to his chest. “Hayden, you were unaware of that when you left her. Why didn’t she tell you?”

“I would have killed my father. Strangled him with my bare hands. Laura knew the consequences my actions would bring about. He’d known she wouldn’t tell me and counted on her silence. He probably taunted her afterward, fueling her fears.”

He released his painful grip on her shoulders. Raked his hands through his hair.

“Two days after my father’s funeral, Laura came to London. I not only refused to see her, I left that day for the Continent. I’m sure the gossip sheets reported my salacious antics while abroad.” He glanced away. “I only came back a month later when I received word from Edith that Laura was dead. A carriage accident.”

Sophia briefly closed her eyes, forcing the new wave of tears pooling in them to stay contained. There had been no reconciliation between them. No words of love or sorrow, no apologies made, and no reunion. That was the crux of the problem. Hayden had loved Laura, and she had loved him. Enough to relinquish him, yet she’d died before the truth lay exposed, leaving him riddled with guilt. If his father had meant to hurt Hayden, as well as Laura, he'd succeeded.

"Hayden, you are not accountable for your father's sins."

"Sophia," he said softly, "you don't understand."

"I do, Hayden."

He shook his head. "Laura left a note at my house, revealing everything. My father was dead and she'd finally felt safe telling the truth, knowing I would not exact my revenge on the bastard. If I'd just returned sooner or not left at all."

Warm tears spilled onto Sophia's cheeks. What horrendous guilt Hayden must have experienced when he'd finally comprehended the sordid truth—read Laura's letter. Realized the secret she'd kept, the pain she'd endured, and that she'd been waiting to tell him the truth.

Sophia gazed into her husband's tormented eyes. Guilt was a terrible cross to bear. Sophia knew it intimately. She'd contended with that emotion after her niece Georgiana's death—sometimes she still did. There was no recourse when the one you loved was nothing more than an intangible memory.

"I'm sorry, Hayden. So terribly sorry."

He scowled. "I don't want your pity. Condemn me, but don't pity me."

Now she knew why Hayden did not reveal he was the mission's benefactor. He sought and cultivated society's censure, hoping to punish himself.

"Hayden, your father is the one who deserves condemnation. You were ill used by a man with no moral compunction, no soul, but you are not that man." She cupped his face. "When I look at you, I see a man capable of tremendous love. A man who loves his daughter—"

He gave a discordant laugh. "Daughter? Celia is my sister."

She shook her head adamantly. "No, I have watched you

with her, seen the love you have for her. She is your daughter. She is my stepdaughter and will be the much beloved sister of our children. If you will help me, we can make a wonderful home for Celia. For our family."

She took his hand, placed it atop her abdomen.

A depth of emotions glistened in his blue eyes.

"Hayden, will you be my partner? Help me through life's adversities and allow me to help you?"

"Do you love me, Sophia?"

"Hayden, when I met you, you made me feel . . . Oh, I don't know how to explain it, but I felt something strange. Something more than physical attraction. It did not make sense in my rational mind. You and I seemed so ill-suited. Now I realize we are not so different. We both suffer from guilt that is not our cross to bear. I could not save Georgiana. I realize that now. Just as you are not responsible for what happened to Laura."

Sophia slipped her hand around his neck and peered into his eyes. "You want to know why I capitulated so easily that night you came to my house. The truth is, I already loved you then. I desperately want the child that grows within me. I want your love. I want a family. And I want to share my life with you. Do you want these things as well?"

He set his hands about her waist and pulled her into a tight embrace. "Sophia. I wish to stand by your side. To love you till we are old and gray."

She realized he spoke the truth. He would not stray. When Hayden loved, he did so with all his heart. She'd misunderstood him. He was more trustworthy than anyone she knew. He'd raised Celia. Given the child his love. She stood on her toes and brushed her lips against his. "Then we shall take this journey together."

Hayden's mouth covered hers. With barely contained hunger, he swept her off her feet and brought her to their bed.

* * *

The next morning, they awoke to someone knocking, none too gently, on their bedchamber door.

"Goodness, are you two ever getting up?" Celia impatiently called out.

Sophia nuzzled Hayden's neck as he informed Celia that Sophia and he would be downstairs shortly.

Then he showed Sophia, one more time, how very much he loved her.

Epilogue

Hayden stared at Sophia sleeping cradled in his arms. Her backside pressed against his body and her legs tangled with his. How many mornings had he spent over the last nine years watching her sleep, feeling her warmth? She was his angel, the woman who had steered him away from self-destruction, the woman who had taught him to love and trust again. He inhaled, drawing in her scent of lemon and lavender, which remained a balm to his senses. Familiar, soothing, evocative.

She wiggled slightly, causing her bum to rest against his manhood.

He grinned. All these years and she still set his blood to boil. He would have enjoyed waking her slowly with his mouth and hands, but she'd stayed up late last night studying for the medical examination she'd soon be taking. He didn't doubt she'd pass, and that left him thinking a great deal about the future and his soon-to-be-doctor wife.

With a little mewl, Sophia stretched. "Mmm, good morning," she mumbled groggily, glancing over her shoulder to offer him a smile.

"Good morning." He pressed a kiss to the top of her head.

She arched one perfectly shaped brow at him. "You look a million miles away."

"Do I? Just thinking how beautiful my wife looks when she sleeps."

She wiggled her bottom again and shifted backward. "You weren't thinking anything else perchance?"

"You always make me think of other things, but I'm taking pity on you this morning."

With a soft laugh, she turned around in his arms. "So tell me what's causing those lines on your brow?"

He took a deep breath. "Dr. Montgomery is retiring."

"Yes, he's moving to the country. Wiltshire, I believe." She shut her eyes and burrowed closer to him.

"I'm contemplating whether we should purchase his London town house."

Sophia's eyes shot open. "Purchase? His residence is one of the largest on Harley Street."

"Yes, what do you think?"

"Why, you're serious, aren't you?"

"Sophia, tell me how you feel when you leave in the mornings to go to Henrietta Street?" Hayden knew the answer. When his wife left to go to the London School of Medicine for Women, guilt assailed her. He saw it in her eyes. In the way she kissed each of their children, not once, but twice before she made it through the door.

He drew his finger over her cheek. "One word sums it up, my love. Conflicted. The house on Harley Street would be perfect. It's already set up as a physician's residence. You wouldn't have to venture out to some office every morning before you made your calls. It would allow you more time at home."

* * *

Sophia kissed Hayden's cheek. The Earl of Westfield was *now* so far from wicked it seemed laughable. He was loving, kind, a wonderful father, a generous lover, and a thoughtful husband.

Four months after they married, he'd surprised her by taking her to South Kensington Museum, where she'd been shocked to see her grandfather's statue on display. He'd purchased the sculpture from his brother-in-law, Henry, and donated the artwork to the museum so the masses could admire it, just as she'd hoped.

Not quite a year after that he gifted her one of her grandfather's paintings. One of the three she'd sold to purchase her Chelsea residence. It took him nearly another two years to track down the last one she'd sold, but he had, and now the landscape hung in their bedroom. And he'd fought diligently to change the law that excluded women from being physicians, until he'd succeeded. However, the best gift he'd given her was their family. Celia, Vincent, Harry, and Michael.

Footsteps raced down the stairs outside their bedchamber door. The boys were already up, and Vincent—named after her grandfather—was most likely leading the pack, driving their poor tutor on a merry chase.

She smiled at her husband. "The cavalry is up."

In the corridor outside the bedchamber, Celia's calm, maternal voice shushed the fast-moving feet.

"Yes, I promised them we'd play a bit of cricket before their studies this morning." He pressed a light kiss to her forehead. "Sophia, my motives for purchasing Montgomery's residence are not completely unselfish. One of those boys is bound to take a tumble eventually, and I'd feel more at ease knowing you were close at hand, for I'm not adept at treating them."

She drew her finger over the small scar above his right brow. Hayden had insisted on being in the room during

Vincent's birth. He'd passed out cold and needed seven stitches. He'd been present for both Harry's and Michael's births, but he'd sat near the head of the bed, holding her hand, his back firmly to the doctor.

"I've made an appointment to see Montgomery's residence today at two o'clock. What do you think?"

Her finger trailed downward, over his cheek to his bottom lip. "I think I love you more and more each and every day."

She moved closer and felt something draw firmly to attention beneath the covers.

He wiggled his eyebrows at her. "I believe the children are going to have to wait a bit longer for that game of cricket to begin."

Laughing, Sophia tugged the bedding over their heads.

Keep reading for a sneak peek at

NEVER DECEIVE A VISCOUNT,

the next in the Infamous Lords series.

Coming soon
from
Renee Ann Miller
and
Zebra Shout!

Emma Trafford tapped softly on her sister's bedchamber door and inched it open. A single candle on a bedside table sent scant light into the dark room. Lily, dressed in a white cotton nightgown, stood before the window, her blond hair and slender twelve-year-old body illuminated by moonlight.

"Lily?" Emma whispered.

With a gasp, Lily spun around and tucked a pair of opera glasses behind her back.

Why, the little hoyden! If that gossipmonger across the street saw Lily spying upon her, the whole of Bloomsbury would know before daybreak.

"Are you watching Mrs. Jenkins?"

"Indeed not. One could expire from boredom observing her snooze all day."

Emma released the air in her lungs and glanced out the window. The London sky was absent its perpetual fog. Perhaps Lily had turned her mind to more intellectual pursuits. "Were you observing the constellations?"

"Ah . . . yes, indeed, the stars." Lily nibbled her lower lip.

One day, when they were old and gray, Emma would

reveal to her sister that Lily always bit her lower lip when she lied. "No, you were not. Now confess."

Lily shuffled her bare feet. Even in the dim light, Emma could see the two red spots on her sister's porcelain cheeks. "I'm observing the woman who recently moved into the town house next to Mrs. Jenkins. Have you seen her? She looks to be your age, perhaps a bit older. She wears feathered hats and gowns with huge bustles. Late at night, a fine carriage pulls up and an exceedingly tall gentleman enters the house."

"You were spying on them?" Emma tried to keep the shrill tone from her voice.

"Well, tonight they didn't close their shutters, and I was ever so curious."

Emma gasped. "Lily, that's scandalous."

"Ha! If you think I'm scandalous, you should see them. Do you wish to hear what they wear to bed?"

She did, but before Emma could lie and say no, her sister barreled forward. "The woman is dressed in a nightgown that barely hides her bosom. And the man, well, he's wearing just his drawers." Shock and titillation colored Lily's voice.

"Oh my goodness." Emma dashed to her sister's side and outstretched her hand. "Lillian Marie Trafford, give me those glasses. Now!"

Lily jutted out her bottom lip and handed over the opera glasses. "Em, the man has arms as thick as Titian's depiction of Mars. And he has the largest—"

Emma clapped a hand over her sister's mouth. She didn't know what Lily intended to say, but the child spent too many hours at the lending library examining books on Renaissance paintings, and Emma feared it wasn't a love of art that piqued Lily's interest.

"Not another word." Emma removed her hand.

"But he looks nothing like old Mr. Peabody when he drank too much punch at Mrs. Green's Christmas party and removed his shirt and trousers." Lily leaned close and spoke in a hushed tone. "He looks more like the paintings of the naked men on the ceiling of the Sistine Chapel. But larger. More powerful."

Oh, my. Emma stifled the salacious images working their way through her mind.

"If you don't believe me, take a peek." Lily pointed at the window, her eyes bright.

The temptation to join her sister in wickedness tugged at Emma. She'd never seen a man wearing only his drawers. Well, except for Mr. Peabody, but his prune-like anatomy and pencil-thin legs had not impressed her in the least. And the one time she'd been intimate . . . that had been a debacle she didn't wish to recall. She set the opera glasses on a table and drew the curtains closed.

"Get under the covers, and promise me you will not spy on the neighbors again. Especially *those* neighbors." She pulled her sister toward the bed.

With a sullen expression, Lily climbed under the blankets and folded her arms across her chest. "I promise."

Emma pressed a kiss to her sister's cheek. "Now sleep well, dearest, and blow out the candle as soon as I close the door."

Across the central corridor, Emma slipped into her bedchamber and padded to the window. The curtain rings rattled on the rod as she pulled the material closed. Unable to resist, she parted the fabric an inch and peered out. The town house across the way glowed like a balefire in the dark night. Their new neighbors certainly didn't want for money.

She moved away from the window. After she changed

into her white cotton nightgown, she settled between the sheets with a book of Tennyson's poems.

A half hour later, Emma stared blindly at a page. Doubtful the man across the way resembled Michelangelo's nudes. Men like that were only in artists' imaginations. She set her reading aside and turned down the wick on the bedside lamp, shrouding the room in darkness.

Boom! The bedchamber door flew open and slammed against the wall.

"Em!" Lily's frantic voice cut through the gloom like a shaft of light.

Heart pounding, Emma bolted upright. "What's the matter?"

Lily rushed forward, her pale face illuminated by the globed candle she held. "You must summon a constable."

"What's happened?" Emma tossed off her bedding.

Her sister's empty hand fluttered in the air. "The man. I-I believe he's killed the woman. He tore the thin material from her body, then settled under the sheets and climbed atop her. Her head thrashed back and forth while he . . . Oh, it was horrid. And when he was done, she just lay there not moving, eyes closed with an odd expression plastered on her still face. *She's dead!*"

More than once, Emma had contemplated the joining of a man and woman—compared it to what she knew. Her single experience had left her sore, shamed, and ruined. But there were times she'd imagined a husband gently removing his wife's clothes in the dark. Or if they were daring, leaving a single candle lit. She'd never imagined all the lights on. Perhaps her imagination was lacking.

"Em!"

Lily's voice startled Emma from her torrid thoughts. "Lily, you promised you wouldn't spy on them."

"I know, but . . ."

Emma scooted to the other side of the mattress and lifted the blankets. "Get into bed."

Her sister's mouth gaped. "Aren't you going to summon a constable?"

She sighed. "Dearest, sometimes married men and women partake in activities in their bedchambers that girls of twelve should not be privy to. They . . . they play games."

"This was not a game. A game would be blind man's bluff or twenty questions. This was depravity. Murder. Just like the murders Inspector Percival Whitley solves."

Lily had a fertile imagination, and those penny dreadfuls she read about Inspector Whitley of Scotland Yard didn't help. "Get into bed," Emma repeated. "I'm sure it was a game."

After setting the candle on the bedside table, Lily climbed next to her. "If that is the type of amusement married couples engage in, I shall become a spinster." Lily grabbed Emma's hand under the sheet. "Is that why you didn't marry Charles? Because you knew once married you'd have to partake in such wickedness?"

Emma's chest tightened as shame overwhelmed her. Charles had asked for her hand three years ago, on her twenty-first birthday, a week after Papa died. She'd allowed Charles to convince her that they didn't have to wait for the sanctity of marriage to join with each other. He'd professed his love and told her he couldn't wait anymore. That madness might overtake him, if he couldn't make love to her.

Three days afterward, he'd called on her and said his father was not in accord with the betrothal. How foolish she'd been to think a baron's son would marry out of his station, especially a portraitist with no fortune.

"We realized we didn't suit," Emma said, shoving the guilt over her reckless behavior aside.

"I'm glad"—Lily snuggled closer—"for I hate to think of you being forced to play such wretched games."

Charles had married last year, an earl's daughter, and his wife was now round with child. She blinked away the moisture filling her eyes. Silly to shed tears. She didn't need Charles or any other man. If she sold enough portraits, she could support herself and her two siblings all on her own.

Forcing a smile, Emma tucked the blankets around her sister's slender shoulders and kissed her cheek. "Good night, dearest."

The morning sun shone through the drawing room's windows, brightening the faded blue walls. Emma sat at her secretaire and perused the bills in front of her. Once she finished painting Mrs. Naples's portrait, she'd have nearly all the funds for Michael's boarding school tuition, along with enough to pay the coal merchant. Though not enough to pay what she owed Mrs. Flynn. The housekeeper continued to work for them even though Emma hadn't paid the woman her full salary in months. For all her gruff ways, Mrs. Flynn possessed a soft heart and a motherly tendency toward them.

The double doors swung open, and Lily stormed into the room with as much drama as the night before.

"I told you that man murdered the ginger-haired woman!" Lily grabbed Emma's hand and tugged her across the room.

"I do not want to hear another word about murder." Emma planted her heels into the threadbare carpeting.

Her sister stomped her foot and pointed at the window. "See for yourself."

The headache that had begun as Emma looked at the

bills grew stronger. She pressed her fingers to her temples. "I insist you cease this spying."

"But Inspector Whitley says one must carefully search for clues, for they will always reveal the villain."

Emma attempted not to roll her eyes heavenward at the mention of the fictitious inspector. Setting a hand on the window's casings, she gazed outside. Two burly men were hefting a large trunk onto a dray across the street. "What is it I'm supposed to be witnessing?"

Lily groaned. "Don't you understand? The woman's body is stuffed in the trunk."

"You know no such thing."

"What else could it be?"

"They might be cleaning their attic."

A tall gentleman with broad shoulders stepped out of the town house. He was impeccably dressed in a navy overcoat and top hat.

"That's him!" Lily clasped Emma's arm, her fingers tight enough to leave marks.

The man lifted his hat and raked his fingers through shiny black hair.

Lily's warm breath puffed on the back of Emma's neck. "Criminals are always dark and dangerous in appearance. And if he isn't dastardly looking, I don't know what one would call him."

Emma swallowed. *She* would call him beautiful. The perfect subject to paint. His face all hard angles. His jaw strong and firm. His nose chiseled. He reminded her of a panther she'd seen at Regent's Park Zoo. Striking, yet if one were foolish enough to reach out to stroke its fur, surely they'd lose an appendage.

Her gaze shifted from his broad-shouldered body to the trunk. It was indeed large enough to hold a woman's body. Oh bother. She was letting Lily's imagination play havoc on her own mind.

"I will not make accusations against him." He looked not only dangerous, but also wealthy—a man financially capable of destroying them if they libeled him. "You have no proof."

"Proof? I told you what I saw last night. Now the trunk. What more do you need?"

"And I told you—"

"Yes, yes, a game. What balderdash."

The drayman's voice calling to the horses to "move on" drew their attention back to the window. A closed carriage with yellow wheels now stood in front of the town house as well.

"See," Emma said, pointing at the fancy equipage. "The woman is probably inside."

Lily bit on the nail of her index finger. "If you hadn't been arguing with me, I might have seen something. I'm going to go outside and peek in the carriage."

Emma grabbed her sister's hand. "You will do no such thing. Anyway it has already started up the street."

Lily wrenched her hand free and pressed her nose to the pane of glass. "Drat, I know what I saw, and I shall prove it to you."